FORTH INTO LIGHT

FORTH INTO LIGHT

A NOVEL BY

GORDON MERRICK

The sequel to the national best-seller
ONE FOR THE GODS

ALYSON PUBLICATIONS
LOS ANGELES

Manufactured in the United States of America.
Printed on acid-free paper.

This trade paperback is published by Alyson Publications Inc.,
P.O. Box 4371, Los Angeles, California 90078.
Distribution in the United Kingdom by Turnaround Publisher Services Ltd.,
27 Horsell Road, London N5 1XL, England.

First published by Avon Books: August 1974
First Alyson edition: October 1996

5 4 3 2 1

ISBN 1-55583-292-X
(formerly published with ISBN 0-380-01195-6 by Avon Books)

For Charles G. Hulse,
who invented this book.
With love and gratitude always.

I t was a bombshell: George Cosmo Leighton had been robbed of almost two thousand dollars! A theft on this tranquil Greek island where thievery was unheard of! The two thousand dollars George had been waiting for for weeks!

Exclamation points could be heard in all the voices commenting on the event.

A case might have been made that the money had simply been lost, but public opinion among the foreigners was formulated around tables set out on the *quai* in front of Lambraiki's grocery store, and the foreigners pronounced in favor of theft. A suspect was quickly found. There had been other small vexing losses—or thefts, as everybody was inclined to regard them now—and the facts could be neatly arranged to point to only one possible culprit. A Greek, naturally.

The case immediately acquired curious and unexpected dimensions. To a not notably well-heeled community, it was a great deal of money. In that summer of 1960, it was enough to buy three or four houses on the island, enough for a foreign family to live for six or eight months, a native family for a year or more. In addition, Leighton was arguably the most distinguished foreigner in residence and certainly the most permanently established. Only Charlie Mills-Martin could dispute his preeminence, with seniority of property ownership in his favor, but in the scale of fame a nearly legendary literary figure generally outweighs a successful painter.

A prominent resident, a sizable theft—it was the stuff for lively gossip, but it quickly became much more than that. Before the day was done, relationships had dissolved, re-formed, taken new directions. By the dawn of another day, rumors had begun to fly that even the Mills-Martins, symbols of stability, had been touched by the mid-

1

summer madness. Arrivals. Departures. Perhaps it all had something to do with the heat.

The day had begun like a thousand others. The sun rose in its accustomed place and cast a saffron spill over the milky Aegean. It took an hour or more for its rays to strike the port, which lay in the close embrace of its twin promontories. By seven, the last rocky barrier had been surmounted and the town was exposed at last to a blaze of white stinging light, and the business of the day had begun.

The fruit and vegetable sellers had removed the canvas covers from their wares and were ready for trade. The water men had filled their square metal cans at the Good Well and were making deliveries with their donkeys among the storefront cafés and restaurants. Small boys carrying blocks of ice in loops of string were spreading out and up the steep, stepped streets into the upper town. One of the three garbage collectors with his two mules, each laden with a pair of big basketwork panniers, was heading out toward the mole to dump his first load of the day.

Since there were no roads on the island and few machines, the sounds were all natural sounds. People shouted at each other, donkeys brayed, cocks crowed as they had been doing all night, cats wailed like babies in the fierce conflict of copulation.

It was a combination of these sounds that slowly awoke George Cosmo Leighton, dragged him unwillingly into consciousness. A fly settled on his bare shoulder, and he shrugged it away. He knew that it would alight again on the same spot. This knowledge obliged him to face the fact that he was waking up. Two women were screaming conversationally at each other nearby, and he winced as their voices cut across his nerves. The fly touched down again, and he twitched and cursed to himself. This small effort brought sweat streaming from him. It was hot, a heat so still and oppressive that his whole body felt helpless, hopeless in its grip.

He wasn't sure whether it was morning or afternoon—a siesta could induce this same deep drugged sleep—but in a moment some time mechanism within him told him it was morning, and his mind fumbled for the events of the day before to confirm this judgment. Something had happened to give the day a particular flavor, something on the whole agreeable. Something...the money had come. That was it. He felt eased and comforted and immediately sank into a pocket of vestigial sleep that contained a trace of consciousness. Sarah. Sarah. A boat. A dog talking to him.

The fly alighted again and jerked him back onto the track of memory. The money had come. Good. And then—yes, there had been the evening, the money flowing, simply because of the comfortable feel of cash in the pocket, probably a week's drink allowance gone in one night. There had been people, the usual crowd. His mind edged forward to the culminating row with Sarah. Had he finally said it all? Had he actually spoken the words that had been locked within him all these months? Had he told her that he never wanted to touch her again, that she was free to have any man she damn well pleased? No. His helpless love for her had made a coward of him. He remembered smashed glasses and a rage to say it at last but control continuing to operate. He unglued his eyes cautiously to see it there were any signs of his having brought the rage home with him.

He found himself sprawled naked on the couch in the big white room, his workroom, on the top floor. His erection was distasteful but reassuring to him. He would gladly renounce sex forever, but he clearly wasn't impotent; only Sarah made him so. Sarah's infidelity. Sarah's *lapse* (on days when he was feeling kindly toward her). Sarah's betrayal. He had thought at first of fighting fire with fire, but he had found that there was more to infidelity than going to bed with an attractive body. It dislocated all the filaments of life, overthrew carefully tended balances, introduced chaos. The island was a festival of sex, strewn with pretty, willing girls, but he hadn't found one with whom he wanted to share the dissolution of his marriage. Renounce sex—except that he suspected Sarah had no intention of doing so.

The touch of the fabric under him became suddenly intolerable, damp, and clinging. His body was covered with a slick of sweat. His shirt and trousers were in a crumpled heap on the painted floor near the door, still holding the vague contours of his body, like a man with the air let out of him. Everything seemed to be in order. There was no litter on the floor—he hadn't indulged in his favorite drunken pastime of tearing up manuscripts. He closed his eyes with relief and tried to swallow some of the thick sour taste in his mouth. His thoughts flew back to Sarah, and he could feel rage still smoldering in him—rage and hopelessness were all that love offered him.

He struggled into a sitting position, gripping the edge of the couch with his hands and swaying slightly. His stomach was in intense disorder, and his heart was pounding dangerously. At least the money had arrived safely. The next few months were secure.

Gathering strength for the further effort of getting to his feet, he felt the erratic beating of his heart accelerate and paused cautiously to ease it. He was practiced in the wiles of keeping panic at bay. *Move around, get the day started. Everything will be all right.*

He headed unsteadily for the little heap of clothes on the floor and, supporting himself on the back of a chair, leaned over and picked them up. He discarded the shirt and disentangled the brief shorts from a fold in the trousers and discarded them too. With difficulty, lurching and losing his balance, first on one foot and then the other, he managed to get his legs into his trousers and pull them up. These feeble exertions reduced his sex and produced rivulets of sweat. It flowed down his forehead into his eyes and trickled down his ribs. His belly was stretched taut with the drink of the night before. He had trouble getting his fly buttons closed.

The feel of the trousers against his thighs brought a memory of the reassuring feel of the thick wad of bills he had been carrying the night before. He slid his hands into the pockets for reassurance now.

There was nothing in them. He reached for shirt and shorts and shook them out and dropped them again. He stood frozen, motionless, and then a prickling chill of fear ran up his spine and across his scalp. Nonsense. The money was here somewhere.

He turned blindly and stumbled to the couch and began to poke about in it. He straightened and made an enormous effort to think clearly. He must have emptied his pockets downstairs. Otherwise, there would be *something* in them, if only his lighter or a box of matches.

He caught sight of a package of cigarettes under the edge of the couch. He lowered himself to his knees and peered under. His lighter winked at him, and he fumbled for it and recovered it. No money.

A wad of bills couldn't roll under the furniture. He dropped back into a seated position on the floor and ran his fingers through his damp and tangled hair. He must have given the money to Sarah for safekeeping. He suddenly remembered having pulled it out at Lambraiki's. To pay for a round? Unlikely, since he always ran a drink bill at Lambraiki's. Still, he had definitely had it there toward the end of the evening. He must have pulled it out to give to Sarah. Had it figured in their fight? Had he flung it in her face in some mad gesture of defiance before he started smashing glasses?

Panic crept through his guard once more—a real, well-founded panic. The money couldn't be gone. It was all they had to live on until he finished his new book. He had stretched his credit with publishers and agents and patrons as far as it would go. The book was going badly, had been going badly ever since—

There was no time to think about that. He had to make sure that the money was somewhere in the house. His writer's mind strayed from the immediate and leaped and faltered among general thoughts of money: the evil engendered by its unequal distribution, the distortion of values that must accompany its acquisition, the necessity of always combating its enslaving grip. Enough of that. He had to find this particular goddamn money.

He pulled himself to his feet and made another fumbling, frantic search of the room before starting down through the maze of the house. It had once been two houses, which added to its vagaries—cramped stairways that were almost ladders, arbitrary changes of level, heavily barred windows giving from one room into another.

By the time he reached the covered balcony that led to the bathroom, he had pieced together additional fragments of the night before. He clearly remembered Sarah and himself struggling home in silence through the dark, narrow, uneven streets with the drunk's determination to steer a straight course, hostilities suspended in the common effort. She had been carrying her shopping basket. It would have been perfectly natural for him to have dropped the money into it. It served as a general catchall.

He paused ritualistically on the balcony to look at the view of sea and rocky hill, but the sun's dazzle made him wince, and he hurried on to the bathroom, clinging to the shade against the wall. His island paradise. The thought was ironic. Unlike most of the people who came here, he hadn't expected to find a panacea for all the world's ills. The long journey across Europe had been undertaken years ago to escape the demands of fame and the more time-consuming aspects of success. He could have as easily chosen a farm in Vermont or a ranch in Montana, but he was married to a romantic girl—yes, she was still a girl in many ways—who was captivated by what she read in books, so their journey had ended on a Greek island, And he had found something here, a redefinition of freedom in his observations of a community released from all constraints, new judgments imposed by the clash of anarchy and order. Interesting. Rewarding. Until Sarah—until Sarah— Fuck the good life. Fuck happiness.

He stood for a long moment in front of the toilet, half-dozing and swaying slightly as the liquid absorbed the night before drained out of him. Then he braced himself to confront the ruin of his face. The mirror over the washbasin offered no pleasant surprises. The eyes were red and puffy, the deep tan looked gray and lifeless, a stubble of graying beard blurred the jaw line. The celebrated George Cosmo

Leighton. Well, perhaps not quite...the *once*-celebrated George Leighton? His flight from success had been perhaps more successful than he had intended. The face, even in its present condition, was marked with sensitivity, in the eyes, around the mouth, but to his frequent surprise, with no trace of weakness. He knew that in an hour or so the fluids and tissues would have worked their mysterious miracle, and he would be once more clear-eyed, strong, and capable-looking. What part did this trick of physiognomy play in his life? If he looked like a derelict, would he abandon hope and be obliged to concede defeat, discard pride, and plead with Sarah to save him?

He turned on a faucet, and a trickle of water dribbled from it and died. *God blast Jeff,* he prayed, exposing his son to divine retribution. He knew that he shouldn't expect a seventeen-year-old prodigy to be always efficient in the performance of household chores, but all he asked of the boy was that he should keep the water tank full, and this he regularly failed to do. He was caught in a sudden gust of rage that spread outward like running fire until it had touched everybody and everything—Sarah, the children, the house and its naggingly primitive plumbing, the island, his publishers, his critics—all of humanity and the whole world. He gripped the sides of the basin until sanity returned and then, trembling slightly and shaken, went to the emergency supply in the earthenware jar in the corner and scooped out a jug of water. He finished his toilet hastily with an inadequate pass at his hair with a comb. Sarah and the money. He had to face Sarah in order to find the money.

The full coffeepot on the stove in the cool, dark kitchen told him that she was already up. The cup rattled in the saucer as he helped himself. His anxiety to check with Sarah conflicted with his reluctance to break his work habits. The morning was sacred to his work; if he exposed himself to the torments that any contact with Sarah risked arousing, the morning would be lost. He couldn't afford any more lost mornings. Here, sustained by the vivid picture of stability and order evoked by the kitchen—dark hand-hewn beams, rosy time-smooth stone floor, glow of copper, bunches of wild herbs hanging from the ceiling, loops of garlic and onions, rustic baskets overflowing with fruit and vegetables—he was almost lulled into feeling that the money didn't matter. And yet—out of some perversity in him, or because of a human inability to come to terms with Eden?—he sensed in the bountiful room a reproach. Was it frivolous to hope to live at peace in a disordered world?

He took a peach from a basket and tested it with his finger, postponing for a few more seconds the encounter with Sarah. He would have to pretend that last night's quarrel hadn't happened, even though he felt it as sharply as if they had attacked each other physically. Out of pride and embarrassment, because it was so alien to the qualities out of which they had forged their relationship, they had both refused to name the issue that lay between them, so that their quarrels were barren, missed the point, and left no opening for reconciliation.

He rejected the peach and set down the cup with a hand that still shook. Get on with it. He wouldn't be able to think about anything else until he had found the money.

He came upon her in the garden, and his first glimpse of her aroused all his unguarded admiration. He made an effort of will to resent her taking such an unfair advantage of him. She was wearing a crisp white blouse and a freshly pressed blue skirt. Her hair was carefully arranged, her makeup impeccable. Everything about her testified to her blamelessness. One couldn't reproach this model wife for having been drunk and disorderly. She had scored the first point of the day.

She was bending over the geraniums, removing the dead blooms with deft unshaking hands. Love, painful and involuntary, surged up in him, love for the quick grace of her movements, for the lovely line of her body, the arm lifted, the breasts nestled forward against the stuff of her blouse, the firm curve of hip flowing into slim leg. She had offered this beauty to another man. He could maintain her right to do so; fidelity, to have any value, must be voluntary. He knew he wanted her as much as he ever had, but there was no longed-for stir of desire in his loins. It had begun with what had seemed at the time a normal physical withdrawal, an instinctive distaste for sharing her body. When his love had finally prevailed, when his need for her had worn down his outrage, it was too late; his punishment of her had trapped him in his self-righteous celibacy. Life had become a torturous determination to hide his impotence from her. He had played this comedy for—less than a year? It seemed like a condition of life; he was doomed to his sterile love for Sarah.

It was doubtless bizarre of him to want only his wife after almost twenty years of marriage, and to expect her to be satisfied with him. Infidelity was an attribute of marriage, but he had always thought of the two of them as exceptions in all things. In the early years, in the full flood of his first spectacular success, he had slipped a few times, the inevitable follies that resulted from being lionized, but he had quickly learned that however much he might hurt Sarah, the loss to himself risked being greater. Ties were loosened, and he had needed the ties that held him to Sarah. He could curse them now. He cursed everything that held him prisoner—the children (hardly children anymore), the house, the shortage of money, the total *nonexistence* of money this morning. He seemed to have lost all control over life—all because Sarah had been to bed with another man. All because she had committed the perhaps greater crime of not really trying to hide it.

"Hi," he said cautiously, approaching her without quite looking at her. He caught the brave tender smile she offered him as she turned. He could guess by the glitter in her tantalizingly expressive but often unrevealing eyes that she had already had her first drink.

"Good morning, darling," she said. Her voice was a musical contralto, self-trained, "affected" to those who didn't like her, capable of subtly provocative meanings. With three words, she could tell him that she forgave him and that she had a great deal to forgive him for.

"You're looking very bright this morning," he said dryly, letting her know that he hadn't been taken in by her painstaking camouflage.

"I *feel* bright," she insisted, resolutely fresh and wholesome. "It's going to be another scorcher."

Someday, he thought, *I'll probably kill her.* There seemed no other imaginable solution. He moved into the shade of the grape arbor and slumped into a chair. The sawing of the cicadas was a thin rhythmic insistent celebration of heat, as nerve-racking as a fingernail drawn across slate. He pushed his hand through his hair. "You have that money I gave you last night, haven't you?" he asked, instinctively phrasing it so that her responsibility was engaged.

"Money? What money? Why should you give me money?" It was a quick, decisive disclaimer, disclaiming in effect any possibility of sharing anything with him.

"I'm talking about *the* money," he said, no longer caring who scored against whom as he squarely, soberly faced the appalling possibility of its loss. "Yesterday's lot. All of it. I didn't give it to you?"

"No, of course not. You mean—" She began in her brisk, unyielding manner, but her voice caught finally on a note of incredulity and alarm. He registered it with harsh satisfaction. She was engaged in this with him whether she liked it or not.

"Are you sure I didn't put it in your shopping basket?" he asked.

"I haven't looked. Oh, God, why did—?"

"Where is it? The basket, I mean." he was already off, moving toward the house.

"It's right there on the chair in the entrance." Her words were breathless, and he felt her following him. It gave him a welcome sense of power over her. He cut across the paved courtyard and entered the house and seized the woven-grass basket. It contained some odds and ends from yesterday's mail, his swimming trunks, a towel, a tin of milk. He fumbled through the things and threw down the basket and stood irresolutely, running his fingers through his hair. He had to think. He had to remember. She stood watching him from the doorway, an accusing but attentive presence.

"You can't mean you've really lost it," she said in a way that canceled out all hope of finding it.

"Lost it?" he repeated angrily. "How do you mean, lost it? It might have been stolen for all I know. All I know is, it isn't here."

"But what are we going to do? Oh, I know, I know. We're not supposed to worry about money. That's all very well when you have some, but that was every cent we could put our hands on."

"That's putting it in a nutshell." He curbed an impulse to soften the blow for her. It had been a function of his love to smooth things over for her, help her skirt issues, add a bright false color to a gloomy picture. Perhaps a head-on collision was what they needed. Perhaps the ghastly predicament that faced them would shake them out of their proud reticences.

"I'm glad you can laugh off what amounts to criminal carelessness," she said, offering battle.

"If it's gone, it's gone. What am I supposed to do about it?" There was an unfamiliar mean, sad pleasure in rubbing her nose in disaster, and he hated it. He knew that to hold her in his arms even briefly would give him strength to face any eventuality and that this was true for her too; they needed each other's support and sympathy, but an embrace could lead to more passionate contact and reveal what he had been hiding all these months. "It probably dropped out of my pocket at Lambraiki's," he said, adopting an optimistic tone in spite of himself. "Stavro will keep it for me."

"If you think there's any of chance of that, you'd better go right down there." From her safe neutral position in the doorway, she felt the reverberations of longing passing between them, and she steeled herself against them. He had shut himself off from her; he had condemned her to solitary guilt. It placed too great a burden on her nerves to respond to every slight lowering of his guard; the instant she did, the guards were raised higher. She permitted her eyes to linger briefly on the painfully open, vulnerable face and saw the torment in it. Her heart ached with rejected love. Accustomed by these last months to clutching at straws, she was almost inclined to welcome destitution as a promise of relief. They would be stripped to essentials, finally broken or reunited.

"This means losing a whole morning's work," he complained, as if he could reduce the loss to a mere nuisance.

"I don't see—how *could* you have dropped it?" she asked.

"Things have been known to drop out of pockets."

"But it's so unlike you."

"Is it?" He rubbed his hand over his eyes, wiping away sweat. He supposed he was still, to her, a model of self-discipline and purpose and efficiency. He didn't feel like a model of anything. Was this failure with her a symptom of a larger disintegration, an indication that he was running down generally, growing mentally and physically flabby, "going to seed," as the transients put it when they were first frightened by the idyllic island atmosphere? "I don't see how you can live here without just going to seed," they said nervously, wishing probably that they had come without their wives or husbands.

He took a deep breath and straightened his shoulders to prove to himself that he was intact. "Well, I'd better get going. You might tell Jeff to pump."

"Oh, dear. I used a lot of water this morning. I needed a real bath."

"You needn't make excuses for him. What if I'd wanted a shower? The tank's supposed to be kept full." He was seared by hate again, the sweeping hatred that embraced everybody and all of life, locking him in a vast cold solitude. He shoved his hands into his empty pockets and doubled them into fists, trying to regain the sanity of tolerance and compassion.

"Perhaps you'd better speak to him," Sarah was saying. "I don't seem to get anywhere with him these days."

No, you don't, he thought. *He was here when you were panting after your pretty young man. What did he see then? What did Kate see?* Hate seethed in him. "If I'm going to do something about the money, I haven't time for Jeff," he said. "Just tell him to pump." He glanced at her as he started to turn away and stood transfixed, once more undone by her. Light enveloped her, striking golden reflections from her chestnut hair, burnishing her skin, caressing the swell of her breast, endowing all of her body with luminous grace. He thought of the way she felt in his arms, the way she folded herself against him, offering herself with passionate generosity, her eyes unguarded and brimming with desire, and he was almost stirred, almost confident

that it could happen; but her eyes held him off and, abashed, he averted his own and turned from her. "I better put some decent clothes
on," he muttered as he left.

She waited until his footsteps had receded into the upper part of
the house and then fled through the dining room to the kitchen. Her
private bottle of brandy stood on the sideboard in among the bottles
of vinegar and olive oil and condiments. It wasn't hidden. She simply kept it here for convenience where it wouldn't be noticed. She
poured herself a generous measure. Her hand shook (what a luxury
to allow it to, after the struggle to pull herself together this morning)
as she lifted the glass to her lips, but steadied as she drained it. Sweat
broke out on her forehead, and she shook her hair back and took a
quick little gasping breath. Everything was going to be all right. He
would find the money. She was free now to go lie on the rocks, where
Pavlo was sure to be. Her mind erupted in a burst of erotic images of
the young man—strong thigh, smooth chest, muscled stomach, taut
heavy pouch of swimming trunks that seemed to swell and strain in
her mind's eye until her legs almost gave way beneath her.

She hunched her shoulders and beat her belly with her fists as if
there were something in her she could destroy. A whimpering moan
broke from her. She thought of her mother, a sturdy Westerner who
had taught school all her life and who had a stock lecture on self-
indulgence. Self-indulgence? One didn't indulge torment; one fought
it. There was no pleasure in her thoughts of Pavlo, only compulsion
and a debasing need.

George's doing. At times, she felt that he was intent on destroying
her. Sex had never been a problem for her. She had never had any reason to think much about it; it was only one aspect of the love that
filled her life with George. Life had always been George. There had
been a few intense awkward teenage affairs before him, and then she
was married to a struggling writer, whose struggle was made pic-
turesque by his being able to take her for weekends to his parents'
great estate up on the Hudson, where there were not only servants but
white servants. To a girl who had been brought up in a Depression-
ridden small town, it was quite dazzling—she had read about such
establishments but hadn't believed they still existed—and she was
soon dazzled further to find herself the wife of the great literary lion
of the day. It was the fulfillment of childhood dreams, dreams nur-
tured by and inherited from her father, himself an incurable romantic, a failed poet turned occasional journalist. Overnight, George had
achieved for her all that her father could have hoped for—freedom

from drudgery and routine, friendship with some of the important talents of her time, firsthand knowledge of the world she had read about, a certain reflected fame of her own of the sort poor foolish Zelda could have enjoyed through Scott if she hadn't been determined to outshine him.

That the dazzle had begun to dim in recent years was the only possible explanation for her having succumbed to Ronnie. Her faith in George hadn't wavered, but the world's had, making her question perhaps, without even knowing it, her complete and exclusive commitment to him. Whatever the reason, Ronnie had made her feel young and at the same time stirred an acute consciousness of the swift passage of years. George had been away on business in New York, a rare separation; she had caught Ronnie looking at Jeff in a way that made her feel that, as a woman, she could play a crucial role in his life; but nothing altered the fact that she had taken him knowing he could offer her nothing that George didn't give her, except physical novelty.

Was it as simple and degrading as that? Was Pavlo the logical next step? Had Ronnie's rather ethereal romantic quality enabled her to disguise with sentiment what was in fact an animal hunger for new bodies? There was no fooling herself about Pavlo. She was obsessed, quite specifically, with his body, with the part of his body contained in his swimming trunks. His prick. His cock. His dick. She forced her mind to shape the words baldly in an attempt to exorcise its spell, but her lips parted and her breath quickened as she thought of seeing it naked, of holding it, of feeling it inside her, of surrendering to its massive power.

She straightened with an effort, brushed the hair back from her forehead, and carefully poured herself another drink. More of George's work. He had been encouraging her to drink ever since he had found out about Ronnie. She couldn't remember when they had last had a sober evening together. Drink helped. She lifted the glass to her lips and swallowed the neat brandy in one gulp. She waited as the floor rocked gently beneath her, and then some spring within her seemed to snap and her thoughts became loose and remote.

No, there wasn't the slightest connection between Ronnie and Pavlo. She had been touched by Ronnie's need and had responded as any woman might, offering herself to help him enter fully into his manhood. She couldn't excuse her infidelity, but there had been nothing base about her motives. Her obsession with Pavlo was loathsome. She hated feeling like a sex-starved bitch in heat, but what normal healthy woman in her thirties wouldn't be sex-starved if her husband denied her intercourse for a year? Normally, she might look at Pavlo and admire his superb body, as women ogled Charlie Mills-Martin's impressive crotch, without wanting to fling herself on it. Sex on such a gross functional level had never had any meaning for her. Yet she could not check the beating of her heart when Pavlo presented himself for her inspection. That was what it amounted to, recognized by both of them almost from the first time he had appeared down on the rocks two weeks ago. He had apparently caught her eyes on him in an unguarded moment and had looked at her with a lazy, complacently knowing smile and thereafter had offered her a generous display of his person. When he climbed out of the sea, he had a habit of darting his hand into the front of his trunks to arrange himself. He soon took to seeking her eye simultaneously and when he caught it, his hand would linger a second longer, his sex would stand out more pronouncedly where he lifted it upright against his belly. When he squatted beside her to exchange some banality, his hand would stray to it, not reticently or for concealment but proudly, thumb and forefinger curved lovingly around stout columnar flesh to define its contours, his eyes willing hers to look. She resisted always, and always gave in, but permitted herself only the most fleeting glances.

Yesterday, he had strolled over to her, the contemptuously knowing smile on his lips, holding a towel casually in front of himself. When he was standing over her, he had dropped the towel to his side and put a hand low on his hip so that the tips of his fingers just touched something she refused to look at and said something about the weather. She felt all the muscles of her face tightening, her head seemed to swim, and she found herself staring open-mouthed at what he had revealed for her inspection. It was clearly outlined, partially or fully erect, held against his groin by the stretched confinement of the trunks and barely contained by them.

Pavlo stood over her while she still stared, his remark about the weather unheeded, and swayed his hips slightly in cautious imitation of copulation. He had laughed and lifted the towel in front of him again and sauntered down to the sea.

What had he expected her to do? Get up and ask him to take her somewhere? She took a deep breath, shook her head angrily, and refilled her glass. This one would get her safely to lunch. She drank it more slowly, in measured sups. When she had finished it a little smile played about her lips. Thank heavens for the heat. It put one right off the whole idea of sex. He would probably be quite disgusting naked. All the great male paraphernalia. Grotesque. Anyway, he had shown her all that he had to show, short of dropping his drawers. Perhaps they would move on to a purely spiritual relationship. She giggled as she recorked her bottle and returned it to its place among the condiments.

Up at the Mills-Martin house on the eastern promontory of the port, overlooking the whole town, the day began in cheerful tumult. The two adult male members of the household were, as was their wont, in bed together. Because of the heat, there was space between them, but each held the other's rigid sex in his hand, the grip firm and caressing when they drifted into consciousness, relaxing as they retreated once more into sleep. A sheet haphazardly covered their loins, their lean, smoothly muscled, heavily tanned torsos sprawled across the bed, tousled blond hair on the pillows, Peter's golden, Charlie's graying but streaked now with gold by the sun. They breathed deeply each other's odors, to both of them the sweet odor of contentment and security and time-tested passion.

They awoke with a start as the children erupted into the room. Charlie rolled quickly onto his stomach, prepared for the onslaught. Peter was gathering the sheet more securely around him as Little Pete charged him and began to drum on his hip with his fists.

"Daddy, Daddy, Daddy," the child shouted.

A glancing blow struck Peter's subsiding sex. "Hey, that's Daddy, all right," Peter protested with laughter. "Cut that out."

"Mummy says it's time to get up," Charlotte said.

Charlie groaned. "As usual, Mummy's probably right," he said from the depths of his pillow. The girl leaned over him and found an ear to kiss. He stroked her pale hair as she did so.

Little Petey had propped himself against his father's slightly turned hip and dropped his arm over his thigh so that it rested near his crotch. Expecting this move, Peter had managed to tuck himself out of reach; the little boy had a way of exploring private areas, leaning against them, letting his hands stray to them. ("His father's own son," Peter had commented when the three parents had discussed it.) A small hand patted his stomach. "Where's your toy now?" the child inquired secretly, conspiratorially, peering up from lowered brows.

"It's vanished. It has a way of doing that." The toy had been invented when Little Pete's hand had made unequivocal contact with his erection one morning; He had claimed to have a toy in bed with him.

The wide inquiring eyes grew lively now in anticipation of a new game. Little Pete shook his head uncertainly, torn between skepticism and the will to believe, and smiled slyly. "No, it hasn't. How can it?"

"It just does. It comes and goes. I never know when it's going to turn up."

Petey settled more of his weight on his father's hip and plucked excitedly at the sheet. "That would be interesting. Why can't I have one like it, Daddy? You said you'd give me one."

"Later. You have to be older to have any fun with it."

"Will you give Lottie one before me?"

"No. A girl wouldn't want one. It's strictly for boys."

The bed began to shake with Charlie's silent laughter. Petey threw his head back as he gazed adoringly at his father and heaved a great sigh as if he could scarcely contain his delight. Peter was constantly struck with wonder as he caught glimpses of himself in the lively eyes, the tilt of the nose, the generous mouth, the shape of the golden head. Everybody found his son beautiful.

"He's so *dumb*," Charlotte said, coming around to the bed to kiss Peter on the cheek. She was a poised, grown-up young lady of nine. Peter put his arm around her and seated her on the edge of the bed beside him. Little Pete went racing off around the room making dreadful noises in his throat. He was a jet or a rocket or perhaps the hydrogen bomb.

"Are you really going to be forty your next birthday?" the girl asked Peter.

The doleful note in the question made Peter laugh. He lifted his hand to her face and let his fingers linger on her cheek near her eyes where she was unmistakably Charlie. "Somebody's been giving away my secrets," he said. "I have a whole month still to be thirty-nine."

Charlotte gazed at him with commiseration. "It sounds so old. I just can't believe it." Her incredulity was shared by everybody who knew them. They had taken good care of their bodies and could still wear clothes they had had for ten years; they kept a few serviceable museum pieces that dated back to when they had first met and fallen in love. Charlie was acquiring a slightly weathered look, and his graying hair marked him with years, but in the right light Peter retained an unearthly youthfulness that made people's mouths drop open when they learned his age.

Peter laughed at the lovely solemn little face that was studying him with such concern. "Just wait. There isn't all that much difference between us. When you're fifty, I'll only be about eighty, and then the joke will be on you."

15

Little Pete exploded in a series of fearsome detonations and ended up on Charlie's side of the bed. He smoothed the sheet over Charlie's bottom so that its contours were precisely delineated. "Hey, Daddy," he said, stroking a buttock. "Why do you and Daddy sleep in the same bed? Kyria Tula says daddies usually don't."

Charlie heaved himself over onto his back. "Because we like to, dopey," he asserted.

"Why else?" Peter agreed. "Why do you like to get into Mummy's bed? It's nice sleeping with people you love."

"He doesn't understand anything," Charlotte pointed out with slightly bored forbearance.

"Then why don't you let Mummy get in with you?" Petey persisted. His sturdy little body was largely hidden by the bed. Eyes full of mischief searched for an answer across Charlie's sheeted and blameless stomach.

"She doesn't like the way we snore," Peter explained.

The look of eager anticipation lighted the child's face once more. "Show me, Daddy," Little Pete urged, already beginning to do a jig of hilarious appreciation. Peter snored hideously. Charlie joined in. They all dissolved in paroxysms of laughter and rolled around on the bed together.

They had expected questions from the moment they had decided to create a family with the unorthodox material at hand (*decided* to live with and for these miracles? What loss would they be answerable for if they had failed to do so?) and had resolved to answer them as truthfully as possible. Martha had already explained to Charlotte that Charlie was her father, but that she had been married to another man so that when she was free she had married Peter in order to have Petey.

"It amounts to the same thing." Martha had pointed out, unconscious that there was anything extraordinary in what she was saying. "They've always been together. They're like brothers, only even more so. When you're older and understand more about love, you'll realize how rare and wonderful it is."

The adoption of a common name had consolidated the family. It had been Peter's idea to go through the legal formalities of combining his and Charlie's surnames into a hyphenated amalgam so that the children, with Martha's former husband's consent, were legally brother and sister, Martha was legally the mother of both, and Charlie and Peter achieved a sort of official sanction to their extra-legal relationship. This had so nicely confused the situation that few remembered for long who was what to whom. There were those who

16

believed that Charlie and Peter really were brothers despite the fact that they were openly and unabashedly in love with each other. Some people were convinced that Martha had worked it out somehow so that she was in enviable possession of both husband and resident lover, though they were inclined to be vague about which was which. On the island, having notably failed to live up to their explosive and scandalous potential, they were regarded as the essence of sanity and respectability. It was generally and reassuringly felt that as long as the Mills-Martins were there, everything would be all right.

"All right now," Charlie said, disentangling himself from immature arms and legs. "Go tell Mummy you've made complete nuisances of yourselves and that we'll be down in a minute." Charlie swung Charlotte into the air above him, and Peter caught her and landed her on her feet. Petey planted a hand firmly and painfully on Charlie's genitalia as he pushed himself off onto the floor. The children scampered off across the big, white, shuttered room and disappeared.

"I've always thought the Mills-Martins sounded like a circus act," Charlie said with a chuckle. They joined hands under the sheet. "God. That's all I needed after last night. What are we going to do about the Leightons?"

"I don't know. I think maybe we're going to have to start keeping them in separate cages. I haven't had a chance to tell you. Young Jeff sidled over to me in the heat of the battle. He wants to have a serious talk."

They turned their heads simultaneously on their pillows and exchanged a look. Charlie lifted his brows. "Has the hour struck at last?"

"I wouldn't be surprised."

"Dimitri?"

"Your guess is as good as mine."

"I hope not, poor kid. I'm afraid Dimitri is not one of our greatest successes. Could it, by any chance, be you he's interested in?"

"More likely you—more of a father figure," Peter said with a spurt of laughter.

"Well, as the elder statesmen of international homosexuality, we have our responsibilities. I hope you'll be able to help. Jeff's a good kid."

"I'll try to handle it the way I hope somebody would if the hour ever strikes for Little Petey."

"The Groper? Are you mad? He's going to be so bored and familiar with the male body by the time he's twelve that he'll be the straightest guy who ever walked down Main Street."

They smiled into each other's eyes. "That'll be his tough luck. You know, if Miss Charlie gets any more like you, I'm going to fall in love with her. Would that be incest? Let me think. You're her father and Martha's her mother and I'm—no, it's perfectly all right. She's just my son's half-sister. What could be more natural?"

They burst out laughing at the complex web of relationships they had created. Charlie brushed the sheet off them and propped himself beside Peter and bent over him and kissed his sex. The heat rather dampened Peter's ardor, but he touched Charlie's hair and made little murmuring appreciative sounds to indicate his willingness if Charlie wanted it.

"Lovely toy," Charlie said and stirred unique excitement with his tongue. He gave Peter's thighs a squeeze, then rolled over, dropped his feet over the side of the bed, and rose. Peter's eyes were fixed on the heavy curve of Charlie's semierect sex as he turned toward the bathroom. After twenty years, it was still to him the most magnificent and exciting spectacle in nature. Presented with Charlie's back, his eyes traveled from the broad shoulders down to the spring of solid hip and buttock. He smiled as his thoughts grew lustful and his sex hardened and lifted from between his legs. "If it weren't so hot, I'd drag you back here and have my way with you," he called after the retreating figure.

Charlie laughed. "It's bound to cool off. I'll still be here."

When they had taken turns in the bathroom, they twisted lengths of cloth around their waists sarong-fashion and set off through the house to Martha, Peter's hand resting lightly on Charlie's shoulder.

Ten years ago when they had bought it, the house had looked a severe, uncomplicated block of masonry; but as they rebuilt it, they had discovered many surprises. Guided by old photographs, they had restored the colonnade along the wide upper balcony, cleared terraces, created loggias, dug out shady inner courtyards. It was spread about the hillside on three levels, a house of big cool marble-paved rooms and unexpected private apartments all giving out onto the port and the town and the islet-strewn sea. It wasn't home to them—they still considered the farm in Connecticut their real base—but it had become more important to them than they expected. As an art dealer, Peter used it frequently as a stopover point on his frequent business trips about Europe. Charlie found it congenial for work. They had acquired a proprietary feeling toward the island, had been alarmed by the increasing influx of tourists following the big Hollywood film that had been made there two years before, had success-fully used their influence with the local authorities to limit hotel and night-club developments. They had the right of discovery. If they hadn't already been there, the Leightons wouldn't have bought, and in the absence of both families, nobody would ever have heard of the place. They were already talking of spending at least half the year here when the children were old enough to travel alone.

They descended a covered exterior stair, crossed a courtyard, and entered Martha's quarters. She was waiting for them at a table set inside open doors that gave onto a balcony overlooking the port. The sun was still behind the house, so the room was dark and shadowy behind the motionless linen draperies at the windows. Through the doors, the lower town built close around the port looked like a minia-ture stage setting.

"Good morning, darlings," she greeted them, holding each briefly to her comfortable breast and giving each a maternal kiss. She had never been thin and, with time, had settled into an appealing amplitude. Her soft pretty features were ageless, but she had an air of settled maturity that her two men lacked. "Were you able to sleep in this heat?"

"We were doing fine until you unleashed the hounds of hell," Charlie said.

Martha laughed. "Did they pay you a visit? I didn't tell them to. You should be flattered. They can't bear to be away from you."

"The fiends. Actually, we had a very jolly roughhouse. Peter's toy failed to put in an appearance."

They all exploded with laughter.

"Call Kyria Tula for your coffee," Martha said, shaking her head in mock reproof.

Peter did so. The kitchen and dining room were on the other side of the courtyard. The three sat in caned armchairs around the table. Powerful binoculars lay on it. Peter picked them up and began to explore the town.

"What a horrid evening," Martha said. "I'm devoted to the Leigh-tons, but they're making themselves socially impossible. You'd sup-pose they'd have worked their way through last year's little trouble by now. Unfortunately, I'm afraid Sarah's headed for real disaster."

"Pavlo?" Peter said from behind the binoculars.

"She can't take her eyes off him. She actually had the cheek to compare him to Charlie. Really! That dull body boy."

Peter lowered the binoculars. "It's obvious where she's been looking."

Martha looked at him with a twinkle in her eyes. "Yes. Well, there may be some slight similarity, but I doubt if he can compete even there."

"Trust my expert eye. He can't."

"For God's sake," Charlie exclaimed. "You two have such dirty minds. Come on. Let's stick to the Leightons."

The Greek housekeeper entered and greeted them all affably. She set cups and coffeepot on the table and withdrew. Peter resumed his scrutiny of the outside world.

"I feel as if we ought to be able to help them," Martha continued, pouring coffee. "They're still in love with each other. I'm sure of that, even though they've been together almost as long as you two. Their financial worries are over for the moment. I thought that might help them settle down. Isn't there some way you could scare Pavlo off?"

"What do you expect?" Charlie asked. "Sarah's making a big play for him. You can't blame him for taking what's offered, especially when it's such a high-class article. He's probably used to little tarts."

"There he goes now," Peter said, shifting the binoculars along the opposite promontory, where the road led out to the swimming rocks. "Off to give all the girls their morning thrill." He swung the glasses back toward the center of town, held them steady a moment, and then inched them back toward Lambraiki's. "Yes, by golly. This is a new twist. Here comes old George himself. He seems to be in rather a flap. I've never seen him walk so fast. Why isn't he at work? If he starts drinking at this hour, the glasses will be flying by noon. In he goes." He put the binoculars aside and picked up his cup.

"Speaking of work," Charlie said, replacing his cup in its saucer, "the master had better get at it." He rose but lingered as Peter's head lifted and their eyes met. "That thing I started yesterday has turned out to be a bitch," he said. "Come up to the studio. I'd like to talk it out with you." He ran his fingers along Peter's upturned jaw. "Beautiful bastard." He leaned over, and their mouths touched briefly in a kiss. He gave Peter's neck a squeeze and trailed a hand affectionately across Martha's shoulders as he moved away.

"Soon's I finish my coffee, love," Peter said, his eyes once more following the back, his smile reborn by lustful thoughts. A surge of the almost tangible contentment that he had learned to accept as a feature of life swept over him.

Martha sat back in her chair with a little sigh as she saw the triumphant light in his eye, compounded of desire and confident possessiveness. It was a familiar look associated inextricably in her mind with a memory of one of the first nights she had spent in this house, long ago, just after Charlie had bought it.

She had been pregnant with his Charlotte, she had been in the first desperate throes of her passion for him, she had been still married to Jack, and she had no faint intimation of what the future might hold. First Charlie, then, more convincingly, Peter had talked of the possibility of her living near them after her divorce so that Charlie could take some part in his child's upbringing. She was still clinging to the hope that she could somehow win him away from Peter, marry him in a conventional way, and bear him more children.

An odd time, fraught with crisis, yet what she remembered mostly about it was a great inner stillness. A spiritual paralysis, perhaps induced by the scene she had inadvertently witnessed. The house had been little more than a ruin then and so different from its present splendor that she wasn't even sure where it had taken place.

She had been below and they had been above somewhere, the pattern for the future already established—she in her quarters, they in theirs—although she hadn't grasped that that was the way it was to be. Slow of her, perhaps, but so much had happened that summer when they had become friends and made the trip to Greece together, she and her husband and the two beautiful young men who made it quite plain that they were a couple.

She had finally accepted the failure of her childless marriage to Jack. She had seduced Charlie and become pregnant by him before she had accepted the fact that his prowess as a lover was no evidence of heterosexuality. She had even had Peter as a lover, at Charlie's insistence, because he rejected any experience that excluded his friend.

On that restless night when she had heard sounds above, she hadn't hesitated to go up and join them for a good-night chat. At the top of the perilous stairs, she had found an open door filled with a glow of lamplight and had taken only a few steps toward it before she realized what the sounds signified. She drew back with an instinctive respect for their privacy, but neither of them had been reticent in telling her about their lovemaking. She was filled with a sudden rebellious urge to see for herself. Simple prurience? A lingering delusion that their sex play could have none of the passion she had offered Charlie? She moved cautiously until she had the bed framed in the door while she remained in darkness.

The lamp revealed Charlie and Peter locked in each other's arms, their limbs beautiful in the soft light but so closely entangled that it took her a moment to define their positions. It was Peter who bore down on Charlie's back; it was Charlie who had been mounted. As she watched, they reared back onto their knees and Charlie slid back into Peter's lap, his hips working, his whole body writhing with submission, his voice crying out his joy at being possessed, the look of rapt ecstasy on his face similar to what Martha imagined a woman would look like being taken by her man.

Mingled rage and horror struck her at the experienced mastery with which Peter was handling him; he was fulfilling desire with blithe possessive authority. She turned and moved silently, as quickly as she dared, away from the light and back down safely to the part of the ruin assigned to her.

She had sat for a long time in the dark; it must have been several hours before she had sorted out all her reactions. She had no grounds for being shocked; they had both made it clear that they engaged in that form of copulation, though she had always imagined their positions reversed. She found the act repellently unnatural, but after the first searing vision of it had dimmed a little, she knew that she found neither of *them* repellent. She was still in love with Charlie, but the fire of it had gone out the instant she had seen the rapture in his face and known that she could never make him look like that. She felt an odd sadness, the birth of a sad sisterly maternal tenderness for him mingled with the love that had lost its fire.

As she sat in the dark, she had decided to leave them both, she had decided to stay and destroy the bond that held them and take whatever could be salvaged of Charlie and make him her husband, while in the midst of these decisions a curious intimation grew in her of having passed through the stress of some initiation.

She had been consecrated the high priestess of the mystery. They had carried her beyond the world of ordinary men and women into some transcendental realm where love was the only law. She would never feel at home elsewhere again. She was the handmaiden of the unknowable that would some day be revealed to her. If leaving them was impossible, she must accept the role assigned to her and fill her life with whatever unknown rewards she might find in it.

Martha looked at Peter as he swallowed the last of his coffee. She loved the curve of his neck and the long lashes that lay on his cheeks like a girl's. Her husband. The father of her son, by Charlie's volition as much as Peter's. She still found it very nearly incredible, even though it was only a technicality. By the time they had all been ready to make a final commitment to each other, it hadn't mattered which she married legally.

Affection had plastered over the cracks where love had proved inadequate. Peter's tax position was the primary consideration, since he had had most of the money in those days. She had chosen a life that most people would find incomprehensible, but it worked. Only rarely, when Peter was away on business and Charlie chose to spend the night with her, did she feel that she had somehow allowed herself to be cheated.

"Don't keep him waiting," she said when he put down his cup.

"What?" He gave her a vacant little smile. The look that Charlie had inspired lingered in his eyes. He made a visible effort to descend from the stars. "Oh, the master. No. I was just going. I was just think-ing about him."

"Were you really?" Martha said ironically. "Do you ever stop?"

Peter laughed, followed by a smile of affection for her. "Some-times. For a minute or two every now and then." He had been relish-ing the pleasure he always felt when Charlie drew him into his work. Charlie had done so only since he had become an established suc-cess, perhaps in recognition of the part Peter had played in achieving it. Charlie hadn't suddenly hit on some new vein in his work. Peter had detected a trend developing in the art market and by shrewd con-trivance had placed Charlie in its van so that he had been catapulted into the ranks of the handful of major innovators of contemporary American art.

Success had seemed to free him from the confines of his ego. He referred to himself as "Peter's commodity." Ever since he had con-ceived his child on Martha, he had allowed everything feminine in his nature to emerge, as if being a father had relieved him of the necessity of asserting his masculinity. Their sexual habits, so long based on Charlie's cherished image of himself as "normal" and Peter's cheerful recognition of his own streak of femininity, had evolved until Peter had finally been confirmed in his role as the male member of their partnership. There was no longer any question of who was the boss; Charlie turned to Peter for everything. There was a new softness in his manner, a habit of deferring to Peter, something in the way he looked at him, certain movements he made toward him that, if more pronounced, might seem womanish. It made Peter smile whenever he noticed it; it was such an unlikely development. Old butch Charlie who had stumbled in the beginning over calling him "darling" in front of Martha. His reserve, the firm check on his emo-tions was still there but so mellowed that people who met him now were apt to comment on his nice lack of complexity.

Peter burst out laughing, which Martha took as an expression of his usual high spirits as he put his hand out and touched hers.

"I'll go check the genius. Shall we go swimming soon? I'd like to find out what's going on. I can't imagine what's taken George away from his work at this hour."

"They *do* worry me. I'm glad you're worrying too. If anybody can help them, you two might be able to."

He rose, reminded of young Jeff. He was a sensitive kid, and Peter hoped to run into him to confirm their date for later and make him feel welcome. He liked the young and their problems because he still felt so close to his own troubled youth. He and Charlie had suspected what Jeff's great problem would be ever since they had first known him, before he was even in his teens. It was hard to say why; something indefinable, something they had both felt. He hitched up his sarong more securely and gave Martha's right shoulder a squeeze. "Okay, old lady. Give me an hour or so. Right?"

"Yes, darling. Try not to be longer. It's so hot." She addressed a well-muscled and shapely back as he jauntily left the room bursting with pride at being consulted about Charlie's work. She felt a brief resentment, but it was quickly absorbed into the almost dense stability she sensed in her household. By comparison, the more conventional lives of their friends seemed fragmentary and ephemeral. They brought so little stamina to their relationships. Like the Leightons. Flying apart because of some past foolishness of Sarah's. Of course, fidelity wasn't a problem for the Mills-Martins. At the beginning she had expected, perhaps even hoped, that other young men would prove to be a disruptive force, but it hadn't turned out that way. Once she had become a mother she had ceased thinking in such terms. She had found childbearing sensually thrilling, more fulfilling sexually than anything she had known with a man except for the first days of clandestine lovemaking with Charlie. Bearing children had slaked her passions by offering her a greater passion. She still sometimes caught herself nurturing a fantasy about Peter falling for a girl and making a new life for himself, but she couldn't really imagine it happening and probably would fight it if it did. There was enough to treasure in what she had. It distressed her to see others less fortunate tearing at each other and courting disaster.

The Leightons. It was doubtless the heat that made her feel something explosive in their estrangement that threatened all of them.

By now, the island could be said to be awake. The dedicated alcoholics were settling down at tables along the waterfront. Sid Coleman and his girl had shared their first joint of the day. One of the more laggard households was that presided over by Joe Peterson, the student of theology.

Joe was wandering naked and befuddled around the kitchen of his rented house wondering how he could make coffee without disturbing any of the dirty dishes that were piled up in the sink and spread out on the limited counter space. The two-burner stove had been selected as the repository for dirty pots. The congestion of the kitchen had its counterpart in the long narrow room upstairs where two splayed and sagging beds contained four bodies, three female and one male.

One of them was Lena, Joe's principal girlfriend for the past week or so. Until Joe had retreated to the kitchen, they had formed a threesome with an English girl called Penny who had turned up from somewhere a few days before. Lena had a wholesome Scandinavian attitude toward sex—the more of it the better and in the greatest possible variety. Heaven knew what she was up to now. The other bed contained the German traveling companions Gunther and Hilda, who had moved in only yesterday.

How any of them could remain up there in this heat Joe couldn't understand. He had never felt anything like it, not even in his native California. It was utterly still, unnaturally still, so oppressive that it felt as if something would have to give. Joe felt crowded by it in the cramped kitchen.

He was a big man, big bones covered with a solid layer of smooth California flesh. His curly brown hair grazed the kitchen ceiling. He had a big mouth that turned his face into a dazzling array of teeth when he smiled.

He stared at the dirty pots on the stove. As long as they were there he would have no coffee. He picked them up and carried them through the bare room adjoining the kitchen and threw them into the courtyard. The clatter seemed to melt into the heat. He returned to the kitchen and scooped water into the kettle from the jar in the corner and put it on to boil. Gunther drifted silently into the kitchen, also naked.

"Hi," Joe said.

"Good morning." The German wandered over to the kitchen table and stood in front of it.

Joe was embarrassed by their nakedness despite the promiscuity prevailing above. "I'm trying to get some coffee going," he explained. He lifted his hand to wave Gunther away from the table and touched his hip. The hip didn't move. Joe looked at him.

The boy's gaze was level. "Enough of girls, I think. You and me, *ja?*" he suggested. His face was expressionless, but his eyes managed to convey his thought. He shifted his hip slightly, reminding Joe that his hand was still on it.

Joe felt himself blushing. He should probably give it a try just to find out what it was all about and what guys did together; it seemed to be the thing to do these days.

Biblical references paraded through his mind, all of them minatory. All the same, he had been tempted to experiment with Costa the boatman a week ago, before Lena had moved in. Costa was the go-between for the foreigners with the local population; he could come up with anything from lobster to pot. He had made suggestive gestures in a joking way late one night at the house and had proposed staying till morning. Joe had sent him away with some reluctance. The island was nutty. What would he be tempted to do next? He found his eyes fixed on Gunther's.

"Well, I don't know," he said. "It's a pretty crazy idea. We'll see." His characteristic tone was eager and innocent, and he sounded perhaps more willing than he intended. He spread his fingers on the boy's waist.

"Is good. We will be brothers. Is different with girls."

Joe found nothing to dispute in that statement and exerted pressure with his hand to move Gunther out of the way. As he did so, without actually looking, he could see from the lower rim of his vision that he had excited the boy. His own quiescence reassured him that he wasn't going to turn queer overnight.

He pulled open the drawer of the table with the insubstantial hope of finding some clean spoons. There were none. He started to push the drawer closed but hesitated and then pulled it all the way out, gazing into its emptiness.

"Son of a bitch!" he exclaimed. "I put a thousand drachmas in here yesterday. Where is it?"

"You lose something?"

"No, goddammit." Joe lifted accusing eyes. It wasn't much in dollars, but it was worth two weeks living here. "My money. It was here yesterday. Somebody's taken it."

"You think I steal? Your money? What for?" For the first time since Joe had met him, Gunther smiled. It wasn't an expansive smile, but it indicated amusement and immediately exculpated him.

"No, not you. Of course not." Joe put his hand on the boy's shoulder. It's slightness was very pleasant to the touch, quite like a girl. "Maybe Lena took it. I'd better go ask her."

Gunther stepped closer to him. "We go to bed now?"

"Not now. Aren't you hot?" Joe's eyes were on the boy's mouth, finding that if you overlooked the slight shadow of mustache above the upper lip, it appeared kissable. "Anyway, I've got to find my money. I don't like being robbed. I wonder what old George will make of it. He's always maintained that nobody steals here. Do you know him? George? George Leighton? The famous novelist?"

"Novelist. Money. What matter is it to me? I offer to be your brother."

"Thanks, Gunther. Later maybe," Joe said distractedly. "I have to look into this. I don't guess the police would be any good. George will be able to advise me." He pushed Gunther firmly aside and went up to confront the girls.

George Leighton was bathed in sweat when he reached Lambraiki's. He pushed his way into the dark narrow store past a knot of shopping women and went on around to the back of the counter, a privilege only he could dare assume. Stavro caught sight of him out of the corner of his eye, but went on weighing out a block of white cheese.

"Good morning, my Yorgo," Stavro crooned, not making the effort to move his lips. The lethargy communicated by the ample figure in a soiled smock was deeply soporific, and the vague fumbling of his hands suggested that he would go on ladling out cheese forever. George sighed as he adapted to the island rhythm. He felt foolish for having practically run all this way. At least, the end of his mission was in sight.

"Listen," he said, pleading. "Did you find any money last night?"

Stavro wrapped the cheese and pushed it across the counter. "What else?" he crooned to the customer and in the same tone, without turning, he said, "Money? What money, my Yorgo?"

"A lot of it. A bundle of thousand-drachma notes. Almost sixty thousand. I must've dropped it at the table last night."

Without giving any sign that he had heard, Stavro counted out change for his customer. There was a monumental deliberation about everything he did that was almost soothing. George half-expected him to withdraw the bundle of bills from his cash drawer with the same expressionless deliberation and hand it over. Instead, he turned from the counter, put his hand on George's shoulder, and, gently easing him around, guided him past groceries into the back room, which in addition to tables and chairs contained a confusion of tin tubs, coils of rope, kerosene lamps, and great barrels of wine and brandy and ouzo. He gave George a little hug.

"You were outside. Then at the end, you were sitting here," he said, stating a fact that George was obliged to accept in faith. "I swept up myself. There was much broken glass. There was no money, my Yorgo."

George's heart had been beating rapidly in anticipation of the conjurer's trick, the rabbit pulled out of the hat, the money suddenly materializing in his hand, and now it seemed to stop entirely as the words soaked with black finality into his mind. "Why were we in here?" Did it matter that he had perhaps caught Stavro in an error? "It was hot last night."

"You were outside. Then you and Sarah came in here. Others followed, the way they do."

"There's no chance you swept it up without noticing it?" he asked, not aware of the incongruity of finding hope in such a suggestion. All the sweepings would have been dumped into the sea hours ago.

"I always notice, Yorgo," Stavro said with tender regret. "People are always losing things here."

"Oh, Christ." Leighton swore helplessly in English. "I tell you, it was a lot of money. I was planning to pay my bill."

"Never mind." Stavro immediately brightened at having found a silver lining. He rocked George in a bear hug and patted him reassuringly on the back. "The bill doesn't matter. You can pay anytime."

With what? George wondered. It was impossible for the locals to believe that the foreigners might have financial problems like ordinary mortals. They were here, far from home, with no jobs and unlimited leisure. They were obviously rich. He would be violating Stavro's trust if he continued to run up a bill under these circumstances. He extricated himself from the big man's embrace with a shrug.

"Well, if it isn't here, it isn't here," he said because he could think of nothing else to say, because the catastrophe had gone beyond the bounds of relevant comment.

"That's it," Stavro agreed, happy to have the unpleasantness disposed of. "Have a drink. I will pay. What will you have?"

"Thanks, Stavro. A beer might help."

"Stamatis, a beer for Mr. Yorgo," Lambraiki called to one of his invisible children as they drifted back together toward the front of the shop. Leighton squeezed past the waiting customers, stumbled into sunlight, and slumped into a chair. Even under the awning, the heat was dense. It clung to him so tangibly that he felt he could remove it, along with his sweat-soaked shirt.

"Oh, Christ damn," he muttered to himself, running his fingers through his hair. The money was gone. The money was *gone*. What was he going to do now? He forced himself to think bleakly about the subject that interested him least in the world—money.

As the son and only heir of rich parents, he had never given much thought to creating an "estate" or whatever it was people were supposed to do. He had spent freely in the big years, and his reserves had quickly dwindled when his last two books had failed to earn anything like what he had been accustomed to making. Still, the picture wasn't all black. He had provided for Jeff's and Kate's educations by setting up trusts for them. He carried a lot of insurance for Sarah. It had some cash-in value, but he was vague about just how it worked. It would take weeks of tiresome correspondence with the family friend who managed such things to realize anything from whatever assets he had left. The missing money was all the immediately available cash he had. What was he supposed to do until he found more?

Work. That was what he wanted to do. He had to be free to work. How was he to finish the new book if he had to spend the next month or two trying to rake up more money?

He felt the prickling of fear down his spine and turned restlessly in his chair, looking for his beer. A small boy with an apron flapping around his ankles approached the table and set down a bottle and a glass. George poured it out gratefully with hands that still shook. The first cold swallow soothed his spirit, and he took a long breath of relief.

At least they were here and not trying to be grand in some city. One of the things he had liked best about it here was that you could spend money all day without thinking about it and end up with change from a couple of dollars. If you had a couple of dollars. The shopkeepers would carry him indefinitely, but he still had to give people bits of metal and paper for certain things. Why not use leaves or blades of grass? Maybe the Mills-Martins would lend him some of the stuff. Jesus. Had it come to that? Sponging off friends? All his debts so far were confined to his professional sphere; they weren't debts so much as options on his future.

He wasn't frightened of being poor; on the contrary, he welcomed it from a philosophical point of view. He had the house. He had put a lot of thought and effort into it, but it was the only material possession that he had ever really cared about. The hell with possessions—but that didn't mean he was careless with money. Even drunk, he couldn't have just left it on the table or thrown it on the floor. He had checked with Stavro because he had had to make sure, but he hadn't really expected to find it. Obviously, it had been stolen.

Facing it finally, after trying to suppress the possibility, brought with it a nasty shock. If it had been stolen, it had been stolen *by* somebody. He didn't know anybody who would steal. There might be thieves among the beats who drifted through, but he didn't know them; he had been with friends.

No Greek could have taken it. Greeks didn't steal. The Mills-Martins, the Varnums, Sid Coleman and his girl—everybody was automatically ruled out. Yet the money was gone. Somebody he knew was a thief, somebody with a mental quirk, perhaps. He must make everybody understand how important the money was to him. Whoever had taken it would return it. Or perhaps somebody, seeing that he was drunk and risked losing it, had sneaked off with it as a joke and a warning. It was the sort of thing Sid might do to teach him a lesson, as a part of his campaign to get him off booze in favor of pot.

By the time he had almost finished the bottle of beer, he had achieved a degree of tranquillity and was wondering whether he should attempt to do some work. He was bound to get the money back somehow. Perhaps another beer? He hadn't quite decided to write off the morning as a loss when Joe Peterson pulled out a chair and settled himself massively at the table with him.

"Hi, George. You're just the man I wanted to see." Joe always wanted to see George. George was one of his literary heroes, and he had come to the island hoping to get to know him. So far, they hadn't achieved intimacy, but Joe was always glad of a chance to call himself to the older man's attention. "Let me buy you a drink. I have a problem."

George's mind sprang to attention. *Had Joe been among the group last night? If he was going to return the money, why didn't he do it and get it over with?* "I might have another beer," he said, lifting his arms and snapping his fingers.

Joe made a face. "Beer? Beer's all right first thing in the morning to take the taste of coffee out of your mouth. But lord, man, the morning's getting on. I think I'll have a gin. It's very good in hot weather. Not martinis. Martinis are no good without ice. But gin and soda's not bad."

"Have you passed this information on to Dr. Barth?" George

asked. "Or are you saving it for your doctor's dissertation?"

Joe drank with pedantic application, as if he were engaged on a research project.

"You probably *could* do something with scriptural references to wines and spirits," Peterson reflected. The child with the flapping apron appeared at George's summons, and they ordered.

"What's your problem?" George asked. If he knew something about his money, why didn't he say so?

"Well, the question is, What do you think of Costa?"

"Costa? Which Costa?" This wasn't at all what he had been hoping for.

"Our Costa. Costa the happy boatman. He's sitting over there with that band of ruffians."

George glanced in the direction Peterson indicated. A group of dock workers and fishermen were seated at a table in front of the admiral's statue, unshaven, barefoot, wearing greasy undershirts and dirty patched pants. In their midst, Costa gleamed, immaculate as always in white shirt and fresh cotton trousers. George caught his eye, and they smiled and waved. He turned back to Peterson. "He's a good man. What about him?"

"I like him, you understand. I consider him my friend. The trouble is, I'm almost certain he's stolen a thousand drachmas from me."

George's first reaction was a sort of dull envy. A lousy thousand drachmas. How would Peterson feel if it had been sixty thousand? He looked at the young man's round cheeks, the wide innocent eyes, the eager, almost girlishly vulnerable mouth, and envy turned to resentment. It was always the innocent, wide-eyed, well-meaning ones who caused trouble, with their milk-fed manners and morals, and it was always the local community that paid. "Costa wouldn't steal," he said flatly.

"It looks like an open-and-shut case, George. I had this thousand-drachma note yesterday. I didn't have anything on—no pockets, you understand. The money had been lying around the kitchen so I stuck it in the table drawer. I don't usually keep money there. Later Costa dropped by, the way he does, and I left him in the kitchen to go to the john. When I looked for the money this morning it was gone."

"That sounds fairly simple-minded. He's the only person who's been in the house?"

"No. I have these beats staying with me, but you know how they are. They couldn't be bothered to steal. Too much trouble."

"How sober were you? You were running around without any

pockets. Did you lure him into bed, maybe? I can imagine Costa taking money if he did something he ought to be paid for."

Peterson laughed nervously. "Hey, now wait a minute. With all this snatch around, why should I do that?" A blush suffused his cheeks, and his face assumed his earnest student's look. "You know I don't go for that sort of thing."

"People do all sorts of things here that they don't usually go in for. I just want to get the whole story." He glanced back at the table at the foot of the admiral's statue as their drinks were put on the table. A memory from last night suddenly came to him. Costa had asked him to change a thousand-drachma note. That was why he had pulled out the wad of bills. It hadn't made sense before. Leighton frowned. If it had been Joe's money, Costa wouldn't have advertised the fact that he had it. And Costa wasn't a pickpocket. "What are you planning to do about it?" he asked abruptly.

"Well, that's the problem. I don't care about the money. Hell, I'd have given it to him if he'd asked me. I just don't like to be robbed. I guess that sounds pretty bourgeois and materialistic, but I just don't like it. It undermines my confidence in the guy."

"You don't want to go to the police. They might not be so easily convinced that your beat friends don't steal."

"I hadn't thought about the police," Peterson assured him. "The thing is, you have a lot of influence. Well, hell, you have the whole island in your pocket. Couldn't you talk to Costa and suggest he give it back?"

"How would you react if somebody walked up to you and asked you to return money you'd stolen?"

"Well, of course you'd have to handle it tactfully. I know he took it. It couldn't have been anybody else."

"Nonsense." George was talking to himself more than to Joe. "These people are sharp, they cheat the pants off each other, but they respect their friendships with foreigners. There's a tradition of hospitality that means something. We've never had thieves here. You can leave things around and come back and pick them up a week later." He sat back and took a swallow of beer. His suspicions had been talked into submission.

Peterson nodded like a bewildered and unhappy child. "I'm sure you're right, George, but I want my money back. If I have to, I'll beat it out of him myself. I just thought you might handle it more diplomatically. Everybody pays attention to what you say around here."

"In that case, I have to be careful what I say. Anyway, I can't get too worked up about your money. I lost almost sixty thousand drachmas last night."

Joe sat back with mouth agape and then uttered a long whistle. "*Jesus.* That's two thousand dollars. Jesus *Christ.* How?"

"I had it in my pocket, like a goddamn fool. It's a nuisance not having a bank here. Costa asked me for a change of a thousand drachmas in the back room in there, so I pulled the whole bloody lot out to give it to him. As far as I know, I shoved it back in my pocket, and that's the last I remember seeing it. When I looked for it this morning, it was gone."

Peterson flung himself back in his chair, his big body evoking squeaks of protest from its flimsy frame, and spread out his arms. "Holy mother of God! What more do you want? I told you, it's an open-and-shut case."

"Except that Costa's not a thief," George asserted. "Anybody might steal if he's desperate. But if Costa were in trouble, we'd know about it. He'd try to borrow before he'd steal, the way I'm probably going to have to."

"I'll leave the psychology to you, George. I just want my money back."

"I want mine back about sixty times more than you do," Leighton said irritably. He squinted out toward the sea. It wasn't its usual tonic blue today, but gray, as still and motionless as cement. The flag out by the cannons at the entrance to the port hung limply from its mast. Down along the broad *quai,* an orange caïque was unloading watermelons as round as cannonballs. Donkeys passed, staggering dazedly under huge loads. It was too hot to worry about money. He would rather forget it than be riddled with suspicions. He couldn't believe that Costa, or any of the locals, would rob him. He had been here too long; friendships had been sealed by too many small reciprocal acts of kindness and esteem. "I'll be damned if I know what either of us can do about it," he said dismissively.

"Good morning, all." A voice spoke from behind them, and Henry Varnum pulled a chair and folded his skeletal frame into it. He had a long clown's face, a long tip-tilted nose with a bulb at the end that looked as if it ought to light up. He put bony elbows on the table and kneaded his eyes with his fists. "Any casualties last night?" he asked in his knotty Australian accent. "No broken bones? You were in a fair way to getting pissed, Georgie boy."

"I'm evidently not the only one who isn't home pecking away at the typewriter," George remarked with a sharpening of interest. *Was this it? Was Henry going to pull the money out of his pocket with a little speech about fiscal responsibility?*

"Shit, eh? I'm in the middle of a blizzard scene. You might be able to do something with it in this weather, but for us lesser hacks, the imagination balks."

"Try an ice pack. Listen, Henry, you were with us last night. Did you notice if I did anything in particular with a fistful of money, like give it to a little blind lady?"

"You were waving it around at one point. I must've been pissed too. As I remember, it looked like all the money in Greece."

"It was a lot. You wouldn't have any way of knowing whether I had it with me when I left?"

"That, no. You don't mean you've lost it? Shit, eh? That's pretty dicey for you, George."

"Almost sixty thousand drachmas," Joe elaborated with awe. "I've been robbed too, but only a thousand."

"Robbed, eh?" Varnum glanced from one to the other. "Well, for what it's worth, so've we. Jenny was missing her shopping money the other day. It didn't seem worth making a bother about, but I wonder. One doesn't think of the people here as thieves."

"Do you suspect anybody?" Joe posed the question eagerly.

"Not enough to really accuse anybody, but strictly between ourselves, I couldn't bloody well help wondering about Costa. What do you think, George? He'd been at the house the evening before. You know the way he sort of drifts in and out for no particular reason. A regular bloody cat man. I like him, blast him. I bloody well don't see who else *could've* taken it. We run a dismally orderly house."

George glanced at Peterson and saw his look of triumph. He felt himself being pushed closer to something he instinctively resisted. The foreigners hadn't the right to unload their troubles on locals; the system was rigged too heavily in the foreigners' favor. "Well, at least you two *know* you've been robbed," he said. "I wish I did."

"All the same, you'll have to go to the police about a sum like that," Varnum said as if it were a foregone conclusion.

"Police? Hey, what's happened? Has somebody been murdered?" Sidney Coleman erupted into the group with explosive energy. George sat up straighter as Sid grabbed a chair. He admired Sid. He was a poet, so there was no room for envy of his striking talent. He was prankish and unpredictable, the most likely person to have taken George's money into protective custody. Joe and Henry Varnum both spoke at once, filling the newcomer in on the putative thefts.

"Hey this is great, fellows," Sid exclaimed, without offering George a word of sympathy. His Jewishness was stronger than any mere nationality, although he also happened to be Canadian. A smile of mad infectious glee lighted his bold Semitic features. "This is a *mystery*. Let's *solve* it. Henry, you've written mystery stories. How do we go about it?"

"This one's too bloody easy. It solves itself."

"Why're you all so sure about Costa? It could've been anybody. It could've been *me*, for Chrissakes. No, no. Hey. Hey, *listen*, men. I know when we ought to do. Hey, listen." Sid rocked back and forth with suppressed glee and jabbed a finger into the air. "We'll *arrest* him. How about that? We'll arrest him and give him a *trial*. Island justice. A regular jury trial, with a *jury*. I'll handle the defense. One of my uncles is a lawyer. I bet I can get him off. Anybody want to bet? I bet I can get him *off*. If he's guilty, he has to give the money back. If he's innocent, we buy him a drink. Hey, this'll be great."

The group was rapidly augmented by female attachments. Joe's Lena arrived lugging an overflowing shopping basket. Jenny Varnum followed with a few small bundles. The Varnums had no children. Passersby, drawn by the animation around the table, hovered briefly and passed on—the English lady who had just married a Greek male prostitute she had picked up in Athens; the gentle young American alcoholic who was watched over and protected by the whole community, both indigenous and foreign; the Italian painter with his Dutch boyfriend.

Sid and Henry were making everybody laugh a great deal. The air was sibilant with the word "police" as the story was repeated to the new arrivals. George was damned if he was going to the police, not for ten times the sum. Their methods were notorious. He had absolutely no grounds for suspecting anybody. His conviction that Sid might have the money was weakening, but he clung to hope. Perhaps they were all in on it and had invented this game as a form of torture before the happy denouement. Island fun.

"Let's get *started*," Sid cried, rocking with glee. "Who's going to arrest him? I demand that my client be *arrested*."

"I'm afraid if we ask the police to arrest him, they'd keep him," Varnum objected.

"The Vigilantes! The Storm Troopers! We'll knock on his door in the middle of the night!"

Before they could get launched on this new tack, George leaned across the table and addressed Sid directly above the babble of voices. "Listen, chum. This is all good sport, but I'm pretty worried. Don't you have an idea what happened to the damn money?"

"Me? What are you talking about, comrade?"

"You were there. I thought you might know something about it. I thought you might even have taken it to keep for me."

"Crazy, man. Why would I do a thing like that? Do you think I want to give you a heart attack? I'd be dead already if I lost that much money."

"I see." So much for hope, frail at best. If Charlie and Peter had picked it up, it would have been delivered at the door first thing this morning. That was the way they were. Punctilious. There had been nobody else. Give up. He caught Joe's eye. "I think maybe I'd better have that talk with Costa after all." At least it would give him the feeling that he's done everything he could.

He pushed his chair back and stood up. He was aware of silence falling over the group as he left. He approached Costa from behind under the admiral's statue and put his hand on his shoulder. Costa looked up and they greeted each other with their eyes.

"Can I speak to you a minute?" George asked. He nodded to the others at the table.

"Sure, Yorgo. Sure." He rose and followed Leighton a few steps into the shade of an awning. He moved with light gliding grace. He had a northern face, Irish or Breton, with fine features, light hair, humor dancing in pale blue eyes. When he smiled, his face lighted with elfin charm.

"I need your help," George began. His heart was playing tricks again under the pressure of his jangled nerves. It was crucially important that he choose the right words if he was to accomplish anything. He was watching Costa closely, trying not to appear to be doing so. "There've been a couple of robberies in the last few days. People are beginning to want to do something about it."

Costa rotated his hand in front of him in a Greek gesture of chastisement. "What do you expect, Yorgo? The kind of people coming here these days." His English was good, picked up on the docks like everything else he knew.

"Yes, I know, but the way things stand, it looks as if it's someone we know, someone who knows our houses. All the money I had last night is gone."

A look of genuine concern crossed Costa's face and he made a hissing sound between his teeth. "But it was very much. This is bad,

Yorgo. You had it with you when you left Stavro's. I saw it. Surely it is at home somewhere."

"You saw it? How do you mean?"

"It made a lump—how do you say?—in your pocket."

"Oh?" Leighton turned this information over in his mind for an instant. His trousers fitted loosely, the pockets were roomy. He could test the story by experimenting with a wad of paper. "Well, that proves what I'm saying. A total stranger couldn't have found his way around in the house at night without waking somebody up. I thought maybe I'd dropped it after I changed your thousand drachmas."

"No, I saw it when you left," Costa repeated. The humor had gone out of his eyes. They were intent and watchful, but friendly.

"All I want is my money back. The same for the others. I thought maybe you could spread the word that if the money's returned, nothing more will be said about it."

"How can anybody return the money without making himself to be the thief?"

"I've thought of that. Would you be willing to act as go-between? That is, let people know that you'll return the money, with no questions asked?"

"And make myself to be the thief? No, Yorgo. I cannot do that."

"This is serious, *Costaiki mou.* If somebody goes to the police and your name is mentioned, you'd be in trouble."

"The police!" he cursed the police with his hand, palm out, fingers extended, pushing at air. "What can the police do for you? And why will my name be mentioned?"

"I don't like to say this, but it already has. Two of the foreigners think it might've been you. I've told them it's impossible."

"Who says this?" Costa demanded indignantly.

"I can't say. The point is, they like you. They don't want to cause trouble."

"Ah, the foreigners." He spat the word out. "They are my friends and then if you lose some money, I am getting the blame. I have nothing more to do with the foreigners."

"Don't be a fool, Costa. I was just trying to warn you for your own sake."

"No worry. Costa can take care of himself." He said it with a swagger, but George could feel him turning dangerous. "The foreigner comes and all he brings is trouble. The drink. The dope. The stealing. All from when the foreigner comes. *I* warn. I warn before. The police maybe arrest that bar boy, Dimitri, Jeff's friend. You better look if

Jeff has nothing in the house is bad for him."

"What in hell are you talking about?" George demanded, unprepared for what seemed a new unrelated element in the conversation.

"I talk about the dope. It is expensive. Where do they all get the money?"

"Are you suggesting that Jeff takes dope?"

"Not just Jeff. If the police they come for me, I must tell all I know. Jeff. Your friends, many of them. If money is stolen, it is for dope."

Leighton couldn't speak for a moment, sickened with himself and Costa. They had exchanged their threats, defined the area in which each could hurt the other, banished friendship. For what? For money. Shaken by being included in a blanket condemnation of the foreigners, he was tempted to put his hand out and touch Costa's shoulder in a gesture of conciliation, but he checked himself. He was just beginning to digest the clear hint of blackmail in what Costa had said: if George made trouble about the money, Costa would make trouble for Jeff. All his carefully suppressed suspicions came rushing to the surface. Why had only Costa seen the bulge in his pocket? Very convenient. He didn't want to go to the police, but he wouldn't allow his right to do so to be challenged. He couldn't afford the luxury of conciliation. He had to get his money back.

"You don't leave me much choice," he said, drawing on all his strength to meet Costa on his own terms. "I think this had better be cleared up. I'll go to the police at six this evening. If you can help me get my money back in the meantime, meet me there. That'll be the end of it. Otherwise—" He shrugged away the shreds of his scruples.

"Yes. Sure. What is Costa next to Mr. Yorgo? The foreigner speak and—hup." Costa joined his wrists together as if they were manacled. Because the gesture illustrated an ugly truth, George was swept by anger. He wanted to seize Costa and shake him until the money dropped out of him and bring an end to this nasty incident. Instead, he turned abruptly and went back to his table. Peter and Martha had joined it. He pulled his chair around so that he could sit beside them.

In his sweet solicitous way, Peter was the first of George's friends to make him feel that his loss mattered. "This is a hell of a thing, George," he said, his clear, extraordinarily direct blue eyes full of concern. "I've just heard about it. What lousy luck. I just want to say, Don't hesitate. If you know what I mean."

"Thanks, friend. I may have to take you up on that." George put a hand on Peter's bare arm and gave it a squeeze. He had never been one for such intimate contacts, but he was aware that he liked to touch Peter. He was so completely pleasing physically. He supposed that in some obscure bisexual corner of himself, he was a bit in love with him. He removed his hand.

"Henry says you're going to the police," Martha said. "Have you anything to go on?"

"I don't know what Henry knows about it. I hadn't intended going to the police, but I've just had a very peculiar talk with Costa."

"He's not involved in this," Peter asserted as firmly as George had earlier. Costa was a friend and a semiemployee of the Mills-Martins; they had an arrangement whereby his boat was always at their disposal when they were here.

"I don't know, Peter," George said, running his hand agitatedly through his hair. "He as much as said that if I go to the police, he'll bust open the drug trade here and implicate Jeff. Why would he say a thing like that unless maybe he did take my money?"

Peter frowned. "That doesn't sound like him. Can you tell me how he put it? His English sometimes goes a bit haywire."

"He said, 'I warn you. I warned you before.' And then a lot about Jeff, and Dimitri at the bar, and all the people who use dope here." George saw Sid Coleman's powerful leonine profile swing toward him, and he was struck by his urgency when he leaned forward to speak through the buzz of conversation around them.

"Hey, now, wait a minute. Now, listen, George. Don't talk so loud. And don't start something you won't want to finish. Jeff's clean. You can take my word for it. I happen to know these things. Don't fool around with Dimitri. Dimitri's all right."

"Blast Dimitri," George said heatedly. "I don't give a damn about him. Costa brought him up. Costa's acting damn suspiciously."

"Just remember," Peter interjected, "if you go to the police, they're going to insist on your accusing somebody. That's the way they operate."

"Well, I *can't* accuse anybody. Joe and Henry say they're sure it's Costa, but I'm not sure of anything. He just told me he saw the money in my pocket when I left last night. I'll check that when I go home. If a wad of paper doesn't show in the trousers I was wearing, I really will suspect him."

"He's been to jail before, you know," Peter persisted.

"I've heard some story. What was it all about?"

"He tells various versions. You know the way he is. I think all it amounts to is that when he was a kid just after the war he took to stealing to stay alive and got caught. The point is, the law here is tough on second offenders. He's told me himself he could get ten years with only a token trial."

George nodded. "Point taken. What would you do if you were in my position?"

They looked at each other for a moment with affectionate concern. George was only a few years older, but Peter looked almost young enough to be his son. Nevertheless, he had an air of authority that commanded George's respect. George waited for an answer, prepared to be guided by it.

"It's a tough one, George. I understand that. Try the test with your trousers. It's too much money for anybody but a real crook to take. That's what bothers me. I'd better have a talk with Costa." Peter glanced over toward the admiral's statue, where he had seen him with George. He wasn't there.

"I wish you would," George was saying. "You know I hate having anything to do with the police. In a reasonable society—" He paused, aware that the man from the telegraph office was hovering behind him, and looked up.

"*Here* you are, Mr. Yorgo," the man said. "I think I have something for you." He fumbled with his pouch and began to go painstakingly through its contents. Eventually, he extracted a telegram and presented his book for signature. *Christ, now what?* George thought. His mother? His father? Signing, he had difficulty controlling the trembling of his hand. He took the telegram and tore it open savagely.

ARRIVING TOMORROW FOR DAY WITH LEIGHTON ARRANGE BOOKISH RECEPTION TRAVELING INCOGNITO NO PRESS PLEASE
    COCHRAN

George stared at this odd communication for some seconds before his mind grasped it. Cochran. Mike Cochran. Could it possibly be? The rich, the successful, the celebrated Michael Cochran? He knew no other Cochran. Old Mike, his classmate and bosom pal, turned playwright, screenwriter, the familiar of presidents, princes, and the big guns of international celebrity. With the caution of experience, he hastily checked the date on the message. The seventeenth. He looked up at the assembly around the table.

"Does anybody know the date today?" he asked.

"It's the sixteenth, isn't it?"

"No, it's later than that. The eighteenth, I think."

"Isn't today Thursday?"

"That's not a date, you cretin."

"I can tell you exactly," Peter said after a moment's thought. "Sunday was the fifteenth. It's Wednesday, the eighteenth."

Naturally, George thought. *Why shouldn't a telegram take twenty-four hours to travel forty miles?* Then "tomorrow" was today, and Mike would be here in less than an hour. He couldn't believe it. Jesus Christ, after all these years. His mind tried to fix a picture of his friend as he had been when they had last seen each other—twelve years ago?—but he caught only a glimpse of a presence adorned with a few physical details—a lank lock of hair, a tough farm boy's frame, a tone of voice, witty and sardonic. He experimented with amendments dictated by the passage of time—the lock thin and graying?—the frame padded out with paunch?—but it was as unconvincing as mustaches scrawled on the picture of a pretty girl in the subway. There was success, big sustained worldly success, as well as time to reckon with—success and money. He folded the telegram and put it in a pocket.

"I think Mike Cochran's coming on the morning boat," he announced.

"Michael Cochran!" Varnum exclaimed. "Crickey. The island's coming up in the world. I read he was in Athens on some cultural thing."

"Really? That explains it." George beamed happily in a way that had become so unfamiliar that it made his face feel uncomfortable. Mike would take his mind off his money for a while; there was nothing he could do about it till evening, anyway.

Everybody was apparently glad to forget the money. Mike's name was picked up and passed around the table to the accompaniment of generally irreverent comments. Peter turned to Martha. "You remember? He was married to Charlie's actress wife for a little while." Peter's eyes strayed, and he threw his head back and uttered his infectious laughter. "Oh, my God."

Martha and others saw what he had seen and laughed with him. A small figure under a straw hat had adopted an unmistakable stance down on the edge of the *quai* and was aiming a glistening arc of water into the port. Peter rose and crossed the *quai* just as the jet ended. Little Petey looked up as his father joined him, and his face broke into a beam of guilty joy.

"You caught me with my pee-pee out," he announced.

Peter laughed. "I sure did." He squatted down to the child's level and began to help him get his buttons into the right holes. He was

41

constantly amazed and delighted that paternal love could arouse him sexually. The toy materialized briefly in the uncomfortable confines of his shorts as he breathed the sweet smell of the little boy. "There's nothing wrong with your pee-pee," he said. "I mean, it's no big secret. It's just considered sort of private. That's why we wear pants. Anyway, you're not supposed to pee in the port, so don't."

"It was fun, Daddy," Petey chortled.

"Good. You've had your fun. Not again, right? What if everybody used the port to pee in?" He hugged his son and kissed him on the cheek.

Petey looked at him, performing solemnity. "All right, Daddy. I won't. Ever, ever again."

Peter laughed at the little fraud and stood and led him to the table with his hand on the back of his neck. He heard George arranging to meet Joe that evening in front of the police station. Joe was looking solemn and self-important, obviously pleased with his central role in the drama.

"You're not leaving, are you?" George asked Peter. "Don't. I want Mike to meet you."

Peter glanced at Martha. "Not now, George. Bring him up to the house. If he's staying, we'll have a dinner for him. We'll arrange something when you know."

"I'd better get cracking myself. I have to round up Sarah and do something about lunch. Anybody seen her?"

The latest arrival, Dorothy, Sid Coleman's American painter girlfriend, turned to him. "Sarah? She's down on the rocks swimming."

"Christ. I do have to run. Be seeing you, everybody." George sprang up with a wave of his hand and hurried off toward the western promontory and the road leading out to the swimming rocks. Peter and Martha exchanged another glance.

Sid reached across the table and clutched Peter's wrist. "Hey, listen, man. Why is Costa talking about Dimitri? What's the connection? Is something going on between Dimitri and Jeff?"

"I don't know. I'm seeing Jeff after lunch. I'll try to find out." Peter signaled to Martha that he was ready to go. Petey, who had been making the rounds of the table tasting everybody's drinks, moved to their sides as they rose. He gave them each a hand and they smiled and nodded their farewells to the assembled company as they circled the table and went to the door of the shop, where Peter called out a message for Costa to the Lambraiki family. They set off with Petey between them for the other side of the port.

"What a lot of excitement," Martha said. "What do you make of it?"

"Sid's worried about his supply of pot. Everybody knows he gets it from Dimitri. That silly little bastard. I wouldn't mind seeing him get arrested. What it has to do with George's money and Costa, I haven't the faintest idea. Maybe Costa was really trying to warn him about something and George took it as a threat. We shall see." He kept his eyes out for Costa at every small grouping of tavern tables they passed. As they approached one that was frequented almost exclusively by locals, his eye was caught by an extraordinarily beautiful girl sitting at a table. He did a little double take as he focused on her. Dark hair swept back from an exquisite profile, her nose tilted deliciously, her mouth looked as if it were about to open in a kiss. Peter quickened his pace in his eagerness to see her full-face. He saw her straighten and then lean forward with her head cocked slightly in an attitude of intense, generous absorption. The muscles of his stomach contracted as if he had been struck. His arms and legs tingled with it. He felt that if she looked at him like that, he would faint dead away at her feet.

"What?" Martha said. "Did you say something?"

"Daddy, you *stepped* on me," Petey protested.

Peter laughed as he tore his eyes away from the girl. "Sorry. A slight distraction. Did you see that incredibly beautiful girl?"

"So that's what it was." Martha laughed with him. "You men."

They were past her before Peter realized that his eyes had been so fixed on the girl that he hadn't seen who had been the recipient of her electrifying look.

Shaved and sweating, George Leighton stood under the awning of the café at the boat landing. In only a matter of minutes, Mike would actually be here. George had found Sarah sitting down on the rocks with Pavlo, the new body boy. He had swept her off to shop. Briefly they had captured their old high spirits as they discussed lunch and ran up bills for a fish and a few bottles of good wine and negotiated with the butcher for an edible piece of beef for dinner. They hurried home, as excited and responsive to each other as they had been in the old days when some unexpected treat turned up. He had left her there to dress and deal with Chloë, who was not a maid so much as a friend they paid to help around the house, and had hurried back to be sure to be here for the boat. He hoped she would make it in time. He wanted everything to look right for Mike.

This reunion was acquiring a significance for him that went

beyond the renewal of an old friendship. Their lives could serve as illustrations of conflicting philosophies. It was almost too pat. They had started off together, they had both achieved success, George earlier than Mike. Mike had courted it, acquiring wealth and celebrity and numerous wives. George had sought a more enduring reality, careless of money and fame. He had even managed to be broke for Mike's arrival.

Yet there was no basis for real confrontation. George Leighton's reputation was secure and distinguished, quite independent of popular or material success, though he had had that too for a while. Mike, whose youthful ambition had been so great, would be the last to claim any high literary merit for his bright Broadway comedies. No conflict there. It had been said that George Leighton was losing touch, but losing touch with what? Certainly not, God knows, with the suffering that lay at the core of human experience. With his country? There was a respectable literary tradition for expatriation. No, there was no need for apologies, nothing to hide. Except the impending ruin of his life.

He wondered what price Mike had paid. He wondered, too, why Mike was coming. If business had brought him to Athens, it would seem natural to look up a friend so near at hand, except that there had been other occasions when they could have arranged for their paths to cross. Had the president appointed him to confer on George Leighton an exalted honor? Or, prompted by some residue of the competitive spirit of their youth, was he coming to assure himself that George Leighton was a wreck and a has-been? George lifted his chin and squared his shoulders. He was confident that nothing showed.

A band of ragged longshoremen was moving down to the edge of the landing area. This was a recent improvement; small boats no longer rowed passengers ashore. The white-uniformed harbor patrol had already taken its station within the railed enclosure. The idlers who daily constituted themselves a welcoming committee were spreading out along it. He noted again the dead gray look of the sea. The heat was more than oppressive—it felt dangerous, as if its pressure would shatter the atmosphere.

He had almost given up hoping for Sarah when he caught sight of her and waved.

"You look almost cool," he remarked admiringly as she joined him.

"The sea helped."

"Mike'll probably want to go later."

"Yes, you should take him down after lunch. You can sit in the sea and talk your heads off. It's too hot for naps anyway."

"I hope to God we all recognize each other," he said with a chuckle. "Twelve years is long time, except that suddenly it doesn't seem like anything at all."

She looked up at him in quick scrutiny and smiled. "You haven't changed much. More distinguished. Of course, we're both black as niggers, which may confuse him."

He took her arm and led her out into the crushing sun and over to a place at the barricade. A dark hungry-eyed boy darted up to them, roughly shoving a smaller boy out of his way as he came.

"Will you need me?" he demanded, looking as if he would attack anybody who refused his aid.

"Yes, my child," George said with a slight smile. "You have your animal? Wait for us. There will probably be baggage."

This was the way he hoped Mike's visit would go—people springing eagerly to serve them, everything working smoothly, all the laws and fissures with which they had to contend in daily living neatly covered over for this occasion. "I told Chloë to plan for lunch at one-thirty. Does that check with you? I didn't think we'd want to prolong the drinking hour."

"Oh, good," she said. "That means I'll—I mean, that means you'll probably be ready to take Mike for a swim by about three."

"Yes," he agreed. She was really determined to get him into the water. Did she think he was going to need sobering up? He wiped sweat from his forehead and out of his eyes. He felt as if the sun were beating him into the ground.

"Here she comes," Sarah announced to the empty sea in what appeared to be a moment of clairvoyance. She had scarcely spoken before there was a blast of ship's whistle and the boat came surging around the steep rocky promontory, pushing its way through the lifeless sea, stirring it to a heavy leaden swell. There was the rumble of reversed engines, lines were thrown, whistles piped, the ship's telegraph clanged. Urgent messages below. The boat bumped broadside against the *quai* and came to rest in a swirl of slapping water. Everybody began to shout. The longshoremen jockeyed the gangplank into position, and there was an explosion of humanity. In an instant, the enclosure was packed with pushing, shouting people, baggage, parcels, packing cases, baskets, odd lengths of pipe, toilet bowls, and a baby carriage.

There was no sign of Mike. People were streaming down the gangplank, but the first flood spent itself quickly. Leighton turned to Sarah. Her eyes were scanning the open upper deck, the wide windows of the first-class lounge.

"Do you see him?"

She shook her head, and he turned back to the scene of confusion around the gangplank. A final trickle of passengers emerged from somewhere in the depths, an ungainly crate was trundled ashore, there was a flurry of white jackets in the shade of the covered deck, and two stewards teetered down the gangplank under a load of handsome matched suitcases. Leighton's attention quickened. These were worthy of Michael Cochran. Why so many? Was he planning to stay a month?

Then he was there, framed in the gangway, like the star entrance in a musical comedy, shaking hands with the captain. George burst into laughter of recognition and welcome. He looked so exactly like old Mike, except that he had a completely unfamiliar elegance now, and the lock of hair had been suppressed by expert barbering. He was apparently in no hurry, though it was obvious that the boat was being held for him. All his movements were deliberate and looked rehearsed, the mark of celebrity. The captain bowed before him profusely, and then he turned and strolled down the gangplank. He was expensively dressed in a crisp summer suit. *It won't stay crisp long,* George thought with malicious satisfaction. The two stewards were waiting by the baggage, and Mike distributed tips with experienced graciousness.

George leaned over the barrier and shouted, "Mike, you son of a bitch, aren't you going to greet the natives?"

Cochran turned and smiled. "I'll sign autographs in the lobby of the hotel in an hour," he called back. Then he laughed, and the self-consciousness dropped from him as he hurried to them. He clapped Leighton on both shoulders and shook him affectionately. He took Sarah in his arms across the railing and kissed her on both cheeks. There was a slight hook in his nose, and the skin was stretched taut over wide cheekbones, as if he might have Indian blood. He had always had great success with women.

"God, this is wonderful," he exclaimed. "Let me look at you. You look divine. How did you find this incredible place? I don't believe it for a moment. It's all painted on a backdrop. The very Cosmo, himself. Why aren't you wearing your beachcomber costume? I was particularly looking forward to it. Oh, lord, how *are* you both? You look superb."

They laughed a lot and exchanged rather incoherent and repetitive pleasantries.

"Well, let's get organized and get out of this sun," George suggested finally. "I take it you haven't brought any of your wives."

"I've run out of wives at the moment. A wife in this heat. What a hideous thought. Sorry, Sarah, old dear."

The ragged child approached George, and he pointed out the baggage, astonished once more at its quantity. "Listen, you bastard," he said. "You haven't brought all that stuff just for the day. How long are you staying?"

"Till tomorrow. But not to worry. I'm not going to be a nuisance. I understand the hotel here is fairly civilized."

"So is our house. Don't be ridiculous. You're going to stay with us."

"No, I'll be better at the hotel. Not that I'd have the slightest hesitation about turning your house upside down. I just like having my own hole to crawl into. Somebody was supposed to arrange it."

George threw his arm around his friend's shoulder and gave him a hug. George was the bigger of the two, which bolstered his confidence. "It's too hot to argue. This kid will take care of your things. I'll see that the manager gives you the best room."

"You're joking," Mike exclaimed as he caught sight of the small boy struggling to attach the luggage to his donkey. "Don't you have child labor laws here?"

"No. Everybody's free at birth to share in the blessings of private enterprise."

"No, but seriously. Is that sort of thing usual here?"

"A lot of kids work, if that's what you mean."

"But doesn't it bother you?"

"Oh, come off it, Mike," Sarah interjected. Reasons for wanting this reunion to be a success were beginning to preoccupy her. She was impatient of the least sign of discord. "Don't start theorizing until you know something about the place."

Memories of college days drifted through Leighton's mind. He and Mike organizing meetings, drawing up petitions. What had they been about? Antiwar? Pro-war? Definitely socialistic. Mike had had firm and dogmatic opinions about everything, and George had welcomed them as revelation. Life had taught him to be more pragmatic and tolerant. Should he be shocked that a ten-year-old be allowed to earn his living? He took a sidelong glance at Mike, dark, slim, stylish—frivolous was a word that came easily to mind—and wondered if he really cared. He wondered, too, with a wrench of regret and misgiving, if it were possible to recapture the old easy intimacy.

They left the controversial child still struggling with the luggage and strolled down around the *quai* toward the new hotel.

"What happened to the twentieth century?" Mike inquired. "Look at all these giant beasts of burden. Don't you have any cars or trucks?"

"Dear God, no," Sarah exclaimed.

"But how do you go anywhere?"

"Go anywhere? We walk—or take a boat."

"Farewell, mechanized world. Not that I'm not tempted to get out at times myself. If only I could afford to."

"Afford to!" George protested. "You must make in a month what we spend in a year."

"That is a secret between me and my tax man. But don't forget my precious wives. They must be provided for in a manner to which I never intended to accustom them."

George laughed. "I suppose there's something to be said for sticking it out with only one."

"Definitely. But not everyone is lucky enough to find Sarah." He and Sarah bowed to each other with mock formality.

Sarah was struggling toward a decision. The invitation was explicit at last. He had come out with it just before George had found them together on the rocks. He would be at home alone all afternoon. The risk had seemed too great for her to accept even though she felt incapable of refusing when she was close to him. Mike's arrival changed everything. George would be safely occupied; she might not get another such opportunity for weeks or months. She couldn't go on living with this obsession. Just once with him would free her of it. He was only a body.

They chatted as they strolled, hugging the sides of buildings for whatever shade they could find. Mike's voice was lighter than George remembered and made everything he said sound rather trivial and superficial. Was there something slightly effeminate about him? No, that was probably the effect of his new elegance. He worked in the theater; some of its artificiality was bound to rub off.

They turned into an interior street on the level that formed the floor of the great amphitheater of the town. Houses rose all around them, but the sun almost obliterated them, flattening them out and destroying perspective so that the effect was of a glaring white wall from which the eye shrank.

"Is your house near here?" Mike asked.

George pointed up and to the left. "Up in there. You can see part of it from here, but I wouldn't be able to pick it out for you."

"Good God. You have to *walk* up there?"

George laughed. "I remember when we were in New York we used to walk all over the whole damn city. There was a question of carfare."

"I suppose we did. We must've been younger in those days."

George looked at him and smiled. Perhaps they would strike the right note yet. The few casual words had sent memories crowding through his mind of that brief period before Sarah, just after they had escaped from the army and were discovering New York together, memories of the tiny apartment they shared over a drugstore, memories of girls, some of them shared too, memories of Mike, still with a New England rawness on him, gawky in badly cut clothes but with the flippantly abrasive humor that had made him seem older and more experienced than himself. Mike had been the leader. A residue of that element in their relationship colored George's response now, strengthening and reassuring him, as if his friend's presence might resolve the conflicts—yes, it was not too strong a word—that were destroying him.

They crossed the walled patio of the hotel and came to a halt at the desk. Mike looked around him. "My God. This is Greece? It looks like something out of Santa Monica."

George took in the familiar lobby with astonishment. They had all been rather proud of the new hotel. It had a private bath with every room, flush toilets, box springs on the beds, and all sorts of unfamiliar luxuries. For the first time, he wondered what Mike would think of their house. He counted on the house to offer irrefutable proof of the felicity of their life here. He slapped the desk and called impatiently for the manager, who shuffled out from some nether region. The deference with which he was greeted mollified him.

"I told the donkey boy to arrange everything. Your bags are in your room," he explained to Mike. "You better go get out of some of the finery before you melt."

"Good. I'll pop into my island drag and be right with you."

A maid appeared and led him away, and the Leightons stood with the manager while George impressed upon him the importance of this guest. He invented vast sums purporting to be Mike's income from Broadway and Hollywood. This might result in his bill being padded, but at least he would get whatever service the hotel was capable of providing. Even as he did it, it struck him as absurd that even he should feel the need of pampering the celebrated Michael

Cochran. What difference did it make if he was slightly uncomfortable for one night? It was absurd, too, that he should be pleased by the luster his friend's celebrity would add to his status on the island, but there was no denying that it counted.

In a few minutes, Mike returned resplendent and immaculately white in fine linen slacks and a sports shirt of some rich loosely woven stuff. He wore sandals on his carefully tended feet. He looked as clipped, trimmed, pruned, and polished as a fashion model. There was no real reason why a writer shouldn't look like that, George conceded to himself, but general they didn't. Mike wasn't a writer, anyway, but a specialist in popular entertainment.

"Everything all right?" he asked.

"I'll survive. You might tell your friend here that there's no hot water."

"I'm afraid he knows. They only turn it on in the morning."

A frown crossed Mike's face. "Ah, well, the Greeks doubtless invented plumbing, so I suppose we must be grateful to them."

"I told you you should've stayed with us. You could've had hot water morning, noon, and night." He was glad to establish this fact for the record, though they never turned the water heater on during the hot months.

"Would you tell them to have a thermos of ice left in the room?"

"You go too far, Cochran."

"You don't have *ice* here?"

"Certainly. But you don't put it in your drinks. Not if you want to survive."

"Why not?"

"Ice is made with water," George explained. "The only water we have is rainwater. The icehouse uses any liquid they can get their hands on. There are ugly rumors that they pee in it."

"You mean if it doesn't rain, you do without water?"

"That's about it. We're closely geared to nature here. It's quite interesting, nature, but I suppose you've eliminated it from your scheme of things. We've learned to control nature. That's interesting too."

"Air-conditioning!" Sarah exclaimed distractedly, aware of a sharp edge in the exchange. "It must be so strange not to know what it's like outside."

"Strangely wonderful. What I wouldn't give for a little air-conditioning right now."

They set out once more under the blazing sun. George led the way through narrow streets that rose gently, broken by occasional steps.

They moved through a dazzle of white, white walls, white streets. Even the boulders that thrust up here and there, forcing the street to detour around them, were washed with white. As they approached the house, he felt the excitement building up in him irrationally. Why should he care whether Mike liked the house? They reached the dark green door in the high wall, and he had an odd sensation of intense exhilaration mingled with dread, like a child opening a Christmas present, as he pushed the door back and stood aside to let Mike enter the paved oasis of trellised vines and citrus trees and glowing bougainvillea that obscured the outlines of the whitewashed house.

"Well, this is more like it," Mike said as he stood and looked around him.

Leighton exhaled a long breath of relief and felt the thrill of pride he always experienced when he showed a newcomer the house. Six years ago this court had been a weed-choked yard, the house a weather-stained ruin. He had done much of the heavy labor himself, which probably added to its value in his eyes. The place was the one element in his life about which he could feel total confidence. "I'll fix us a drink and then show you around if you'd like."

A bottle of ouzo had been set out on the table under the vines, and a thermos of ice water. He poured them drinks, allowing himself a stiff one—he had had nothing but beer so far—and lifted his glass to Mike.

"Well, here you are," he said, feeling that now at last they could really get through to each other. "Welcome."

"If the rest of it's anything like this, it's gorgeous," Mike said, raising his glass in turn. "I do hope I don't start envying you."

"Come along. As a matter of fact, the tour is compulsory."

They went through the lower rooms, rich with polished woods and gleaming brasses, the walls lined with books and pictures, the floors of stone or tile, the ceilings of intricately patterned wood characteristic of the island. They went upstairs to the wide, awninged terrace that commanded a sweeping view of the town above the port below and the encircling sea. They completed the tour in Leighton's big workroom on the top floor.

"Well, you've certainly done yourself proud," Mike admitted. The house had completed his discomfiture. He had come to perform a rescue operation, to pick up the pieces of George Leighton and send them home. The drunken derelict he had been told to expect was in aggressive good spirits and apparent good health, emanating self-confidence and prosperity. He had been prepared to offer a substantial loan if necessary, but George was living like a king. In Hollywood or around New York, a comparable house would cost more than a hundred thousand dollars. It diminished his own achievements, threw into question the validity of the course he had followed, stirred unfamiliar guilt about the compromises he had been obliged to make. It was disconcerting. He was determined now to find the flaw beneath this apparently untroubled surface—the flaw that lay buried in every life—and expose it so that even George would be forced to acknowledge it. He wouldn't want to leave until he had done so. "What I don't understand," he said, "is how you afford it. I've never been able to hold on to any loot."

"Neither have I."

"Oh, come on. I know you've made a pot, but Hanscombe told me what your last couple books have done. You haven't been living on them."

"Of course I have. You don't realize—if we really pay attention, we can live here for about a hundred and fifty dollars a month."

"You're kidding. I couldn't keep my dogs for that."

George cursed his habit of truth. Modesty wasn't the line for this new Mike. "I said we could," he pointed out. "I didn't say we do."

"All right. Then what's the trick?"

George felt his grip tightening on his glass. Why couldn't the damn fool let well enough alone? Couldn't he conceive that a man might go on struggling to give the best of himself even though the rewards constantly diminished? He thought of the stolen money and almost hurled his glass against the wall. He was being hemmed in, his very survival threatened. And Mike sat looking cool and elegant, talking about what it cost to keep his dogs.

"For one thing, I've never cared all that much about money," he said carefully, amazed that he sounded so calm. "That's something you're bound to remember, even though your attitude has changed. It's pretty old-fashioned of me, but I still don't believe in the money-success standard."

"That's one in the eye for old Mike. Of course, you've got rich parents."

"That might make a difference. I suppose in the back of my mind the fact that someday I'll have a steady income relieves some of the pressure, even though I can't count on it for another fifteen or twenty years."

"Well, since we're having this moment of truth, I'll tell you straight, Cosmo. I've been more or less commissioned by Hanscombe to bring you back alive."

"Oh, Christ. Is that why you're here? What does Hanscombe care? He gets my books regularly."

"That's not necessarily enough. Hanscombe makes no bones about it. He thinks at the rate you're going you won't have any public at all in a few more years."

"Hanscombe seems to've been shooting his mouth off a good deal."

"He's just thinking of your interests. Hell, you could make a good living at home. There're all sorts of possibilities for a prestige writer like you. Your name would mean something on the lecture circuit. If you were back where people could see you, even the movies would probably use you."

"When am I supposed to do my work?"

"Ah, yes. The dedicated artist. There's nothing wrong with reaching a popular audience. Even Shakespeare was a hack. What's special about you?" As he asked the question, Mike knew there *was* something special about him. There was an undeniable aura that clung to his name out of all proportion to Mike's evaluation of his accomplishments. If this weren't true, if Leighton didn't figure among the nation's cultural assets, Mike wouldn't have come. Failure embarrassed him. "I'll tell you frankly I think you're missing something. Your stuff's getting remote. People want to be socked between the eyes these days. If you got back into the world, you'd feel it. I suppose it's a matter of losing touch."

George almost laughed out loud at the line he had so accurately anticipated. "What in hell does everybody mean by 'losing touch'?" he demanded. "Do they expect me to write like the new kids? I'm not interested in armpits and vomit and urinals and pot. I don't know anything about boys screwing each other. If I wanted to find out, I'd have plenty of opportunity here. What people can't get through their heads is that life here is just as dirty and sweaty and fucked-up as it is everywhere else."

"Then why not come back where the big things are happening? The world is moving. Greece had her say two thousand years ago. It's our turn now. Hell, the black thing alone is one of the biggest things of our time."

"The black thing! Christ, I'm not a Negro. If a black wants to marry my daughter, he's perfectly welcome to her. Seriously. I have nothing else to contribute to the cause."

"But she's not likely to meet any Negroes here, is she?"

"Why in God's name not? The island's crawling with them. They come off the boat in droves. Regular little Harlem we've got here."

Mike laughed briefly, dismissively. "Well, Cos," he said, "I don't suppose even you would pretend that this is an important center of cultural and intellectual activity."

"I might, you know. There's an element of the eternal here that goes beyond current fads. It's something I'm trying to get into my work. I may not be big enough to do it, but that'll be my fault, not the fault of the place."

"Do you expect to go down in history as the only American artist who wasn't hurt by expatriation?"

"Henry James? Tom Eliot? What would they have been if they *hadn't* been expatriates?"

"There's no point in playing guessing games. The fact is, you're an American writer. Your best work is one hundred percent American. You need the country just as much as the country needs you."

Leighton remained silent for a moment. He was damned if he would admit that what had started as a voyage of discovery with Sarah had become an economic necessity. He wasn't ready yet to tell Mike that he found him shockingly transformed by playing the success game. And he couldn't tell about the curious loss of nerve he observed, with anguish, in himself. He felt already shattered by their brief exchange, uneasy and at bay. There were all the good things he had found here, but when he tried to put them into words for Mike, They became terribly elusive. Too many shadows fell across them.

"You know, Mike," he said, making a grueling effort to achieve conviction and authority, "I see a lot of people from your big world. They come limping in here, riddled with ulcers and neuroses, and it's fascinating to watch what happens to them. They take their clothes off and lie down in the sun, and they positively blossom. They can't stop talking about what hell their lives have been wherever they've come from, but as soon as they get well, as soon as they're whole and happy again, they begin creating their hells around them, and sooner or later it all blows up and they go. I would like to believe that man is capable of bearing happiness, and there's lots of material for research here. When I've answered that one, maybe I'll be ready to leave."

"You can't be happy at home?"

"Good God. I'm not talking about *my* happiness." George rose abruptly and walked over to the bookshelves to hide his face from Mike. He took a long swallow of his drink. The drink was helping, but he wasn't going to be able to take much more of this. He looked up at his five published novels. They took up scarcely five inches on the shelf. Fifteen years of thought and feeling and plain hard labor. He had scarcely begun. If he could just hold on a little longer, if he could just get through to Sarah again, he'd show Mike and Hanscombe and all the rest of them what writing was all about. *And* make another pot while he was about it. He turned and managed to give his friend a composed smile.

"Come on. Let's adjourn this meeting of the Save George Cosmo Leighton Society. We probably have time for another quick one before lunch."

"Not for me. One more of these and I'd be flat on my face."

"You're getting old, Mike. The debilitating effects of civilization." He snapped his fingers and went to his desk and began tearing typewriter paper into strips. "Just a minute," he said over his shoulder. When he had torn what he judged to be enough, he gathered the strips together and folded them into a wad.

"Has the heat finally got you?" Mike asked.

"Just a minute. Just stay where you are." He hurried to the head of the difficult stairs and went down them as fast as he could. He found the trousers he had been wearing the night before in a closet and quickly changed. He put the wad of paper in a pocket and climbed back up to Mike.

"Now, then. See if you can tell if I have anything in my pockets," he instructed Mike.

"Is this the sort of game you play here? What am I supposed to do, admire your basket?"

George walked back and forth in front of him. "Tell me. Can you see anything?"

"Poor old Cosmo. His brain has finally snapped. No, I can't see if you have anything in your pockets. Maybe a pack of cigarettes in the left one?"

George put his left foot up on a rung of a chair. The wad of paper was clearly outlined under the cloth. It looked as much like a rather crushed cigarette pack as it did a wad of paper. Experiment inconclusive, but damaging for Costa. Had he put his foot on the rung of a chair?

"Will we be vouchsafed a word of explanation?" Mike asked.

"We were having a discussion this morning. It's too complicated to explain. Come on. Let's go down. Lunch will be ready soon."

In apparent harmony, they retraced their steps down through the house.

"I see you have some nice pictures," Mike said. "I've become quite a collector myself. The Impressionists, mostly. Do you know Peter Mills-Martin?"

"Sure. He wants to have you for dinner if you're staying."

"I've met him once or twice, like that, at big parties. Wonderful guy. I knew he had a house here. I did a bit of business in his line while I was in Athens. I'd like to have a talk with him."

"Nothing could be simpler. We'll probably run into him later. Otherwise, I could send word up to him."

They found Sarah in the garden stretched out in a chaise longue reading. George noticed with mingled surprise and pleasure she didn't have a drink beside her.

"Have you two caught up on old times?" She greeted them with a bright smile. George noticed the way she snapped her book shut with quick nervous fingers. There was something febrile and overeager about her that puzzled him. It was different from the drink-induced tension he knew so well. There was a sort of pent-up joyousness or anticipation about it, as if she were about to perform some miracle. Perhaps she was pleased with the way lunch was turning out.

"Mike's been paying his duty call on the house," George said.

"It's fantastic. The palaces of the East."

"You're not having a drink before lunch?" George asked her.

She shook her head. "We're going to eat in a minute. I thought Mike would probably be hungry."

The nearby table was already set with bright pottery and coarse linen place mats, a loaf in its basket, a bottle of wine in its ice bucket. Everything was as George would have wished it, simple but handsome, suggesting good management and rustic abundance. If the meal were ready, the miracle would be complete. They usually managed to assemble a few scraps anytime between two and four. Sarah was responding to the day's challenge like a champion. He stood over her and gave her shoulder a little caress. "Has anybody seen our son and heir?"

"I think I heard him in his room."

George turned to the house and called up, "Jeff, about time for lunch."

"What about your daughter?" Mike asked.

"She's staying with a little friend in Athens," Sarah explained. Mike continued to ask appropriate questions about the children, their ages, where they went to school, and so forth, exerting great charm. Beneath it, Sarah sensed a watchfulness that puzzled her, and she became defensively chatty.

In a few minutes, Chloë emerged with a platter on which lay an excellent-looking fish, and Jeff came slouching after her. They were both introduced to Mike.

"What's all this fuss about?" Jeff remarked, gazing darkly at the table. It was the sort of thing that Jeff, with almost belligerent tactlessness, could be counted on to say. But since he growled rather than spoke, George was confident that Mike hadn't heard. Chloë fetched a great salad and took her place at table with them.

"Servants are part of the family in Greece," George explained. "There are really no class distinctions here. It's one of the nicest things about the place."

"We don't usually make much of lunch," Sarah said accurately. "I hope this'll be enough."

"Good lord, have you forgotten how we eat at home? I usually have a sandwich."

Except for a few abortive attempts by Mike to draw Jeff out, met with sullen growls, the talk was a lively triple exchange as they traded their news and gossip. Sarah only sipped at her wine instead of gulping it by the glassful as she usually did. George was quick to snatch at any hope. If she could muster such self-control for Mike, perhaps her drinking had not yet got a real grip on her. Buoyed by the good talk and the wine he had drunk, he dreamed of life resuming its old happy pattern. It *could* be good here; an hour or two with Mike and the glimpse he offered of the great world was enough to dispel any doubts. Nothing had been damaged yet beyond repair. If the new book had a better break than the last one, they might even have enough money to get away for a bit, to Paris perhaps, or London, and replenish themselves at the old sources—theaters, friends, exhibitions, shops. Sarah had always been fascinated by shops. He smiled to himself as he thought of her eager acquisitiveness. It had been a long time since she had been able to indulge it.

"When are you two going for your swim?" Sarah asked. "That is the plan, isn't it?"

Jeff had excused himself, mumbling about having to see somebody; the table had been cleared, coffee had been served. She posed the question pointedly, as if to firmly mark the end of the lunch interlude. The famous swim—well, she had certainly earned her nap.

"It might cool us off," George agreed. "How about you, Mike, my boy?"

"I think I could do with a bit of a snooze first. Fifteen minutes will do to recharge the batteries. And no more cracks about getting old. I'm simply following your example and sinking into the island torpor."

"Why don't you stretch out here? It'll be a little less hot than the hotel. I have some business at six, but we have plenty of time."

He took Mike up to the guest room and, returning below, went to the kitchen and checked Sarah's bottle of brandy. He had been right. The level had not appreciably fallen. He went back to the garden to look for her. She was stretched out in the chaise longue again. He went around in back of her and kissed her on the top of the head, then sat at the foot of her chair.

"That was wonderful, Sal. You really did us proud."

She smiled and shrugged, but there was an edge in her voice as she said, "I usually do, don't I?"

"Oh, of course. But I wanted it to go particularly well today. I think he was impressed."

"I can't stand him lording it over you. As if making a lot of money in Hollywood has anything to do with writing. He's changed so. If I see too much of him, my act might wear a bit thin."

"Well, you're in the clear till this evening. Thanks for making the effort. I'd like to keep things peaceful for old time's sake."

"And what about all that chummy bit with Jeff?"

"What do you mean?"

"Just that. Women can spot it a lot quicker than men. I saw the way he looked at him. I don't care how many women he's been married to. Psychiatry is turning everybody nuts in the States, and they dare come here and tell us there's something peculiar about the way *we* live."

"Oh, well. He's only going to be here one night. We probably won't run into each other again for another twelve years."

"I wouldn't be so sure. I'll bet not many people bolster his self-respect the way you do. You treat him as if he were still worth something. You're too nice to do otherwise. Now that he's seen the house, he'll probably become a regular visitor."

"That might a bit of a trial. Anyway, you were marvelous." He put his hand on her ankle and gave it a squeeze. He dared touch her because of Mike's presence in the house. It could lead to nothing. He dared look at her unguardedly. Let his eyes be totally absorbed by her. He didn't know if she was beautiful. He knew only that to him she was the sum of all that was attractive and desirable. The eyes that could flash fire, the mouth that had shape and meaning and expression, not a flabby orifice like so many mouths, the texture of her skin, the way her neck flowed into her shoulders—if he were creating a woman, this was the way he would make her. He moved his hand back and forth on her ankle caressingly. Their eyes met. Hers were guarded, but he could read an ambiguity in them, something reluctant and questioning, in which desire was somehow mingled. He felt a stirring in his sex, and his breath came quicker. It was actually happening. With her. Dangerous games—too dangerous to play sober if it weren't for Mike's inhibiting presence.

He waited for the thought of being alone with her to have its usual effect of quelling his response, but desire continued to work through him. Was he delivered at last? There was no question of putting it to the test now, but he felt close to daring it. Tomorrow, with Mike gone, perhaps the moment would come again. Her eyes flickered in his, and a taut little smile twisted her lips.

"If you're going, shouldn't you go?" she said sharply, shatteringly. "It must be after three-thirty."

He stood up, thrusting his hands into his pockets to arrange his instantly shrinking sex. The link between them was totally severed. He experienced a sense of physical removal, as if he were spinning off into space. It was a not unfamiliar sensation, a sort of hallucinatory spell that seized him occasionally and into which he fell willingly, for it freed him from what seemed while it lasted the trivialities of daily existence. He felt as if he were looking into the very eye of life. He was alone, and all of life's secrets were his.

"I'll wander along," he said, barely aware that he was speaking to her. "I won't let the police keep me long. I'll be back no later than seven."

She waited until he was out of sight and then closed her eyes and gripped the arms of her chair and arched her back. With a long exhalation of breath she let herself go limp. How much longer must she wait? Time for George to get ready, for Mike to pull himself together. Another half hour? She was gripped by necessity; if there had been any doubt, she now knew that it had to happen. For a moment, George had looked at her in a way he hadn't for a long time, as if he wanted her, and everything in her had recoiled from him. She despised herself for it. To restore herself to him required one further treachery.

She made an enormous effort to hold herself in her chair. She fought against going to the kitchen for a drink. She didn't want it to happen in a daze of alcohol. She wanted to experience it coldly and conquer her craving for new young bodies.

At last, she heard voices and a door close. When nobody appeared in the garden, she supposed they had gone out the side door. She sprang up and went directly to her room—their room—but it had become more and more hers. She pulled the cover from the big double bed and mussed the sheets and punched the pillow. She stripped off everything she had on and put the clothes neatly away. She avoided looking at her body. Its hunger shamed her. She pulled on a straight sack dress and slipped her feet into sandals and was ready. She stood for a moment, listening to the house. She heard nothing. She went out to the foot of the steep stairs that led to George's study and, as an extra precaution, called his name. There was no answer. She slipped noiselessly down the stairs and through the garden and was gone.

Peter opened the letter he had saved for last from the batch that had come in on the morning boat. The house was very still. Charlie was working. Martha and the children were having their afternoon naps. Peter was waiting for Jeff in the room that was officially his bedroom but in which he never slept. It was furnished as his office, with a bed thrown in.

The letter was from a friend, Raoul Bertin, who had a famous restaurant in the south of France. Peter had kept it for last because it was the one that interested him most in today's lot. He had read the newspapers a month earlier about the robbery at Raoul's restaurant. In the French tradition, Raoul had fed a great many needy painters over the years and had been given a great many pictures. Some of them had been painters who later had become important names in contemporary art, and they formed the nucleus of a collection to which Raoul had extensively, if not judiciously, added. It was a quite important but uneven collection. A month ago, a large part of it had been stolen. Peter ran his eyes over the letter, finding, as he had hoped, that it was about the theft.

> ...I have a very good idea who did it...transporting themselves by yacht...the pictures will be divided into lots and disposed of around the Mediterranean, in Spain, Egypt, perhaps Turkey and Greece...this is not certain knowledge but suppositions fabricated with what I have heard...I do not cooperate with the police. In recent years, I have had reason to believe that some of the pictures are fakes. Have you not suspected yourself, my friend, that some were not quite right? The insurance is very good. I will be able to console myself if I never see them again. Because you are there, you may hear noises of them. For myself, I will be happy if you

seal your ears. You are a man of big scruples and may feel obliged to act. That will be your affair. I write so that you do not concern yourself very much for a friend's loss....

Peter finished the letter with a smile and tossed it down on the desk in front of him. After a moment's thought, he tore it into very small pieces and went to the bathroom and flushed them down the toilet. A waste of precious water, but Raoul really shouldn't have written that he was prepared to cheat his insurance company. Peter had been sure that quite a lot of the collection was fake but had never said so; he had tactfully refused when Raoul had hinted that perhaps Peter might arrange the sale of some of them.

He started back to his desk and then remembered that he was naked and picked up his loincloth from where he had dropped it and hitched it around his waist. As he did so, he heard the front door open and close down below. It had its particular sound. Costa? Jeff? He had told Jeff where he would be so that he could let himself in without disturbing any of the household. Nobody ever locked their doors here. Costa always seemed to know instinctively where he would find anybody he wanted. In a moment, he heard footsteps crossing the room next door, and he went to the door to greet his visitor.

"Hello, young 'un," he said, standing aside to let Jeff enter. The boy offered him the ghost of a smile as he slouched in. He had very wide shoulders, but the rest of him was still in the formative stage, so that he looked rather as if he had been hung on a coat hanger. He had big hands and feet that suggested he still had some growing to do. He would probably be as tall as his father, a couple of inches taller than Peter, who just grazed six feet. Jeff slumped into a chair, his arms and legs all whichaway. Peter pulled the chair out from his desk and placed it near him. "Do you want anything? Coffee? A cold drink?"

"No. I'm fine." Jeff's voice was deep and pleasing. A lot of dark hair fell over his forehead. Heavy brows rose into it. He had a strong straight nose and a delicately sculpted mouth. His face would probably be slightly craggy, handsome and masculine, when finally formed, but there was still something softly androgynous about it that didn't appeal to Peter. His eyes were enormous and fascinating, full of intelligence and dreams; they roved constantly to Peter, to the ceiling, to the shuttered windows. He had never been seen with a girl, although the intensity of his manner seemed to herald the birth of passion. It was one of the things that had made him and Charlie wonder.

"Any news of the family fortune?" Peter asked as he sat.

"The money?" Jeff shrugged and ran powerful fingers through his hair, a mannerism he had presumably acquired from his father. "Dad's probably put it somewhere in the house. He's so drunk most of the time, he doesn't know what he's doing. He'll find it."

"It would be too bad if Costa gets into trouble if it's as simple as that."

Jeff's eyes shot to him and away. "They can't do anything to him if they don't have any evidence."

"I hope you're right. Did your celebrated guest arrive?"

"Mike Cochran? I like him. There's something peculiar about him."

"Really?"

"The way he looks at me. He's supposed to have had all these women." Jeff flung his long bare brown legs about and dropped his head onto the back of the chair. He looked at Peter through half-closed eyes. "I guess you know what I wanted to talk about. I'm in love with Dimitri."

"I see." Peter had expected a more roundabout approach. ("Is it possible for a guy—" Or, "I have this strange feeling...") He should have realized that, growing up here, Jeff would take for granted all the permutations in the range of physical love. "Let me think. You're almost eighteen, aren't you?"

"I'll be eighteen when I go to Harvard in the fall. Are you thinking I don't know anything about love? I don't." He pulled himself forward and propped his elbows on his knees and gripped the sides of his head with his hands. He stared at the floor. "All I know is that I've been passionately attracted to him ever since he came back in the spring. That's why I had to talk to you."

Peter was touched. Jeff was almost two years younger than he had been when he had met Charlie and had his first sexual experience. He tried to imagine what it would have been like for him to have had this sort of conversation at the time and realized that it would have been impossible. He rose and went to his desk and found that he had nothing to do there. He turned back to Jeff. "Do you want to talk, or do you want me to ask you questions?"

"Either way. You can ask me anything you want." He lifted his head and dropped his hands. The unabashed adoration in his great dark eyes made Peter's throat tighten. The gift of youth engaged his responsibility. Jeff went on, "You and Charlie are my gods. You must know that. I couldn't talk to Charlie like this—he's so sort of aloof and above it all—but I worship him too."

Peter cleared his throat. "We're very fond of you, Jeff. We've talked about you and wondered. We thought something might be going on with you and Dimitri. What's the matter? Has it gone wrong? Is he giving you a bad time?"

"You don't understand." Jeff slumped back in the chair with his hands between his legs. The ghostly smile hovered on his lips. "Nothing has happened. I mean, nothing. Ever. Not with Dimitri or anybody else. I haven't wanted sex until Dimitri, and he wouldn't have anything to do with me. He said I was too young. He was afraid of having trouble with my father."

"That sounds surprisingly sensible of him," Peter said, returning to his chair.

"That's changed now. Something's happened—I can't tell you all of it—he's agreed to let me stay with him tonight."

"Ah?" An unformed thought strayed through Peter's mind and was gone. "Well, there's not much anybody can say at a moment like this. Are you sure you know what you're getting into? You're too intelligent for me to tell you that we all go through phases and that sort of thing. I just wish it weren't Dimitri."

"I know. I know all about him. I know he'll go to bed with any man who comes along. I had to pretend I'd had a lot of experience before he'd even look at me. I haven't the slightest idea what sex is all about. That's why I had to come to you. I couldn't talk to the queers around town. They'd just try to make me, and I don't want that. Please, Peter. I want you to tell me what I ought to know."

"That's a big order, love. Do you know what he likes in bed, for instance?"

"Oh, yes, I know that. I can't imagine doing it. All the kids here sodomize each other. They've tried to get me to join them, but they're so ugly, and it seems so animal. I know size means a lot to him. He never stops talking about it, but I don't even know if I'd be considered big or little. I'm terrified. I don't want tonight to traumatize me for life."

Peter suppressed a smile. His solemnity was comic, but also touching. "You sound a bit mixed up. There's no law that says you *have* to go to bed with a boy."

"Oh, I know about myself. I always have." He pulled his hands out from between his legs and ran them up, palms flat, over his stomach to rest on his chest, wide fingertips touching. The insidious, unconscious seductive wiles of youth. The ghostly smile brightened. "I should've been born in Delos. I would've been a naked dancing boy and performed unspeakable rites before a monumental phallus. I've known about myself even before I knew anything about sex. I

63

remember reading about Apollo and Hyacinth when I was a kid—one of those children's mythologies with all the sex and meaning taken out—and I almost fainted, it was so beautiful. I understood completely without knowing *what* I understood. I knew the story was about Apollo being in love with a beautiful boy, and it almost made me swoon. Literally. Who'd mind having a discus between the eyes if they'd had erect Apollo? To me, the phallus is the most thrillingly beautiful form in nature. I see it in everything. It's life itself. I don't see how anybody can help worshiping it. I wish mine was a yard long. When I masturbate—I do a lot—I think of you and Charlie with huge erections. Two beautiful huge phalli."

"Goodness. I do believe I'm blushing." Peter was glad to be able to let himself laugh. "Charlie probably qualifies, but there's nothing very special about me."

"I wonder how people get to be homosexual. I should think everybody would be, but since they're not there must be some reason for it. Does anybody know? I mean, I know the theory about the dominating mother and the inadequate father, but it hasn't been like that for me. Dad's always been wonderful until recently. I realize that knowing you and Charlie, seeing what a wonderful life you have together, and knowing you're in love with each other—that helped me not to be ashamed of it; but even if I'd been brought up in the States where it's supposed to a fate worse than death, I'd still worship men. The divine phallus. Do you know why that is?"

Peter smiled and shook his head. "Not a glimmer. It was different for me, but the result was the same. I grew up without knowing anything about it. As far as I knew, I'd never even seen a queer, but when Charlie looked at me the day I met him, I knew exactly what I wanted." Peter lifted his head and laughed. "The only way it makes sense is if we're all bisexual and some of us suppress the homo part more than others. Maybe I'd have been for girls if I hadn't fallen so in love with Charlie. The important thing is not to close yourself off to any development. You might have a surprise yourself someday."

"You're so relaxed and sure. You make me feel as if I can say anything to you. Would you let me see you naked?"

Peter was startled, but managed not to show it. "I'm fairly naked already. Would a little more make any difference?"

"Of course. You know that. If you'd let me see you naked, I'd get an erection. If I were naked too, you could tell me if I'm anywhere near big enough to interest Dimitri. Don't you understand? I know that anything you tell me will be right. You make everything seem good. I don't want it all ruined tonight because of my abysmal ignorance." He flung a leg over the arm of the chair and dropped his head back and stared at the ceiling. His long neck had a prominent Adam's apple. It bobbed up and down as he spoke musingly. "Do you know that thing—Homer or somebody—about the birth of Apollo? 'He came forth into light.' Maybe gods do. Everything has always seemed pretty dark to me." He suddenly dropped his head forward and covered his face with his hands. "It's so damned important to me," he said in a deep painful growl.

Peter was moved by him, but not remotely tempted. It had been years since he had even thought of making love to a boy, not necessarily out of loyalty to Charlie or because his basic sexual drive was any less unequivocally homosexual but because he was simply no longer interested.

Peter didn't quite know how it had happened; it was one of Charlie's miracles. He had demonstrated to Peter, by insisting that he share Martha, that he was capable of giving pleasure to women and could derive pleasure from them. The discovery had broadened and opened out the world for him. His occasional heterosexual experiences offered the revivifying titillation of novelty and the comfort of knowing that they were incapable, through some private chemical eccentricity, of throwing him off course emotionally. As Charlie had doubtless hoped, they had somehow eliminated the temptation of boys.

Peter looked at the tormented boy in front of him and chose his words carefully so as not to let their conversation get out of control. He didn't want to add to his torment or make him feel rebuffed. "I don't have to see you with an erection to have a pretty good idea of how you're built," he said. "You're all right."

"You've noticed?"

"Sure. I'm no longer in the market, but I still take a scholarly interest in guys' crotches."

Jeff looked up, and his smile was suddenly boyish and vivid. "You're extraordinary. You're so natural. I don't know any grownup like you. To be perfectly honest, I don't feel any age difference between us at all. You might not think that's a compliment, but it's meant to be. It's amazing. You *will* let me see you naked, won't you?"

"I've never been shy about stripping, but I'm not sure it's a good idea under these particular circumstances."

"You mean because of Charlie?"

"How do you mean?"

"You're faithful to him, aren't you?"

"Of course, but stripping for you wouldn't be unfaithful to Charlie. Anyway, we found out long ago that we *can't* be unfaithful to each other. I have a girl every now and then, but he likes that. We all have our queer patches. That's Charlie's. He gets a kick out of thinking of me with a girl." He paused, thinking of the girl at the port at noon. He directed his attention back to Jeff. "The last time I was almost unfaithful was with Dimitri, God help us, and that was ten years ago when we first came to Greece on that cruise with Martha and her husband. When we bought the house."

Jeff's eyes had widened with interest. "What was he like?"

"About the same age as you are now. Very innocent and appealing. Not as beautiful as he is now. Quite small, by the way, if that's as important to you as you make it sound."

"It's important to *him*. I don't know what's important to me," Jeff burst out, flinging himself about in the chair. "I haven't wanted sex until now. It seemed dirty to me. I realize that that's because with kids there's no love. I'm ready for love now. I've got to come to terms with sex. If I don't, I'll end up with fantasies about you and Charlie and Apollo, and masturbating for the rest of my life. Is it mad for me to be a homosexual and think I can have a good life? Is it very difficult?"

"I suppose so. Maybe more difficult than for other people, but making a good life isn't easy for anybody. I have no complaints, but—" He paused, and his habitually sunny expression clouded briefly. "It can be weird sometimes. Being queer, I mean. You go along leading a good life—I mean, really good—loving and living for love the way everybody agrees is good—and then some trivial little event of the day reminds you that you're supposed to think of yourself as a monster. Charlie fought it at the beginning. He threw me out to get married. I mean a regular marriage, not the nutty setup we have now. Well, you've probably heard about that. For a long time after we got together again, we tried to hide it. You know, pretended with everybody that we were just good friends. That does a lot of damage. Then Martha came along, and by some fantastic freak of luck she turned out to be the one woman in ninety million we could work things out with, to have the children and everything. The thing I don't tell most people is that if she hadn't come along, we'd have been fine without her. It's been marvelous, but as much as I adore the family, Charlie is still the center of life and always has been. People may be fooled by us, but we've never fooled ourselves about that. Yes, dammit, of course a homosexual can have a good life."

Jeff was staring at him. Peter was astonished to see that his eyes

66

were liquid with tears. "There's so much love and understanding between you," he said wonderingly. "Why isn't everybody like that? When I think of what goes on at home, it makes me sick. My father turning into a drunken wreck. My mother running after young men who aren't much older than I am. And they never *talk* to each other. They fight, but they never say the truth. You weren't here, so you didn't meet Ronnie, but you must know all about it. He was after me. I wouldn't have him, so Mother grabbed him instead. That's why tonight is so important to me. I've got to start sometime. I've got to make a life for myself. I may really be in love with Dimitri, but I'll never find out if I go to him like this, all tied up in knots."

His voice strangled on his words. He lifted his fists and pressed them to the sides of his head. "I'm going out of my mind. He'll see that I'm an inexperienced kid and throw me out. Oh, God, Peter, you could help me so." He closed his eyes, and tears spilled down his cheeks.

Peter checked an impulse to go to him and put an arm around him. The boy was already emotionally overwrought; tenderness might further undermine his control. Showing him his body seemed a more straightforward alternative. He hesitated for a moment and then stood up. "All right, Jeff. Let's get some of those knots untied." He went to the door and locked it. He unhitched the cloth from around his waist and tossed it aside and turned back to Jeff. They had swum together so often with very little more on that he couldn't imagine his nakedness being much of a thrill. "This is what I look like," he said, approaching the boy.

Jeff's eyes were fixed on the bit he had never seen. When Peter stopped in front of him, his chest heaved with a deep convulsive breath. "You're so incredibly beautiful. You and Charlie are the most beautiful men I've ever seen. I knew it. You're bigger right now than I am with an erection."

"I doubt it, but if we're going to pursue our comparative study, you'd better let me see."

Jeff disentangled himself from the chair and stood. He kicked off his sandals and peeled off his shirt. In a moment, he had got his legs out of his shorts and underpants. He kept his eyes averted.

"Good lord. You actually *do* have an erection," Peter exclaimed. The boy's torso was still hairless, but there was a shading of down on his chest and across his flat belly. Only the pubic hair had developed. From it, the pale sex rose at a steep angle, giving an impression of great vigor. Its adult virility was a shock in juxtaposition to the tanned, coltish, angular boy's body. "It's just what I told you. You have a good average cock. If anything, a little bigger than average. I'm afraid my vocabulary isn't as elegant as yours. I can't refer to our phalli."

"Is it bigger than Dimitri's?" Jeff's eyes were still averted.

"Considerably, unless he's grown."

Jeff looked up with an urgent plea in his limpid eyes. "I still don't know what we're supposed to do. If Dimitri and I were like this, what would happen?"

Peter smiled at him. "If you were like this, you'd be in bed together, and nature would take its course."

"But I don't know anything about nature. How does one start?"

"Any way that strikes your fancy. Making love is an expression of desire. It's supposed to be fun. If I were Dimitri, what would you want to do?"

"Can I tell you the truth? Kiss your—I don't see how I can say it, but it's true—I want to kiss your cock. Is that ridiculous?"

Peter laughed. "You can't expect me to think so. I've been rather partial to kissing cocks in my time. Lots of people are, women as well as men. You won't go down in history as the inventor of cock-sucking."

Jeff looked at him gravely. "Would you let me?"

"Are you kidding? Of course not." There was a sharpness in his refusal which he immediately regretted. He wasn't angry. He felt a deep affection for the boy and, now that his first surprise at developments had worn off, completely at ease. Being naked together made him feel like a kid again, but that wasn't unusual for him. He often wondered if he would ever feel fully grown up. Did he feel young because he looked young, or was it the other way around? Maybe when he was forty at last, he'd crumple with the weight of years. Meanwhile, it was very pleasant to see an attractive youth with an erection. He couldn't wait to tell Charlie about it. He approached Jeff but stopped before he was within reach. "In the first place, you couldn't give me a hard-on. That's not because you're not a damned attractive kid, but it's just the way it is. A lot of people think queers will go for any guy they can get their hands on, but you must know better than that. So let's stick to Dimitri."

"How can I think about Dimitri with you here?" His eyes dropped once more to the object of his cult. "It's absolutely ravishing. I could kill myself with envy. It's obviously twice as big as mine."

"Don't be silly. Bigger maybe, but so what? All this fuss about size is silly. It may be important to Dimitri, but it isn't particularly to most people. I've always enjoyed having a little extra to wave around, but it hasn't been a big thing in my life."

"Is Charlie much bigger than you?"

"Oh, Lord. He really *is* twice as big as you are, but he's a phenomenon. I admit I'm nuts about it." Peter laughed. "I've always wished he could make a cast of it. It would be quite a hunk of hardware." Jeff lifted his great adoring dark eyes, and Peter felt the contact between them beginning to flow directly and easily. The boy's expression had cleared. He was excited and curious, but his adoration wasn't primarily sexual, fervent but not passionate. He looked at the tenderly curving lips and experienced a stunned moment as he realized that this was the kid he had watched grow up, young enough to be his son, here naked with him, the persistent erection still lifted before him. "I have a sneaking suspicion I rather hoped you'd turn out to be one of us," he said with a smile. "You're certainly the most attractive boy we know. I suppose you've never been kissed, have you? If you put your clothes on, we might do something about that."

The ardent young face lighted up; the yearning eyes dropped for another lingering look at Peter's midsection. Then he pulled himself up and, with more grace and purpose in his movements than Peter had seen in him before, returned to where he had dropped his clothes. The erection gave him the pagan look of a naughty Greek vase painting. Peter retrieved his sarong and hitched it around him. He was glad he hadn't made a great mystery about his body. They could deal with each other as friends now on an equal footing with no meaningless strains or tensions between them. He wandered over to Jeff while he tucked himself back into his shorts. Jeff looked at him expectantly as he finished buttoning up. Peter took a step closer and tilted his head toward him with the back of his hand, and their mouths met. Jeff's was closed. Peter ran his tongue lightly along his lips, and they opened with a gasp. Their tongues touched, and then Peter pulled back with a laugh. "You mustn't keep your mouth closed when you're consumed with passion." He was thinking of the thousands of distasteful open-mouthed male kisses he had received at "gay" cocktail parties in the old days.

Jeff's eyes were aglow with wonder. "Oh, my God, Peter. That's fantastic." His voice had deepened with emotion. "That's the most thrilling thing I've ever imagined. I'm in love with you, of course, but not like with Dimitri or some ordinary mortal. It's good you don't want me—not that I ever thought you did—but it would be too much.

Show me more—tell me everything while I'm still innocent. I don't want it to be an ugly shock. Just tell me everything people do. You can't corrupt me, because I intend to find out anyway. I guess I know already, but tell me exactly what I'm supposed to do with Dimitri."

Peter ran his fingers along the sharp line of jaw, then dropped his hand and took Jeff's and led him to a chair. He sat opposite him. "If you know, you know," he said baldly. "He likes to be fucked. He'll want your cock inside him."

"Yes, but doesn't it hurt? I should think it would be better for me to be small if that's what he wants."

"That isn't the way it works. Guys who like to be fucked like to feel it. The bigger the better. I happen to know what I'm talking about."

"And you say that I'm maybe a bit bigger than average? All right, what do I do? How do I go about it?"

"You'll be in bed, of course. It doesn't strike me as all that mysterious. Hell." Peter sat back with a helpless little chuckle. "When you're in bed with somebody you want and kissing him and all that, you just let yourself go. You'll probably find yourself kissing him in the most unlikely places. I'm sure you won't think of anything that'll surprise Dimitri."

Gloom seemed to be descending on his audience. "You're not telling me," Jeff muttered heavily. "I mean, how do you get in the right position and that sort of thing?"

"Oh, dear. I guess I'm going to have to write the script. Look, you don't have to leap at him and plunge yourself into him. Maybe you'll find some entertainment along the way. If you want to suck his cock, I'm sure he'll be delighted. When he comes, swallow it. You know that much, don't you?"

"No. I've wondered. It doesn't make you sick or anything?"

"Of course not. It's good for you. Some guys spit it out. It creates an unfriendly atmosphere." He rose and went across to a drawer in the bedside table. He pulled out a tube of lubricant he kept there. He and Charlie used the room sometimes because it was safely isolated from the children.

He returned to Jeff and perched on the arm of his chair. "You have to use something to make it easier. Even some girls do. Dimitri will undoubtedly have something, olive oil or Vaseline or God knows what, but it's much better with this. You can get it at the pharmacy. Take some with you tonight. It'll show him you know what it's all about. When an opportune moment occurs to make free with his bottom, spread it around and have at him."

Jeff looked at the tube without moving. There was a moment of silence, and then he burst out querulously, "I knew it. I knew it couldn't possibly work."

"What's the matter?" Peter dropped a steadying hand onto his bare shoulder.

"I've had an erection until this minute," he protested, as if he'd been somehow cheated. "Thinking about all this, it shriveled right away. That stuff, having to stop everything to put it on. The trouble is, I probably don't even want it that way. Looking at your great golden phallus made me realize that I'm just like him. I want—I'll want him inside me. The whole thing's ridiculous."

Peter checked his laughter. Jeff's young confused innocence made his throat ache. He settled himself more comfortably on the arm of the chair and lifted his hand and began to stroke the boy's hair reassuringly. The head dropped against his rib cage. It gave him a nice little paternal thrill, which, as he had learned with Little Pete, linked up somehow with sexuality. "I don't think it'll be any great loss if things don't work out tonight," he said sympathetically, "but if you're really in love with Dimitri, don't worry about the sex part. Maybe with you, he'll learn something new about himself. It can work both ways, you know. Charlie and I found that out. He'd kill me if he knew I'd told you that. He doesn't like us to talk about our sex life, and he's probably right. I'll make an exception for you. I'm making a lot of exceptions for you." The head pressed closer against him, and he smiled down at it. "Right from the beginning, Charlie always took me, fucked me, and I couldn't imagine it being any other way. But then, just about the time we were getting together with Martha—he decided he wanted it the other way around. He's very mental about things. I'm just a cheerful idiot. I thought he was mad and thought it would spoil everything, but of course it was bliss, like everything with him. I think he thought it was time for me to develop the more aggressive, sort of masculine part of me and that it would help me have a try at girls, and I guess he was right. It's what I said earlier— it's good to keep yourself open to new experience. I'd certainly never *looked* at a girl before, and I'm glad he changed that, even though I don't exactly go chasing after them very often. It's just that it's good to respond to *everybody* as much as possible. That's why I think everybody is probably meant to be bisexual instead of being pressured one way or the other. The point is, he's always made life bigger and better by paying attention to the way we've developed and making something of it. Even when we were having problems—my problems mostly, such as infidelity—once, believe it or not, but there were temptations—he was able to help us through them by adapting and finding ways of making even bad things work *for* us. He drives me wild sometimes when he gets going on some new line, always all of it working away inside him, but I think that's behind us now. He's made life marvelous. That's why I take love seriously. That's why I'm talking so much. I'd like you to understand how good it can be. I don't believe much in your rendezvous tonight. Dimitri doesn't care about people."

Jeff reached up and seized his hand and clung to it as if he were frightened. "I guess that's the sort of thing you have to learn by experience." His voice came out deep and full of pain. "Isn't it natural to think that somebody you're all involved with is going to be different with you than he is with others?"

"Natural enough, but it almost never works that way. I wish we could find you somebody who would make you forget all about him."

Jeff's shoulders lurched with the rumble of a chuckle. Peter wanted to be able to look into his face for what was coming next, but he kept his head averted. Peter pressed it to him briefly and stood and withdrew his hand. Holding the boy, thinking about Charlie, talking about the intimate wonders of their life, had stirred his sex. It lifted against his loincloth, and its increased length and weight made it swing conspicuously when he walked. He hitched the cloth more firmly around him and returned the tube to the bedside table, circling Jeff so that he was able to keep his back to him until he dropped into a chair and faced him.

"Now, listen, Jeff, honey," he began incisively. "Why don't you cancel your date? You're obviously not happy about the whole idea."

"It's too late." Jeff clawed at the hair Peter had lovingly smoothed and dropped his hand over his eyes. "I've made such a big thing of it. I have to go through with it."

"Look at me, for God's sake. What is all this? I've been waiting to ask you something. Are you mixed up in this dope business with Dimitri?"

Jeff shook his head. "I know about it, but I'm not really mixed up in it."

"Then what is it? There's something you ought to tell. I'm sure of it."

"No. Really, I can't—"

"Listen, Jeff. Aside from his fairly sloppy sex life, Dimitri isn't a very nice guy. There was some nasty trouble with a rich Englishman in Poros. Dimitri had to get off the island. If we'd known the story when he came here and talked about opening the bar, we'd have tried to stop him. You've got to tell me if you're involved with him in any way except for planning to go to bed with him."

Jeff lifted his head and revealed his eyes at last. They were troubled but candid. His mouth worked briefly before he got out any words. "That's really all it is. The complications have to do with that. Everything will be all straight after tonight. He's had an enormous hold over me, but you've made me see I've been an hysterical child. It's because I haven't had a sex life. Any initiation will do. Just the idea of its being messy scares me. I suppose that's part of being immature. One shouldn't expect everything to be all moonlight and roses."

"No, but it's not as messy as you might think. When Charlie kicked me out, I had myself fucked by every attractive guy I could find. I know."

A peal of laughter burst from the boy. "You really are extraordinary. You make everything seem so healthy and natural. I've been noticing lately how rare that is."

Peter rose on an impulse to go to him but found that he was still in a noticeably aroused state and turned hastily and took refuge behind his desk. He didn't know why he went on feeling so sexy. It certainly wasn't Jeff. A mood of the moment. Maybe he should go find Charlie The word he considered the ugliest in the language crossed his mind: *tumescent.* It was joined by his second ugliest word: *penis.* He had a slightly tumescent penis. A horrible disease. Jesus. He smiled to himself and looked at Jeff. "Don't forget, honey. We belong to each other a little now, so if you hurt yourself you'll be hurting me too. Don't forget that. Come to me if there's something you want to talk about. After this, you can tell me anything."

"How could I forget? It means so much to me." His eyes wavered, and an uncharacteristic little playful smile sprang to his lips. "You know, that little skirt is much more revealing than you may realize. Your—your cock is much bigger than it was. I have to go. Let me see it first."

"Don't you think we've done enough stripping for today?"

"You stripped too soon. That's a cheat." Jeff rose. Standing straight, he was a tall and distinguished-looking youth. His eyes were fixed on the sarong.

You know how cocks are," Peter said. "You never know what they're going to do next. I long ago gave up taking any responsibility for mine."

"Then it's all right if I see it. Looking at it draped like that just inflames my fevered imagination."

Peter threw his head back and laughed. "God forbid I should do that." He pulled the sarong off as he came out from behind the desk. Glancing down, he was surprised to see that things had gone so far. He hadn't felt *that* sexy, but there was nothing to do but make a joke of it. "Here we are. Time for the second showing."

Jeff approached, his eyes wide and intent on it. "Oh, Peter," he said in an awed murmur. "You're sublime. It's what I imagined, only more so. How can you say size doesn't matter? I'd sell my soul for something like that." He stopped and reached out and ran his hand down the length of it.

"Hey. Who told you you could do that?" Peter demanded without moving.

"You don't have to tell me. I know I can touch without its being a big thing between us. You know I'm not going to do anything wild. You have me completely under control. You know that."

"Okay, but don't let's push it." At the first caressing touch, his sex had lengthened with a little leap and stiffened slightly, but he could feel that this was as far as it would go. A pity in a way. Jeff was such an appreciative audience. He deserved to see the complete production. With a little surge of exhibitionism, he thrust his hips forward to give it greater prominence. It slanted down away from his body, lifting with only a hint of erection but extended almost its full erect length.

Jeff gazed at it and crooned a paean of praise. "This is the first time I've seen a man with even the beginning of an erection. It must be absolutely enormous. It's huge right now. Staggering. It's so smooth and so—so powerful, long and straight like a dagger. No wonder I'm queer. How could anyone help worshiping such mystery, such beauty. Oh, God, Peter, there are so many things I'd like to do with it, but looking is enough. I know now men are really made like this. It isn't all my imagination."

"Well, that's it, as far as I'm concerned. I've shown you all I can." Peter gave the boy a pat on the shoulder and moved back from him. He flipped the sarong over his shoulder. "I've got to be ready to cover up. I'm sort of hoping Costa may turn up." He saw the boy's expression cloud as he finally tore his eyes from him and turned away nervously.

"I have to be going," Jeff said as he pulled on his shirt without tucking it in and stepped into his sandals.

"There's no rush."

"No, I have to see Dimitri about something."

"I'll be waiting to hear all about it."

Jeff faced him. The ghostly smile was on his lips. He seemed tense and withdrawn again. "Yes. I wouldn't be surprised if the best part is telling you about it. Can I come see you again tomorrow after lunch?"

"You can come see me any time you like, love. Just don't let him upset you."

"This has been the most wonderful hour of my life. I'll never forget it."

They looked into each other's eyes, and then Jeff's dropped inevitably to the sacred area as they moved toward each other and remained there as Peter put his arm around his shoulder and walked him to the door and unlocked it. Jeff gave him a last lingering look, then turned with a growled "so long" and slouched out.

Peter turned back into the room and stretched his whole body. Sex. Sex. Sex. His damn cock was beginning to get on his nerves. He thought of the girl again. If there was ever a girl he would gladly chase, she was it. That extraordinary look. The way the features were so delectably put together. Thoughts of the girl accomplished what Jeff had not. In one long deep satisfying surge, his cock lifted and locked into erection. So that was what was the matter with him. He looked down at himself and laughed. Poor Jeff had missed the finale. He must tell Charlie that he hadn't forgotten his duties to heterosexuality. He threw down the sarong, trotted to the bathroom, and got under a cold shower.

Fragmentary thoughts skipped through his mind. Something was eluding him. Something about Jeff's reluctance to keep the date with Dimitri. He felt as if he knew more than he could coherently formulate, as if some information had been passed on to him that he hadn't quite grasped.

He decided that if Costa didn't turn up soon, he should go look for him. There was something fishy going on. He could feel it in his bones. And because usually there was so little going on, fishy or otherwise, he suspected that it all linked up in some way—George's money, Costa's uncharacteristic threats, Jeff and Dimitri. He added the letter he had flushed down the toilet to his little collection of anomalies. Could the stolen pictures have something to do with it too? It was the sort of thing Dimitri might have a finger in. He hoped Jeff had been telling the truth. He felt responsible for the boy. The juxtaposition of naked bodies, even chaste, struck resonances beyond ordinary human intercourse. He marveled briefly at Charlie's miracle, marveling that he could get through such an encounter without even a twinge of temptation. He would do what he could to keep the boy out of whatever mischief was afoot.

George and Mike lay side by side on towels spread out on a cement platform in the shade of a rock, apparently mending the strands of intimacy that had bound them so long ago, while Mike's determination hardened to break through the facade George had erected for him; his picture of life here was too idyllic to be convincing. He suspected that George intended to make his own successful life seem empty and meretricious.

"You're living in a dream world," Mike insisted. "Do all your kindred spirits here live in palaces like yours? Incidentally, how does a whole family, and guests too presumably, manage with just one bathroom? I'd go out of my mind."

George laughed. "God bless America. Do you realize that there wasn't a single bathroom on the island when we arrived? Well, the Mills-Martins were first, but no matter. You'd be amazed at the things you can get along without."

"No, I wouldn't be. When I was a kid, we had an outhouse in the backyard. We didn't even have electricity until I was twelve. We got along. But who wants to? There's something unnatural about turning your back on progress."

"Progress doesn't mean anything if it bypasses the human spirit. I remember you saying something of the sort years ago."

"I used to talk a pretty fancy line in the old days. I doubt if it was any more profound than the things most kids say."

"I think it was. It meant a lot to me. I left the States because of certain feelings I thought we shared. I'm not sure of things the way everybody is over there and being famous all of a sudden didn't help. I found myself getting fixed in a set of public attitudes when I wanted to go on exploring. I didn't want life to get flattened out for me, all neat and simple and sanitary, the way it tends to get in the States. If there're any rough edges, go to a psychiatrist. He'll smooth them out."

"As a matter of fact, he probably will. What's wrong with that?"

"Oh, Mike, what about the struggle? What about hopes and dreams? What about suffering and happiness? What about death?"

"You sound as if you'd caught the European disease of self-flagellation. It's so self-defeating. Frankly, you wouldn't have to worry about being famous anymore. You may be able to live here on what you make, but you couldn't in the States. Not comfortably. You're not earning up to your potential. There's something wrong there. It may not sound stylish intellectually, but money counts."

"Of course it does, but not in any of the important ways." All the money in the world wouldn't help him get back to Sarah. Money. It would soon be time to do something about it. They had been lying here for nearly two hours, with frequent dips in the sea, and he had been surprisingly successful at keeping his mind off the money. Now he felt his nerves knotting. A drink would help. *Watch it,* he warned himself. *No drunkenness while Mike is here.*

He felt increasingly that Mike was seeking the confrontation he had envisaged that morning and dismissed as being without valid grounds. He could feel him probing, trying to catch him out in some way. Was he trying to force some acknowledgment from George for his glittering achievement, or was he so unsure of it that he had to demonstrate that it was at least greater than George's?

George had felt flashes of malice in him, and they had so saddened him that he had tried to ignore them. Once upon a time he might have enjoyed meeting him head on, heaping him with scorn, and taunting him for having so readily come to terms with the commercialism that had earlier been a target of his invective, but he felt no fight in himself now. He was struggling for his own survival; he had no energy to spare for a conflict that was basically foreign to his nature. He had loved Mike; something worth preserving *must* remain.

They both stirred at the same moment and sat up and wiped sweat out of their eyes.

"I'm about ready for another dip," George said, "and then I'm going to have to think about getting along to the police."

"What's this big police deal?" Mike asked, rising.

"Oh, nothing. Just helping out a young American with some business." He was reticent about telling Mike about the money. It was just the sort of thing he could seize on; such a lot of fuss about a miserable two thousand dollars. He was probably bound to find out about it, but Costa might yet come through with something; something might happen at the police station that would put an end to it.

His heart accelerated. There was an emptiness in the pit of his stomach. Just one drink would do no harm. He stood beside Mike, looking down on him and relishing his physical superiority. Stripped of expensive clothes, Mike lost his new elegance. He had a sturdy farm boy's body, trim and vigorous, a boxer's body. The paunch George had imagined this morning was definitely not in evidence.

His looking so like he used to look endeared him to George and stirred memories of their intimacy when they had shared girls.

"Is there any crime in your ideal community?" Mike asked idly.

"Damn little. The police are political agents more than anything else."

"I've heard as much. Well, that's one advantage of being an expatriate. You can sit back and shrug at what's going on around you."

"Nonsense, Mike. If this is a police state, it's because we've encouraged it to be one. There was a civil war here after our war, apparently a pretty nasty one. A lot of people are prepared to put up with strong-arm methods to avoid any repetition of it. I don't pretend to like it, and I do everything I can to resist it. There's no such thing anymore as expatriation in the way you seem to mean it. We're all part of the same world."

"I wonder. I'm quite active politically at home. I have some voice in what's going on over there. I wouldn't have much scope here, would I?"

"As a foreigner, of course not."

"There you are. Isn't that another indication of your abdication? You're accepting too many limitations, George. It's bound to affect your work."

"I don't want to be in politics, dammit," George said with more heat than he had intended. Mike had touched a sensitive area; he had given it a good deal of thought and had decided that as long as he wasn't cramped by the system, he had no obligation to take a stand against it, any more than he would at home. "A man has just so much time. I've always felt that my work was more important than anything I could do as an amateur politician. Everybody agrees that things are more or less the same here as they've always been. Until the Greeks get fed up I don't feel any need or right to mount the barricades."

"Old Juggernaut George. No wonder we want you back." Mike covered his retreat with laughter. He had no taste for heavy debate; hit-and-run was more his style. He had George on the defensive. It would be interesting to see where it would lead.

They clambered over the rocks together down to the edge of the sea. On the way, George noticed Pavlo had arrived and nodded distantly to him. He was flaunting his body as usual in the smallest bit of bikini the law would allow. He didn't matter. He hadn't liked finding Sarah sitting with him this morning, but he knew that she couldn't be interested in such a blatant hunk of exhibitionistic flesh.

78

Dreamy young intellectuals were more her line.

Disagreeable things happened in his chest and stomach, but he got a grip on himself. Farther along, he saw the fancy little Swiss faggot they had all been laughing at frolicking with a group of cadets from the merchant marine school. His sense of possessiveness toward the island came to the surface, and he frowned. If he had his way, he'd set up a control on the port and turn away the undesirables. They brought their civilized sicknesses with them and left a trail of corruption behind them. He was aware that plenty of homosexuals were decent human beings, but they were beginning to give the island a definite flavor.

He dived into the leaden sea. He and Mike returned to their bit of shade. He lay again long enough to get dry; then he rose and pulled his trousers on over his trunks and put on his shirt and sandals. "You want to stay on a bit?" he asked Mike.

"I might as well. There's no point in getting any hotter than I am already."

George frowned again as he looked down along the rocks to where the Swiss was still surrounded by cadets. "That looks like trouble," he said. "Some of those cadets are tough. They lead the boys on and then beat the hell out of them."

Mike propped himself on an elbow to see what George was talking about. He smiled up at him. "They look to me as if they were enjoying themselves. You really feel you own this place, don't you?"

"Perhaps, in a way. You see, there wasn't much here until we came."

"And now you control the police."

"What do you mean by that?"

"Don't you? How could you help this American if you didn't?"

"Oh, I see. No, you misunderstood. I'm just going to interpret for him. I'll meet you afterward at that grocery-tavern I pointed out to you. You'll recognize it. Just look for the statue of the admiral. I'll be along about seven or so. We'll have dinner at home."

Mike nodded agreement, and they lifted their hands to each other in farewell. George climbed up the rocks to the rough road that led into town. He didn't pause to admire the panorama as he rounded the last steep spur of rock that hid the port. The compartment of his mind in which he had somehow managed to confine his anxiety about the money had totally collapsed, and he was plunged into harassing thought. He was doing the only thing he could do. He had given Costa a chance. If he brought the money, or some news of it, well and good. He knew everything that went on here. Nobody could steal two thousand dollars without his hearing of it. The money was all that mattered.

The money. The word jangled in his mind like a torn nerve. He couldn't understand how he had got through the day with such apparent calm. What did he think they were going to do without money? Peter, in his usual sweet thoughtful way, had made his offer, but did he mean he would cover all of it? It would never occur to anybody that that was all the money he had. If Mike were still the same old Mike, he would have been a godsend, but he couldn't even tell him about it now. Mike and his dogs. Christ. He wiped his sweating palms on his trousers and ran his fingers through his hair.

Entering town along the western arm of the port, he passed the Americanized tourist bar where Jeff was frequently to be found lounging with his friend Dimitri, but it was deserted now. He turned onto the wide *quai* facing the harbor and saw Joe Peterson sitting at Lambraiki's, a pile of books beside him, a glass in front of him.

"Have you tried this Greek vermouth?" said Joe in greeting. "It's not bad as an afternoon drink."

"I admire your unflagging spirit of inquiry. Come on. Finish that thing and let's get it over with."

"You really think this is the best way to handle it?"

"It's the only way. I told Costa what we were going to do. What's the matter? Have you changed your mind? Do you think one of your beats could've taken your money, after all?"

Joe flushed but answered without hesitation. "Oh, no. No question about it. It was Costa. I just hate to call in the coppers. It seems unethical somehow."

"I don't think you'll amount to much in the pulpit. Come on." He stood nervously rocking a chair while Joe drained his glass.

"Okay. I might as well leave my books here." He stood up and moved into position at George's side, and they set off for the police station. It was up a side street at the end of the port. When they reached it, they found Peter waiting in front of it.

"Well," George exclaimed, not happy to have Peter as a witness to this not very felicitous occasion. "A gathering of the clan. What are you doing here?"

Peter nodded to them both and addressed George. "I've been looking all over for Costa. I hoped he might be here."

"So did I. It's past six."

Peter's usual ebullient high spirits were shadowed by concern. "He's usually around somewhere. His boat's there. I wonder what he's up to."

"Do you think I gave him a scare and he's run off with the loot?"

"On the contrary. I'm more and more convinced he had nothing to do with it. I've got a hunch, but it's too vague to talk about. If I'm on the right track and Costa knows, I can understand his wanting to stay out of it."

"You're sounding very mysterious, chum." George put his hand on Peter's shoulder, unnecessarily but compulsively, and gave him a little shake. "Why don't you tell me what's going on in that beautiful head of yours?"

Peter smiled briefly. He remained preoccupied. "What are you planning to do?"

"Two thousand dollars has disappeared. I'm going to report it to the police. If somebody picks it up I want them to know it's mine."

"That's fair enough. But for God's sake, be careful how you bring Costa into it. I like the guy. I'm sure he didn't take it."

"I like him, too, but I can't afford to be sure of anything. I tried the trick with the trousers. The bundle of paper I used was bigger than money. You couldn't really see it."

"I see." Peter studied the ground for a moment. "I wish you'd wait till I find Costa."

"I told him what I was going to do. If he had anything to add to what he said at noon, he'd be here now."

"That's true," Peter admitted with evident reluctance. "Jeff came by a little while ago. He thinks you might have put the money away somewhere and forgotten it. It didn't sound very likely to me."

"Thanks." George spoke with an ironic edge in his voice. "You'll learn, if you haven't already, that children never credit their parents with any sense. I'm sometimes hazy when I wake up in the morning, but I've never gone through a day without remembering the major events of the night before. Putting two thousand dollars away would count as major to me."

"But—" Peter began, but found there was nothing he could say that wouldn't risk betraying Jeff's confidence. George could be trusted to act fairly. "Sure. You're right. You'd better go tell the police. Good luck."

Peter and George parted with affectionate taps on the back. Peter nodded to Joe and left. George and Joe entered the police station.

The door gave onto a long flight of wooden steps that thundered underfoot so that there was no danger of the police being taken by surprise. At the head of it was a sort of common room with doors opening off it. When George and Peterson thundered up to it, they found two old men waiting stiffly on a wooden bench, but a policeman greeted George by name, and he was immediately ushered into the captain's office. A woman in black sat huddled in front of the captain's desk, but she was prodded to her feet and ordered out. Was this what it meant to control the police? Or was it only the normal extravagant courtesy shown any foreigner? The captain rose, crisp and resplendent in a tan uniform, belted, buckled, beribboned, and shook hands with George across the desk. He nodded severely at Joe. Orders were barked, chairs were shifted, the two foreigners and the captain sat down.

"It is a pleasure to see you, Mr. Yorgo," the captain said. "You will have coffee. How do you take it?" He included Joe in the invitation menacingly, as if it were too much of a strain on his official manner to be cordial to two people at the same time.

He barked orders for coffee, and the policeman withdrew. He produced a box of cigarettes and pressed one on George. He pushed the box toward Joe as if he were offering him a dare. In civilian clothes he was a quite nondescript-looking man, with unusually small neat features for a Greek, but the uniform possessed him and transformed him into a forbidding figure of authority. Even with George, his conversation had rather the air of an interrogation.

He asked about Sarah. He asked about the children. He wanted George's opinion of the tourist season and how it compared with the season before. George knew it was necessary to go through these formalities before it would be seemly to discuss business. Coffee arrived. More cigarettes were offered. Joe was ignored. Finally, George judged that the amenities had been sufficiently observed.

"You know Mr. Peterson here," he said, indicating Joe as if he had just entered the room. "He has the Gripari house."

"Yes, yes, of course," the captain said, stiffening in his chair and frowning as he assumed his official role.

"Mr. Peterson has just been robbed of a thousand drachmas. I suspect that I've been robbed of nearly sixty thousand."

The captain jumped as if he had been shot. "Sixty thousand drachmas! It's not possible."

"In my case, I have no real facts to go on, but Mr. Peterson feels quite sure where his money went." George told their stories, scrupulously emphasizing the fact that he might have lost his money.

The captain threw up his hands in angry disbelief. "Ah, no, Mr. Yorgo. I do not believe you are the sort of man to lose such a sum. That would be the act of a young fool. You are known and respected.

82

You don't go about losing sixty thousand drachmas. No. No. No. Mr. Peterson is right. It was doubtless Costa. He is a man with a police record. We keep our eyes on him. This morning he spent almost one hundred drachmas on beer alone. Where does he get the money? Don't worry. You must tell me everyone who was with you last night."

George was disinclined to tell him he was too drunk to remember. "The usual crowd," he said. "You know, all the foreigners. My friends."

"I know the house owners and those who have established residence. What of the transients we are getting now? I wouldn't trust all of them."

"I know very few of them. I know none of them were with us last night." He was sure this was true. He had remembered enough of the evening to know that there were no unfamiliar faces among their party.

"And Greeks? The local population?"

George hesitated, studying the end of his cigarette. Facts were facts. "Costa," he said. He heard the captain slap the desk and forced himself to look at him. The captain seemed to have grown. He loomed with authority.

"Very well. We know you had the money in your hand at one point. We know the Lambraiki family would never keep it if you left it there. Costa knows your house well. He follows you home. He waits for the lights to go out. He runs no risk. If anybody finds him in the house, he can invent a reason for wanting to see you. It is very simple, Mr. Yorgo." The captain snapped orders. George found the staccato handling of the language difficult to follow, but he understood that Costa was to be brought in immediately. He shifted in his seat, preparing to rise.

"Thank you," he said as soon as the policeman had left. "You understand that Mr. Peterson and I don't wish to make any charges. We just want our money back."

"It is now in the hands of the police, Mr. Yorgo. Sixty thousand drachmas! A man can live for a year on that."

"Well, we might as well go along. I'll be anxious to hear what you find out."

"Sit. Sit, Mr. Yorgo. You must be here to accuse him."

Another policeman came staggering in bearing an enormous typewriter which he placed on a small table against the wall. The captain issued another stream of orders.

"Now please repeat what you've told me," he said, scarcely altering his tone as he turned to George. "We must have your official accusation."

Resistance stiffened in George. It was all happening too fast. He hated the easy simplification, the condemnation without evidence, the brutal atmosphere of the proceedings. He had known he shouldn't come to the police. He stood up. "I can't possibly make an official accusation. You can question him. Perhaps he'll return the money and that will finish it."

The captain stared up at George with outraged astonishment. "Ah, no, that will not finish it. Theft is theft, regardless of whether the money is returned. Costa is a troublemaker. Probably a Communist. I don't know why you foreigners have made him a friend. All these loafers are Communists. Sit, Yorgo."

"I can't stay now. I have people waiting for me."

"You do not wish to recover your money?" the captain demanded coldly.

A direct question to which there was only one answer. He couldn't afford niceties of sensibility. He had to get his money back. Perhaps by staying he could assure Costa of proper treatment. "All right. All right. But I can't stay long." He sat down. He was being trapped into something he hadn't bargained for. Perhaps the police wouldn't find Costa. Peter hadn't been able to.

"What's going on?" Joe inquired. "What's it all about?"

"He wants to put it in writing," George grumbled. He outlined once more the circumstances of Peterson's loss, addressing the policeman's back while he typed laboriously. When he got to his own story, the captain began to interrupt frequently, altering phrases, giving the whole story a more pointed and incriminating flavor. When George had finished, the captain added with scarcely a pause, "I accuse Constantine Petropoulos of this theft."

"Now, just a minute," George protested. "I've told you I can't accuse anybody."

"You agree that it's not like you to lose such a sum," the captain reminded him.

"Yes, of course." He was glad that he had at least the decency to blush.

"And who is the most likely thief?"

"Nobody is likely. I can't believe Costa's a thief. I can only say he's the only person I can think of who *could* have done it."

"Very well. You accuse him."

"I do *not*. I might suspect him. There's a big difference."

84

The captain drummed his fingers angrily on the desk. "Mr. Yorgo, for the purposes of the police, there must be an accusation. Suspicion limits our action. It's only a technicality."

"Mr. Peterson feels able to make an accusation. I don't."

"Very well." During this exchange the policeman had torn the sheets from his machine and placed them in front of the captain. The latter picked them up and shook them at George. "It is all here just as you said. Do you want it written all over again? For what? For a technicality. We have Mr. Peterson's accusation."

"Cross out the last line." He saw the captain's eyes flash with exasperation as he picked up a pen and did as he was told with an angry slash. He knew that his statement was more strongly worded than he should have allowed it to be, but Joe had provided the accusation the captain had been determined to get, so he hoped it was of no great importance. The fact that Joe wouldn't have come if he hadn't encouraged him lingered in the back of his mind as a reproach.

The captain held out pen and document, and George took them and signed. He was appalled by himself the moment he had done so. An outright betrayal, though he couldn't quite define what or whom he was betraying. He had known that just to mention Costa's name to the police would seriously jeopardize the Greek. His own principles? He believed that police powers should be strictly limited, but he recognized the necessity for them in an imperfect world. The conviction remained that he had done something very wrong; it might seem less wrong if he could put a name to it. His disapproval of himself expressed itself in a generalized anger at being here, at the waste of time, at police methods everywhere. He turned to Joe. "Come on and sign this thing and let's get out of here."

Peterson had time only to unwind himself from the chair when Costa was flung into the room. At least, that was the effect his entrance made. He was followed by two policemen. He had no sooner recovered his balance in front of the captain's desk when they manhandled him some more, pushing and pulling to no particular purpose. George met his eye, and he spat ceremoniously, ejecting no saliva but making the motions with his mouth. George felt something in him recoil, not with outrage but with shame for himself. He wanted to hide. A policeman struck out at Costa's face. The captain's harsh voice was rattling out oaths and orders. Costa had lost his swagger but not his fight; in the back of his eyes there was the murderous gleam of fear.

George turned away, trying to dissociate himself from the scene.

He heard the captain shouting phrases from his statement. Costa shouted back, sounding close to tears. There was the sound of more scuffling and the thud of a blow. They were all shouting at once, their voices rising to such intensity that it had the effect of physical violence, painful and numbing. George wanted to shout them all down. The money wasn't worth this. The man who had spat at him had been his friend. He heard Costa proclaiming his innocence, offering to give Peterson a thousand drachmas if he needed money so desperately. He heard Jeff's name shouted, and the numbing chaotic din came to an abrupt halt. George swung back to face the scene

Costa stood in front of the desk with a bundle of hundred-drachma notes in his outstretched hand. The captain was glaring at him, but the glare was lighted with interest. The two policemen shuffled awkwardly on each side of their prisoner.

"Drugs, you say?" the captain said after the brief healing silence.

Costa stuffed his money back in his pocket and shot George a sidelong glance. "His son and Dimitri at the *Meltemi*—I think they are partners. Dimitri supplies marijuana to the foreigners."

"I won't have this," George broke in, advancing on the group. He was glad to focus his anger outside himself, to use it to obliterate his shame. "You're not going to drag a seventeen-year-old boy into this."

The captain lifted his hand without taking his eyes off Costa. "Please, Mr. Yorgo. One moment. We know something of marijuana on the island. You say Dimitri is the source?"

"For all the foreigners. It is known to all but you."

"We try not to concern ourselves with the foreigners, but Dimitri is Greek. What has that to do with your stealing?"

"I don't steal. But perhaps Mr. Yorgo's son has. I know he gave Dimitri money this morning. I saw him counting out many thousands of drachma notes. They hid it when they saw me."

The captain turned to George. "Is it normal for your son to have large amounts of money, Mr. Yorgo?"

"Certainly not. I give him thirty drachmas a week for pocket money."

"Whoever deals in drugs makes much money." The captain swung back to Costa. "Why should such a person have to steal?"

"How do I know? I say only what I know."

The captain banged his fist down on the desk and raised his voice once more to a shout. "And what about Mr. Peterson? Where do you get the money you're so willing to give Mr. Peterson?"

"I have money. I have my boat. I work."

"I know all about your work. It's terrible how hard you work. Now I'm going to give you a rest. You will spend the night here to think things over. If you have nothing new to tell me in the morning, you will be on the first boat for the jail in Piraeus. You will doubtless find old friends there. With your record, the statement I have here should guarantee you at least five years of rest. Take him away."

The policemen seized Costa and dragged and pushed him out of the room.

"Jesus, this isn't very pleasant, is it?" Joe muttered unhappily.

The captain rose, crackling and military in his splendid uniform. He seemed refreshed by the episode and smiled broadly. "Very well, Mr. Yorgo. I think our friend may have changed his mind by morning. He will not have a peaceful night."

"Yes. Well, perhaps a night in jail won't hurt him. I didn't like his trying that idiotic story about my son." George was unable to respond to the smile, but briefly took the hand the captain held out to him. "I must remind you I have influential friends. I don't want Costa harmed in any way." George saw an alteration in the captain's expression. His eyes grew steely while his smile became more genial.

"Very influential friends. Yes. I believe Mr. Michael Cochran has come particularly to see you. A great honor for the island. I've been instructed to do everything possible to make his stay pleasant. It is the first time I have received such instructions about any foreigner here, though you, too, are doubtless very influential, Mr. Yorgo."

Would it never end? All he needed was to have his nose rubbed in Mike's importance. It had been stupid to give the impression that he was threatening the captain, but he refused to relinquish his point. "I'm simply pointing out that I'd feel personally responsible if Costa is mistreated in any way. You would regret it."

"A police has many regrets, but he must do his duty all the same. It is interesting what he says about this Dimitri. Already, we know Dimitri is very much too fond of boys. A harmless vice, perhaps. But drugs? It is true that your son has been friendly with him. The last thing I would want is to have to take action against an alien minor. You understand me?"

He understood. It was his turn to be threatened. Coming from this symbol of overbearing authority it was hard to swallow. It struck at all his protective paternal instincts. "I intend to speak to him about this, but Costa's story is ridiculous. As you said, what has peddling dope got to do with stealing? It was just a stupid attempt to divert suspicion from himself."

87

"We have our own ways of sifting true from false. We will encourage Costa to tell us more. Come by in the morning. Perhaps we will have your money for you."

Doors opened and closed, stairs thundered. Peterson followed him like doom. He wanted to be alone. He was filled with disgust, his pride was battered, he felt as if he were on the point of total disintegration. He didn't know where he was going to find the strength for the necessary session with Jeff. He stopped in the street and turned to Peterson. "Did you understand all of that?" he asked.

"Not much. But I didn't need any Greek to see how they were treating Costa."

"Well, this is their country. You'll probably get your money back. You'd better stop by here in the morning."

"Okay. Let's go have a drink. I need one."

"I've got to go home. See you later." He nodded and made off down a side street, fleeing like a criminal. He slowed down, trying to recapture his self-respect, trying to feel like the reasonable, intelligent human being he knew himself to be. He was not responsible for the police. He had taken a perfectly normal step to recover some money, yet he couldn't suppress the feeling that it wouldn't have happened this way once upon a time. There was a loss of resilience, of confidence, a fumbling uncertainty of touch. His drunkenness last night. His craving for a drink now. Disintegration. The word stuck in his mind, casting a new chilling light on the episode in the police station. He had bungled it from beginning to end. The words and acts of the successful become outrageous or merely foolish in the failure. Yet he wasn't a failure; it was simply that recognition had slowly been withdrawn from him so that he felt suddenly that the personality that had been shaped by the early years of glory had become inappropriate to present circumstances. Could Mike be right? Had it been unrealistic and perverse of him to allow himself to reach a point where the loss of two thousand dollars could alter his whole life? Jeff and the bar boy. He had disapproved of the friendship, but he had lost the authority to cope with it. Here was a chance to redeem himself; at least as a father. He had to succeed with Jeff. He couldn't afford any more losses.

He was hurrying again, almost running, and he was panting when he entered the garden gate. He must catch Jeff before he started his evening ramble. The house steadied him. It was a refuge. It offered him its handsome assurance that his life was good. He paused, letting his eyes absorb the beauty of the courtyard, remembering the way it was when they had bought it, feeling a pride of achievement as well as responding to the aesthetic satisfaction offered by the big gnarled central olive tree and the smaller citrus trees beyond, which created a false perspective and a sense of great depth. The covered balcony they had added for additional access to the bathroom provided an asymmetrical and curiously romantic note to what had been rather stark cubes. The great burst of bougainvillea filled the other wall with color. He moved slowly into the lush green shade he had built, almost as palpable as the masonry that enclosed it. His air. It smoothed from his mind the uglier aspects of the experience he had just undergone and insulated him against it. No police state entered here. He could offer Jeff the guidance and understanding he needed. He felt a sudden deep longing for Sarah. The house was so completely and essentially a joint creation, as fully shared as an act of love; she was central to his satisfaction in it. As if in answer to his thought, she appeared in the door.

"Hi, there," she greeted him. You're back. Any news?" She gave him a smile radiant with warmth and welcome as she joined him. He felt it as a shock to his whole system, as startling and beneficent as a plunge into icy water on this sweltering day. His experience with the police made him feel unworthy of it, and he received it with humility and gratitude.

"I don't know what's going to happen. No money yet. The police seem to think they'll get it back."

"Somebody *must've* taken it. It couldn't just disappear. Who could it be?"

Her eyes were full of sympathy. He could feel the free flow of it toward him, unlike this morning when she had been so quick to dissociate herself from him. He realized that he hadn't had a chance to talk to her about the money since then. He took her hand and squeezed it. "The police seem to suspect Costa."

"Our Costa? Oh, no, he wouldn't."

"Well, there's no point guessing. We'll just have to wait and see what they find out. Is Jeff here?"

"Yes, he's in his room."

"I want a word with him. It looks as if his chum Dimitri might be in for some trouble. Ready for a drink?"

"I can wait. What about Dimitri?"

"I'll tell you in a minute. I'll be right back. We can have a drink together before we go down to collect Mike." He lifted his hand and touched her breast. "You look as if you'd had a good rest. You look wonderful."

She flushed with pleasure. "I've been milling about in the kitchen. Dinner's pretty well organized."

He looked into her eyes and smiled. Something he saw in them charged him with irrational confidence. He gave her a little pat and reluctantly turned from her. He entered the house and climbed the stairs and quickly changed his clothes for the evening. He went along to Jeff's room and knocked on the closed door.

"Yeah," was the grudging reply from within.

George opened the door and looked in. Jeff was at his desk, bent over a forbidding tome of the sort he was partial to. "I'd like to speak to you for a minute," George said, trying to sound friendly rather than parental.

Jeff turned a dark guarded young face to him, the large eyes so strikingly like Sarah's that he felt a pang of love for both of them. "What's up?" Jeff demanded.

"I'll tell you. Come on upstairs to the study. It might be cooler up there."

He waited as Jeff slouched and shuffled out of his chair and then preceded him up the difficult stairs. He closed the door behind Jeff and went to the couch where he had slept the night before and seated himself. Jeff ambled to a chair and arranged himself in it—legs flung about, the base of his spine on the edge of the seat, head resting on the back. His eyes roamed restlessly, avoiding his father's.

George curbed an impulse to reprimand him. This was the current affectation of the young. They thought it old-fashioned to sit up straight. They didn't believe in moving their lips when they spoke. They cultivated a bored and insolent look. It would pass. There was a more important issue at stake. "We've always been able to talk to each other, Jeff." He heard the wheedling camaraderie in his voice and was embarrassed for himself.

"Yeah, sure." Jeff had the good grace not to sound completely indifferent.

"Well, let's get right to the point. It looks as if your friend Dimitri is about to have some serious trouble with the police. I've just heard about it. For your own sake you'd better steer clear of him. You may feel it your duty as a friend to warn him, but otherwise I don't want you see him again." As he spoke, George saw the boy's arms and legs begin to twitch, and at his last words Jeff gathered himself together convulsively and hugged himself with his arms. His eyes blazed up with startled life.

"Not see him again? What's he supposed to've done?"

"It's serious. Peddling drugs. Costa has accused you of being in on it with him. I don't take that seriously, of course, but anybody who sees a lot of him is automatically suspect to the police."

"How can I be? I haven't done anything." The note of querulousness in Jeff's voice reminded George how close the boy was to being still a child—his child—and he felt a wrench of tenderness for him. He leaned forward and gave the boy's leg a pat.

"I'm sure you haven't, but appearances count. Costa says you gave Dimitri a lot of money this morning."

Jeff forced laughter and pulled his legs up under him. He made a swipe at his hair. "Where would I get money? He came sidling by the way he does when I was helping Dimitri with his accounts. Does holding money mean that I'm giving it to him?"

"I see." So Costa hadn't been lying; he had seen Jeff and Dimitri handling money together. "If you're on those terms with him, knowing about his money and all that, it's even more serious than I thought. You make yourself an accessory to anything he's doing."

Jeff's dark eyes widened and wavered into contact with George's, then pulled quickly away. "Adding up his accounts for him isn't a crime. Why are you so interested in the police all of a sudden, anyway?"

"I'm interested in the police because I've got to get my money back. Who do you suggest I go to?" George resented being made to feel apologetic. He added curtly, "As a matter of fact, they're holding Costa for questioning now."

Jeff's eyes stared into George's with wild incredulous reproach. "But how could you? It's against everything you believe in." Jeff sprang forward in the chair and gripped the seat with his hands. "How could you drag an innocent man into it? The money's obviously in the house somewhere. You don't know what you're doing half the time."

George's mouth dropped open with astonishment and snapped shut again with anger. "Just what is that supposed to mean?" he demanded.

"It's true, isn't it? I live here too, remember? I see what goes on. You're a drunk. Everybody knows you're a drunk. You and mom both. You came staggering home last night. You probably shoved the money in a drawer somewhere and forgot it. That's the way you are these days. Did you tell the police how drunk you were? Did you tell them you can't remember half the things you do?"

George waited for the first impact of the words to pass. Even if they were justified, he was stunned that his son could say them. Instinct told him that there was more involved than Costa and his going to the police. An angry reprimand died on his lips. He had to win the boy's confidence, not alienate him further. "Jeff," he said quietly, "you're surely old enough to understand that drinking too much sometimes and being a drunk are two different matters. You've never spoken to me like this. There must be something very serious on your mind. Speak up. We're here to help, you know, and stand by you."

Jeff subsided back into the chair and pushed at the hair on his forehead. "I can't stand hypocrisy," he growled in his deepest tones. "How do you expect me to react to a big paternal scene? What do you know or care about my feelings? You're too busy fighting with Mom and getting drunk."

George thought of his parents. No conceivable circumstances could have provoked him to speak to his father in this way. It had always been "yes, sir" and "no, sir" and the seething rebellion underneath, so that when he had finally freed himself, there had been nothing left, no basis for any sort of relationship. Jeff would at least know who his parents were. He almost envied him being involved in some way with a drug peddler. It sounded so dangerous and grown-up. At that age, George had been thinking about school teams and debutante balls. At least, he supposed that was what he had been thinking about. He couldn't remember.

"If you'd just calm down a bit," he said persuasively, "you'd discover that I do care. Very much."

"In a pretty peculiar way. You pay no attention to anything I'm doing, and then all of a sudden you lay down the law and tell me I can't see one of the few people I like here. Who am I supposed to see, for God's sake?"

George admitted the point. There was no organized social life for young people here. There was no intermingling of the sexes. Jeff had long since passed beyond the possibility of finding intellectual satisfaction with his immediate contemporaries. The local boys, those who didn't go to work long before school was over, had simple interests that probably included some casual sexual play until they were ready for their virgin brides. Not a stimulating scene. He couldn't blame Jeff for being drawn to the larger world of the tourist bar. "You know I'm not much for laying down the law," he said. "I hardly know Dimitri. It's generally understood that he likes boys, but I'm sure you know enough about that sort of thing to handle it as it suits you. You're too old for me to choose your friends for you.

Even if he were the devil himself, I wouldn't interfere unless I had some good reason. All I can offer you from here on is advice if you care to ask for it, and understanding. I'm pretty confident I have more of that than most people. Let's stick to this drug business. What do you know about it?"

"Drug business? A lot of people here smoke marijuana, if that's what you mean. You can get it easily enough."

"So I'm learning. I hadn't really been aware of it, except for Sid. Have you ever used it?"

"Once. It made me sick. Are we going to have an inquisition now?"

"I just want to know how the land lies. You knew that Dimitri supplies it?"

"There's no secret about that. Everybody gets it from him."

"You say Costa didn't take my money. He keeps trying to make a connection between it and you and Dimitri and the dope. What do you suppose he's driving at?"

Jeff threw his head back and opened his mouth. His big Adam's apple worked as if he were trying to get air. "I can't stand this," he burst out. "None of it would've happened if you'd been sober. Do you think I stole your money? Go on. Say it. Accuse me. Say the truth, for once." He jerked about in his chair, his coltish legs kicking out disjointedly.

"Take it easy, for God's sake. I'm not accusing you of anything." he had offered understanding, but he couldn't understand Jeff's behavior now. Maybe he and Dimitri actually were in business together. Or perhaps he had uncovered a serious love affair. "Listen. I just wanted to warn you that your friend is in danger. I know boys your age are sometimes under terrific pressures. I know you're not a thief, but anybody might steal if they're in a bad enough jam. I wouldn't condone it, but it wouldn't be the end of the world. I'm proud of you, dammit. There's nothing bad in you. That's why I don't want anything bad to happen to you."

"What's bad about seeing a friend?" Jeff attempted a defiant note, but his voice caught on tears. "That's all I'm thinking about. He's expecting me this evening. We're—he's—I want to be his friend."

"And I want to respect your friendships. The trouble is, I'm responsible for you for three more years. I can't have you running risks with the law. It involves me. You mustn't have anything more to do with Dimitri until we see how all this turns out. If you want, I'll go explain it to him with you. If he values your friendship, he'll understand. Now. Have we got that straight?"

Jeff began to tremble all over. "It's all so awful," he burst out, and his words tumbled out chaotically. "I find somebody who likes to have me around and—he's not perfect but I like being with him. If you knew anything about what's going on around here—why don't you leave me alone? What about Mom? Don't you have some responsibility for her? Maybe you'd like to know where she was this afternoon. She was up at Pavlo's house. I saw her when I—"

George was on his feet, towering over him. He swung his hand hard across Jeff's face. The boy made little whimpering sounds in his throat. He swung again and struck so hard that he almost toppled Jeff out of the chair.

Jeff was doubled over, his arms over his head. "No. Don't. I didn't—I don't know what I was saying," he cried. He was shaken by racking sobs.

George didn't hear them. He didn't know how he had got to his feet. He was gripped by a rage of despair, trembling as violently as his son. He reached down and seized Jeff's arms and grappled him up out of the chair. Jeff resisted feebly. George caught him as he almost fell and thrust his arms around him and pulled him close against his chest. He had nothing more to offer him, nothing more to offer anybody out of the empty ruin within him. Perfectly empty. Perfectly ruined. The comfort he derived from stilling Jeff's sobs was irrelevant. He pressed his face into the boy's hair and kissed the side of his head.

"Get out," he said when he could speak. "Go to your room. I didn't want to hurt you." He half-supported Jeff as he stumbled to the door. George didn't see him go. He was having trouble with his vision. He found his way back to the couch and sat on the edge of it, holding the hand that was still numb from striking his son.

Of course it was impossible. Jeff was a hysterical kid. He knew it was impossible. He had proof. For the moment he couldn't think what it was. Slowly it came to him. He had seen Pavlo on the rocks. He and Mike had left for their swim well before four. She had been here then. Pavlo had been on the rocks when they arrived. No. He had seen Pavlo arrive. When? Just before he had left Mike to go to the police. He rubbed his hand and tried to remember having seen him earlier. It was no use. There had been time.

He passed his fingers lightly over his forehead. If it was true, he would have to kill her. *If?* Hysterical or no, Jeff hadn't made it up. It had burst from him involuntarily.

She had been with Pavlo this morning. She had arranged it then, practically under his nose. A bitch in heat. He would leave her to it. She could have all the Pavlos she wanted. He would simply get on a boat and go. Disappear.

No. Why should he let her get away with it? He would confront her with it, beat her, throw her out. It was the end of everything. Nothing he could do would make any difference. Except to make an end to himself. The infinite relief of nonexistence.

He lifted his hands to his eyes and covered them. He remembered the curious state she had been in at lunch, drinking little, unusually lively and keyed up. He had sat at her feet later and touched her and felt some sort of anticipation vibrating in her. Of course. Thinking of that obscene hunk of male flesh. Panting for a screw.

He surged up and seized the chair Jeff had been sitting in and hurled it against a window. It clattered to the floor in a shower of glass. He strode to the shelves and pulled books from them and flung them about the room. He grabbed a lamp and smashed it to the floor. He would wreck the whole goddamn house. Home sweet home. Through the tumult he was creating, he heard her voice calling from below.

"George? Darling? Are you there? What's happening?"

He froze, holding his typewriter in his hands, and remembered Mike. He couldn't face her now and go on to a pleasant evening with Mike. Mike mustn't know. He somehow had to get through the next few hours treating Sarah as if he knew nothing. His arms ached with a longing to hurl the typewriter down the stairs, catching her where she stood at the foot of them. Only a half hour ago she had welcomed him with eyes full of interest and love. Satisfied eyes. He put the machine down hastily. He had to answer her. If she came up, he wouldn't be able to restrain himself. If was too raw and fresh in him to pretend with her.

"It's all right," he called, finding that his voice was under control. "I knocked over a lamp."

"Broken?"

"It can be fixed. Are you ready? I don't want to keep Mike waiting."

"I'll be ready in a minute."

"I'll be right down." He moved silently around the room, gathering up books and shoving them back on the shelves. He set the chair upright. The window was smashed, but he could fix it himself. The lamp was a ruin. He took a final look around. Nobody could tell what had happened. He would have to think of some explanation for the window.

He hurried downstairs on tiptoe and went to the cabinet in the living room where liquor was kept. He poured out two generous measures of brandy in quick succession, gulping them down. After the second one, he paused with the bottle in his hand and looked around him to gauge the effect. Better. Much better. Something was terribly wrong, something was broken, but he could bear it for the moment. He heard steps on the stairs outside, and he poured more brandy into the glass and swallowed it down. He couldn't look at her. He couldn't touch her. It would be all right as soon as they were with people. She called his name unnecessarily loud, assuming he was still in the top of the house. He put the bottle back and started out.

"Coming. I'm in here." He joined her at the door. It was still all right. With doors to open and close and the street to walk down, she wouldn't notice that he was avoiding looking at her. She was just a presence beside him. She had no identity, no power to hurt or stir him.

"Dinner's all taken care of," she said. "I told Chloë we'd be back at about nine."

"Fine." Everything was in order. Everything was perfectly normal. He stumbled slightly as they set off down the rough cobbled street, and he concentrated on holding himself steady. It wouldn't do to look as if he were drunk. The sun was lowering in the west, and color was beginning to creep back into the town. A vine bursting over a wall in front of them was a vivid green. All day it had been black.

"You and Mike have a good swim?" she asked conversationally. She noticed that he had been drinking and wondered. *Had he and Mike got started on a bender?*

"Sure. Fine." They had had a fine swim while she—that was where the drink came in handy. While she what? He knew, but the answer was like a great blank ache in him, formless, like the knowledge of death. They walked on. Was she saying something? Had he answered? He held as aloof from himself as from her, putting his feet carefully one in front of the other.

They reached the shops, and he greeted people automatically. Out on the *quai,* he saw Peter and a girl heading in the direction of the Mills-Martin house. He didn't immediately identify the girl, and his mind was too abstracted to bother with a second glance. The sun was about to perform its daily miracle. All the houses on the eastern arm of the harbor were beginning to flush with a golden glow, and fire was springing up in their windows. In another fifteen minutes it would be dusk.

The tables in front of Lambraiki's were full. As they approached, he spotted the Varnums and Sid Coleman and his girl and Joe and

Lena sitting together. At a table near them, Mike was sitting with the Italian painter, Roberto, and Paul, his Dutch friend. He wondered where Mike had picked them up. He turned away quickly as he caught a glimpse of Pavlo a few tables from them.

Mike waved. "We've saved chairs for you," he said as they approached. The three men stood for Sarah.

George remained standing for a moment, exchanging remarks with the group at the next table. He was sorry the Mills-Martins weren't here. Charlie was always an impressive presence to display to visitors. He was aware of a recently arrived French contingent whom he hadn't met looking at him and nudging each other. He had been successfully translated into French. A big frog in his little pond. He sat down carefully and braced himself to make small talk with the others. Only a few more hours. Mike would be gone tomorrow. Roberto and Paul immediately began asking questions about Costa. It was apparently the latest sensation, for lack of any more-scandalous gossip. Roberto and Paul were inclined to be indignant about his being held.

"How can they lock him up when they have no evidence?" Paul demanded.

"They do pretty much what they want to do," George said indifferently. He wanted a drink. He clapped his hands and ordered for Sarah too when a Lambraiki boy came running.

"I hear he offered to give Joe's money back."

"Yes. Perhaps that's the way it'll be settled. We'll know in the morning."

"Even if he does, can you imagine the police letting him go?" Roberto insisted. "Because he's had trouble before, they'll keep him for years. I heard about a case like this in Athens. It was four years while he languished in prison."

"Why didn't you tell me about all this?" Mike inquired. "You said you were just going to interpret for an American. I understand you've been robbed of seventy thousand drachmas."

"By tomorrow, it'll be a hundred thousand."

"What is all this?" Sarah chimed in belatedly. "Costa's been arrested?"

George was muddled. Hadn't he discussed it with Sarah? How had Mike found out about it? Not wanting to be reminded of it, he stated the bare facts to the table in general, not mentioning Jeff. "Joe is certain about Costa," he concluded. "Otherwise his name wouldn't have come into it."

"Yes, but the police!" Roberto and Paul wouldn't let it go.

"It's not unusual for the police to be called in when there's been a robbery."

"George is a cynic," Mike said lightly. "If the police abuse their power here, you must grin and bear it."

"You don't really know anything about it, Mike," Sarah said, giving, George thought with a burst of hatred, her usual performance of unshakable loyalty. "Roberto and Paul are upset because we all like Costa. He hasn't anything to worry about if he's innocent."

George didn't want her as an ally. He didn't want anybody as an ally. He had always been recognized as the final authority on island affairs; he was unused to the criticism implied in Roberto and Paul's comments. He must set them straight. What about? The drink was beginning to hit him. A moment of concentration. Now then: "That's not quite true. Ordinarily, he might just be taken off and forgotten about. I won't let that happen. I'll see that he's treated fairly."

"Of course, that makes a difference. They'll pay attention to you," Paul agreed. George shot him a grateful glance. Drinks arrived, and he took a long swallow of his.

"Big man on island," Mike said. "I'm amazed they haven't made you mayor."

George wondered if he'd been drinking too. The sneer was undisguised. Well, if that was the way he wanted it. "We can't all be chums with the president," he said with a warning edge.

Roberto and Paul seized on the reference and began questioning Mike about the White House. George finished his drink quickly and ordered another. He was aware that Sarah was trying to catch his eye, and he pretended to be following the conversation. A pressure was building up in him that shook him physically. He had to drink it into submission or he would explode with it. Pavlo was sitting only two tables away. Sarah was performing with sickening credibility; it made everything about her false, an affront to all they had ever been to each other. Mike was parading his important connections with graceful modesty, and Roberto and Paul were drinking it in. How much more of this was he supposed to take? He looked over heads across the port. The light on the white houses had deepened to a rich copper and seemed to come from within. As he watched, it faded rapidly, and the air itself turned gray. He drank.

"Come on, everybody. Time for another round," Mike said. "This party is on me."

"We must go. We have a date," Roberto said. Paul finished his drink, and the pair rose together. They thanked Mike and drifted off. George wondered who would take their places. There was usually a rush for any empty chairs at his table.

"I like those two," Mike said. "Your friend Peter Mills-Martin's not among us this evening?"

"I saw him a little while ago. He'll probably be along."

"Roberto and Paul are very nice," Sarah said. "I feel terribly sorry for them."

"Really? They struck me as being quite pleased with themselves."

"She means because they're queer," George said, and then told himself to stay out of it. It was too much like actually speaking to her. Dangerous.

Mike laughed. "Women can't stand seeing any man escape their clutches."

"Is that all you see in it?" Sarah objected. "I mind for their sakes. They have so much love in them. If it had been channeled in a normal direction, their lives would be so much more complete."

"You mean they could have wives and babies?" Mike was laughing at her.

"Yes, that. And more. All that can exist between a man and a woman that goes beyond just physical coupling."

"How do you know it can't exist between a man and a man?"

"How can it? There's none of the natural duality of male and female. It's all on one note. Can you imagine a whole community of homosexuals?"

Certainly. Hollywood. Everybody's as queer as a toad. Lovely people."

"I suppose it's possible you don't really know what I'm talking about," Sarah said, brushing aside his flippancy. "You obviously didn't find it in your marriages."

"You can say that again."

George found his hands clenched into fists beneath the table. Physical coupling! There she sat, looking so clean and fastidious, an almost spiritual light shining from her great lovely eyes, talking about the beauty of marriage. He wanted to smash her into the ground, kick her, stamp on her. And Mike too. Smug, flippant, arrogant. He didn't give a damn about people. That was it—he'd felt it all along but hadn't wanted to admit it to himself. Total self-absorption.

"Perhaps we're talking at cross-purposes," Sarah was saying with the disinterested air of one who seeks enlightenment. "Perhaps you're trying to tell me that you're a homosexual too."

Mike laughed comfortably. "My wives would be astonished to hear it. But I like queers. They're generally fun to be with."

"Considering your exalted position," George broke in, "I should think that might be rather dangerous."

"You mean, What will people think? You really are out of touch, Cosmo." He snapped his fingers at the passing boy and gestured for more drinks. "They're all over the place these days. I could name you some names that would amaze you. Everybody knows it's just one maladjustment among others. It's something for the headshrinkers to work out."

"Headshrinkers! Tolerance in the U.S.A. We're just smearing—smoothing over all distinctions between right and wrong."

"You tolerate Roberto and Paul."

George took a swallow of his drink. It dribbled over the side, and he brushed at his chin as he steadied himself against the table. "Not tolerate. I *accept* Roberto and Paul because they're two people living decently for each other. I don't accept the predatory strays who corrupt the locals and consider anybody fair game, including my children."

A look of sharpened interest came into Mike's eyes. He had learned a lot about the Leightons since his swim. George's drinking was confirming his suspicion that his earlier air of assurance and well-being was a heroic but fragile pretense. "And what about the predatory heterosexuals?" he asked.

George lurched forward against the table, spilling drinks. "What in hell do you mean by that?" he demanded.

"Just that." He was playing his cards with the watchful concentration of a dedicated gambler. "Observation has led me to suspect that marriage doesn't represent perfection in human relationships. Surely there's as much hanky-panky going on here as anywhere else."

George studied him intently, trying to keep himself steady in his chair. Did he know something? At least Sarah had the good grace to keep quiet. He was conscious of the three empty chairs among them. Why didn't people come as they always did and put an end to this impossible conversation? Now that it was started, he didn't know how to stop it. "I wonder why you really came here, Mike," he said musingly, almost to himself.

Mike seemed to be expecting the question and to welcome it. "That's a good question. I could have said for old time's sake and let it go at that, but I'm not much for reviving the dear dead past and all that. Let me see. Possibly in the back of my mind I wanted to know

100

if you'd got hold of something that I'd missed. It's always interesting to check your own—whatever you want to call it—progress, accomplishment against somebody you more or less started out with. Primarily, a lot of people led me to think I might be able to help you."

"Help me?"

"In the ways we've talked about. Get your career back on a working basis. If you decided to come back, I could drop a word in the right quarters. I really do happen to have a good deal of influence. You'd find it pretty rough trying to reestablish yourself on your own. Especially in Hollywood. You've got to play hard-to-get before anybody really wants you. That's where I would come in."

George took a long swallow of the fresh drink that had been put before him. The drinks had carried him to another stage. He felt very lucid and detached now, free of the dictates of pride or shame. "Would it make you feel your visit had been worthwhile if I asked you to lend me a thousand dollars?" He was astonished by the words as he heard himself saying them, but they seemed to make complete sense. What a splendid idea. What a simple solution to the money mess.

Mike straightened himself in his chair as he absorbed the full extent of George's ruin. The camouflage had fallen apart with a vengeance. Here was the drunken deadbeat he had expected to find. It was rather an anticlimax. "I thought you might be in a financial bind," he said, all affection and kindliness in the face of George's abject surrender. "But would a thousand really make much difference?"

"Oh, I though I might buy a couple of dogs. Liven the house up a bit."

Sarah's hand was on his arm. "Darling, do you think this is worthwhile when he's going to be here such a short time?"

He pulled his arm away. "You stay out of this. We'll get around to you in a minute."

"Now, listen—" Mike began to protest, but George lifted his hand. "Let's stick to business, Mike. Well, what do you say, yes or no?"

"Of course. I assume you mean to come home. I wouldn't want to be responsible for subsidizing more of—well, more of this."

"But we're not—" Sarah began.

"I told you to stay out of it," he snapped without looking at her. "*This*, did you say, Mike boy? Drunkenness and adultery. Is that what you mean? You don't have any of that over there in your antiseptic, brainwashed, air-conditioned, all-American hell? No, probably not. You probably have a pill. Anything to dull the pain so you can get on with the serious business of beating up niggers and bombing civilians and making money. Money! There's the all-purpose pill. Well, come on. Let's get on with it. What about that *money*?"

Mike looked slightly pained, but picked up where he had left off. "I'll tell you what. If you'll write me a letter outlining an idea for a scenario—it doesn't matter what it is—we can make it a business deal. I'll deduct it, and you won't have to think of it as a loan. It'll be money earned."

"All right. Make it two thousand."

"The tax people might not go for that much unless I do something with it. Fifteen hundred. There could be more once you're there."

"Deductible. You do me a favor, I do you a favor. We're both satisfied. How about that, boy? Fifteen hundred bucks for two minutes' work. I'm still in there fighting. Do you have your checkbook with you?"

"I do, as a matter of fact. But don't you want to wait till tomorrow?"

"No, no. A deal's a deal. Sign on the dotted line."

Mike studied him for a moment, wondering if even now George were playing some sort of complicated joke on him. George faced his scrutiny with a mad grin. Without taking his eyes off him, Mike reached into his pocket for checkbook and pen and then, with a slight shrug, leaned over and wrote out a check. He tore it out and handed it over. George acknowledged it with a bow. He studied it a moment as his expression set and hardened into a look of malevolent fury. He turned to Sarah and shook the check under her nose. "Do you see that? Do you know what that is?" His voice was strangled with rage.

She drew back and lifted her hands, palms out, as if warding off a blow, looking at him beseechingly with great liquid eyes. "Please," she murmured, but it was only a feeble whisper in the storm that was breaking over her.

"This is a one-way ticket out of here. Single. The children are provided for. You can stay and sleep with every man on the goddamn island. I'm afraid you'll have to get paid for it. I don't see where else you're going to get any money. But whores *should* get paid. You have every right to demand it."

She glanced about her instinctively, and then her expression closed in with something very like boredom. "You'll be sorry for saying these things in front of Mike, let alone anybody else who wants to listen."

"Why should Mike care? He's a whore too. His friends are whores. The whole world is one big goddamn brothel. And now I'm a whore." He shook the check at her again. "I'm picking up my winnings and walking out. Out, do you understand? You can have the precious island and your pretty boys all to yourself."

"That's enough, George. I'm going now." She made a move to rise.

"Sit down," he roared, and heads turned.

She subsided into her chair. Her hands were trembling, and tears were welling up in her eyes, but she managed a tremulous public smile. "Very well, darling. If it helps you to say these things, I'll try to listen. But maybe Mike would enjoy doing something else."

"Don't you believe it. Let me tell you about Mike. He's come here to see what a wreck I've made of my life, and I wouldn't want to see him go away disappointed. We've played our little comedy for him, but it wouldn't be fair to let him think it had anything to do with real life. I feel it my duty to tell him that that was the first civilized lunch we've had since the last time visitors came through and that by evening you're usually too drunk to know whether there'll be any dinner."

"If this is the moment of truth," Sarah said in a voice filled with sorrow, "perhaps I ought to tell him why we drink."

Although George was looking at her, his rage blinded him so that he was spared any real communication with her. Mike was simply a shape beside him, as impersonal as a priest in a confessional. "Oh, I'll tell him. It's because I don't give you a normal sex life. My problem is that I can't take infidelity lightly. There's something about touching a body that somebody else has—" His voice wavered and broke, and he bowed his head over the bottles and glasses on the table. "Oh, shit," he said.

"Please, darling. We can't go on torturing ourselves for something that's all over and done with. We've held on to it long enough. It's part of the past."

His head jerked up, and his eyes burned into her without seeing her. "You filthy lying bitch. Go away. Go start on your evening rounds. You might as well get some practice."

"I'm sorry, Mike," Sarah murmured. She pressed a trembling hand to her forehead as if she felt feverish. "You see how it is."

"Go, goddamn you." He kept his voice low so that it came out like the hoarse echo of a shout. "Go before I kill you."

As he spoke, all the lights of the port blazed on. They were lifted from intimate dusk and placed on a spotlighted stage. They all blinked.

"You mustn't try to order me about, George." Her poise remained intact, and she communicated a sort of bruised valiant dignity. "I wanted to go ten minutes ago, but I stayed because I thought it would help you to get this out of your system, whatever it is." She was sure he couldn't know about this afternoon. She may have made some blunder—could he have come back to the house after she left?—that might have aroused his suspicions, but he couldn't *know*. For his sake as well as hers, she must do nothing that even hinted at guilt.

"For the love of God, go," he said in an agonized whisper, the muscles of his face and neck knotted in an agony of control. "Don't you see what you're doing to me? Do you want me to knock you out of your chair in front of everybody?"

She wasn't afraid of him. She knew the limits beyond which he would not go. At this most violent, he would never hit her. She finished her drink composedly and picked up her straw bag. "This certainly isn't very enjoyable for any of us," she said. "I'll wait for you at home. Sorry, Mike." She rose and left.

George made a grab for his drink and spilled it into his mouth. It dribbled over his chin and splashed his shirt and trousers. He lurched heavily and almost tipped over. He shot out a foot and steadied himself. "That's better. Just us boys together. Drink up, Mike."

Mike looked at him coldly. His hair had fallen over his eyes. His lips and chin glistened wetly. His shirt was wet and wilted. He swayed in his chair. Mike shook his head slightly in response to a question that had formed in his mind. Had he really supposed that this wreck represented some secret value, some criticism of conventional success? He looked across at the ruin of his friend from the rampart of his large bank account, his numerous profitable interests, his celebrated and important friends, his efficiently luxurious establishments in New York and Hollywood, his nearly one million dollars' worth of uncompleted contracts, and he knew that even if he were inclined to sentiment, he would scarcely feel sorry for him. There wasn't enough left to feel sorry for. George had made his bed. He had helped all he could, but the money would surely offer only a brief reprieve from the final inevitable collapse.

"I think you'd better go home too," he said. "*If* Sarah will let you in. I wouldn't if I were she."

"Wouldn't you now? A fat lot you know about it. God, what a prick you've turned into. Sad." With Sarah gone, his venom flowed freely over Mike.

"If you'd look at yourself in a mirror, you'd see something truly sad. But I don't think it's worth discussing. Let's call it a day, George."

"Good idea. Let's call it a day. I don't think dinner would really be much fun. You should find plenty to amuse you around town. Sarah thinks you've got the hots for Jeff. Don't try anything, or I'll have you run off the island."

"Christ. Little Napoleon. Another crack like that and I may just have that check stopped."

George lifted his hand, fumbled for the lock of hair that hung over his eyes, and tugged it. "I forgot I was your indentured slave."

"Since we knew each other when we were kids, I suppose it's natural for us to revert to this schoolboy nonsense, but I don't really find it amusing."

"So frightfully sorry. I must go have my head shrunk. God, what garbage." *Let it all go,* he thought. *Throw away the past. Stamp on affection and gratitude.* He wanted to hold out his hand to Mike and weep with him.

"Will you ask that child how much all this is? I want to go."

George clapped his hands, and the boy came running. He wept within himself while Mike paid the bill. Would there be a chance at the end to salvage at least some talisman of the old love?

"Well, that's that," Mike said. "I'll count on that letter from you. There may be other papers you have to sign to help create the fiction that you're capable of having an idea worth fifteen hundred dollars. My lawyers will take care of it."

That finished it. That snapped the final tie. "I know you mean that as an insult, Mike, and your intention is noted. But truthfully, if I thought I were capable of writing the sort of crap you do, I'd turn in my typewriter and go get an honest job." He chuckled happily to himself.

Mike rose, rigid and tight-lipped. "I'll wave to you on my way to the bank, funny man."

George was alone. He sat, breathing heavily, not thinking but aware of the thing building up in him again that made his body feel too small. It would surely crack under the strain. He gripped the straw seat of his chair and wondered if he should have another drink. It would do no good. Drink helped when he had to confront others, but he was alone now and must confront himself. He felt suddenly terribly conspicuous, indecently exposed in the midst of this brightly lighted, laughing, convivial crowd. Somebody might try to join him at any minute. Yet moving would require a superhuman effort. He had to make it. He had to get away. Mustn't croak in public.

Slowly he pulled himself up and steadied himself for a moment against the chair. The first step was the tough one. After that he would be all right. He took it, lurched as he had known he would, righted himself, and then began to thread his way through the tables. People called to him in the accents of half a dozen nations. Hands reached out to him, but he eluded them. Darkness was his goal. Each step threatened to bring him crashing ignominiously into a chair or table. He began to chuckle softly as he thought of the havoc he would create if he ended up in a tangle of legs and broken bottles and over-turned tables. He gained confidence as he went along. He was perfectly all right, really. He'd just been sitting down too long.

He got clear of the café without mishap and headed out around the port. He didn't know where he was going. Anywhere where it was dark. American jazz blared at him as he passed the tourist bar. He hugged the edge of the *quai,* staying as much as possible in shadow. In another few moments, he had passed the last buildings and was in the clear, climbing the road that led up and around to the swimming platforms. Away from the lights of the town, the sky was suddenly unfolded above him, thick with stars.

At the fig tree, he turned off the road down steps and stumbled across rough terrain until he came to the first platforms. He stayed up away from the sea, following the ramparts of the old fort toward the place where he knew now he had intended to go all along. The ramparts curved back and joined the massive retaining wall of the road, which continued to rise high above him. He went on, his left hand maintaining a light contact with the wall. The tumble of rock on his right narrowed gradually so that as he advanced the sea came closer to him, until he came to a ledge little more than a yard wide, backed by the wall with a sheer drop of a hundred feet down to some sub-merged rock outcroppings and the sea. Here, he lowered himself care-fully, his back against the wall, his knees drawn up under his chin, his feet only a few inches from the edge of nothing. He had made it.

He laid his head back with a sigh and looked up at the sky. Stars throbbed and whirled against his eyes. In quick succession, three of them were dislodged and hurtled blazing fireworks across the heavens. It was as unnerving as watching the Creation. He looked down at the sea, dark below him and motionless. Small islets, humped or jagged, rode on it. Opposite him, the mainland was a flowing line of dark hills. A world of beauty that stirred vague yearnings and an inti-mation of peace.

The soft breathing of the sea sent eddies of warm air whispering around him. He was alone between the dark sea and the blazing sky, totally alone. His mind felt quite sober, with the tired confusion of awakening. Proportion swayed and dissolved as he felt himself shrinking to the small handful of matter that was his consciousness, a poor thing, easily disposed of. He had only to get up suddenly, and the very momentum would carry him over the edge. Or he could simply go to sleep in this position, and he wouldn't even have to make the choice. His body would pitch forward over and away.

And why not? What would be lost? His life had reached an impasse; there was no way out. He had known that money had nothing to do with it, despite today's exaggerated anxiety.

He was rather vague about the transaction he had just concluded with Mike, but the point was that money had turned up at the eleventh hour, as it generally did. When he had told Sarah he was taking the money and leaving, where had he thought he was going? Back to the States? He told himself that it didn't matter, but he felt a hard knot of resistance in him. He could go back only when he was in complete control of the circumstances, his independence guaranteed. He would never accept Mike's conditions, using people and being used to ends he didn't believe in.

The yawning gulf at his feet exerted a stronger pull. Provisions had been made. He didn't remember if there were suicide clauses in the various policies, but nothing could be proved. He often walked along here seeking a secluded spot to swim. Drunk, he could easily slip and fall.

The alternative was to stay. Stay in a place where every stone, every vista, the air itself evoked a few unthinking words spoken by a hysterical boy. The struggle of these months, as he passed through layers of pride and shock and hurt in an effort to reach the living nerve of his need and love for her, praying that it would take charge of his body, had been dishonored. He had felt at moments that he had almost reached his goal. A ravaged dream. Surely she had known or guessed, felt somehow his long slow voyage toward reunion. She could at least have waited with him. Drink had made it possible to avoid any overt rejection of her. Because their lives had always been so closely attuned to each other, she had drunk with him. Anesthetized by liquor, they had dodged the issue she had created. What more did she want? The answer to that was plain enough. Legs spread, she panted for her emptiness to be filled. Happiness? He had offered her happiness, and she had rejected it in favor of a quick immediate thrill. It required too much effort to sustain happiness or to reconstruct it when it was lost.

How did one exorcise love? After all that had been done and said, it was still there, gripping him in an unrelenting, paralyzing vise. He couldn't command his release any more than he could command his body to perform its function. He had almost fought his way back to her once; it was a struggle that couldn't be repeated. He had reached the point he had known awaited him: if he couldn't live with her, he couldn't live without her. Couldn't. Wouldn't. His mind drifted. Something about a dog. Mike's dogs. No, a dog that talked. A dream? A dog that possessed the secret key to life but enunciated badly. What would a dog know? Mindless devotion? Wagging tail? There were no secrets, only unrecognized truths.

His eyes closed. His head slipped sideways against the wall. He slept.

Peter's walk was jaunty, but his thoughts were troubled as he turned away from George and Joe to let them get on with their business with the police. He was worried by not finding Costa; he hadn't realized how important it might be until a light had flashed on in his mind regarding Jeff's visit and the odd ambiguity of his attitude about his date with Dimitri. Had Jeff discovered that Dimitri had stolen his father's money? It would explain the coincidence of Dimitri's agreeing to go to bed with him on this particular night; it would be his way of keeping Jeff on his side. Jeff's tormented manner required a more convincing explanation than sexual ignorance. Conflicting loyalties were more like it.

Peter couldn't work out a very convincing scenario for the actual theft, but it wouldn't take a Raffles to rob George these days. By last night, everybody on the island knew that he had received the money by a bank courier. Dimitri had probably been to the Leighton house and knew his way around in it. Jeff might have caught him in the act.

It didn't quite hang together, but it was more convincing than casting Costa as the culprit. If Costa knew or suspected, he would be the last person to help George unravel the mystery. Costa's fundamental kindness would impel him to protect George from making any disagreeable discoveries about his son. Peter felt confident of being able to handle Dimitri and Jeff thereafter.

When he reached the *quai*, he turned toward home but after a moment circled around and headed in the opposite direction. Dimitri might be at his bar; a chance word might help fix or dispel his suspicions.

In this pre-drink hour before the sun finally released the port from its punishing glare, there weren't many people about, but he kept a lookout for the girl of noon. He very much wanted to see her again. Unless she left on the afternoon boat, he was bound to run into her sooner or later.

Sooner.

She was just rounding the turn in the *quai* that would bring her straight toward him. Here she was, moving closer with the serenity of beauty. He could see now that she had the kind of figure he liked a girl to have (*boyish, of course,* he thought with a smile) with slim hips and breasts that didn't strain exaggeratedly at the patterned shirt she was wearing but nestled, round and firm, within it. His pace slowed, and he adopted a collision course.

Her head was turned inland, the exquisite profile lifted, the lips slightly parted as if she still expected a kiss (he touched his own lips with his tongue as he looked at them), apparently searching for something among the shops and taverns that fronted the harbor. She kept glancing in front of herself to make sure of her footing.

They were within speaking range when her glance included him. He could look her full in the face at last. Her eyes were as beautiful as he had known they would be, exquisitely shaped, dark, velvety, with long lashes. His heart gave a leap as he realized that her glance wasn't slinging past him noncommittally, but their eyes were holding. A slight smile lifted the corners of her mouth. She was going to speak to him! He wondered if she was going to ask him for a light. His answering smile became a grin.

They came together as if they knew each other. He found it difficult not to kiss her immediately on her expectant mouth.

"You *are* Peter Mills-Martin, aren't you?" she asked stunningly. "I've been wanting to meet you."

The accent was unmistakably American, but there was none of the harshness in her voice that he regretted with so many of his compatriots. Now that she was in front of him, he saw that she wasn't a girl but a young woman in the full bloom of beauty, probably in her late twenties. No untouched virgin. He felt a blithe stirring in his loins. "I've been *dying* to meet *you.*" He smiled delightedly and nodded down the port. "I saw you this morning. I've been thinking about you ever since. How do you know my name?"

"That's a long story. I wonder—"

"The longer the better." Peter took her arm and turned her around and led her back toward Dimitri's bar. "Let's see if we can find a long drink to go with it."

109

"Don't you want to know who I am?" She looked up at him with amusement but no flirtatiousness in her lovely eyes.

"It doesn't matter so long as you look the way you do."

She laughed with composure. "My name is Judy Menzies."

A very down-to-earth name for such a glamorous creature. "You don't look like a Judy. Miss or Mrs.?"

"Miss." She shot him an easy, knowing smile. "A female on the loose. Be careful."

"I'll be very careful not to let anyone else get you." He had already come to the conclusion that her beauty masked a shrewd and businesslike nature. Although she didn't look it, he had already revised her age upward to the early thirties. She had an air of cool, experienced competence, as well as a sensible awareness of the potency of her looks that took her out of the twenties.

"How long have you been here?" he asked.

"Just since this morning. It's extraordinarily beautiful. Actually, I came to see you."

"What a wonderful idea. Are you an art collector?"

"In a sense—for the time being."

"I can't wait to hear all about it." He led her into the shade of the *Meltemi*'s awning. The place was deserted. He called through the door into the dark interior, and a homely young man appeared. Dimitri permitted no competition on the premises. They settled on ouzo. "With ice," Peter ordered. Dimitri somehow provided ice cubes, though the island's electricity was shut off for most of the day. They sat in Dimitri's comfortable outdoor chairs. The proprietor's absence absolved Peter of giving any more thought to the money mystery. Instead, he admired Judy Menzies's pretty legs as she crossed them. He looked at her hands and saw that they were shapely and delicate. Everything about her delighted him.

"You've read about the Bertin art robbery, of course," she said.

He sat up. "Funny coincidence department," he said. "I've just had a letter from Raoul Bertin this morning."

"It's no coincidence *my* being here. I told you, I came to see you."

"Oh, dear. Don't tell me you're an international art thief. I'll never be able to turn you over to the police."

She smiled. "I'm Timothy Thornton's secretary." As she spoke, she straightened her shoulders slightly and leaned forward, her head tilted, and looked into his eyes.

His heart stopped. Not even the mention of Tim's name could divert a flicker of his attention from her. His sex did things that made him cross his legs. It was the attitude that had taken his breath away this morning. The tilt of her head, the line of her neck and shoulders, the look in her eyes, everything about her seemed to make an offering of herself, meltingly generous and unstinting. He managed to breathe again. "Who were you with when I saw you this morning?" he demanded.

"This morning? Oh. Sitting over there? Just a girl I'd talked to earlier."

"A girl? In that case, there should be a law against your looking at people like that. You make me feel I'm the most sensational man you've ever laid eyes on. You looked the same way at that girl. It's not fair." He thought he detected a blush under her tan as she sat back in her chair. She gave her head a little toss to settle her hair back from her brow.

"You're very disconcerting," she said. "And quite sensational, too. But you're right. I mustn't go about giving people devastating looks. Nobody's ever told me before."

He smiled at her as he sipped the ouzo that had been put before them. "That's better. If you stay like that, I can look at you adoringly without wanting to fall on my knees in front of you. Where were we? Timothy Thornton. How *is* old Tim?"

"Fine. The company that insures the Bertin collection is a client of his."

"Aha, as they say in the detective stories." Tim was a highly successful lawyer and a pillar of respectability, but twenty years ago he had almost won Peter away from Charlie. When Charlie's marriage had collapsed, Peter had been living with Tim, had been presented with the choice, and had found it briefly difficult. Peculiar to think of having a life with Tim. He had married a very rich woman rather older than himself and kept a succession of young lovers in the deepest secrecy. He wondered if Judy Menzies knew about them. "Well, it's nice to know you're on the side of law and order."

"Oh, yes." She smiled at him enchantingly, revealing perfect teeth. "It isn't always the winning side. The police apparently aren't getting anywhere. I was here on vacation—at Mykonos, to be exact. Mr. Thornton cabled me asking me to go to Athens to see if I could find out anything. He has an exaggerated opinion of my abilities. I hadn't a glimmer what he expected me to do—slouch around low bars picking up tips from gangsters? He even insisted on providing me with a yacht. For thrilling chases across the Aegean? It's over there. The third one in from the end. That power cruiser or whatever you call them."

Peter reluctantly stopped looking at her long enough to glance in the direction she indicated. He saw a big glittering speedboat tied up at the newly reconstructed outer mole that had been put in for yachts. He turned back to her with a laugh. "This place is mad. You never know what's going to happen next."

"I've had several long letters from the boss. He mentioned your being here. It seems that whoever took the pictures aren't ordinary crooks. They have important connections. At least, that's what he thinks. He has some reason for thinking they're operating by yacht. Customs people are apparently intimidated by yachts. Anyway, there seem to be a great many of them about. The police can't search all of them."

"Where do I fit into this fascinating tale? Does Tim suspect me of dealing in hot pictures?"

"He said if I mentioned his name, you'd help me in any way you could." She smiled again, this time with open delight in herself. "Funnily enough, I've had some success. It's not difficult for a girl with no striking deformities to cut quite a swathe in a small town like Athens. I've been meeting everybody who is anybody. I've heard that Michael Cochran picked up some pictures while he was there. I'm not exactly trailing him, but I thought it might be a good idea to talk to you while he's here. I suppose you'll be seeing him. He might mention having bought some pictures. You could ask to see them. You know the Bertin collection, don't you? You could identify anything from it?"

"Yes, but is Cochran apt to discuss stolen pictures? I've met him a couple of times at parties. He's very attractive and turns on terrific charm when he wants to. I probably shouldn't say it because I hardly know him, but he struck me as slippery. I can imagine him trying a fast one with stolen art if he thought he could get away with it."

"Oh, I don't necessarily think he would know they're stolen. He could buy them in good faith. Don't misunderstand me. I don't know if he has anything from the Bertin collection. It's just that it's the only art transaction I've heard of since I've been playing detective. It gives one food for thought."

They looked at each other and burst out laughing. They had nothing in particular to laugh about; it was a way of telling each other that they were enjoying themselves. In this season of thefts, the Bertin collection was more interesting to Peter than George's money, much as he wanted him to get it back. "Well, well, well," he said with lively relish. "If it turns out your hunch is right, what would you do about it?"

112

"That's the sticky part. Mr. Thornton would have to take over. Or you, if you see a way to handle it. Michael Cochran is a very big gun. He's a personal friend of the president. The government here is making a tremendous fuss over him. He's practically an unofficial ambassador. He'd have to be handled with kid gloves."

A twinkle came into Peter's eyes. "You know, I've never told Raoul, but I'm pretty sure that a lot of his collection is fake. Mike Cochran would look a fine idiot if he's not only bought hot pictures but hot fakes."

"Fake? How could they be fake?" The efficient businesslike side of her became more pronounced. "If they're insured, they've surely been authenticated."

"They don't do things by halves in the forged art racket these days. There're plenty of fake authentications around. Modern art is a field I approach very warily."

"The boss will be hopping when I tell him that. Are there any fakes among the things that've been stolen? He'll be very unhappy letting his clients shell out for fakes."

"I haven't seen a complete list of what's been taken. I've just read about it in the papers."

She reached down into the capacious linen bag on the ground at her side. The way she held the arm of the chair with her other hand stretched the fabric of her shirt taut so that Peter could see her breasts clearly defined for the first time. They were small but firm and full, breasts that would lift excitingly if she were naked. She brought out a folded paper and handed it to him. He opened it out and made a little whistling sound between his teeth as his eyes ran down it.

"They got away with all this? It's quite a haul."

"Are some of these the fakes you're talking about?"

"Do you have something to write with?"

She handed him a ballpoint pen. He called for more ouzo as he took it. He put the list on the table and checked off a Pissarro, three Bonnards, five Modiglianis, and two Utrillos.

"Those are the ones I'm almost certain of," he said, pushing the list across to her. "There may be others."

"That's about a third of all that's been taken," she said indignantly, studying his notations.

That such beauty could be animated by everyday, practical concerns made him laugh; thoughts came to mind of the Botticelli *Venus* dealing with a plumber or the TV repairman, piquant and absurdly inappropriate. "Not in terms of value," he pointed out, picking up the fresh ouzo. "The Picassos and Braques and Matisses are superb, but Raoul knew them before most people did. I'm afraid too many painters have painted too many pictures that all look alike. It makes it easy for the forgers. I know of cases where famous painters have denied their own work. Can you imagine a Vermeer being taken for anything but a Vermeer?"

"I might not know a Vermeer if I saw one," she said with forthright simplicity, her expectant lips still asking for a kiss. "Everybody says you're a very good dealer. It's certainly a lot more fun talking to you about the wretched pictures then traipsing around alone after them." Little bubbles of laughter began erupting from beneath her surface. "You *are* fun, aren't you? People aren't as a rule. You will help me with Michael Cochran, won't you?"

"I thought I'd made it clear that I'd do almost anything for you so long as you don't go away." Peter touched her wrist lightly with his fingers. He was immediately attacked by this horrible disease in its most violent form. He removed his hand hastily. "Cochran shouldn't be difficult to approach. I'll get him talking about pictures and ask him if he's bought anything lately. We'll see what that produces. Let's finish our drinks. I want to take you home and introduce you to the family."

"That would be lovely. Is your brother here? I do know *his* work."

"You mean Charlie?"

"Yes. Have you others?"

"Other brothers? At last count, I had four. They, along with my father and a good many uncles, are the backbone of the United States Army. Charlie isn't my brother. He's my beloved friend and very distant cousin. As a matter of fact, his name is Mills and mine is Martin. We merged."

"How very peculiar. You're married, aren't you?"

"Yes, indeed. I don't usually bother to explain all this to people but I like so much to look at you that I thought I'd better make it clear right from the start."

"You're making it clear?" She leaned back with laughter. There was a girlish note in it that struck his ear with delight. "You're too absurd. Doesn't your wife mind your picking up stray females on the port and bringing them home?"

"It doesn't happen every day. She'll be very pleased. I think maybe we'd better just let you take it as it comes." He drained his glass, his eyes lively and teasing as they noted her mystification. In addition to being strongly attracted to her, he was beginning to like

114

her very much. He wanted her to be prepared for his unconventional family life.

He dropped money on the table, and they rose. "Can I go like this?" she mused, more to herself than to him. "I thought a shower—"

"No. You're perfect." He hadn't really looked at what she was wearing, he knew only that she looked trim and fresh and that her breasts were covered with expensive-looking silken stuff in tones of blue and green. He registered now that she was wearing a green linen skirt and immediately imagined her without it, without any clothes, being naked with her. With women, he had always felt it a matter of take it or leave it; on the occasions when circumstances had been favorable, he had gladly taken. What he felt for Judy was surprisingly close to the urgent driving desire he had felt long ago for boys. He lusted to please her, to give her pleasure. Standing close to her made him acutely aware of how well-matched they were, of how perfectly they would fit. She was tall, only a couple of inches shorter than he. She was dark as he was blond. He felt a need to be joined to her like a necessity of nature.

They set off at a leisurely pace, retracing their steps across the inner edge of the port. They walked side by side, but he avoided touching her. In the old days, had she been a boy, they would have exchanged open invitations to bed by now. She was allowing him to exercise his male prerogative of taking the initiative. A connection had been made, and he was ready to let it ripen in its own time. He felt that she had accepted his extravagant flattery in the spirit in which he had intended it: a tentative sexual approach lightened by self-mockery that hadn't required her to accept or reject him. He sensed a great self-containment in her, an inviolability, and ascribed it to her beauty. It exempted her from flirtatiousness; she was capable of making men swoon with a look. And a girl this morning? He wondered.

"The light is absolutely amazing," she said. The sun was getting low in the west. It bathed the white houses on the eastern promontory with a rosy, coppery sheen. "Where're we going?"

He pointed up at the house that dominated the hillside. "The one with the colonnade."

"And all those terraces? It looks magnificent."

"It's quite a house."

"When do you think you'll see Michael Cochran?"

"I haven't so far, but he's here to visit a good friend of mine. You know, George Leighton, the writer. You'll have dinner with us up at the house. We'll come down later and cruise the port. He'll be around with George. When it's as hot as this, everybody's inclined to stay up all night."

"I'm so glad you're taking charge. It wasn't fair of the boss to unload the pictures on me. This is more like a vacation. I'm beginning to love the place. Have you had your house long?"

Peter explained that he and Charlie had bought it for two hundred dollars after they had seen it in the course of the yachting trip with Martha. He didn't attempt to explain that the yacht had belonged to Martha's first husband or that before the cruise was over Martha had been pregnant with Charlie's child. If the evening ended in the way he ardently hoped it would, perhaps he would explain it all to her in bed.

He saw George and Sarah emerging from their side street and waved. They didn't respond. He led his girl through narrow streets and up steep steps, climbing slowly so as not to feel the heat too acutely. They paused frequently while she exclaimed at the glowing amphitheater of the town and the red globe of the sun sinking toward the rim of the flat sea and the vast panorama of distant islands and mountainous mainland. The sun was only a point of fire on the horizon when they reached the house, and then it was gone, leaving only a hot glow in the west and the gathering twilight.

"Now it's supposed to cool off," Peter said. "It doesn't feel as if it's going to." He opened the door for her and escorted her up through the sprawling, multileveled structure.

"But it's a palace," she exclaimed as they crossed a living room that gave onto the long colonnaded loggia.

"We're prone to palaces here," he said. "They cost about the same as a hen house at home." He led her across a courtyard and smiled as he heard the children's voices. They mounted stone steps to a garden in the rear. This was a property they had acquired more recently for Charlie's studio. It was protected from the sun most of the day and had no view. There were a few big trees, olives and almonds and, along the back, the single story of the studio.

As Peter reached the top of the stairs, the children were upon him, clamorous with welcome. They clutched his bare legs and seized his hands. Little Petey managed to butt his crotch with his head. Peter backed away, laughing. "Hey, now. Wait a minute. Hold on. Quiet, everybody. We've got a visitor." He put his hand on Charlotte's shoulder and urged her forward. "Charlotte, this is Judy. The blond bombshell is Little Petey."

Charlotte performed her neat curtsey. Petey smiled up from lowered brows and said something in a language of his own.

"She's a very pretty lady, Daddy," Charlotte said judiciously.

Judy leaned down to her and took her hands. "And you're a beautiful girl," she said.

"Is she a mummy, Daddy?" Petey demanded, reverting to English.

"I don't know. You'd better ask her."

"Are you, lady?" Little Pete persisted.

"I'm afraid not. I'd like to be your mummy. You look like a wonderful little boy."

Little Petey looked at her with wide eyes and then turned and scooted off across the stone paving toward the studio. "Daddy, Daddy," he shouted. "Daddy's brought a pretty lady."

Judy gave Peter a slightly questioning look as they moved into the garden. The children's indiscriminate use of "Daddy" always alerted strangers to the fact that they were confronted with an unusual situation. He was wondering if he should tell her that they weren't both his when Charlie emerged from the studio wiping a brush with a rag, wearing his short sarong. Peter's eyes went automatically to the folds that fell from the bunched-up cloth at his waist. He knew at a glance which fold draped the prodigious sex; his practiced eye could discern its outline faintly lifting the cloth and its slight swing as he walked. Peter moved toward him. "How goes it, mate?" he asked.

"Pretty good, mate." Charlie placed a hand inside the collar of his shirt and held his neck. They exchanged a look and a smile that asserted their total possession of each other and excluded the whole world.

Peter turned back to Judy, presenting her to Charlie. "Look what I found. Have you ever seen anything like her?"

"Who is she? Hedy Lamarr? Elizabeth Taylor?"

Peter saw Judy's astonishment as she looked from one to the other.

"I'd have *taken* you for brothers," she said to Peter. "You're so extraordinarily alike."

"It's growing with the years. You know what they say about people who live together. This is our resident genius. Charlie. Judy Menzies. She's Tim Thornton's secret agent. She's hot on the trail of Raoul's pictures."

"And desperately in need of your assistance." Charlie winked at Peter and exerted a little extra pressure on his neck before releasing him. He went to their guest and took her hand. His smoky purple eyes studied her intently for a moment. "Forget those dames I just mentioned. You're much more beautiful than either of them. You're the real thing. Peter's an expert." His smile was warm and welcoming. Peter moved to them, propping an elbow on Charlie's shoulder. "What's the news?" Charlie asked. "Did you see Jeff?"

Peter threw his head back and laughed. "I sure did. I'll tell you about it later. How about a drink? Where's Martha? The sun's down. Let's go to the loggia."

Charlie handed the brush and rag to Charlotte. "Put that in there with the others, will you, sweetheart?"

Little Petey charged him, tugging at his sarong and threatening to strip him. "Horsie, horsie, horsie," he chanted. Charlie grabbed him and swung him up onto his shoulders. They all descended the stairs and passed through the house to the long colonnaded terrace. Both Peter and Charlie called to Martha as they went. A table with bottles and glasses and iced water awaited them. Handsome garden furniture was set about. Columns framed the view. A telescope mounted on a tripod stood at the stone railing. Peter went to it and trained it on Lambraiki's.

"There's Mike Cochran," he said to anyone who was listening. "He's a damned attractive guy. The Leightons appear to be in good order."

"This is the most beautiful house I've ever seen," Judy said.

"Hello, darlings, one and all." Martha appeared, wearing one of the long loose robes she wore around the house, more dress than dressing gown.

Peter turned from the telescope and went to her and took her hand. "Come meet our dinner guest," he said, leading her to Judy. "This is our resident wife." He was aware of a slight stiffening in Judy as the women shook hands.

"What a beautiful creature," Martha said, all ease and smiles. "Is this the girl who had you falling all over yourself at noon? You're staying for dinner? I'm so glad. I'll tell Kyria Tula."

Charlie handed them all drinks. They settled down in comfortable chairs. Little Petey engaged Peter's attention with a rambling story about a fish he had caught that afternoon. The fish had a complicated and incoherent family life, with numerous fathers and mothers. He had ended up back in the sea, but had failed to swim away. "He died, Daddy," the child announced dolefully, barely able to conceal his glee at this tragic ending.

Peter caught fragments of the conversation Judy and Charlotte were having, sitting side by side on a sofa. He heard Judy say, "...then back to school in the States?" And, "...because he's my *particular* father," from Charlotte. He saw Judy's shoulders straighten, and his breath caught again as he watched it happen—the forward sway of her body, the tilt of her head, her eyes melting with generous absorption. He understood now that it was a trick, a physical mannerism that meant nothing and of which she was apparently unconscious, but he felt it still all through him, in his loins, in the tingling of his arms and legs.

The lights around the port blazed up, and he applied his eye to the telescope once more. "Uh-oh. George looks as if he's getting started early. He's giving the word to Cochran," he said, turning to Martha.

"Oh, dear," she replied with a troubled frown. The lights were a signal. She rose. "All right, babies. Time for your supper." She waited while the children made their prolonged good nights and then herded them out.

"That means our dinner will be along soon," Charlie said. "I better go slip into something less comfortable." He drained his glass and touched Peter on the arm as he followed Martha into the house.

Peter wandered over to Judy. "You're very good with children," he said.

"I'm glad you invited me. It feels like such a happy house."

"We get along. It's especially happy with you in it."

She was looking up at him. He saw a muscle beside her mouth give a little twitch as she turned away. It was the first hint that she had nerves, that there might be tensions beneath the serenity of her beauty. It excited him. He thought again of their being naked together, of stirring her to abandon her cool self-containment. His heart began to beat rapidly.

"I'm not sure I understand it all," she said, breaking a brief silence.

"You will. I want you to."

She turned back to him quickly, looking up with questioning eyes. "You do?"

He looked at her mouth, and his lips parted. He lifted his eyes and met hers. "I think it's definitely a necessity," he said.

George woke up slowly, stiff and uncomfortable, wondering where he was. He wanted to stretch out, but some memory printed on his mind cautioned him to restrict his movements. He straightened his head; it felt as if it were resting against rock. He opened his eyes and saw star-filled sky above him. He lowered them and found himself staring into black emptiness a foot away. It all came back to him with a rush—the scene at Lambraiki's, his suicidal flight over these rocks. How had he managed to perch himself here without going over?

His head swayed, there was a hollowness in the pit of his stomach, and the cramp of fear in his feet. He couldn't stand up. The slightest slip would be fatal. With infinite caution, he inched himself around, still seated, so that his body was parallel to the wall. Using his hands and feet, he moved himself along, a foot at a time.

After a few minutes, during which all his attention was concentrated on resisting the pull of the sheer drop at his side and not feeling the sharp stones cutting into his hands, the ledge began to widen, and he was able to move faster and with less care.

As soon as he felt safe, he pulled himself upright against the wall and stopped to catch his breath. His heart was racing. He was trembling from head to foot. He became disagreeably aware of other organs. The pain in his back was kidneys. The burning sensation in his chest was his outraged liver.

Having accepted and escaped death, he now presumably wanted to live. He ought to feel lighter, stripped down somehow, stripped to the bare bones of his essential values, equipped for decisions. There were plenty of them looming. He was still here to make amends to Costa; he could do what he had said he was going to do and see that he was given a fair deal. There was a decision to be made about Mike. If he was going to keep Mike's money—he was very vague about it, but he knew Mike had given him a check that more or less covered his loss—he should be able to do so with gratitude and an acknowledgment of its importance to him.

He felt for the check in his pockets and pulled it out and ran his fingers over its crisp surface. Security. He tore it in two. He thought of Sarah and fingers tensed and he continued to tear at the check until it was in shreds. So much for their life together. He couldn't remember all that he had said to her, but he knew he had ripped everything apart as effectively as he had the check. He had said it all at last. Why hadn't a merciful providence nudged him off his perch? Why had he taken such pains to work himself back to safety? He needed a drink. Drink gave him the illusion that there was something to live for without her. He would never see her again.

He pushed himself away from the wall and continued over the rocky uneven terrain. He had no idea what time it was. He could have been asleep for fifteen minutes or four hours. By the time he had climbed back up onto the road, he was sweating profusely. A few feet back from the sea, the heat offered an almost palpable resistance. He had to push against it.

When he rounded the last bend in the road, he was startled by the dazzle of lights on the port. As he approached, he saw that the taverns were crowded and clock in the bell tower pointed to just after ten. He slowed his pace. Still dinnertime. He didn't want to eat. He couldn't go home. He didn't want to talk to anyone. Drink was the only answer.

He was approaching the *Meltemi*. Jeff's hangout. He had to help Jeff get straightened out. Was this reason enough to live? Jeff and Kate? Kate was an easygoing, good-tempered, quite ordinary girl, but Jeff was special. His outburst this evening indicated that he was perhaps more special than George had realized. George had promised himself not to let the boy get swept away in the general wreckage. He could make a start by taking a closer look at Dimitri.

He had never set foot in Dimitri's bar, though it was reputed to serve more sophisticated drinks than anywhere else in town. Music blared from it into the leaden night. It was too early for the after-dinner crowd. A few people were at the tables outside. George went inside: it was almost deserted. Two youths were sprawled out on a banquette, inert, only their feet moving to the beat of the loud music. Dimitri rose from somewhere behind the bar. George stood in front of him.

"But it's Mr. Leighton. Good heavens. This is an honor." A shadow of nervousness passed across the young man's face and was quickly gone. He had a classic head that somehow lacked character, but was lightened by gaiety. He flashed white teeth at George. "You must have a drink on the house. A whiskey?"

"It needn't be anything so fancy." George's voice sounded odd to him, as if he hadn't used it for a long time. He cleared his throat. "An ouzo would be fine. You can make it a strong one if you want."

"I wouldn't dream of using the measure for you." He gave George a sidelong look and lifted his finely arched brows flirtatiously. His light brown hair waved prettily. His lips were very red in his deeply tanned face. He wore a white shirt of some sheer stuff unbuttoned to the waist, revealing a beautiful bronzed torso. Lightly muscled, graceful and willowy. His black trousers were skintight. Although he didn't appear to be so grossly endowed as the repulsive Pavlo, he had arranged his genitalia in some way that made a conspicuous, smoothly rounded bulge at his crotch. When he had put George's drink in front of him, he stood with it thrust forward, his hands low on his hips, fingers pointing at it.

"This is the first time you've been here, isn't it? Did you come to see Jeff?"

"Oh? Is he here?" Hadn't be forbidden Jeff to come here again?

"Yes. I thought—"

"Where?"

Dimitri tilted his decorative head toward the rear. The room was deep, formerly a boat builder's workshop, tunneled into rock. A loft had been inserted into the front end; at the rear it rose a full two stories to the rough-hewn arched-rock ceiling. A wooden staircase led up to the loft.

"You mean upstairs? Do you have living quarters here?"

Dimitri smiled and looked at George through partly lowered lids. He gave his hips a suggestive little forward lift. "It's an office, but I sometimes spend the night here. I live with my mother up behind your house—but you know how it is with mothers. One sometimes wants privacy."

"I'm sure you do." George finished his drink in a gulp. Dimitri took the glass in a long, well-manicured hand and turned with a flip of his narrow hips to display the voluptuous curves of his buttocks while he refilled it. He returned the replenished glass to the bar. George arranged his face in a friendly expression. "I'm glad to have a chance to talk to you," he said lightly.

Dimitri's red lips parted, and he ran his tongue over them. "I'm very flattered, Mr. Leighton."

"Jeff thinks the world of you. You must be the best friend he has here."

Dimitri smiled with another flash of white teeth. "We've become big friends this year. He's a very good boy."

"Are you having an affair with him?"

Dimitri drew back with a display of consternation. "Please, Mr. Leighton—"

"Come now. We're both grown men. Everybody knows your tastes. You make no effort to hide them. Why should you? I admire you for being so open about it."

Dimitri's flustered air lingered only a moment, and then he uttered merry laughter. He moved closer, leaned against the bar, and looked at George with new interest. "Good heavens. Who would have guessed you'd be so nice?"

"Did you expect me to be an ogre? Jeff is a bit young for me to talk freely to him. Are you having an affair with him?"

"I have not, to this moment, put a finger on him." The note of incredulity in his voice made it almost comic but convincing.

"Can you swear to that? No, don't bother. I'm sure you can lie as well as I can. Perhaps you think I haven't the right to ask the question; and you might have a point. The only thing is, I want to be helpful to Jeff, and I don't know much about this sort of thing. He's reached the age when sex must be very much on his mind. An affair with another boy of his age doesn't necessarily mean he's going to be queer, but if he is I'd like him to be happy. Has he passed on my message to you?"

Dimitri was drawing designs on the bar with his index finger. He lifted his eyes and gave George a long calculating look. He drew his head back and smiled fetchingly. "Yes. Thank you. You've been very considerate. I have done what is necessary. I'm not worried about the police."

"Good. The fact remains, you're mixed up in this dope business. It's against the law. I can't allow Jeff to be associated with it. I've told him I don't want him to see you anymore, but if there's something serious between you I'd take that back. It's hanging around here that I don't like."

"Good heavens. You're very surprising. Jeff is lucky to have such a father."

"I wish I were sure of that. I'd appreciate your not telling Jeff I mentioned any of this. Do you mind asking him to come down here?" George took the last swallow of his drink.

Dimitri immediately seized it and refilled it. "One second," he said, his eyes briefly on George's with provocative speculation. He laughed again—cheerful, empty-minded, somehow callous laughter—and ducked down under a shelf at the end of the bar and went back to the foot of the staircase, his hips swaying. He stood, dwarfed by the cavernous ceiling, and called up. His voice was drowned by the music. He returned to the bar as Jeff appeared on the stairs, too quickly for him to have been undressed. George had wondered. Jeff slouched across the stone floor and ducked down behind the bar after Dimitri.

"Hello, youngster," George said easily.

"Hi." Jeff kept at a slight distance from his friend.

"I came in for a drink, and Dimitri told me you were here. Did you have dinner with your mother?"

"After a fashion. She seemed upset. I don't think she was drunk."

"Please, Jeff. That's not a very nice way to talk about your mother." He took a long swallow of his drink. He was aware of Dimitri watching him closely as if he were expecting trouble. Jeff was a little taller than the Greek and struck a definitely masculine note beside him. "I thought I made it clear that I didn't want you to spend another evening here."

"I wasn't with him. You saw for yourself. I was upstairs checking some accounts."

"He's very good at arithmetic," Dimitri interjected.

George kept his eyes on his son. "I've just told Dimitri about not wanting you two to see each other." He lifted his hand as he saw that Jeff was about to speak. "I've decided that that was going too far. I absolutely forbid you to come here again, but you've got a home. You can receive anybody you like there. I've told Dimitri that as far as I'm concerned he's welcome to come to the house."

"Why should I want him to come to the house?" Jeff's great eyes burned with the intensity of desperation. "How could we—I don't want him there. I don't want to be there myself. This is the only place I can come to get away from the house."

George closed his eyes while he made sure he had himself under control. When he opened them he saw that the two friends had moved closer together, almost touching. Dimitri was slightly behind Jeff, as if counting on him for protection. "I'm sorry you feel that way about home, but if that's the way it is, there's not much I can say. I wish I could promise you that things will be better. I don't know. You'll be going away soon. Your mother and I—" His voice caught. He drained his glass hastily and held it out. Dimitri reached for it, and their fingers touched. Was there an insinuating caress in Dimitri's? He pulled his hand quickly away at the risk of dropping the glass. One more drink would make it all right; he would find it quite reasonable for his son's presumed lover to make a pass at him. All that really mattered was for him to make his point with Jeff successfully.

A fresh drink was on the bar in front of him. He picked it up and swallowed some of it. "Look. The house is quite big. You have a comfortable room of your own. You have a door with a lock. You have only to turn the key and forget the rest of us exist. Good God, Jeff. I recognize your right to a private life. It's not too much to insist that a minor stay out of a bar. You seem to forget that all this talk isn't necessary. I have only to tell the police you're not supposed to be in here and they'll keep you out."

"The police! All your talk about understanding and you always end up calling the police."

"I mention the police because you won't listen to reason. Can't you realize I'm not trying to break up a friendship but talking about this particular bar?"

124

"Your son is very stubborn. I've found that out." Dimitri laughed gaily and grabbed the back of Jeff's hair and gave his head a shake. It was a natural affectionate gesture, and George liked him better for it. It lightened the atmosphere.

Jeff pulled away with a normal boy's impatience. "I don't understand it. I've been coming here for weeks, and now all of a sudden it's forbidden."

It was the first hint of his yielding. George warned himself to let the boy come around in his own way. "That's the point you keep missing," he said mildly. "I've learned things today. You're in danger. You're a foreigner, for God's sake. Do you want to get us all deported?"

"I don't care what happens to me. What difference does it make?"

George prayed for patience. Jeff was suddenly so like the child he had recently been, a child having a tantrum. He wanted to grab him by the scruff of the neck and lead him out from behind the bar. "Please, Jeff. Nothing has changed except not coming here for the time being." To his dismay, he saw Jeff's eyes fill with tears.

"I just hope you don't expect me to leave now." The boy's voice was choked. He ran his fingers through his hair. "We've—I can't—if I'm not coming here anymore, I have things to do. I've got to explain certain things to him. We have have to talk. I'll be home later."

George took a deep breath of relief. He had somehow managed it. "Very well. Let's make a bargain. I'll let you stay this last time if you promise not to hang around down here. Go back upstairs and stay out of sight. Get whatever business you've had together settled and done with." He drained his glass once more and put it on the bar. He nodded and smiled in their general direction and turned and left.

He found that he was having trouble walking straight. His sleep hadn't sobered him as much as he had thought. A few ouzos shouldn't affect him like this. Still, he hadn't disgraced himself with Jeff. The boy was going to be all right. He would damn well see to it that he was all right. A challenge for the next few weeks. He had been through enough for tonight. He could get as drunk as he liked.

Outside, to his increasingly muddled senses, there seemed something sinister about the heat. Something was definitely wrong. Maybe it was the ouzo. Dimitri must have really socked him with it.

His effort to keep a steady course caused him to walk with great purpose, but he had not idea what he was going to do. He headed automatically for Lambraiki's. He was hailed from a table and veered aside and fell into a chair opposite Sid Coleman and his girl.

"Great, Yorgo," Sid greeted him. "That was a great landing. For a minute there, I thought you were going to overshoot the field."

"What're you guys drinking?" George demanded, peering at the glasses on the table.

"Apple juice. Great stuff. Tell him, Dorothy. Tell the man about apple juice."

"It's made of the juice of the finest selected apples, scientifically ripened and untouched by human hands." The line emerged appropriately from Dorothy's scrubbed, fresh doll's face. She had dimples in her cheeks that made her smile bewitching.

"How about that, Yorgo? It says so right on the bottle. Selected. *Chosen*, like the Jews. Want some apple juice?"

"You two are nuts. Get me some brandy." Hands were clapped and orders were called.

Sid leaned forward earnestly. "You drink too much, you know that, Yorgo? Why don't you let me fix you up with some pot? You really ought to try it."

"Very friendly of you and all that, but I tell you I don't like the stuff. You kids think you've discovered it, but I tried all that years ago." He filled a glass with brandy as soon as the small tankard was put before him and drank it down.

Coleman shook his head sadly. "That stuff's *bad* for you, man. Pot's the thing for you. Sarah would love it, I bet. Jeff could get you all you needed. A family that smokes together flies together. Look at Dorothy here. All I have to do is give her a few puffs and she thinks I'm Marlon Brando. It's great. Isn't it great, darling?" They leaned toward each other and exchanged a look of naked and tender desire.

"You better watch out," George warned, finding that the minatory note made him feel more sober. "They're about to crack down on dope here."

"Jesus! Don't say that. You hear, darling?" His fine Semitic features flared and swooped dramatically. "You mean all that stuff about Costa and Dimitri? Don't let them, Yorgo. This isn't the right season for growing your own."

"You grow the stuff? You're mad. When are you going to stop playing games and wake up to reality?"

"Wake up to *reality*?" Coleman gave an extravagant impersonation of incredulity. "Did you hear that, darling? He thinks we should wake up to reality. Do you know what her idea of reality is, Yorgo? Marriage. She wants us to get married."

"What's so funny about that? You've been living together for two years. Why shouldn't you get married?"

126

"You hear that, lover?" Dorothy said with lazy satisfaction. "You hear what the man said?"

"Jesus Christ. Women are chattels. You know that, Yorgo. By nature, they belong in the stable with the cows. Give them a nice clean stall and plenty of hay. Service them regularly. That's all they understand. I *like* cows, but I wouldn't want to marry one."

George poured himself another generous measure of brandy and swallowed half of it. "There's a lot of stru—truth in what you say, Coleman."

"There is. There definitely is. How about some other realities? You're the reality man, Yorgo. What other realities do you have to offer?"

"They'll come to you, boy. Even up there in your marijuana patch, they'll get through to you."

"That's it. That's *it*. Can you think of a more harmless—no, I'll go further. Can you think of a more exemplary life? Living in harmony with nature. I sow. I watch the tender shoots struggling up toward the sun. I tend them. I give them *water*. But it's not all clear sailing, I can tell you that. What if there's a sudden freeze? Or hail. Do you have any idea what a sudden hailstorm can do to a crop? Wipe it out in the twinkling of an eye. Hail. It's really murder. I'm wiped out. I have to start all over again, at grips with nature with nothing but my bare hands. The dignity of man. Persevering in the face of adversity. It's the theme of all great literature. You know that, Yorgo."

"I'll say one thing for you, Sid. You're a cheerful bastard. I hope you can keep it up."

"You know what the trouble with you is, Yorgo? You believe in things."

"Do I?"

"Sure. The flag. Mother. You believe it all means something. Now you take—yes, take Peter. Peter could be a saint or the devil. How about that, Yorgo? It doesn't matter. Right? He's the pagan life-force. He lives. Peter *lives*. He doesn't go around finding meaning in everything."

"Not meaning. That's religion. Faith. Faith in man, in his ability to make a good life with what he's born with." Astonished to have said so much without stumbling, George pushed on. "You can't take Peter. I'm taking him. He's what I'm talking about. He's the only person I know who has the courage to—to make a consistent try for happiness. I'm not sure creative people have any business hoping for happiness, so go ahead and louse up your life, but you have no right to tell everybody else that happiness doesn't exist. Peter's happy because he respects his capacity for happiness and is prepared to make sacrifices for it. Most people don't and won't. There's a reality for you." George was impressed by his lucidity and coherence. The words were coming slowly but made perfectly good sense. His body might be drunk, but his mind wasn't.

He opened his mouth to continue when the ground moved under him. A bad sign. The table lurched and retreated from him. He made a grab for his glass. The ground shook under him again as if it were trying to unseat him. There was a crack like the snap of a bullwhip followed by a thunderous crash. George found himself lying on the cobbled paving with an arm lifted over the back of an overturned chair. This wasn't good. He was making a public spectacle of himself. He heard Coleman saying something near him and realized that all the lights had gone out. He pulled himself up quickly and made out Coleman's figure bending over his girl on the ground. There were lumps of broken masonry scattered about. No immediate explanation came to his mind, but he was suddenly filled with an urge to run.

"Come on," he cried. "Get her out of here." He lunged forward and pulled at the girl's legs.

"Are you all right?" Sid asked dazedly.

"Get her out of here. The goddamn building's falling down."

Coleman followed his example, and they managed to gather her up and move her down toward the water. Staggering and lurching under the load, George became aware of people milling about all the length of the *quai,* the mumble of voices, an occasional shout, a scream.

"What *is* it? What's going on? What happened?" Sid kept repeating as they staggered to the edge of the *quai.*

They stretched the girl out on the cobbles, and she moaned. "Darling, are you all right? Come on, darling. Everything's all right. Come on, darling, sit up." Sid's incantation continued until Dorothy struggled into a sitting position.

"What happened?" she gasped. "God. My head."

"You got conked. There, just sit there for a minute. You'll be all right."

George's eyes were beginning to see in the dark. He looked back to where they had been sitting. A building had definitely fallen on them. But which one, and why? He was struck by a change in the town's low skyline. Something was different. Something was missing.

"Jesus Christ," he exclaimed. "The clock tower. The whole bloody clock tower fell on us."

"You're kidding."

"Look there. You see? That's where it should be." The line of roofs was all of a level against the star-pricked sky, no longer dominated by the ornate square tower. As they looked, the air was filled with a curious roar, growing in strength, like the approach of an enormous wave. In another moment, people began spilling out of the streets that led back up into the town. They came in increasing numbers, and the roar became a din of a thousand voices and the slap of running feet. The whole town was assembling on the waterfront.

"What's going *on*?" Sid complained again.

"It's an earthquake, silly," Dorothy announced as if it were an everyday occurrence. "Didn't you feel it?"

"So that's what it was," George exclaimed. "I thought it was the drink. I guess it *was* an earthquake."

They helped Dorothy to her feet.

"Do you think there'll be more of it?" Sid demanded.

"I've felt tremors from time to time," George said. "Nothing like this. There hasn't been a real earthquake here since the eighteenth century."

"That was real, man. That was real enough to suit me. We could have been *killed*."

George laughed at the shocked indignation in Sid's voice. He looked back at the gap in the sky where the tower had been. People streamed past them in the dark. Where were they going? Perhaps there was some safe place they all knew about. Flashlights winked among them. Lamps were beginning to appear at the taverns along the front. He heard the Greek word for earthquake being repeated excitedly. "*Sismos. Sismos. Sismos.*" Keening women clutched children. He noticed that it was suddenly much cooler. A breeze had sprung up from somewhere. He thought of Sarah and steeled himself not to go look for her. He knew that if he hadn't had so much to drink, he would already be rushing home. He was in no mood or condition to rush anywhere. Home. He understood how Jeff felt about it. Let the earthquake bring it crashing to the ground. And Sarah with it. It was his only hope of freedom.

Joe Peterson emerged from the crowd with the Swedish girl, Lena, at his side. "Is that you, George?" he demanded in his boyishly enthusiastic voice. "Hi, everybody. How about *this*?"

"We hoped you'd like it," George said. Dark figures whom he didn't recognize moved in beside them, a boy, two girls.

"Why aren't we having a drink? How about it, George? Do you

think the Lambraikis could dig us out some champagne? I think champagne for after an earthquake is definitely the right idea."

"Shouldn't we be *doing* something?" Sid asked. "Digging people out from the rubble? Stamping out bubonic plague? Purifying the *water* system?"

"I don't think we'd better get started on any of that until the lights come on," George said.

Jeff and Dimitri were still behind the bar where George had left them, their voices unnecessarily low under the blanket of music, discussing his visit. They were standing so close together that Dimitri had only to lift his finger to run it teasingly over the back of Jeff's hand.

"I tell you," Dimitri insisted, "he practically said he doesn't mind if we go to bed together."

"No. I couldn't. Not at home. Don't you understand? They'd all know what was happening."

Dimitri laughed and ran his fingers over Jeff's hand again. "Of course they'll know, my Jeff. I'll love that. It will be like having a new family. If you're a good lover, I'll spend the night with you quite often."

"Maybe if you—"

The floor moved under their feet and brought them together with a bump. They steadied themselves against the bar and exchanged a puzzled look.

"Why did you—"

The floor moved again, and there was a crash of glasses from the shelves behind them. The whole building shook, there was an enormous crash outside, and the lights went off. Dimitri was gripping Jeff's hand and pushing him out from the bar under the shelf at the end. They ran to the door still hand in hand. Dimitri stood close against Jeff while they peered into the dark. The great crash still seemed to echo in the air. They heard people calling out. The *Meltemi*'s handful of customers were dark shapes in front of them, all standing and talking excitedly.

"An earthquake?" Jeff repeated, not yet grasping it.

Dimitri laughed. "At least this building won't fall down. It's solid rock." He withdrew his hand, and Jeff's heart gave a great leap as he felt it exploring for his sex under cover of the dark. A thought of Peter flashed through his mind, and he conquered an impulse to draw away, to hide himself. Immediately, all sense of place and circumstance was obliterated by the fact of a man making intimate amorous contact with his body. He reached out and encountered the sheer shirt and smooth bare skin, and Dimitri was somehow enclosed in his arms. Their mouths found each other, and their tongues met. Jeff's heart raced wildly, responding to the willingness he felt in the body he had desired for so many months. He dropped his hands and found the full curve of buttocks. Muscles danced and quivered under his touch. His legs began to tremble. Eager hands worked his stiff sex up inside his trousers until it stood upright against his belly. They shaped the cloth around it and moved up and down on it. He was going to have an orgasm.

Dimitri drew his mouth away with soft laughter. "Good heavens. You're not a boy, you're a big man. Tonight will be exciting."

Jeff's chest was heaving with the inaugural impact of this love play, electric with desire. He realized how carefully Peter had handled him this afternoon, instructive but unengaged. Driven by the orgasm gathering in him, he reached out again and pulled Dimitri's head back to him and took his mouth with his in a way he hoped suggested experience. He slipped the flat of his hand down inside the front of the tight trousers until his fingertips thrillingly reached fine hair and hard flesh. He withdrew his hand and moved it around inside the shirt and slid it back under the waistband of the trousers, giddy at taking these liberties with an unknown body and at knowing they were wanted. This was life at last. His fingers caressed the velvet upper curves of buttocks and lingered at the cleft between them. He felt all of Dimitri's body melt into his.

Thrilled though he was, he had an intimation of inadequacy. Dimitri had always been to him a figure of dazzling self-confidence and worldly authority, an older man of sophisticated tastes whom he could hardly hope to interest, yet he held in his arms a supplicant, all soft and compliant and yielding to male demands. It denied the child Jeff still felt in himself and called for an aggressive masculinity whose secret he didn't possess. He had learned his true desire with Peter, but this was life, and he hoped it might offer some further revelation.

Dimitri pulled away with laughter that had become slightly breathless. "You mustn't undress me here," he whispered with a hint of delight that suggested he would like nothing better. He turned his back quickly, gripped Jeff's hips, and pulled them up against him. Jeff's hands slipped under the shirt again and caressed smooth skin of chest and abdomen, and they remained locked together for a moment while Dimitri worked his buttocks against Jeff's upright sex.

With only a few layers of thin cloth separating him from the performance of the unimaginable act, Jeff gasped as orgasm threatened once more. A little whimper escaped him as he realized that the danger had suddenly passed and that his erection was subsiding.

The side of Dimitri's head lay against his. "Like that, my Jeff. In a little while," he whispered. To Jeff's vast relief, he broke away. "Now we must get out lamps. Come help me."

They both knew their way around the deep cavernous room. A row of lamps was always kept ready on a table in the rear to fill in the gaps of the town's erratic electrical supply. They went back to them together, guiding each other with their hands in the dark, and Dimitri struck a match and got one going. In its growing light, they exchanged a glance. Dimitri smiled gaily into Jeff's dark passionate young face.

"You mustn't look at me like that. Not yet. I have my work to do first. We're going to be very good together."

Jeff lowered his eyes, wondering if he would ever again feel anything so intensely as their first brief embrace. They checked and adjusted wicks and lighted the other lamps.

Jeff set them about on the bar and the tables, thinking about the bargain with his father. He knew he shouldn't be down here still, but surely an earthquake was an extenuating circumstance. As soon as he had helped Dimitri get organized, he would go upstairs and wait. Thinking it, he knew that if they had their talk now, his father could quite easily persuade him to go home. He still wanted it to happen with Dimitri, but the moment of physical intimacy had stilled his ardor almost as much as if the act had been completed. The undeniably small phallus he had briefly held couldn't match his dream of the soaring male mystery possessing him. He was entranced by Dimitri, but Dimitri wasn't worth the things he had done for him, certainly not worth the childish outbursts with his father. This knowledge enclosed him once more in solitude. He was already beginning to learn something about life.

Dimitri winked at him as their paths crossed. "I'll sweep up behind the bar. We'll probably need more glasses. Bring down the carton that's upstairs."

Jeff hurried to obey. There was very little more he could do to help. Upstairs, he was aware of a growing din around the port. Apparently half the town was out. When he carried the glasses down, Dimitri was in back of the bar once more, and he could see more people gathering outside.

"I think this is going to be good for business," Dimitri said with brisk anticipation, not bothering to flirt with him. "Take those last two lamps outside, will you?"

Jeff went to fetch them, resolved that this was the last chore he would perform. It would be taking advantage of his father's tolerance to hang around any longer. He took the lamps out and placed them. The tables were filling up rapidly.

He had started to turn back when Mike Cochran emerged out of the night. At his side was the blond Swiss boy everybody had been making jokes about for the past few days.

"Aha," Mike said, approaching him. "Is this where the island's youth and beauty congregate? I'm glad to see you survived the earthquake."

"Good evening, Mr. Cochran. I was just going." Jeff could feel his manner growing surly and withdrawn in spite of himself. There was something about the man that made him shy.

"Oh, dear. Couldn't you at least make it Mike?" He stepped close to Jeff, put his hands on his biceps, and held him in a firm and friendly grasp. "I wondered if I was going to see you again. You're the member of the Leighton family I most wanted to make a good impression on."

Jeff looked at him and looked quickly away. He was very sleek and handsome in the lamplight. He radiated the glamour of his successful world. He was rich, he was famous, he knew everybody. He had had a lot of wives. Mike Cochran couldn't possibly mean what he seemed to mean, yet there was something special about the way he looked at him. There was the corroboration of the Swiss boy.

Jeff edged away from him. "I'm sorry, Mike," he blurted. "I have to go. Orders."

"I see. I'm sorry. We're fated not to become friends." He exerted an extra little pressure on Jeff's arms and let go.

Jeff felt it as if some current had been turned off inside him. Mike's magnetism was direct and compelling, somehow inflaming to his imagination. He was a satyr, faintly diabolical but irresistible. He turned his dark eyes back to him and tried not to let his shyness make his voice sound hostile. "We're sure to see each other tomorrow. I have something to do in there. I'll tell somebody to get your order." Their eyes held a beat too long, a beat during which Jeff felt that he had completely given himself away; he had told Mike Cochran that he responded sexually to men. He didn't want to let himself be ashamed of it (Peter said that was bad), but with Mike Cochran it was getting a bit close to home. He turned and fled, his heart drumming in his chest.

Mike watched him go with a touch of relief. He was very tempted by the thought of having George's son—it would place an outrageous seal on his total triumph over his old friend—but those great passionate eyes were dangerous. Available, but at a price. Better stick to the easy bits like this little Swiss faggot or, he thought as he saw Dimitri approaching with a breezy swing of his hips, this quite gorgeous bar boy.

The lights blazed up suddenly all around the port as if on cue to celebrate the beautiful half-naked body; there was a great deep-throated "ah" from the crowd as if in appreciation of it. Mike met flirtatious, inviting eyes as Dimitri stopped in front of him and immediately dismissed the little Swiss faggot from his evening's plans.

Sarah lay stretched out on the bed in their room, dressed, freshly made up, an untouched drink on the table beside her. By remaining absolutely still she could just barely prevent herself from sweating. She had never known anything like it. It was getting denser and denser, as if gathering for some sort of explosion. Somebody on the rocks this morning had said it was earthquake weather. That's all they needed. George's explosion was enough for one evening.

She was trying to imagine what mood he would be in when he came home. Something was happening; the mold into which their lives had frozen was breaking up. Now that he had actually expressed in words his case against her, anything might happen. She felt she ought to put herself through some sort of mental shadow-boxing, like a fighter tuning up for a match. She suspected that she was going to need all her resources for the next round.

After all these years, she still wasn't sure what curious twists and turns might be dictated by his gentle, sheltered background. She had been trained to fight for what she wanted. It had been a struggle in the early years to adjust to his consideration of others, his respect for people he didn't particularly like, his assumption of goodness where nobody else could see it. Too often, it seemed soft and self-abnegating until she had learned his strength and adopted his values.

She must be prepared to fight again to keep him if he had talked himself into thinking he had to leave. She could surely find a way to make it impossible somehow, although Mike's damn check was no help to her. She needed him just as he needed her. Even if it could lead only to mutual destruction, they must see it through to the end.

Should she pretend to be sick? It had worked once before in the early days of his fame when he was taking too much interest in a girl he didn't really want. What sort of sickness could she pretend to have?

The bed moved under her, and she sat up hastily, startled by what might be an attack of some sort. It moved again, more violently. There was an odd wrenching, crumbling sound, and the lights went out. She heard a succession of thuds outside, heavy objects falling to the ground. She leaped up from the bed and instinctively turned toward the window. Her eyes were caught by stars, much higher than where the window was. It took her a moment to grasp the fact that she was looking through the wall. A wide rent ran down it beside the window. Her breath caught, and she took several little running steps in different directions.

She heard shouts in the distance and then a strange rumbling roar that seemed to be growing. Since she couldn't identify it, it terrified her. What was happening? The Bomb? Would the world really come to an end? She had to get out before the roof fell in on her.

She made a rush for the door, fearing for an appalling second that it might be blocked, but it was open, and she picked her way as fast as she could through the dark house and down the stairs.

Seeing the way clear to the open door, she ran out into the garden and stopped, panting and soaked with sweat. With her feet on solid ground and the sky above her, her panic subsided. She stood transfixed by the rent in the wall. A memory stirred in her. Something about earthquakes and a structural defect in the house when they had bought it. Could this really be an earthquake? She looked down at the rubble strewn over crushed flowers. As her mind encompassed the extent of the damage, she almost burst into tears. Then it occurred to her that she had an excuse to go look for George; the house wasn't safe.

She uttered brief faltering laughter. She didn't have to pretend to be sick. He would have to stay to put the house together again.

She became aware of the roar again but beneath it now, near at hand, she could distinguish its component parts—the sound of running feet and the babble of a thousand voices. She went to the garden door and found the dark street full of people all hurrying toward the sea. She had to find out what was happening. She stepped out, pulled the door shut behind her, and plunged into the crowd. Its urgency was contagious, and she found herself hurrying too, almost running. All around her she heard the word *"sismos"* being spoken. So it *had* been an earthquake. Those brief lurches of the bed. Nothing, really. She had always imagined the earth opening and swallowing everything up.

The port was chaos. People were running about and shouting and bumping into each other. She tried to get out of the crowd, but it was everywhere, so she resigned herself to being jostled and pushed wherever it led her. There was no question of looking for anybody. At least George and Jeff had been out, presumably down here on the *quai*. If anybody had been hurt, there would be screaming and a concentration of people around the victims, rather than this aimless milling around. She heard something about the clock tower and, looking up, saw that the vertical accent of the tower was gone. The tower made her feel better about their wall. They hadn't been singled out by a vengeful Providence. She bumped into a policeman she knew.

"Has anybody been hurt?" she asked, raising her voice to make herself heard.

"Who knows? I think not here on the port. The clock tower fell down, but mostly into the courtyard where there was no one."

"Thank God." They were jostled away from each other, and Sarah let herself be carried on, heading toward Lambraiki's. She wanted to find George as quickly as possible so that the urgency of events would help them over his rage.

She found herself crowded up beside Mike. On the other side of him, she caught a glimpse of the little Swiss who had been making himself so conspicuous on the rocks. Of course. She had known all along.

"Lively little town you've got here," Mike shouted.

She didn't know quite what manner to adopt with him, but he seemed friendly.

"Where were you when it happened?" she asked. "Did you feel it?"

"Just a few bumps. We were walking along over there somewhere. I saw the tower going over just as we were blacked out. Does this happen often? Have we more in store for us?"

"I hope not. They talk about earthquakes, but there hasn't been one for years."

"I suppose that explains this enthusiastic turnout. Do you want me to help you out of this mob?"

"No thanks. I'll just drift along to Lambraiki's."

"I think I'll look for a lamppost to cling to till this simmers down. Ta."

The crowd separated them. Sarah saw that lamps had been set out at Lambraiki's. She moved into the calm oasis of tables. She passed

Helen Mansfield and the Greek whore-boy she had just married and spoke to them. She heard Sid Coleman's voice above the general din and made for it. She found him sitting with Dorothy.

"Hey, isn't this great?" Sid greeted her. "Have you come to see the victim? We have here a genuine victim of the great 1960 earthquake. Come on, darling. Show the lady your bump."

Sarah's hand was laid on the back of Dorothy's head. There was indeed a bump. Sid told her about the bell tower and of George's part in the rescue.

"He was here?" Sarah asked.

"Sure. Sure. George the Lion-hearted. He just left a minute ago with Joe and some other children. They're looking for *champagne*."

"Has anybody seen Jeff?"

"He was with his pal Dimitri a while ago."

"Have you heard if anybody's been badly hurt?"

"They say an old lady fell into her cistern. They've gone to pull her out."

"I'll just go make sure Jeff's all right," Sarah said, rising. "If George comes along, tell him I'll be right back. There's a big crack in one of our walls."

"Hey. No. Really? Hey, did you hear that, darling? The Leightons' house has fallen down. This is a night that'll go down in island history."

Sarah walked the short distance around the bend in the *quai* to the *Meltemi*. It, too, had lamps set out. She started in, but as she did so she saw Jeff hurrying across the floor toward the bar carrying a carton. She felt a glow of pride at the sight of him; he looked so grown-up and manly in the lamplight. She turned away. He was busy; she didn't want to be a tiresome mother.

She couldn't quite approve of Dimitri as a companion for him, but it didn't really worry her. Being friendly with homosexuals didn't make you one. When Ronnie had shown a more than casual interest in him, Jeff hadn't given the slightest sign of responding. He was quite open about liking Dimitri; he wouldn't advertise it if there were anything unnatural about it. Dimitri's promiscuous conquests were common gossip; it was a guarantee that he wouldn't take that kind of interest in a gawky schoolboy. He was after men with money. At least, he wasn't encouraging Jeff to chase after girls. There would be enough of that later.

She made her way back to Sid's table and was about to sit when the lights came on. There was a great "ah" of relief from the crowd.

The air of crisis immediately passed. The crowd streamed into the taverns and filled every available outside table. Now that everybody was out, they were apparently going to make a night of it.

"I suppose I ought to go home," Sarah said, without moving. "George may have gone to look for me."

"A husband going to look for his wife?" Sid exclaimed. "You see, Dorothy? You see, darling? You see how marriage damages the brain? George has gone off on a toot, Sarah love."

"In that case, I might as well have a drink," Sarah said composedly. George would hear about the disaster at home sooner or later and come get her.

The great crash reverberating up from the port was followed by a smaller crash in the Mills-Martin house. Charlie and Peter were busy in the dark getting lamps and candles lighted in the efficient routine they had evolved in the course of many power failures. When they were done, Martha took one of the lamps.

"I'll go see if the children are all right," she said.

"What was it? Is anything wrong?" Judy asked.

"I felt a slight jar just before the lights went out," Charlie said. "Didn't you? I guess it might have been an earth tremor."

Peter was at the telescope beside the loggia railing. "I'm not sure I've got this damn thing pointing in the right direction, but the clock tower seems to have disappeared."

"Is that what made all the noise? Come on. We'd better check the house." Charlie handed Peter a lamp, and they excused themselves to Judy as they set off on a tour of the premises.

As soon as they were out of sight, Charlie dropped an arm around Peter's shoulder, pulled him close, and kissed the side of his face. "She's a honey. She's very self-possessed, but she's obviously mad for you."

"You think that about everybody. Silly darling."

"It's usually true. Tell me about Jeff."

Peter did so, making light of it but not leaving anything out. "So I let him take his clothes off for a minute to pass judgment on his cock. Very presentable. I was sort of like an old madam breaking in a new girl. He's a total virgin."

Charlie removed his arm from Peter's shoulder as they started up a flight of stairs. "I suppose he hoped you'd be the first," he commented when Peter had finished his story.

"No, he's too sensitive and intelligent to've thought I'd be inter-

138

ested. Anyway, it was obvious I wasn't, right from the start. We're like family to him, and heroes. He says he thinks about us doing all sorts of wild things together when he jerks off. He'd faint dead away if he ever saw you naked. He's a bit mental about cock. He literally worships the phallus, preferably monumental."

"Another recruit for the cause. I guess it's surprising, even though we expected it. You'd suppose a kid growing up here with the locals would absorb the local attitudes—play with boys maybe but keep your eye on the ultimate goal, an obedient bride. It isn't as if there were a great taboo against a touch of homosexuality."

Charlie returned a hand to Peter's shoulder. The twinge of outrage he had felt at the thought of Peter and Jeff naked together was only a pale reminder of what he would have felt once upon a time. Storms. Probably lying in wait to get Jeff off by himself because he always had to take over any experience that might have touched Peter sexually. Even allowing the boy to worship his "monumental phallus" lest there be any question of its preeminence. God. And now all he felt was a mild displeasure that Jeff had been granted the privilege of seeing Peter naked. Peace and tranquillity. Is this what he had been striving for during the years when he had adopted any wile or stratagem to subdue his jealousy? Was it possible that jealousy had once been capable of pushing him to the edge of murder?

He thought of Peter's infidelity—the first salvo in that summer of the heavy guns when they had discovered Greece with Martha and husband. Charlie had lost count of his own infidelities during the separation imposed by Peter's military service, but he hadn't been able to allow Peter even one. Nor had he been satisfied to simply break up Peter's affair; he had had to do so by taking Peter's French lover for himself to establish, as always, the supremacy of that monumental phallus. It had always been ready to swing into action in those days if crisis threatened. He had deployed it for Martha primarily as an egotistical retreat from the dead end into which Peter's infidelity had seemed to have led him.

The jealous rage in him had been channeled finally into the bounds of safety, but the effort had brought an element of calculation to his love, an atrophy of spontaneity, a reinforcement of the cold core of self-love that had always been in him. He longed to love as Peter loved, freely, courageously, without guards.

He squeezed Peter's shoulder and laughed. "You're a saint," he said, to resolve the Jeff episode in his mind and dismiss it. "I'm not sure I'd trust myself naked with an attractive and worshipful youth,

139

though I can't imagine finding myself in such a spot."

"You know how queer you've turned me. That adolescent girlish look he still has. If I want somebody girlish, I'd rather have a girl."

They laughed together. "You've found a beauty," Charlie said, appeased. Wiles and stratagems. He had known that his insane jealousy wouldn't extend to women. He had made a "man" of Peter, gambling on the probability that it was too late for him to find genuine fulfillment with a woman. He had made himself safe from the possibility of being hurt. Peace and tranquillity. Was that what he had really wanted?

He presided over the most peculiar household he had ever encountered, and it was as staid and proper as any he had known in his native Philadelphian suburbs. Had anybody ever gone mad from a surfeit of stability? Occasionally, surrounded by love and the visible evidence of his success, he wondered why he was living. Happiness? Of course he was happy—sanely, suffocatingly happy. There had once been a fire in life that had threatened to consume him. Sometimes he could still feel it flickering deep within him, and he would almost will it to leap up, burn, cleanse, destroy, leave him raw and exposed to the terrors that stalked mankind, to be one once more with the world he had disciplined into subjection.

They reached the studio and held their lamps aloft and saw that it was in order. In the soft light, Peter looked no older than when they had first met. Charlie's breath caught at his beauty, and his chest strained with the fierce pride of possession that was the most passionate element in his love for him. Charlie put his hand on the back of Peter's neck and pulled him to him so that they were facing each other.

"You're not to be believed. I swear you haven't changed in the slightest since I first got you out of your clothes. Twenty-one years. It's incredible."

"You're doing all right." Peter laughed. "You're much handsomer, and I'm twenty-one times more in love with you."

Charlie exerted pressure on his neck. "If you have a late night, I'll see that everybody lets you sleep in the morning." He waved his lamp toward a picture on an easel. "I'm going to have to get up at dawn to rebuild with the blue. You were absolutely right. I see it now."

They kissed lightly and turned back toward the rambling house. Peter was obviously eager to get off for the evening on his own with the girl, and Charlie shared his expectant pleasure vicariously. Peter was the pulse of life that vitalized the whole house. Taking an active compassionate interest in George's money troubles, prancing about naked to help a young friend sort out his sexual confusion, picking up an enchanting girl on the port. In varied and enthusiastic contact with life, on his own up to a point, just as Charlie wanted him to be. Even so, he wondered if he would be so sanguine about Jeff if he himself had ever had any erotic stirrings toward the boy. As a matter of fact, the girlishness Peter had mentioned, lurking behind the nascent masculinity of the features, *had* struck him as singularly appealing at times. Masturbatory fantasy figures and phallic worship? No. The reign of the monumental phallus was over.

In the lower room they found that one of Charlie's larger works had fallen off the wall. They inspected it, Peter more carefully than Charlie, found no damage, and returned to the loggia.

Martha had already rejoined their guest. "Sleeping like angels," she reported. "What *is* all the hubbub down on the port?"

"There seem to be a lot of people out," Peter said, his eyes gazing with delight at what lamplight was doing to Judy. "Maybe there was more of it down there. We've got solid rock under us."

"I hope nobody's been hurt," Martha said.

"I'll check when I take Judy down, but I don't get the feeling of disaster somehow. Come on. Let's have a drink while we wait for the lights to come back. My God! do you feel something? It's cool. There's a breeze coming up."

They had just been settling down on the loggia after dinner when the crash had brought them all to their feet. They settled down once more. The evening had gone very well, full of easy conversation and quickly flowering intimacy. Peter wanted Judy to himself now, but he sat near her and watched her while she talked to Charlie intelligently about his work. A great "ah" rose them from the port when the lights went on. Martha and Peter went about blowing out lamps and candles, chatting casually. They agreed they had never seen the *quai* so crowded.

Charlie rose. "You're going to have to excuse me. I've got to be up for the first light in the morning. It's the only time I can see color properly here." He went to Peter and put a hand on his shoulder. They smiled into each other's eyes. "If you see Cochran, congratulate him for having survived Hattie."

Peter laid his arm along Charlie's, and they stood in a loose embrace. He was aware of the girl's eyes on them. "Get a good sleep. This breeze will make a big difference."

"Have fun, mate."

They broke apart after exchanging another amused private look. Charlie went to Judy and took her hand. "Make him bring you again. It's been nice." He turned and kissed Martha on the cheek as he left.

"There's something I want to speak to you about," she said to his retreating back. "I'll be right up." She made a warmly cordial fuss of her farewell to Judy. Peter saw that the girl responded with none of the wariness he had noticed in her earlier. The evening had worked out just as he had wanted it to.

When they were alone, he stood in front of her and held out his hand with a smile, looking at her with the directness of established friendship, the way he had looked at her from the start. "So now do we beard Mike Cochran?"

She took his hand with an answering smile, accepting him as a friend. "I suppose we should. It's been such a lovely evening. I don't want him to spoil it."

He led her down through the house, comfortable now about touching her, putting his arm lightly around her waist, taking her arm, holding her hand, accustoming himself to the slight, exquisite feel of her body. Not far along the rough road outside, there was a low wall where land fell away steeply to the sea. He stopped and turned her to him, then bent and kissed her mouth. She seemed to expect it and responded easily, but she didn't let her body go to him, nor did he attempt to draw her to him. He pulled his head back after a moment and looked at her. Light from a street lamp fell on them. He put a hand on her waist and slipped the other into his pocket to arrange himself more comfortably. She had a very basic effect on him.

"I've been longing for that since noon," he said. "Your mouth was made for me to kiss. You may not have realized it, but it's a fact."

"You're such fun and so nice." It was a simple statement without any embellishments or hidden meanings.

"Do you understand everything now?"

"Quite a lot, I think. Martha's in love with Charlie."

"Bang on."

"And you and Charlie are beautifully in love with each other."

"Thanks for putting it like that. We have no secrets from you."

"Have I from you? Haven't you guessed that I've been known to be attracted to girls?"

"Really? We're a couple of queers?" He laughed, mostly at himself for resenting her admission. Here he was all steamed up, and she might not be even faintly interested. At least she didn't seem to mind being kissed. He put his arms around her, pulled her to him, and indulged his passion for her mouth. He held her close this time, so that she was bound to feel his hard sex against her. He was careful not to move it suggestively so as not to give her the impression that he regarded it as something to make a fuss about. He would be quite content to do everything with his mouth if that was what she preferred. He caressed breasts that seemed to strain now against her shirt. Their kiss grew breathless and their mouths parted, but Peter still held her close against him. "Are you as broad-minded about heterosexuality as I am?" he asked, his smile almost touching her lips.

She touched the side of his face with her fingers, and the light caught the uncertainty in her eyes behind her smile. "I think that's the part I don't understand."

"About us? About me? It's simple. Believe it or not, this is the first time I've felt it, the whole breathless works with a girl, the hot pursuit, the way it used to be sometimes with a boy. If you were a boy, I'd have locked myself in the house and not come out until I was sure you were off the island. What about you? Do you like men at all, or am I an exception? I mean, something seems to be happening between us."

She put a hand on his chest and moved her fingers slightly as if testing her reaction to him. "You're certainly an exception. I can't help thinking of them back there. Tell me a little more."

"You don't have to worry about the family. I'm in love with Charlie. You know that. Otherwise, it's all wide open. He knows what I'm up to. He doesn't mind about girls. As for Martha, I'm just a technical husband, as you can see. You make me feel as if I was made to make love to you. I'd like you to love it, too. I'll certainly try if you'll let me."

She looked up at him thoughtfully but with a twinkle of humor. "I've tried with men often enough, God knows, but it's never quite worked. I'm always thrilled when I think it might. With you, I'm more than just thrilled. Electrified, maybe."

"That sounds good. Will we be all right on your yacht?"

"Oh, yes. The yacht. I'd forgotten all about it. Maybe being on a yacht will make all the difference." A spurt of laughter burst from her. "The way I looked at you this afternoon seems to have been true, even if I didn't know I was doing it. You *are* the most sensational man I've ever laid eyes on." She lifted a hand and stroked the golden hair over his ears with her fingertips. She lowered her hand and laid her forefinger briefly on his lips. She pressed her open palm flat against his chest. She dropped her hand to his sex and let her fingers stray along it, looking into his eyes with a hint of mockery. "You men. My, my, my. Isn't there rather a lot of it?"

"Whatever there is, that's it. You make it work at full capacity. We can pretend it isn't there is if you want."

Her laughter broke from her freely. "That would require a good deal of pretending. I'm suppressing a shameful urge to unfasten your fly. How's that for heterosexuality? I want to see it, and all of you. Such a struggle not to keep my eyes glued to you all evening. I've never wanted so badly to see a man naked."

Peter lifted her hand to his lips and kissed her fingers as he spoke through them. "Well, that's settled. I'm glad our minds are running along the same track. It saves so much time. Frankly, I can't possibly keep my mind on Raoul's pictures. I hope Cochran doesn't keep us too long."

It was an effort to break the intimacy their bodies were creating, but he took her arm and they found a rhythm that was a foretaste of physical union as they descended the rough steps to the town. They were silent, their bodies instinctively moving toward each other and finding excuses for contact. An uneven step brought their hands flying together. A rock in the path obliged Peter to put his arm around her. It was definitely cooler. For the first time that day, he wasn't sweating.

They found the port swarming with life. A hum of talk and laughter rose from it. Peter waved to many people as they made their way along the front looking for George and Cochran. He spotted Sarah with Sid at Lambraiki's, but Cochran wasn't there, and they went on. Peter's eyes conscientiously searched the crowd, but his heart wasn't set on finding the visiting celebrity; it seemed much more important to get Judy to the yacht. There was only one more place to look, and then they would be free to concentrate on each other.

Rounding the bend in the *quai* and approaching the *Meltemi,* Peter saw him sitting out in front with the little Swiss faggot. Dimitri stood over him. As Peter watched, Dimitri leaned closer, flirtatiously, and said something. He straightened, and he and Cochran burst out laughing. Peter remembered something he had heard in New York. If that was the way the land lay, what about poor Jeff? When he was close enough to see the expression in Cochran's eyes, he knew that Jeff was going to have some heavy competition. He smiled to himself. He rarely thought about it socially, but he always felt a small special confidence doing business with people who shared his sexual tastes. It shouldn't be difficult to find out if Mike knew something about Raoul's pictures.

He turned to Judy. "I've forgotten. Did you say you'd already met him?"

"Very casually at a party the other day."

"Well, I think he knows me. He looks slightly occupied. Maybe we should leave serious talk till tomorrow. Do you mind?"

Judy laughed softly. "I told you what I'm thinking of. More and more. It's quite indecent."

Peter gave her hand a squeeze and nodded to Dimitri as they came to a halt in front of Mike's table. Cochran glanced up and then sprang to his feet and greeted Peter with slightly self-conscious charm. Embarrassed at being caught at play? "I've been planning to look you up if I didn't run into you," he said. Peter pronounced Judy's name, and Mike took her hand and held it lingeringly. "Of course. We met in Athens. I'm not likely to forget a face like that."

They exchanged additional pleasantries, but Mike didn't invite them to sit, nor did he introduce his little Swiss friend. They all obviously had their minds on other matters.

"We hoped you'd come up for dinner if you're staying a day or two," Peter said.

"It's very kind of you. Actually, I'm a great fan of your friend or cousin or whatever he is—Charlie Mills-Martin. My ex-wife's ex-husband. We have something in common. It would be an honor, but I'm afraid I'll be going along tomorrow."

"What a shame."

"I've been hoping to take advantage of your being here to get some expert advice. I picked up a few pictures in Athens under rather odd circumstances. If it wouldn't bore you, I'd like to know what you think of them."

"You brought them out here with you?"

"Easier to travel with them than arrange some place to leave them. Besides, the whole deal has been like that—sort of—"

He was interrupted by Dimitri, who moved in between them and put a hand on each of their shoulders. "Please, Peter. Why you don't sit with your friend? I bring you drinks. The lady—"

Peter shrugged the hand off. "That's all right, Dimitri," he said pointedly. "We'll let you know if we want anything."

"But of course you must join me. By all means. Let me buy you a drink." Mike was cordial, but it was clear he wouldn't mind if they refused. He ducked down around Peter to pick up his drink. As he did so, he murmured close to Peter's ear, "A very tasty piece."

"Trouble," Peter said as Mike straightened. The latter shot him an amused, worldly-wise look and touched Peter's arm to acknowledge the warning. Peter liked him better than he had on previous meetings. He seemed more natural; perhaps he was glad of a chance to let his hair down. He was very good-looking in a hard masculine way. Peter's smile was open and friendly. "It's awfully crowded here. Why don't I come by the hotel tomorrow—noon, say?—and have a look. They're not antiquities, are they?"

"No. French Impressionists. That's my line."

"Good. You wouldn't believe the things they palm off as antiquities here. Really scandalous."

They exchanged a few more friendly words, including Judy in the date for tomorrow, and parted on the best of terms.

"He seems more than ready to show us what he's bought," Judy remarked as they strolled on. "They're probably not the Bertin pictures at all."

"At least they're French. Whatever they are, I'm afraid nobody's particularly interested in them tonight." Peter laughed. "We're all so funny, smiling like mad and dying to get on with the action."

"I didn't realize about him," Judy said.

"I've heard it."

"And all those wives? You men do make life complicated for yourselves. Poor Mr. Thornton. I can't help knowing a good deal about him."

"Yeah. Poor Tim. He's never been lucky. He'd had a rough time even before he met me."

"You mean, you and he—"

"Oh, very much so. A big affair. The only one I thought might be for life. I never count Charlie. He *is* my life. That's never changed, even when Charlie was married; but it might've worked with Tim if Charlie hadn't wanted me back." Peter uttered a single note of rueful laughter. "The only way I could forgive myself for ditching him was to swear to make it perfect from then on with Charlie."

"You've obviously succeeded."

"We've come pretty damn close." Thinking of time brought sober thoughts about Judy. Had he made it absolutely clear to her how things stood? It was all very well to talk about everything being "wide open," but he didn't like playing with people's feelings. Judy seemed very self-possessed and level-headed. It wasn't likely that she would suddenly fall in love with a man— Enough of that. The idea of falling her falling in love with gave him an egotistical little thrill, but he would take care that she didn't. It wouldn't be any good for either of them.

146

As if sensing some withdrawal in him, she said, "if you've got perfection, what's the point of anybody else? What's the point of me?"

He looked at her. Her face was averted from him, and light from somewhere picked out her exquisite profile from the dark. "Maybe you're part of the perfection," he said, seizing the opportunity to eliminate any possibility of ambiguity. "What do you think about fidelity? Do you think two people can be faithful to each other for life? I did, but then I lost my head over a silly French boy, so I don't count. Charlie thought we'd be more and more unfaithful as time went by, but he helped me discover that I'm not all queer, and the problem was solved. As far as I can see, infidelity is infidelity, whether it's with a girl or a boy, but I don't feel guilty with a girl because Charlie doesn't care. He likes it. Don't ask me why. Maybe he thinks it proves that he hasn't perverted me. He's never taken easily to being queer himself. I'm attracted to other people—he was right about that—but I don't *need* anybody else. Not really. Not deep down. There are times, like today, like that French boy years ago, when it feels awfully like needing. I admit it's surprising to feel it for a girl. I do, you know. I'd hate Charlie to know what I'm feeling right now. Not while it's going on. I'll tell him later, of course. Does all this sound too self-centered and impersonal? Do you want me to go away?"

She looked at him with a quick intake of breath. "No." She exhaled with self-deprecating laughter. "How's that for a straight answer? I'm a simple creature. You electrify me. I wouldn't let you go even if I knew it was going to end with a broken heart. You've turned me into a helpless female. All I can think of is that you're going to make it good for me for the first time. I knew you could almost from the minute I saw you."

"I certainly want to. If the queers can't teach the straights a thing or two, what are we good for?"

They laughed, and their bodies moved close to each other again as they turned out onto the yacht mole. He was amazed at the pleasure he felt with her, the same pleasure he had felt years ago when he had found a new boy who was particularly congenial, the pleasure of establishing lines of communication that he had thought could be known and recognized only by someone of his own sex.

The gangplank was down at the big power cruiser she had indicated, and the wide afterdeck was lighted. Peter saw a figure huddled in the dark bow. It stirred as they came aboard and Judy called out, "It's all right. We don't need anything."

Chunky comfortable-looking outdoor furniture stood about on

deck. There was a table with many bottles on it. Judy went to it, took the top off a thermos, and looked into it. "There's ice. I've never seen so many different kinds of booze as they have on board. It'll give you something to ponder while I'm gone." She drew back as he stepped toward her. "No. Don't come near me. If we start anything I won't be able to stop. You've already talked me out of one shower today. I've got to assert myself while I still can. I won't be more than five minutes."

"Are we all right about the big problem?" he asked as a reminder.

"Don't worry." She turned from him and disappeared down the companionway.

He poured himself an unadventurous whiskey and wandered over to the rail, looking up at the house. Lights showed in Martha's windows, but the rest was dark. The warm glow he felt when he thought of the family spread through him. Charlie filled the front of his mind, perhaps asleep already, sprawled out on the bed with his fabulous erection lifting the sheet. Little Pete crowded into the picture, curled into a fetus with his fists clenched. Briefly, he wished he was back with them. It was nice to know that if he ran, he could be back in six minutes flat.

He left the rail and moved forward to the navigational area. There was a wide panel of dials and meters. He saw that it was a twin-engine job, very powerful. It seemed only a moment later when he heard a sound behind him. He turned and his mouth fell open. "Oh, my God," he murmured.

Her dark hair was combed out softly around her face, which was scrubbed of makeup. She wore a long silk dressing gown under which she was clearly naked. She was barefoot. The reduction in her height sent a surge of protective tenderness through him. He started forward and checked himself as he became aware of boats around them and the openness of the deck where they were standing.

"We'd better get below quickly if we don't want to do it in front of the whole town."

Her irresistible lips lifted in the smile that made her look so young, and she held out her hand to him as she moved back swiftly to the companionway. He had an arm around her by the time they were at the foot of it and a hand had drawn aside the silken stuff of the gown, uncovering one breast, small, round, firmly lifting as he knew it would, her deep tan fading out to milky white below the jewel of the nipple.

"My God. Beautiful," he said, holding her and running a finger along infinitely soft flesh.

148

She put her hand on the top of his trousers and gave a little tug. "In here," she whispered and broke from him, pulling her dressing gown around her. She led him forward through a short gangway to the master cabin in the bow. Peter unbuttoned his shirt as he followed her and pulled it off as he entered. He kicked off his sandals as she closed the door behind them. He made note of the bed that filled the cabin from bulkhead to bulkhead while he pulled his slacks and undershorts over his feet. He turned to her naked, his sex straining up before him as she dropped her dressing gown. They stood transfixed for an instant as their eyes met and then darted over each other.

"Peter." It was a little cry of astonishment and admiration. He started toward her, but she made a slight restraining gesture with a hand. "Wait. I want so to look at you. If you touch me, I won't be able to see you. I want to see what makes me feel like this."

"Hurry. I don't know how long I can keep my hands off you. God, you're gorgeous." She was, in fact, as close to what he thought of as the ideal woman as any he had ever seen. He knew it wasn't every man's ideal. Her breasts were small, her hips rounded but not wide, her legs long and slim. Her pubic hair was trim and sparse (she didn't look bearded like some women he had seen) so that he could see the way the insides of her thighs flowed into her torso and the little folds of her vagina. It had taken time for him to get used to the female's secret genitalia, but the void had been filled by his knowledge of the excitement he could arouse there. There was an exquisite fragility about her narrow shoulders that moved him deeply. He wanted to hold her gently and stroke her glowing skin.

She approached him slowly, her eyes as intent on him as his on her. "How beautiful you are," she said wonderingly. "As beautiful as any girl I've ever seen. I didn't know a man could be beautiful like that. Your chest is so lovely without any hair, but hard and powerful. Your behind is beautiful too. I saw it." She had moved within reach. Peter laughed and lifted his arms to her. She drew her head back with a little shake. "Just one more minute. This is the most amazing of all." She put out a hand and ran the back of her fingers along his sex, lifting it slightly. Peter gasped, and his hips gave a little forward leap. "There is a lot of it, but it's so smooth and pale and graceful, not all angry and swollen-looking like the men I've seen." The tips of her fingers brushed his testicles.

"Jesus. If you go on like this, I'll come, standing right here."

Peter took a step toward her, and they both cried out as their bodies and mouths met and their arms encircled each other. In another moment, they were on the bed, continuing to cry out at the initial exploration of each other's bodies.

The pleasure Peter found in women was rooted in the pleasure he could give them; giving pleasure excited him sexually. There was a smell, a taste, an ooze of mysterious essences that he knew were supposed to make him lustful, but they never had. He had learned to isolate his senses from them and concentrate on the nerve patterns he could play on the erogenous areas. His passion was liberated when he found that her body sent out only very subtly those primeval signals. He made love to her with his hands and mouth. He wanted (he smiled to himself as he thought it) to prove to her that a man could rival a woman as a lover. She shuddered and beat her feet on the mattress and tangled her fingers in his hair as he took her with his tongue. He chuckled to himself and brought her to her first orgasm without bringing his own thrillingly aching sex into play. When he knew she wanted it, he entered her slowly as she directed him with her hands. They rocked together to her rhythm, her hands on his buttocks, working him into her. The duality of his nature was such that an awareness of his own body contributed to his excitement, just as he could share with her the thrill of being entered. A glimpse of his sinewy hand on her tender breast, his long-muscled arm extended to brace himself, his sex springing out from his groin to claim her—all gave him little jolts of pleasure at the splendor of being a man. Identifying with the male-female in her, he let her roll him onto his back, and he lay passively and brought her almost immediately to a second climax as she assumed the dominant position and moved her hands down over his belly so that she could hold the base of his sex and use it as if it were her own. His loins tingled with the massive orgasm building up in him, which he had so far managed to contain.

He felt something surrender in her, melt under his pressure, and he was once more on top of her, driving harder into her as she urged him on. Her hips lifted to him. She slipped hands between his thrusting buttocks and found his testicles and fondled them. The tension was too great for him to postpone any longer; he felt her wanting him now with all of herself. He took a decisive grip on her and, as if she sensed that the moment had come, she flung her arms back above her head and uttered a great cry of triumph as her body was shaken by another orgasm. She yielded up her body totally to receive him. He felt as if he was being torn apart as everything in him burst and he drove his orgasm into the jubilant welcome of her body. They continued to cry out for some moments, their bodies leaping and thrashing together. They lay still finally for a few more minutes until Peter's shrinking sex slipped from her and he rolled off her onto his back.

"My goodness," he sighed. "How glorious."

She moved in close against him. He lifted an arm to draw her closer. She laid her head in his armpit, her lips just brushing his chest. "Glorious," she murmured. "Glorious. Glorious. I know at last. You have all the sweetness and tenderness I've known with women—and this." She ran her hand down over his body and rested it on his moist sex. "It has such strength and yet it's so gentle. It caressed and soothed everything in me until I wanted it to have all of me. I think it's bigger than the others I've known, but it doesn't bully. That's what's extraordinary. Do you know what I mean?"

"Not really. I obviously wouldn't know anything about heterosexual men, the ones who make a point of being he-men."

"Yes, well, those are the ones a girl like me is apt to attract. You can't believe what some of them are like—as you say, proving that they're he-men. Are we going to do it again?"

"Preliminaries are under way. Any minute now."

"I feel it happening. Do you know how I'd like it this time? I want you to do it all with this—what shall I call it?"

"What? Oh. Anything but penis. That's the dirtiest word in the language. As far as I'm concerned, it's my cock."

"All right, I want you to put your cock into me again and make me come as often as you can until you're ready to have another great orgasm in me." At this, it reared up and escaped her hand. They both laughed. "Take me the way most men do—just fuck me with your cock. When you do it, it's so marvelous that I can't imagine wanting anything else. No substitutes. I'll have to find a man exactly like you and live happily ever after. I wonder if I could, even if I did find him."

He propped himself on an elbow so that he lay on his side up close against her, and they smiled questioningly into each other's eyes.

"One plain old-fashioned fuck without any trimmings, coming up," he announced with laughter. "It seems unworthy of your divine body and my exotic skills. Maybe it'll make a he-man out of me. I may not hold out as long as before."

"That doesn't matter There're all the other things I want to do later. We have all night, haven't we?"

They had all night, and they spent most of it in various acts of passion. As the sun began to light the sky, they fell into a deep, exhausted, satiated sleep. Neither of them had let drop a word of love.

Mike Cochran stood at the bar waiting to settle the details of his acquisition of Dimitri. The latter was behind the bar, pouring drinks into six glasses on a tray. While he did so he put on a little burlesque show for his famous customer. He flipped his hips when he turned to reach for a bottle; he added ice to a glass with a comically limp wrist; he turned his back and flexed the muscles of his shapely buttocks as he gathered up some paper napkins and looked over his shoulder at Mike and winked. When he had completed his preparations, he put the tray on the bar and swayed close to the older man's face, finger pertly under his chin, his lips parted, his eyelids lowered.

"So now, Mr. Cochran? What can I give you? Do you want another drink? It is a great honor for you to spend all evening here."

Mike looked at him without moving, a slight smile on his lips. He had spent the past couple of hours admiring the youth's physical charms, and now he wanted to take possession of them. The seductive body so tantalizingly revealed by the open shirt and tight trousers was as desirable as a boy's could be. Mike hadn't indulged his taste for young men until his success was established and the failure of two marriages had convinced him that his relationships with women were probably doomed to be fleeting. He made a point of restraining it except on his travels, when there was less risk of dangerous or embarrassing entanglements, and occasionally in New York or Hollywood, when he was with people he could trust absolutely. He had first become aware of this element in his sexual makeup when he had recognized with incredulity the strong current of physical desire in his feelings for George Leighton. While he chased girls with him, making a show of equal enthusiasm, he was tortured by love for his friend.

By the time he had quelled this unwanted passion, he had resolved to make no room in his life for the awkward and unprofitable comedy of love. Experience had quickly demonstrated that humanity could be neatly divided between those who were hurt and those who did the hurting. He was determined to range himself among the latter. Sex was too readily available to allow it to become a tiresome obsession with any one individual.

Dimitri had been busy with his customers all evening, but he had found time to single out Mike for special attention. Mike was used to this; many young men hoped to use him to further their careers, but with Dimitri it obviously wasn't ambition—he was bed-prone. He radiated desire for what Mike intended to give him. He had whispered at one point that he wasn't free later, but with so little conviction in his pretty face that Mike had dismissed it as a bargaining point. "Aren't you going to close up soon?" Mike asked.

"Yes. Very soon. Fifteen minutes, maybe."

"Good. Will you come to the hotel or do you have a better idea?"

"But I tell you. Not tonight. It's not possible." He swayed a little closer and fluttered his eyelids. "Tomorrow all day. Any time you say."

"I haven't been hanging around all this time for nothing." Mike kept his eyes on Dimitri's and reached into his light jacket for his wallet. He pulled it out and laid it out flat on the bar. He opened it slightly to reveal the bill within it.

Dimitri's eyes flickered down to it and he drew back with a little mime of indignation. "What are you thinking? Can you believe I take money? I only go with those I like. I like you very much. Why should I take money?"

Mike wished he wouldn't talk. There was an intrinsic falseness in every word he spoke that was very boring. "I'm sure you don't take money, but why shouldn't I give you a present if you have to change your plans for tonight?"

Dimitri dropped his hand and laid it on the bar so that it just brushed against Mike's and the wallet. He leaned closer and ran the tip of his tongue along his upper lip. "What can I do?" He looked at Mike with bewitching but vacuous eyes. "It is very hard to refuse you, but I have a friend for tonight. He is waiting."

"Young and attractive?"

"Oh, very. Very young. Only a boy, but a real man where it matters."

"Then what's the problem? Three can be fun."

"Very much. But this is a special." A finger twitched against Mike's hand, and Dimitri dropped his eyes.

Mike dug his finger into the wallet and separated three bills from the others.

"*Very* special." Dimitri inserted a finger beside Mike's and added three more bills to the ones Mike had selected.

"As special as all that?" It was nearly two hundred dollars. They lifted their eyes simultaneously and looked at each other.

Dimitri's smile had become complacent. "You know my friend," he said. "He may be very angry with me for this. He is in love with me. It is Jeff, Mr. Leighton's son."

"Jeff!" Mike almost knocked over the remains of his drink with astonishment, accompanied by a tremor of lustful anticipation as his mind was filled with thoughts of the two youths together, of his taking Dimitri with Jeff as audience, of debauching George's son. The boy was young enough to be led; he and Dimitri could do anything they liked with him. He smiled with acquiescence and removed the six bills from his wallet.

There was a flick of Dimitri's wrist, and the money disappeared. Dimitri winked naughtily. "I am very wicked. But so are you, I think. I don't know what Jeff will think of us." He turned efficient as he ducked out from behind the bar. "I will tell the customers they must finish their drinks. Already, the police give us an extra hour because of the big event."

"Where do you meet Jeff?"

Dimitri gave him a sly, sidelong smile. "We will go to him together. I think you must teach him what you want. He says he likes only the other way. You can teach him while he has me. He will be lucky."

Mike followed Dimitri out and went to the table where he had been sitting. He had sent the little Swiss on his way an hour ago. A number of people had approached and introduced themselves. He had managed to dismiss them all gracefully. He was glad for a moment alone to prepare himself for the evening's next phase. So George's son was a fairy; the extraordinary appeal of the look he had given him just before disappearing earlier in the evening had been as good as a declaration. His being already an adept lessened somewhat Mike's triumph, but if Dimitri was right about the boy, Mike would teach him some new tricks and leave his mark on him. Everything in him tightened, and he unconsciously clenched his jaws at the thought of mounting Jeff, of fucking George's son.

He watched one table after another being vacated. Soon the place was empty, and he rose and returned to the bar where Dimitri was emptying the cash drawer. He glanced at Mike with a smile and a little leer.

"Business has been very good this evening." He left the bar and crossed the room to a panel of switches and turned out all the lights. He approached Mike in the dark and assessed his sex with his hands.

"There seems to be quite enough. You and Jeff. This is my lucky night." He darted from him, and his splendid body was briefly silhouetted against the night as he closed the doors. He was again in front of Mike, taking his hand and leading him back into the high room.

"What about Jeff? Where does he come in?"

"He's here. He waits upstairs."

"You bastard. I could've been with him all this time!"

"And use up all your energy so there is none for me?" Dimitri laughed and started up the stairs, still guiding him by the hand. He opened the door at the head of the stairs, and light flooded from it.

Over Dimitri's shoulder, Mike saw Jeff start up, dressed, from the bed where he was stretched out. The boy's eyes widened as he saw that Dimitri was not alone and filled with an odd mixture of delight and consternation as he sprang to his feet. Dimitri was immediately on him, babbling nonsense while Jeff pulled back from him and whispered frantically. Mike passed a bathroom door and entered the room.

It was quite large, furnished in a nondescript fashion, both office and bedroom, with a window giving onto the port. Mike watched as Dimitri subdued Jeff with a kiss. He could see the suspension of resistance become active participation, and the two began to pull at each other's clothes.

Dimitri had Jeff's shirt unbuttoned and was progressing with the trousers. Jeff wrenched his head away, his mouth open, his flat chest heaving under the open shirt, and once more, over Dimitri's shoulder, shot Mike a look of stricken but intense appeal. There was shrewdness and innocence in it, a young and contradictory look, calculating and open, dependent, fierce. The great eyes burned with untapped, undirected passion.

It sent a shock through Mike's system. He would have to tame this boy quickly, break him like a colt before he threatened his guards and became a potential danger. He stepped to a chair and began to slip rapidly out of his clothes.

The tumult that was raging in Jeff was too great for him to direct or identify. From thinking that he must greet Mike politely and act as if this were a perfectly normal social occasion, he had been plunged into intimacies with Dimitri that made social conventions irrelevant. It apparently was permissible for two lovers to kiss and exhibit an uninhibited interest in each other's bodies in front of a third person. He remembered Peter's admonition to enjoy sex and forced himself to follow Dimitri's example.

Hands reaching for his sex, intent on bringing it out into full view, shocked him into resistance, but the look in Mike's eyes when their glances caught was so amused, so approving, and, after a second to two, so intent with secret meaning that again Jeff tried to adapt to the situation and participate in an assured, grown-up way.

Except for the open shirt, he was naked now, and Dimitri was holding his sex and praising it. Jeff's hands hesitated on the top of Dimitri's trousers, wishing for privacy, jealously reluctant to let Mike see the young man who had somehow become his rival. His determination to conceal his inexperience forced him on, and in a moment he had stripped Dimitri and flung off his own shirt.

The beauty he uncovered seized his attention. His ideal men, Charlie and Peter, had athlete's bodies, renaissance bodies with sculptural definition of muscular structure. Dimitri was a classic drawing, all graceful line, unbroken by muscle or sinew, a body made not for physical exertion but for play. As in a drawing, his sex was discreet but satisfyingly in scale, shadowed with only a light blur of pubic hair. Otherwise, his smooth tanned skin was hairless.

He was so perfect in his way that he momentarily aroused in Jeff a desire to take him in the male way he had thought of as inconceivable. Jeff reached for him, but Dimitri dropped down and began to fondle his sex with his mouth. Jeff stood, his cheeks flaming, exposed and self-conscious, excruciatingly aware of being witnessed, though he had lost track of where Mike was, and prayed that he wouldn't lose his erection.

It was only a momentary fear. His body gave a leap, and he cried out as Mike took him in his arms from behind. His heart raced, and his eyesight seemed to dim as his senses were concentrated in the feel of strong arms encircling his chest. He managed to lift his hands to them and press them closer. He became aware of working the muscles of his buttocks, as Dimitri had done with him, to take firmer possession of the flesh that was pressed between them. It felt very bulky. He ran his hands down Mike's flanks and gripped his hips and pulled them to him.

He choked with the heaving of his chest and dropped his head back onto Mike's shoulder. Mike laughed against his ear.

"You like it, do you? I sort of hoped we'd get together. Have you had it like this before?"

Jeff shook his head and blurted, "Never." He didn't have to pretend experience any more. He wanted Mike to know he was taking a virgin. He was aware of wishing Dimitri would leave him alone. He suddenly wanted everything to come from Mike.

Dimitri rose with a laugh. "It's very hard, very stiff for me. Come. We are all ready now."

"Later," Mike said with sharp authority, as if he had read Jeff's mind. "Jeff and I have something to settle between ourselves. You can watch but don't interfere. Understood?"

"Oh, no. You can't take—"

"Have you forgotten our arrangement downstairs? Do you want me to—?"

"No, no," Dimitri agreed hastily. "But if that's the way it will be, you must promise that I'll be next."

"Don't worry. You're going to get fucked. After all, you're the pretty one." It was true. There was no question which of the two Mike would ordinarily find the more attractive. But there was more to it than physical appeal with Jeff. There was something about him—a purity that demanded to be defiled?—that nagged at him and taunted him. To make his possession of him more exclusive, he turned Jeff around to face him, concealing his genitals from Dimitri.

Not as an act of resistance, but in order to engage Mike's attention more completely and consciously, Jeff made himself a dead weight. As he was turned, his eyes tried to encompass all of Mike's body and imprint it in his mind's eye.

He saw a plain man's body, with no beauty but the beauty of strength. A satyr, with a satyr's coarse body, shaggy and priapic. It was spare and tough and functional. The hair on his chest running down to his belly and over his thighs was the hair common to most men. His romantic dreams dissolved as he embraced reality. Mike's phallus when pressed up behind him had felt extravagantly big, but as he caught a glimpse of it in close proximity to his own he saw that they were not conspicuously unequal. Mike held him by the biceps and stared into his eyes with a look that was assured on the surface but strangely troubled beneath.

Mike pulled him in roughly and took his mouth. Jeff let himself sink against the chest. Mike's hands were moving over him and finding places that made everything in him sing. His body was being tuned into a vast humming response to the man who held him. Michael Cochran. He repeated the name in his mind to give familiar substance to the experience he was undergoing. Mike Cochran. Handsome. Celebrated. Mike was going to be his first lover. Mike wanted him. He had chosen him over Dimitri. Mike was going to introduce him to his adult self.

Mike bit his lips hard, and Jeff made strangled moaning sounds in his throat but clung closer to him. Mike's hand slid down between his buttocks. Jeff was seized by a series of small convulsions. A finger probed. Jeff's body leaped out of control. He tore his mouth from Mike's, uttering a cry, and tightened his arms around him and hung on him, his body writhing against him.

"Jesus, you're really hot," Mike said. "Come on."

Jeff let himself be guided to the bed. He had left the tube Peter had told him to buy on the bedside table, and he handed it to Mike without a word. He dropped onto the bed and stretched out on his side with his back turned. Immediately, he was obscurely disgusted to be taking part in this group activity, but he knew he was too easily disgusted and steeled himself to find it perfectly natural. He heard Mike and Dimitri exchange some words, but he couldn't grasp their meaning. All his thoughts and feelings were so absorbed in Mike that he found himself growing indifferent to Dimitri's witnessing the act. He had probably watched before. Mike would transport them into a world where only the two of them existed.

His heart was racing and his breath coming in quick gasps. He began to tremble all over. When he felt Mike moving in over him, every exhalation became a groan. Mike moved him over onto his stomach and straddled him and lifted his hips so that he was propped on his knees and elbows. He bit his forearm to keep his teeth from chattering. In a moment he felt Mike guiding his sex between his buttocks. Jeff's teeth clamped down on his arm as he felt the initial penetration.

Both Mike's hands were holding his hips, placing them, steadying them as he slowly forced his sex into him. At first, all Jeff felt was terror that a disgusting accident would occur. He was being opened up, his control was giving way, all his insides were bound to spill out. He made a desperate effort to find muscles that would avert the disaster, and then pain struck. He was barely able to choke back a scream. His teeth ground on his own flesh in an attempt to redirect the pain. He had no choice but to forget control and force his body to relax and accept.

The pain instantly became less intense. He felt the penetration growing deeper. His mind reeled and spun off to find comfort in what he had been told. Dimitri's gauge of pleasure was size. Mike must know by experience that it would work, or he wouldn't attempt it. He forced his buttocks to meet and hasten the excruciating invasion. Mike's grip tightened on his hips.

"Take it easy," he warned sharply.

"I want it." Jeff managed to wrench the words from his heaving chest. It was true, although it was no longer a question of desire but a determination to submit to whatever agony Mike had in store for him. His sex had shrunk limply.

158

He felt Mike shifting his hips slightly, felt the pain alter direction, and then Mike's groin came slamming up against his buttocks. For a split second, he was sure that the disaster had occurred, that all his insides were being torn from him, and then the pain vanished so suddenly and completely that within an instant he had forgotten it and was filled with a pride of submission to the column of flesh that had driven into him. He lifted his head and gave a shout of triumph. Mike ran his hands up over his back, gripped his shoulders, and pulled him in on himself. Jeff rotated his hips to take him deeper, to savor Mike's possession of him. A man was using him for pleasure. He felt his sex filling out and lifting once more.

Mike began a rhythmic thrust and withdrawal that gave Jeff the first darting pang of orgasm. A low wail began deep in his throat and continued, climbing the scale and growing in volume, as his body was gripped with ecstatic worship of the flesh within him. Passion whipped his hips and buttocks to a frenzy of welcome. The wail rose, and his mouth opened to release it. He heard Mike laugh, and then his hands were on his chest and he was pulling him up and back so that he was able to drop his head on Mike's shoulder once more as the grip of his orgasm tightened. The wail ended in a succession of hoarse barks. All of his body was convulsed. Mike dropped a hand over his sex to contain the ejaculation and massaged his sperm onto him as it jetted from him.

"You," Jeff cried. "Oh, God. Now you."

He didn't know whether he was sobbing or laughing. He felt totally fragmented, as if he would never be whole again. He was buffeted by a storm of sensations and emotions, conscious of nothing, not even that he had had an orgasm. It bore no relation to anything he had ever done for himself. As the storm subsided he found that all his tensions and cravings had been assuaged, and he was lulled into deep contentment by the sliding movement within him.

He accompanied Mike's movement with a slow rotating lift of his hips so that at the final limit of Mike's penetration they were locked together for a moment in profound union. His erection was slowly restored. Little by little, Mike's movement accelerated until he was thrusting into him hard and fast. Jeff laughed with joy and excitement. His body was a receptacle for Mike's lust.

He worked his hips rapidly to Mike's rhythm, giving him his body so that he would make them one. He laughed again as Mike's breathing grew rapid and he began to make broken little moaning sounds. He cried out at the thought of Mike discharging his passion into him and continued to utter cries in time to the hard pounding of Mike's body. They communicated with brief grunts and growls.

Jeff was stunned by the depth of their intimacy. The assured and worldly Mike Cochran had become this panting passionate lover. He hadn't dreamed it was possible to feel so close to another being. Suddenly, Mike bit his shoulder hard, his sex was immobilized and swelled hugely so that Jeff felt another stab of pain, and then Mike's legs were flailing and his body lurching about on Jeff's back while he clung to his shoulder with his teeth. Jeff lifted his hand to his head and stroked his hair. After a few moments, Mike had his body under control, and Jeff felt the sex shrinking inside him. His first lover. He had been had by a man.

"I want it again," he whispered. "Again and again and again. I'll be better next time."

Mike made no answer. In another moment, his sex slipped from Jeff despite his effort to keep it within him, and Mike sprang up and was gone. Jeff felt a shock of emptiness in himself. Dimitri materialized from somewhere at his side. He pushed at Jeff's hips to get his sex out from under him and held it.

"It looks like he gives you a good time." He laughed and snuggled in closer and kissed him and squeezed his sex. "I want it very much. Shall we now or must you wash?"

Jeff lifted himself over him and pushed him back on the pillow and kissed him deeply while his hands caressed the exquisite body, wondering if he could strike in it some spark of the male drive that he knew now his body was intended to serve. He was aflame with his new knowledge; he had discovered a rare and precious gift in himself; he knew how to satisfy the needs of the supreme and mysterious phallus. It was such an immense discovery that he was filled with a burning longing to use it to the utmost, but he was far from sure that Mike would come to him again. He had sensed something shutting off in his lover almost before Mike's orgasm had spent itself.

He held Dimitri's modest sex and thought how sweet it would be to feel it entering him. If Mike caught them at it, jealousy might shatter the mask he hid behind and take him one more step toward admitting his need for Jeff, the need he had enacted in him with such devastating power. Jeff felt nothing in Dimitri but a passive delight in being held. He disengaged himself from his friend, sprang out of bed, and hurried to the bathroom. Moisture was beginning to seep down the inside of his thighs.

Mike was standing in front of the washbasin drying himself. He

160

turned as Jeff entered and smiled at him easily, charmingly, with no acknowledgment that a bond had been created between them. His eyes dropped to Jeff's still-rigid sex.

"Still raring to go? I can't believe that was your initiation. You certainly took to it with enthusiasm."

Jeff looked at him unashamedly. "I told you. I want you to do it again and again. You've taught me how. Can't we go now? I want to spend the night with you."

"You're very flattering, but mightn't that be going a bit too far?"

"What are you afraid of?" Without waiting for an answer, Jeff crossed to a primitive-looking shower in the corner, passing close to Mike, hoping to provoke him with his eyes. Mike's eyes didn't waver, but Jeff could see that there was something going on in them that Mike didn't want him to see. He was too good an actor for Jeff to be able to quite identify it, but he had felt the effort Mike had made not to reach out for him as he passed.

Still looking at him, Jeff turned a tap. A feeble spray of water issued from a dented pipe, but it was sufficient for him to wash himself, and he did so thoroughly, facing Mike, flaunting his body, not because he was proud of it (he found himself depressingly flat and angular and callow) but because the tradition in mythology and literature placed such emphasis on the seductive effect of youth on older men that he assumed there must be some truth in it.

At least, Mike stayed where he was, trying to look as if he were waiting for him casually, but held by him, unable to leave. Jeff could see that much. He soaped his sex and kept giving it little caresses to keep it erect, looking challengingly at him. He was playing a game whose rules he didn't know. He knew only that if somebody did this in front of him he wouldn't be able to stop himself from participating.

Mike made an excuse of checking his nails to drop his eyes to Jeff's caressing hand. A ghost of a smile hovered around Jeff's lips as he turned off the water and began to toy with himself more purposefully. Mike made no pretense of not watching. Jeff saw his sex lengthen and curve out slightly from his body.

"Do you want me to go ahead and do it?" Jeff asked.

"Don't you think you ought to save it for our host?" Mike looked up with his mask in place.

Jeff released his sex and left the shower to stand close to him. "Are you going to let me have Dimitri?"

"Let you? Aren't you planning to fuck him? I thought it was all arranged."

161

"It was." Jeff reached out and ran his hand under Mike's lengthening sex. He felt it grow heavier as he held it, and its head began to rise. "I give you an erection. Why don't you take me away so that you can have me all to yourself?"

"That wouldn't be very considerate of our friend next door. I want to watch you fuck him. I can't think of a more delightful sight than two handsome lads making sport with each other."

"Do you want him?"

"I hadn't quite decided, but you do seem to make me feel sexy. Why not?"

For answer, Jeff darted his head forward and took Mike's mouth in his. He felt the sex lift into complete erection in his hand. Mike's arms were around him, pulling him close. Jeff raised his other hand to the back of Mike's head and drew his mouth deeper into his. Mike's hands were traveling over his wet body, drying him, declaring a passion that his eyes denied. Mike bit his lips again. He protested in his throat but didn't draw back. He let Mike devour his mouth until his breathing became so labored that he was almost suffocating. He pulled his head back and stared into Mike's aroused eyes. He took a deep shaky breath.

"I think I'm going to be in love with you," he said, smoothing the hair back from Mike's forehead.

Mike pulled his head back and laughed harshly. "I should think you'd want to spare yourself that. Ask my wives what it's like."

"Why do you have wives? You like young boys. I like men. I think you might be in love with me. I don't care if you don't want to say it." Mike smile was derisive and unforced. The mask was very effective, but Jeff couldn't imagine why anybody would want to conceal everything interesting about himself.

"What nonsense. You're a silly romantic child. I'm old enough to be your father. You're a very good lay. I'll grant you that. Most boys your age don't admit enjoying it so much. I want to see you fuck your pretty boyfriend. When you're finished, I'll fuck him too. My sperm will mingle with yours. How does that strike your romantic fancy?"

"I don't think you really want him, not the way you want me, but there's nothing I can do about it. I want you to fuck me again."

"I've rarely been in such demand. Maybe we can work it in tomorrow sometime." Mike risked touching the boy on the cheek. It made his heart skip a beat, but he didn't think his expression had altered. He hadn't felt so near to losing control in years. Jeff stood all intense and dewy before him, asking to be hurt. Watching him take the Greek hustler, taking the Greek himself, should shatter the spell Jeff exerted on him.

Its components were so obvious and banal that Mike could laugh at himself for being ensnared by them. He was George's son. He looked like George with lingering traces of Sarah's feminine beauty. He offered his coltish body with an abandon that Mike had rarely encountered. Although they had hardly spoken, he communicated the activity of an original and questing mind, which was more intriguing than physical beauty. He was young. He was an instrument Mike could play in any way he fancied. If he fancied anything, it was to push him to the edge of the hysteria he felt in him, reduce him to an ecstasy of abasement, break him. He was too solicitous of himself to undertake such an experiment in power at the risk of breaking something in himself.

He lingered another moment with his hands on the young body, aware of their sexes lifting against each other, and then pulled away with an effort that caused him a little stab of pain and took his arm to lead him toward the door. "Come on."

Jeff was acutely sensitive of the way he was being handled. Mike obviously didn't know he was giving himself away. His hands were possessive, authoritative, and established a relationship that words could deny but not alter. Mike had made him his because he wanted him to be his. Dimitri was a diversion. When they had disposed of him, Mike would have to acknowledge the special bond that had sprung up between them. Mike had said it himself: "Jeff and I have something to settle between ourselves." It said everything.

"At last," Dimitri welcomed them as they entered the room. "You have been making each other hard again. I thought so. At least you bring them to me." he was lying on his stomach, his elbows propping his upper torso, his legs spread. His eyes were on the erect sexes as they approached. "A fine pair. I don't know which I want most. Don't put anything on them. I have had much time to get ready." He spread his arms out on each side of himself, dropped his head onto the pillow, and smiled up at them voluptuously. "For him who waits, I will gladly give fun with my mouth."

Mike pushed Jeff forward. Jeff straddled Dimitri, and the latter lifted his hips, reached for Jeff's sex, and pulled it to him.

"Oh, my Jeff," he murmured as he directed it into himself.

Jeff felt a greater reluctance than he had imagined at having to perform the act. It was a violation of the masculinity he worshiped. Reluctance was tempered by the immediate thrill of entering another body, of fitting himself into snug containment. Dimitri purred with delight as he continued the penetration. Thinking of the pain he had suffered, he was careful to restrain himself, but Dimitri made a movement with his hips, and all his sex was within him in one lunge. Jeff cried out, and his body collapsed as his orgasm brought the attempt to an abrupt end. When the spasms ended, he heard Mike say, "He must be fantastic if he makes you come that quickly. Come on. Move over and let a man take charge."

"I couldn't help it," Jeff muttered into Dimitri's ear. The orgasm left him relatively intact, more like his solitary play than the mind-numbing fragmentation he had experienced with Mike. He slipped out of Dimitri, leaped up on the opposite side of the bed from Mike, and ran to the bathroom, determined not to see Mike take his place.

He washed himself in the basin without looking at himself until he was sure he must be clean, while he tried not to hear the sounds from the other room. Dimitri, with all his experience, would know how to please Mike much better than a novice. There was no competition as far as looks went; Dimitri was a beauty. Jeff looked at himself in the mirror and saw that his lips were swollen. His shoulder hurt; he touched it cautiously and found a welt where Mike had bitten him.

He had expected to hurt elsewhere, but he felt only a slight smarting and an empty longing for Mike to be there again. The sounds he was trying not to hear told him Mike never would be. Nevertheless, the weight of solitude in him had lifted. He had learned a great deal. He had a gift around which all his lifetime of dreams and yearnings was taking the shape of reality. The world of men was opening to him at last. He need never be alone again. It was unbelievable that only this afternoon he had been plaguing Peter with childish questions.

He had come close to breaking through to Mike. He was sure of it. When he found another Mike, he would be sure enough of himself to play his part more skillfully. Above all, he should avoid threesomes. The bursts of laughter and cries of passion were continuing. He wanted to leave, but his clothes were in the other room.

He was suddenly conscious of silence. It seemed to go on a long time while he remained propped against the basin, his head bowed, waiting. Mike had probably forgotten he existed.

There were sounds of movement finally and, in another moment, Mike entered the bathroom. Jeff expected him to be altered, shaken in some way by what had sounded like a tumultuous and ecstatic encounter, but he looked just the same, the same detached, slightly amused expression on his face. It was the final blow to Jeff's hopes

164

of holding his interest. Nobody could touch Mike.

"That's quite a—" Mike began, but Jeff ducked past him and hurried out, closing his ears to whatever he was saying.

He made for his clothes, irrationally determined to go with Mike or, if Mike stayed, to go alone and wait for him outside. Dimitri was standing by the bed, doing something with a towel. He dropped it onto the floor and glided toward Jeff, swaying his narrow hips, smiling with complicity. They had been had by the same man. He was a note of grace in the squalor they had created in the room, the soiled and rumpled sheets, the discarded towels, the lubricant open on the bedside table. So much for dreams; at least this was really happening.

Dimitri stood in front of him and ran the tip of a forefinger down the middle of his body, from chest to navel to quiescent sex. "There is still this for me," he said, running the tip of his finger up and down on it. "I think it will not stay like this for long."

Jeff hesitated, seeing Dimitri's modest but shapely sex stir into life. Mike would come in at any moment. He didn't want to be found still climbing in and out of bed. Why not? Mike didn't care. Mike had had him. There was the consolation of Dimitri's beauty and his conscienceless but comradely eyes. Jeff was already so accustomed to their promiscuous nakedness that he felt no self-consciousness. Not even at being seen in an unexcited state. What difference did it make if he didn't get an erection? The torments Dimitri had caused him seemed very remote. He remembered with a jolt the important talk he must have with him. He couldn't leave with Mike. He put an arm around the lovely torso and let a hand stray over the smooth tanned skin of the chest as they returned to the bed and stretched out together.

Dimitri held him and played with his hair. "So. Now we have shared our first lover," he said contentedly. "He's a fine man, his cock not so big as some but very exciting. You think so?"

"Sure. I don't know why I haven't tried it before." Jeff still wondered about the preoccupation with size. He had always dreamed in colossal terms, but he would gladly be taken by Dimitri no matter how obvious it might be that it would be more exciting in the mind than in fact. He could wish even Mike, who had felt enormous in him, had been able to drive still deeper into him to make his conquest more immense. There was no end to it. "I guess we're a lot alike. I've always been fascinated by cocks. I haven't seen as many as I pretended. Yours is beautiful."

"Ah? You are my sister now?" Dimitri burst into his cheerful mindless laughter. "We'll share other lovers, perhaps. Even sisters can have much pleasure together."

Jeff supposed he should resent being referred to in the feminine gender, but he didn't. There was a sort of truth in it. Peter would doubtless disapprove, but Peter and Charlie represented an ideal, remote and perhaps unattainable. He couldn't blame Dimitri for offering himself to every man who came along. It was a manifestation of the gift they shared. "It's wonderful being with you like this after chasing you so long."

"Even if my sister is not so much in love with me anymore?" Dimitri laughed again, then pulled Jeff's head down and opened his mouth to be kissed. He did exciting things with his tongue while his hands strayed teasingly over Jeff's body. In a moment Jeff's sex was standing upright against him. Dimitri felt for it and purred and wriggled down. He knelt between his legs, crouched over it, and took it in his mouth.

Mike reentered the room. Jeff made a quick movement of his hand to pull Dimitri's head away, but reconsidered and dropped it caressingly on the crisp curls. Mike had been quick enough to dispose of Dimitri at the beginning. Perhaps seeing them like this would impel him to take charge of him again. Nothing else had worked. He looked at Mike and waited for their eyes to meet, his heart suddenly beating rapidly. Mike surveyed the activity on the bed and then lifted his eyes to Jeff's with a look of slightly scornful amusement. For an instant, Jeff saw deep in the look a summons that almost brought him leaping from the bed. It was gone so quickly that Jeff almost believed he had imagined it.

Jeff tugged at the head that was bowed over him. Dimitri straightened, registered Mike's presence, and giggled. "We have company," he said unconcernedly.

Jeff leaned forward, held him in the kneeling position, and drew him toward him, watching the neatly elegant erection bob about with Dimitri's movements. He knew exactly the picture he wanted to compose. He hunched himself up against the pillows when Dimitri reached him so that his mouth was on a level with the cock. Yes, cock, he thought determinedly, adopting plain words. He put his arm around Dimitri's hips and held him close, directing the cock with one finger so that it brushed against his open lips. He let his tongue play over it while he darted quick glances at Mike, watching clothes transform the tough, intimately known body into the elegant figure of the famous Michael Cochran. It was insane to suppose he could make

166

this formidable celebrity jealous, but he was going to do his best. He thought he had found the key. Why did Mike keep himself turned slightly sideways to them? He said he liked to watch. Why didn't he watch?

Dimitri was cooperating by uttering brief giggles and little purring sounds of pleasure. If it weren't for Mike, he wouldn't be able to take his eyes off the exquisite cock. It wasn't monumental, but it summoned him to worship. He leaned forward and took all of it in his mouth until his lips brushed against soft pubic hair. You couldn't do that with a monument. He drew back slowly and saw out of the corner of his eye that Mike was turning to them at last. He held the cock in his mouth another instant so that Mike would see and then released it. His breath caught with a gasp as their eyes met. The summons was there, unequivocal, boring into him. Jeff's eyes widened, and he felt as if they were flooded with acquiescence to Mike's will. He had to struggle to keep himself from springing up to him. Mike would be bored by an easy victory.

Keeping his eyes on him, his heart racing, Jeff deliberately hoisted himself into a more nearly sitting position and pulled Dimitri down to him so that he held him nestled against his side. He moved Dimitri's hand to his sex, and Dimitri obligingly lifted it away from his belly and began to stroke it.

Mike had resumed his mask, but Jeff could see that it was far from secure. He joined his hand to Dimitri's and moved it lazily over himself, challenging Mike with his eyes.

"Very pretty," Mike said with sardonic amusement. "I admire your youthful endurance."

"I have to—" Jeff blurted out before he could stop himself. He wanted to say that he had to stay and talk to Dimitri, but apologetic explanations wouldn't do. "I'll see you later," he said, between statement and question, and was delighted at how assured he sounded.

"Later?" Mike repeated. "I have a date at noon. Come by after lunch if you like. Both of you. Now that we all know each other, we might have a delightfully depraved hour together before I go. Ta." He performed impeccably. He gave Jeff a meaningless wink before he turned and strolled to the door.

Jeff felt all his muscles gathering to leap up and follow him. He turned quickly to Dimitri and engaged his mouth in a long kiss while he absorbed the shock of letting Mike leave without him. He would rejoin him in a few minutes as soon as he had done his duty. Mike wanted him. Jeff had found the way to break down his reserve. His imagination made a great leap into the future; if Mike were jealous, anything could happen.

His thoughts were suspended in the pleasure of the kiss. He was amazed at the warmth generated by physical contact. He had never expected to find comfort and affection with Dimitri. Mike's watching had intensified the excitement of holding him, but it was sweet holding him now. He was glad to have a sister. If Mike hadn't come along, they might even have worked out some kind of relationship. He would have to tell Dimitri he wouldn't share Mike again. He relinquished the soft welcoming mouth with regret.

Dimitri laughed and squeezed his sex. "It's very hard, maybe bigger than Mike's, I think. You were so quick before, but it felt very wonderful in me. You can fuck me for a very long time, and we will be happy, just the two of us."

"Yes, I want to, but first we've got to talk," Jeff said distractedly. It was very difficult to think clearly while they were entwined with each other. He ran a hand down his neck and over a shoulder and down his chest, caressing the small nipples. He could *feel* beauty. The way spare flesh was laid over the perfect symmetry of the frame was a tactile delight. If Dimitri made a move to take him, he wouldn't be able to think at all. He took a deep breath and made a determined effort to discharge his duty. "I've been worrying all day. We've got to get the money back to my father."

A petulant look marred the bland mindlessness of Dimitri's handsome face. "The money? It's not going to be easy until everything is quiet again. Yes, bigger than Mike's. Oh, my Jeff. I've arranged things with Sid. Maybe he will be able to help. What can I do if the police watch me?"

"They'll stop watching you if we stick to what you said. You promised you wouldn't keep the money for more than twenty-four hours." He held Dimitri's arm to stop the insinuating movements of his hand.

"But my Jeff, what can I do if I cannot do my business? You know all about my money."

"Not all. I know you must have a lot put away somewhere."

Dimitri's smile grew complacent, and he lowered his eyelids and swayed his head forward languorously to touch one of Jeff's nipples with his tongue. "What I have put away is not easy to get in my hands. That is why I let you give me your father's money. You insisted it was all right."

"It was, but don't you understand? It's important for you too." He gripped the curls and pulled Dimitri's head up to face him. "Unless I fix it so that Dad finds the money in the morning, there's no telling what the police will do with Costa. They've got to let him go. You promised."

"But all is different. Don't worry. A week, maybe two, all is all right again.

"A week's too long," Jeff protested. Surely, Dimitri must feel his anxiety. Their physical intimacy must have struck some chord in him of concern for each other. He mustn't let himself get rattled. His emotions had been battered by the secret struggle with Mike. Dimitri couldn't know how close he was to going to pieces. Hysterical pleas would simply glance off his decorative surface. Jeff made an effort to speak calmly. "I know you could get sixty thousand if you had to. That's why I wasn't worried about letting you have it for a day. You know I had no intention of really taking it."

"We both know why you let me have it." Dimitri wriggled his way in closer to Jeff and stretched against him voluptuously. "Maybe Sid will have an idea in the morning. Now you have what you want. Why not enjoy it? Your cock is very ready. Talk about promises. Why don't you do what you say you do?"

"Not yet. Please. I want to, but we've got to get this settled."

"You suck my cock very nicely, if you don't want the other."

"You know how much I've wanted you. You're divine. It's thrilling to see you naked at last and to have you with me like this. Please don't spoil it by acting as if you don't care about our agreement."

Dimitri smiled mischievously, dropped his head onto his shoulder, and ran his tongue around Jeff's ear. "You will suck my cock, and I will suck yours. I like that very much. We will be sisters again. If you are very good maybe it will make me think of a way to give your money back."

He went into action, laughing, wrestling Jeff's hips down onto the bed. His cock bobbed enticingly close to Jeff's mouth. Dimitri's mouth was on his, and then he dropped down beside him and they were joined in mutual worship of each other's manhood. Perhaps this was the only way to win Dimitri over; threats were empty and might turn him stubborn.

Jeff thought he heard a sound downstairs and held himself motionless for an instant. Had Mike waited for him? He must hurry. He ran a hand over Dimitri's buttocks and trailed caressing fingers between them. Dimitri's hips leaped, and he chortled with pleasure as his sex jumped about in Jeff's mouth. Jeff rolled his tongue around it hungrily, hungry for its essence. Peter wouldn't have had to tell him to swallow it. He wanted to savor the taste of it and drink it in. He knew all aspects of his craving now. He would learn how to perfect his gift. Dimitri's expert mouth was making his breath catch and stimulating his appetite for the silken flesh that darted between his lips.

He heard what sounded like a door opening, but even if it were Mike returning the wonder of knowing a man in this way gripped him too deeply for him to think of stopping.

"Jeff," Dimitri cried out, and the voracious contact was abruptly broken. He tore himself away and was out of the bed, dragging a sheet with him.

His mouth still open, Jeff swung his head and, his vision blurred and disbelieving, saw two policemen he knew standing near the door. Dimitri had draped himself in the sheet and was shouting at them shrilly.

Jeff reared up, flung his legs over the side of the bed, and started to spring to his feet, but realized he had nothing to cover himself. He fell back and hugged himself to make himself invisible and to control the tremors that had begun to shake him. His cheeks were burning. Had he been committing a criminal act? He didn't know the Greek law. He would never be able to face his family again. He would be branded for life. He sat huddled up on the edge of the bed and tried to force himself to grasp what was being said behind him while his heart hammered against his ribs and his trembling became uncontrollable.

The belligerence in Dimitri's voice was reassuring. The policemen sounded embarrassed but determined. Slowly, Jeff was able to listen coherently. From a jeering remark, it appeared that Dimitri had been intimate with one or perhaps both of them. Jeff's hopes rose. A few more exchanges revealed that they had accepted Jeff's invisibility. The beating of his heart slowly subsided. They had come to arrest Dimitri on a drug charge. Dimitri suggested with a sneer that they search the place. Their orders were to seal the bar and take Dimitri to the station house. A thorough search would be made in the morning. The conversation became sporadic, and Jeff was aware of Dimitri moving about the room, going to the bathroom and returning. When he came around the end of the bed he was once more superb in tight trousers and sheer shirt. He handed Jeff his clothes.

"You heard all that?" He shrugged contemptuously but without alarm. "You must leave. They wish to close the place officially for a search. Poor silly men. I will make great trouble when they find I am innocent."

170

Jeff pulled on his clothes without rising. When he was covered he stood and took care of the final tucking and fastening. Dimitri moved in close to him.

"You know who I said," he murmured without moving his lips. "The Jew. Go in the morning."

Jeff looked at him and nodded. He forced himself to turn and slouched toward the door, his head down. The policemen greeted him as if he had materialized from nowhere. He mumbled a reply but was unable to look at them. Once on the stairs, he hurtled down them and rushed out into the night. He broke into a trot as he headed for the new hotel. Mike couldn't turn him away now. He had an excuse for seeking aid and advice.

A somnolent clerk gave him the room number. He leaped upstairs. The door opened in response to his light knock. Mike stood in it, wearing a short, belted thigh-length linen gown or jacket. He looked briefly astonished, and then a number of transformations took place behind the veil of his eyes that Jeff couldn't interpret but counted to his advantage. Neither boredom nor dismissal had been part of them. He longed to be taken in his arms or at least touched in come way, but Mike only opened the door wider and stood aside to let him in.

"So soon," he said, closing the door behind him. "I rather expected you, but not till morning. You looked very agreeably occupied."

"You know that didn't mean anything, but it doesn't matter. I have to speak to you." Jeff saw that the bed hadn't been touched yet. He went to it and dropped down on it, looking up at Mike. Away from the atmosphere of indiscriminate sex in Dimitri's room, he found it hard to believe that this man had made love to him. The short robe was very becoming. He looked handsome and expensive and far too worldly for an eighteen-year-old boy. "Dimitri's been arrested."

"What an extraordinary place this is. How do you mean?"

"Just now. The police walked in when we were— They locked up his place and took him away. It's about dope."

"I see. There were a couple of policemen standing outside when I left. Do you use dope?"

"No." He dropped back across the bed, propped himself on his elbows, spread his legs in front of him, and looked up at Mike with his chin lifted, willing him to come sit beside him. The brutal interruption with Dimitri had left all his nerves on edge. Mike stayed where he was standing, as if he expected this to be a short visit. "Are you really leaving tomorrow?" Jeff asked. "Well, I mean—I guess I mean today."

"Yes. I understand there's an afternoon boat."

Jeff heaved a long complicated sigh that caught several times in his chest before it was done. He was suddenly confronting the biggest moment of his life. *Just keep it businesslike,* he warned himself. "Can I go with you? I mean it. No—wait a minute. I'm going to the States in the fall anyway. All you have to do is pay for my trip and let me stay with you until school starts. I'll have my own money then. We could be lovers. Nobody would think it peculiar for you to have George Leighton's son with you."

"Except possibly George Leighton." Mike turned away with a nice show of nonchalance, caught sight of a litter of papers he had left on a table, and went to them, finding them a reasonable excuse for withdrawing slightly while he digested Jeff's proposal. He sorted them—plane tickets, letters, hotel bills—while he rapidly sorted his thoughts. He had known when he left Dimitri's loft that this time, once had not been enough. Jeff had an uncanny way of getting through to him. It wasn't love; a reasonable man past forty couldn't fall in love with a teenage boy. It had nothing to do with George anymore. Jeff had become a menace in his own right.

He had told himself that a good sleep would clear his mind of the boy and restore him to the sanity of his self-sufficiency, but now he was here, his great eyes blazing with innocence and something unsettlingly like love, proclaiming by his very presence that he had something to offer him. Silly kid. Did he suppose that love was happiness, that life could be conquered by giving in to sentiment or the impulses of the heart?

He could send him away this minute, but it might be more satisfying to hold on to him another day or two, demonstrate to himself once more the fallibility of the big emotions, leave him robbed of innocence and with at least an intimation of reality. To guide and assist his making a silly little fool of himself would be insurance against being haunted by unresolved desires.

He stacked the papers neatly and turned back to the boy on the bed. "I wonder. Does your father know you're a fag?"

Jeff kicked off his sandals, lifted his feet, and scooted himself back on the bed with his elbows until he was resting against the headboard. He put his hands flat on his thighs, framing his crotch. "Does he know you like boys?"

"I've never been averse to a romp with a pretty boy when the occasion arises. That's about all it amounts to."

Jeff admired his aplomb. He had said it without too much emphasis or any trace of annoyance. "I don't believe you," Jeff said. He slowly unbuttoned his shirt, keeping his eyes on Mike's. When he had bared his chest he unfastened his trousers, worked his shorts down on his hips, and lifted out his sex. His boldness had aroused it, and a few strokes of his hand completed the process. He continued to caress it as he spoke, holding it upright and away from his belly, the way Dimitri had done. "I saw the way you looked at me right from the start. At lunch. You're very good at hiding it, but I saw. I saw and felt things tonight too. I don't know if you're in love with me, but I know I mean more to you than a romp with a pretty boy. I'm not even pretty. It's something you can't help. I'm in love with you. At least I guess that's what it is. I've obviously never felt anything like it before. I doubt if I'll want sex with anybody else as long as you want me, if that means anything. I'll bet you're getting an erection. Why do you keep that thing on? Don't you want me to see?"

A light leaped up in Mike's eyes that was exciting and dangerous. "Getting a hard-on and being in love are hardly the same thing, you silly faggot." Mike opened his robe and shrugged it off. Jeff saw what he had expected to see. Mike's sex was rigidly immobile as he approached the bed. "I told you you're a good lay. I imagine you're an expert cocksucker, too. How about it?"

Jeff sat up and pushed himself to the edge of the bed, triumphant at this further victory in his struggle and eager to display his gift, though Dimitri had been no preparation for this. He reached for Mike's hips and ducked his head to take it. It swelled as his mouth played with it until it made his jaws ache. Mike seized his hair with both hands and held his head as he thrust it deep into his mouth. Jeff gagged and choked. He wrenched his head back and forth and tore himself free, finding a new strength in the conflict. Mike's mask was slipping. There was violence in his hands.

"You don't have to force me," he gasped. "I want it."

"You'll do it my way or not at all." Mike gripped his hair again and held his head steady. "Open your mouth." Mike directed his sex into it. "Wider. That's better." He forced his sex in as far as it would go and held it there. He began to agitate it slightly so that it tickled the back of Jeff's throat and made him retch. "I'm not Dimitri. Is it too big for you?" He pulled Jeff's head back and forth on it, forcing his mouth open as wide as it would go. "Look at me," he demanded. Jeff rolled his eyes up, and Mike saw a masochistic submission in them that demanded a sadistic response. To keep him off balance, Mike released his hair and stroked his taut cheeks gently. "Go ahead. Let's see how quickly you can make me come. I've never known a kid who was so nuts about cock."

Freed, Jeff applied himself with dedication, thrilling at the thrills he felt stirring in Mike's body. They began to communicate once more in grunts and cries. After a few moments, he felt Mike's body vibrating with an impending orgasm, and his heart began to pound in anticipation of this final initiation. He moaned with longing to swallow Mike's substance. He heard a cry above him as the sex in his mouth leaped so vigorously that it almost escaped him, and he gagged as his mouth was flooded with a thick fluid, odd but not disagreeable to the taste. He swallowed it joyfully. It left a strong musky aftertaste. Now he knew. His mouth clung to the sex, drawing all of it into him until he was pulled roughly from the edge of the bed and flung to his knees on the floor.

"There. Go ahead. Jerk yourself off," Mike ordered thickly. "That's what you've been wanting to do."

Jeff fell back against the side of the bed. Through lowered lids, he watched Mike put his robe on again. He held his rigid sex, even more frustrated than he had been by the arrival of the police. Mike wanted him, but he still wouldn't let himself indulge a shared desire. Jeff's hand moved to obey Mike's order, but he was immediately aware of the defeat implicit in the act and stopped. "You're in love with me. You wouldn't try to hate me if you weren't," he said boldly, coldly, logically. He was learning. He arranged his tangled clothes and pulled himself to his feet. "You *are* going to take me with you, aren't you? To the States, I mean."

"What will your father think of the idea?"

"That's just it. He wouldn't care. He's having problems of his own."

"So I gather. Well, if it's just the trip you want, I might give you that. I came prepared to bail out the Leighton family."

"I want a lot more than that. I want to live with you and be your lover. When I go to college, there'll be the holidays. It'll be interesting for you to see how I develop. I'm intelligent. We're right for each other physically. I think we'll like being together."

"You sound as if you were proposing marriage."

"I am."

Mike laughed, trying to make it sound dismissive, not quite succeeding. "I've been married to some to the brightest, most attractive women in the world. Why do you think I'd want you?"

"You want to be loved by a boy?"

174

"I've had that."

"They weren't clever enough for you." They stood facing each other across the room, motionless, their eyes watchful. Jeff moved closer and stopped again. "Can I spend the night with you?"

"That may be. There's a fascinating element in the situation. You seem to think that when two people look at each other, they promptly fall in love. If I was ever in love with anybody, it was with your father, if you want the truth. A very disagreeable experience, which I've taken pains not to repeat. It's quite pleasant in an obvious sort of way having his son at my feet, begging for me. Such a fine manly lad, too, quite extraordinarily handsome. I'm sure you're the apple of your father's eye. There's that in your favor, as far as I'm concerned. If you're as intelligent as you claim to be, you should find a way of taking advantage of it."

"I'll try to. Thanks." Jeff moved in to Mike until his body brushed against the short robe. He took Mike's hands, lifted them, and put them on his chest, reveling in the desire he felt in them. He leaned forward and touched his lips lightly with his own, then drew back. "You don't have a son, do you? Take me. You'll be my father and my lover. I'm going to stay."

Mike's face was fleetingly marked by deep lines of strain, and then the mocking smile came. "If you're happy on the floor, I couldn't care less one way or the other." The first lesson, one that his wives had always had great difficulty learning: if anybody chose to attach themselves to him, they did so on his terms.

"Good. Whenever you feel like fucking, just say the word. That's when I'm really yours.

"We'll think about that in the morning."

"I certainly will." Jeff released Mike's hand and moved away. He took a cushion from a chair and the cover that had been folded at the foot of the bed and stretched out where Mike could touch him if he wanted him. He closed his eyes and listened to Mike moving around the room, wondering if he would be capable of leaving him on the floor. The light snapped out. He heard the creak and rustle of the bed. Then there was silence except for their breathing. Jeff held his for an instant to synchronize it with Mike's and smiled as they inhaled and exhaled together. That was one form of union his lover couldn't deny him.

At dawn, a brisk northerly breeze sprang up, keeping the temperature down in spite of the blazing sun that rose from the eastern sea. All over the island, bodies stirred and moved toward their partners in the unexpected comfort of being cool.

Sid Coleman and Dorothy, his girl, lay side by side naked in bed. They had started the day, as usual, by sharing a joint. They took long puffs on it, holding the smoke in their lungs so that when they exhaled, little emerged. They lay straight and flat on their backs with nothing over them.

"Holy moly! This stuff is terrific," Sid exclaimed as he passed the dwindling stub to Dorothy. "Look at me, darling. Hey, *look* at me! Coleman the great Erector Set. What would you say to a nice sophisticated little blow job? How about that, darling? Do you realize we have about three thousand dollars' worth of this stuff under that rock in the courtyard? Dimitri is a genius."

"Be quiet," Dorothy said in a voice that drifted from some remote reverie. "I'm beginning to see it all clearly. I'm going to be able to put it all into simple words that even you'll be able to understand."

Coleman's body was rocked with laughter. "How can you speak, how can you even *think* with a situation like this staring you in the face? You must be going mad with desire. Aren't you a woman? Hey, aren't you a *woman*? Now, wait a minute. That's a question that requires investigation. Maybe I've been sleeping with a goddamn boy." He slipped a hand between her thighs and made a thorough exploration. "Reassuring. But you can't trust anybody these days. Maybe you've had an operation. Come clean, darling. I don't have any prejudices against boys. I just like to know where I stand." He lifted himself on one elbow and gazed down at her breasts, flattened but still ripe and generous and as evenly tanned as the rest of her. He traced the curve with one finger and stroked the nipple. There was no reaction. "Hey, you must be dead or something. Darling, speak to me. Say something. Are you dead?"

She brushed his hand away and spoke. "It's really quite simple. The whole point of being married is that—"

He flopped over onto his back and howled. "Oh, no! Oh, no, darling. Now, just listen. Oh, Christ! Jesus, look what you've done to me. You've ruined me. Do you want Coleman, Homo Erectus, or do you want Coleman, a little shriveled-up husband? Do you think that bump on your head has affected your brain?"

"You don't even know what I'm going to say. Marriage is just—"

"Stop saying it! A lobotomy. Maybe that's what you'll have to have. Look at Henry Varnum. Look at George Leighton. I like them. They're fine. But they're *married.* That means they want to break

176

out. It's human nature. Think what repression does to people. I *want* to be afraid you'll run off with some other guy. If you do, then I'll wish I'd married you. That's human nature. Hey, look! Look at me, darling. I'm in love with my own voice." He rocked with laughter and stubbed out the cigarette. "Come on, darling. What're we waiting for? It's your turn to make the first move."

She sighed and lifted herself, presenting her face to him. She gave a tug to her hair, and it fell over his head like a golden curtain. There was a knock at the door. Sid's hands tightened on her arms. "Don't go. There's not a soul in the world I want to see. Isn't that great? If I'm not careful, I *might* ask you to marry me."

"If you did, I'd refuse you. That's what you're too stupid to understand." She rolled away from him, gathered up her hair, and rose. The room was long, with many windows and little furniture. She went to the end window, dropped to the floor so that only her head and shoulders were visible, and looked out. "It's Jeff. Good morning," she called down. "Come in. I'll be right down."

She picked up a man's shirt that covered her to the knees, crossed the room, and disappeared down a stairway. In a few moments, Jeff mounted it.

"She said I could come up," he said, pausing at the top.

Sid had pulled a sheet over himself at the sound of Jeff's footsteps. He sat up. "Sure. Hi. Come in. What's doing?"

"Dimitri's been arrested."

"Hey. Wow. You're joking. Jesus. That's no good. When did you hear?"

"It happened last night. I was with him. We were just talking about how he'd have to be careful and about arranging things with you when the police walked in. He told me to come see you this morning."

"In front of the *police*?"

"Not so they'd understand. I knew who he meant because we'd been talking about you. Did he give you the last delivery?"

"Yeah. Yesterday evening. It's hidden downstairs. Holy moly. I wonder if it's safe. Sit down." Sid arranged himself in a Buddha pose in the middle of the bed.

Jeff sat at the end of it. "He seems to think you know how to dispose of it," he said urgently. "He needs the money. He's got to pay it back."

"Money should be the least of his worries. Even if they can't pin anything on him, they'll be watching him now. All of us, for God's sake. This must be Costa's doing. I don't blame him for trying to protect himself, but informing on us, that's shitty. What's money got to do with it? Hey! Are you by any chance trying to tell me that Dimitri stole your dad's money?"

"No." Jeff crossed his legs, hugged one knee to his chest, and leaned his cheek against it. "It's all so complicated. He was short of cash, and he had a chance to pick up that stuff cheap, so I let him have it. Just for a day. He was supposed to give it back this morning."

"For God's sake! Why don't you tell your father that? Why don't we go to the police and get Costa out?"

"And accuse Dimitri of stealing or say what he wanted it for? He's not afraid of trouble—they can't hold him once they've searched his place—you've got to make him understand that it's important for his sake for Dad to get his money back. Once Costa is cleared, the whole thing will be finished with. I've tried to explain it to him, but I'm not sure I convinced him. I probably won't see him again before I go. I don't have much time. I'm about to leave with Mike Cochran."

"Leave? Hey, wait a minute. What's going on? What're you talking about?"

Jeff uncrossed his legs and stood up, running his fingers through his hair, then sat down again. "Mike's taking me to the States. I was going in six weeks, anyway. What's so peculiar about that?"

"Nothing. An old pal of your father. I just had the impression that things weren't going very smoothly between them last night."

"What difference does that make to me?"

"None. Hey, now, listen. What're you going to do when you get there? Are you going to stay with Mike?"

"Of course," Jeff announced defiantly. "At least until I go to Harvard. I don't care what people think."

"Why should you? I don't have anything against homos, comrade. A man has the right to do what he wants with his own body. I mean, it's basic. It could even happen to me. But Mike Cochran. He's a very ornate character. I thought he might like boys, but he isn't going to take any risks for one. You're too—I know this is a terrible thing to say to a guy, but it's true—you're too young and inexperienced for him. Have you talked to Peter or Charlie about this?"

"No." He was grateful to Sid for taking his liaison for granted. He wondered what it would do to him to be in a community where he couldn't count on such easy acceptance. Was that what was the matter with Mike?

"Well, don't you think you ought to? I mean, they'd really know what they're talking about."

"If they told me not to go, I'd probably think I shouldn't, and I've got to." He sprang up and flung his arms out, and his face twisted into a tormented grimace. "I can't stand it with my parents anymore. I'm in love. I know I'm too young and inexperienced, but I'm going to get some experience now. Just tell Dimitri to do what I say. If you can help raise money on that stuff, everything should be all right. You can handle it with Dad any way you want. Tell him I took it. Tell him it was a mad schoolboy prank. I know what I'm doing. Mum and Dad needn't worry, if they notice I'm not here. I'll go to school when I'm supposed to. Will you tell them that? You don't have to tell them about the sex part unless they bring it up. I think Dad has a pretty good idea about me. I've got to go."

"Go in peace, comrade." Sid lifted his hand in benediction.

"You're a good guy, Sid." Jeff turned and flung himself down the stairs.

Peter awoke with Judy's head on his shoulder. When he stirred, she stirred with him, and their bodies automatically moved into position for making love. With morning, they had become practiced lovers, delighting each other with known pleasures, so that they were quickly locked in the throes of a shared climax.

Only after passion had receded did Peter wonder about the time. He sat up in the enormous bed, trying to remember where he had seen the clock. He spotted it behind him, built into the paneling of the bulkhead. It was almost eleven-thirty. "My God," he exclaimed. "Sweetheart, I never want to see you in clothes again, but shouldn't we meet Mike Cochran?" By the time he had completed the question, he was lying out in the bed again with his mouth on her breast.

She ran her fingers through his tousled hair and held his head for a moment, then pushed it firmly aside and sat up in her turn. "You sleep so beautifully. You make love so beautifully. I want to see if you're beautiful when you're being a serious art expert."

She left him and was quickly, efficiently bathed and dressed and looking beautiful, despite their active night, when he joined her on the covered deck. They had a cup of coffee together with only a few minutes to spare before their noon date.

He was glad they were going to be occupied for the next hour or two. He needed a little time to adjust to what had taken place, was still taking place between them. Except during business trips, he had never before spent a whole night away from home. He was feeling more unfaithful than he liked, even though he knew Charlie wouldn't mind, might not even know it if he had got up early enough. He kept his back turned to the eastern arm of the port, and the house. He had had one of the most sexually satisfying nights of his life—with a girl!— and his body was restless for more. Fortunately, they hadn't time; getting out among people would break the absorbing physical connection he felt with her.

He glanced at the chronometer and finished off his coffee. "Nobody ever does anything here when they're supposed to," he said, "but Cochran's from another world. We'd better run."

She didn't indulge in any maddening little feminine delaying tactics but was immediately on her feet ready to go. He didn't allow himself to touch her until they were on the gangplank. When he put his hand on her arm, he immediately wanted to turn her around and rush her back to the enormous bed. They went dutifully ashore. Passing the *Meltemi,* Peter noticed that it was closed, which was odd at that hour. The port looked unusually still, with few people about.

Sid Coleman and Dorothy were conspicuously alone at Lambraiki's. Sid gestured frantically as Peter and Judy approached and hardly waited for introductions to be performed before telling about Dimitri's arrest and Jeff's morning visit.

"He's left with Mike," Sid concluded. "How does that figure to you?"

"Left? How could he? You mean already—on the morning boat?"

"Michael Cochran? On the regular boat? No, a special caïque. Laid on by the police. They're taking him to the mainland and *driving* him to Athens. Don't you wish you wrote movies?"

"How peculiar. We had a date with him." Peter and Judy exchanged a glance. "Did Jeff say anything to explain the big rush?"

"I gathered they were eloping, friend. Maybe they didn't want to explain to George and Sarah."

Peter frowned. "Jeff's a fast worker. I wonder how he and Mike got together. Did he tell you what they're planning to do?"

"Just that Mike's taking him to the States. I advised against it, but who listens to my advice? But wait. Now, listen. There's more. They've taken Costa to Piraeus. *He* went on the morning boat. Manacled. Stavro told me."

"Oh, damn." Peter's frown deepened.

"And you know what? He didn't take the money. Jeff did, to lend to Dimitri."

"You're kidding! You mean it? The silly little bugger. Why didn't he tell me? I came pretty close to guessing. We've got to make your pal Dimitri give it back."

"Don't worry. He will. I've got him by his busy little balls."

"What an idiotic mess. The only person who gets hurt is Costa. Dammit, I don't like that." He stared thoughtfully at the table for a moment and turned to Judy. "Do you know when Mike's planning to leave Athens?"

"Not a definite date. As I understood it, he was coming out here just before he went home."

Their eyes held for a moment, and Peter gave her a little nod before turning back to Sid. "Are you going to stick around down here for a while?"

"I don't know. Where *is* everybody? Until you came along, I was beginning to think we were the sole survivors."

"They're all probably sleeping it off. Look. Stay here and wait for George. He'll be along any minute. Tell him whatever you think you ought to tell him, but get him to go to the police and throw his weight around to get Costa back here. They may not believe he's got his money back unless they see it. I wish I had the cash to leave for him. I'm going to make Jeff come clean. We'll have Costa out by tomorrow morning at the latest." He looked at Judy and found her radiant eyes on him, her expression alert with eager anticipation. "Tim wasn't so dumb to give you a yacht. We can get there about the same time they do."

"We're going up on the yacht together?"

"It seems to make sense." His voice added a private message to the simple words while he looked into her eyes. He took a deep breath and burst out laughing. "We're not safe in public. You better go back to the boat and tell your crew to get ready to shove off. I'll run up to the house and get a few odds and ends. I'll be with you in no time."

They both stood. Sid looked up at them. "This is great. You're beautiful people. Is there anything else you want me to do? I mean, you're really getting some action going."

"Get word to Dimitri that you want to see him as soon as he's let out. You're sure you'll get the money from him? Then get it to George as soon as possible."

"No sweat, comrade. Maybe not today, but tomorrow sure."

"Good. I suppose it all has something to do with your precious dope, but I don't have time to hear about it. Jeff will tell me." He held Judy's hand and exerted a slight pressure, and they exchanged another look. He turned from her hastily and was off.

By the time he had reached the house, he had decided he wouldn't interrupt Charlie's work. There wasn't time to talk about Judy. Charlie would question him in his approving, loving way; he wasn't sure he was ready yet with quick answers.

The house was quiet. The children would be down swimming. He had his story ready for Martha, but after he had tossed some toilet articles and a change of clothing into an overnight bag he decided there was no need to go look for her. She was probably swimming too. He wrote a quick note for Charlie and left it on their bed:

Love—Rushing. Taking advantage of Judy's yacht to try to spring Costa. They've taken him to Piraeus. Sid knows the whole story. Also helping Judy with Raoul's business heavily mixed with pleasure. Back tomorrow or next day.

I love you.

Circling the port once more he saw that Sid's table was filling out with familiar faces, but George and Sarah were not among them, so he didn't stop. At the boat, he found the motors running, a sailor performing nautical chores forward, and the captain at the wheel. A steward in a white jacket asked if he wanted a drink. He inquired for Judy and was told she was below.

He turned away absentmindedly without ordering anything and restlessly paced the deck. The throb of the motors under his feet, the sense of being catapulted into adventure that leaving port on a small boat always gave him, contributed to his awareness that he was committing himself more positively to the unknown. He had told himself that he had to hurry in order not to give himself time to think; he knew that he hadn't wanted to see Charlie at the house, that he wanted to keep his feelings for Judy intact, undissipated by sharing. For the first time in years he was allowing another person to divert the inner flow of his attention from Charlie. He didn't like it, even if Charlie didn't care. He wished impatiently for Judy to come and make him feel that he really wanted to do what he was doing.

In a few minutes, she joined him, and the look they exchanged did much to still his conscience. They sat together on the covered deck and ordered beer as preparations for departure continued.

"How marvelous we're chasing Mike together," she said. "That *is* what we're doing, isn't it—going to look for Mike?"

"That, and trying to straighten out the island idiocy."

"I'm a bit confused about that. The lovely thing is that it all seems to fit together."

"Like us."

"Yes. I adored ordering lunch for us just now. It gave me a lovely little feeling of keeping house for you. If I spend another day with you, I'll turn into a nice normal little housewife."

"We're certainly going to have another day together. Am I going to be stuck with a normal little housewife?"

There was an earthy note in her laughter that hadn't been there yesterday. "I don't think even you could turn me into much of a housewife. There's something missing in me. I found out a great deal about myself last night."

Their eyes flew to each other at the reference, brimming with scores of intimacies and ecstasies, and then a light of humor came up in Judy's, and they simultaneously burst into laughter. To Peter, it was exonerating laughter. It cleared the air. Whatever was happening to them, they hadn't got in too deep.

"Aren't you going to tell me?" he asked.

"Tell you what?" Her eyes were sparkling.

"What you found out."

"Of course. But not yet. Not now. I have to make sure I know how to say it."

The look she gave him was intriguing but reassuring. He watched the gangplank being brought aboard with a deep sense of relief. Once they were on their way, so that he would have no choice between being here or with Charlie, he was sure it would seem more right to enjoy himself.

After all, he wasn't just dashing off for pleasure. It was important for him to see Jeff, he was determined to extricate Costa, and he might even do Tim a good turn. Judy made it fun, but he had a serious purpose.

The stern lines were clear now, and they were moving out on the anchor chain. He took a last quick, less guilty look up at the house. This was a business trip, really. It wasn't the first time he had left them here to go off on a business trip. He would be back tomorrow or the day after.

The rattle of chain ceased. The bow swung around to the harbor's entrance. The motors became a muted roar under them, and they were off. Their eyes sought each other again, and they laughed with the simple pleasure of being together.

George Leighton woke up in a strange room. In a strange bed. With strange bedfellows. He awoke with a sudden rush into consciousness and struggled upright as he became aware of the unfamiliarity of all his surroundings. The first thing his mind registered was that he was still wearing a shirt and trousers and that two naked girls were asleep in the bed with him. One of them was Lena, Joe Peterson's girl. This was as much as his senses could encompass for a moment.

His head pounded, his stomach heaved, he almost dropped back onto the bed again, but his eye was caught by the bed on the other side of the room. It contained a trio of reverse sexual composition— Joe and the pretty German boy and one girl, all naked. Fragments of the evening before began to fall into place. His mind collided into the scene with Sarah, his heart leaped up in panic, and he struggled to his feet. Bodies on both sides of the room shifted and snorted and whimpered and were still again. He swayed on his feet and careened a few paces across the floor.

Sarah and the earthquake and Joe's group taking him in tow. The money. That was the night before. Joe and his group and drinking himself into oblivion. Whether quickly or slowly he couldn't remember. He still had his clothes on. He fumbled for his fly and found it closed. Still celibate?

His head swung heavily about as he tried to find a way out of the unknown room. He saw a staircase opening in the floor and made uneven progress toward it, trying to make as little noise as possible. He felt on the edge of physical collapse, as if his body could never be put right again, but there was a deadness or tranquillity in him that made this awakening less daunting than any he could remember for a long time.

When he reached it, the staircase looked perilously steep, but he picked his way down it without mishap. The house was a primitive island dwelling with a kitchen but no sign of a bathroom. He went out into a courtyard and relieved himself of last night's drink. He saw that the sun was oddly high in the sky.

He returned to the kitchen, which was crowded with dirty dishes, and doused his head under the spigot affixed to a small tank hanging on the wall over a table bearing a basin. He began to feel as if he might recover, but only after several days' total rest.

His ears picked up the sound of loud ticking, and he realized that there must be a clock somewhere. He followed the sound and found a dented old alarm clock on a cupboard shelf. Its hands pointed at one-twenty. It had to be wrong.

Yesterday's unpleasantness with the police had reassembled itself in his mind. He remembered asserting airily that he wouldn't allow Costa to be victimized. He and Joe had been due to go to the police first thing this morning. The hell with Sarah. The hell with Mike (had he kept a check Mike had given him?), but he hadn't conceded defeat on all fronts. Costa was still his responsibility.

He found a fragment of mirror hanging on the wall and ducked down to look at himself. He was shocked, almost indignant to see how much his recuperative powers had already accomplished. He looked quite presentable except for his sprouting whiskers. His clothes were dirty and rumpled, but there was nothing to be done about that.

He had to see the police chief immediately. It was doubtless later than it should be, but it couldn't be afternoon. He ran his fingers through his hair, hitched up his trousers, and found he could manage his body as he went out again through the courtyard.

He got his bearings and realized where he was. The house was quite low in the amphitheater of the town. A maze of narrow streets separated him from the police station. It was so much cooler than yesterday that he found he could walk quite briskly without working up more than a light sweat.

Nearing his destination, he came out onto a small square shaded by great spreading umbrella pines on which was a tavern much favored by the local population. He started across it and caught sight of the police chief among the scattering of somnolent drinkers. He was sitting at a table alone and very upright, his military cap in place, in front of a glass of ouzo. George altered course and approached him. When he saw him, the captain rose slightly with a crisp bow and indicated the chair beside him.

"Ah, Mr. Yorgo. I had expected to see you earlier. Will you join me?"

George seated himself. "I was just on my way to see you now."

"At this hour? Surely even a poor policeman may have time for his lunch."

"The clock at home must be slow again," George said hastily. So it *was* after one.

"What may I offer you?"

"A beer might be a good idea."

The captain snapped his fingers and issued orders. "You joined in the celebration last night?" The captain's sharp little eyes flickered over George's untidy clothes.

"I had something to celebrate. I was sitting right under the bell tower when it went." Was that worth celebrating? If it had fallen on him, he wouldn't have had to face today, homeless because he couldn't go where Sarah was, poorer by the loss of a friend, washed up.

185

"The whole island had reason to celebrate. No one was seriously injured. Only minor damage. I believe the clock tower was the most serious. We were lucky."

George took a thirsty swallow of the beer that had been put in front of him. His head reeled slightly, and then he felt everything inside him settling into place. "And what about my money? Any luck there?"

"Ah, no. I am sorry. So far, we have failed. Costa is very stubborn. My men tried many forms of persuasion, but he would tell nothing."

"In that case, he's innocent. You'll have to let him go."

"Let him go?" The captain's stare dismissed the suggestion. "We sent him to Piraeus on the morning boat."

George leaned forward. "What does that mean?"

"It is normal routine. He will wait for four or five months in a very uncomfortable prison until his case is heard. He has a record. With Mr. Peterson's accusation, he will certainly get a year. How much more because of your—suspicions, it is hard to say."

"Without any evidence?" George objected.

"With stolen money, what evidence can we expect to find? Do you think Costa will go around with sixty thousand drachmas in his pocket?"

George was momentarily silenced, his disgust with himself reviving as he was presented with the result of his failure of nerve. His protests yesterday seemed feeble in retrospect; his behavior seemed completely foreign to the way he was used to conducting himself. Wreck a man's life for the sake of two thousand dollars? He must have been out of his mind. He drained off his beer and sat back with decision. "Very well. I'll have to go to Piraeus too. I'll find the best lawyer in Athens. I'm going to get Costa out."

"As you wish. You are a philosopher, Mr. Yorgo. Such matters are not for a policeman. I do my job as best I can. To me, Costa is a troublemaker. If he has a few small bruises, can I allow him to display them and claim the police gave them to him? No, no, no. You want quite rightly your money back. I do what is required to get it. With what result? I arrest Dimitri because Costa accuses him of peddling the dope. I search the bar. Nothing. Costa makes a fool of me. He gives me a list of Dimitri's customers because people who want dope will steal for it. Am I to lock up all your foreign colony? No, no, no. I will catch the source. If it's Dimitri, I will catch him soon. No fear. But dope is a serious matter. Costa takes his story with him. We will have special—do you say narcotics?—yes, special narcotics police here spying on everybody. You hear him put blame on your son with his story of passing money to Dimitri. You want to free such a man? Forget your philosophy, Mr. Yorgo. Leave Costa to me."

"I can't. I'm responsible for him." He had seen how Joe lived. His certainty about Costa's guilt was an absurdity. Anybody could have picked up his thousand-drachma note without even wondering whose it was. "I can't sit back and see him taken off for months for something he probably didn't do."

The uniform crackled ominously as the captain took a sip of his drink. "You were sure yesterday that he did do it. Why did you sign that paper? You weren't forced."

"I lost my head. You made it almost impossible for me not to. You're good at your job, Captain." He was almost glad that Costa's difficulties hadn't been resolved. It gave him a cause. His stiffening determination to free the Greek made him feel that, at least until he had succeeded, life might still be worth living. His memory of the talk with Jeff and Dimitri was a bit fuzzy, but he had the impression that it had ended on a note of friendly understanding. If he could free Costa, if he could establish a link with Jeff as he moved into adulthood, there was still hope for decency and integrity. He was glad for anything to divert his thoughts from Sarah.

The captain was smiling with self-satisfaction. "You have noticed how you signed even when you were maybe a little unwilling? I have pride in my work. I tell you, it would be not convenient in the performance of my duty to have Costa back at this time. He would make it look as if I had made an error. Get him a lawyer if you wish. He has the right to one. Then drop it."

"You mean, you don't think a lawyer could do anything for him? All right. I have important friends in Athens. We'll see what they can do."

The captain put his glass down with a little bang. His uniform seemed to fill out dangerously. "Again your influential friends? If you mean to interfere, I must warn you. Your permit will expire in five—six weeks? I have the authority to refuse to renew it. The foreigners are welcome so long as they remain with their own affairs. You may do as you like, but don't fool yourself about the consequences."

"You mean, you'd have me expelled?" It was George's turn to stare incredulously. "On what grounds?"

"Grounds can always be found, Mr. Yorgo."

"You'll get yourself some headlines if you try it." The more obstacles that were put in his way, the more value attached to his cause. If his very existence here were jeopardized, the fight became a major challenge.

"Headlines are quickly forgotten," the police chief said. "But come. I am neglecting my duties as a host." He snapped his fingers again. More beer and ouzo were put before them. "I was surprised you didn't appear this morning to say good-bye to your son."

"Good-bye to my son?"

"That's not correct? You don't say good-bye to one who is leaving?"

"Yes, indeed. But who's leaving?"

"Your son and Mr. Cochran, of course. We arranged for Mr. Cochran—" The captain stopped, doubtless startled by the look of consternation in George's face. "But surely you knew. You will not tell me that Mr. Cochran took your son—"

"No, no. Of course not." With an effort, George got himself under control. He took a swallow of beer while he tried to organize his thoughts. "I was thinking about something else. Yes. My wife—"

"I thought it a wise decision. He will be well with your friend, Mr. Cochran. He and Dimitri were—" The captain hunched his shoulders and tilted his hand back and forth, suggesting ambiguity, a lack of balance.

"I had a talk with them last night," George heard himself saying, while incoherent questions tumbled wildly through his head.

"Ah, yes. Confidentially, when my men went to arrest Dimitri, they found him in bed with your son committing an unnatural act. We all do many things when we are young that mean little in later life, but it is well perhaps for him to be with your distinguished friend now."

George remembered his parting threat to Mike, something about not trying any funny business with the boy. Had Mike taken Jeff off simply as a final taunt? Sarah, with her suspicions, would never have permitted it. If she were right, if Mike had set out to seduce a romantic and susceptible boy, nothing he could do would be sufficient punishment for the crime. "It all came up rather suddenly," he said carefully, hoping not to further betray his ignorance. "I had expected Mr. Cochran to take the afternoon boat."

"Of course, but when your son explained to me that Mr. Cochran was eager to be away, we naturally attended to it. They were to catch a plane to the states, is that not so?"

"Yes, a plane to the States," George repeated. In his mind he was replaying the scene with the boy yesterday afternoon. Jeff had made it clear that he hated life here. Perhaps the banning of the bar had been the final straw. Perhaps he had sought Mike out and asked to go with him. Perhaps he had said things that had made Mike agree as a discreet act of friendship. In all fairness to Mike, it was a possibility. He could hope that that was the way it had been.

He drank his beer and made the necessary replies to the captain's remarks. Courtesy required that he stay a few more minutes. When he indicated that it was time for him to go, the captain gave him a portentous look.

"Don't forget what I have told you, Mr. Yorgo. These are not idle threats. I prefer to direct events here in my own way. It is for the best of the many. I do not permit interference."

"I'm going to look into it. I have to do what my conscience dictates. Thanks for making your position clear."

They nodded to each other, and George rose and left. He crossed the square purposefully, but as soon as he was out of sight, his pace slowed. Out of the chaos of thoughts and feelings in him, he singled out his indifference to the captain's final warning as a guarantee that his principles couldn't be shaken. Justice was justice. His commitment to it was unwavering.

Admirable, unless it was based on an inability to believe that it could happen to him. Countries didn't expel the George Leightons of this world; he had a whole cultural apparatus behind him. If he could be expelled, he had deceived himself about all the foundations on which his life and work were built, and Mike Cochran was right.

Mike Cochran. He mustn't admit his suspicions about Mike; he couldn't permit himself to imagine Mike finding pleasure in his son's body, or all his purpose would be swept away in mindless rage. Their old intimacy would forbid it; it would be incest of an inexpressibly obscene nature. He and Mike had loved each other deeply, so deeply that it had always hovered on the verge of some physical expression. At the time, he would have been indignant at the suggestion of homosexuality, but with the passage of years, understanding and tolerance of himself as well as others had opened his eyes to the fact that only the slightest alteration in the chemistry of either of them could have turned it into sexual passion.

In that sense, his son was their son, and no matter how depraved or perverse, Mike would be as incapable as he himself of having a physical relationship with the boy. No, Jeff had seen in him a godsend and had talked him into giving him the trip. After all, he was due to leave in a few weeks anyway. As for Dimitri, if that was the way Jeff was going to go, better for him to be where his choice wouldn't be limited to bar boys. He couldn't be deeply concerned about the "unnatural." He could think of no act of which the body was capable that could reasonably be deemed "unnatural."

Sarah would know the details of the boy's departure, but he couldn't speak to her. Not yet. Perhaps Jeff had left him a letter of explanation. If not, he knew several trusted friends who could check up on him in New York or Hollywood or Cambridge or wherever he ended up.

He came to a street that led down to the port and hesitated but went on. Everybody would be heading home for lunch by now. Since he was powerless to pursue Jeff and was uncertain whether he should even if he could, Costa remained his first immediate responsibility. He was shocked by his ignorance of the country's legal system. He would have to go to Athens and find out. There were a number of people he could go to for guidance. But to go to Athens involved going to the house, and he couldn't imagine any confrontation with Sarah that wouldn't leave him permanently crippled and incapable of action. Perhaps only expulsion from the country would force an awareness on him of how finally and completely and thoroughly his life here had run its course.

He came to a street that led back and up and would eventually, in a roundabout way, take him past his house. He turned into it and started climbing. He might try to sneak in without seeing Sarah. Or perhaps she was off being consoled by Pavlo. An image of the naked girl he had been sleeping beside passed through his mind. He remembered that she had been very sweet and willing up until the time he remembered nothing. Peterson's girl. Lena.

He would have to borrow some money for the trip to Athens. He thought of Mike's check again. He felt his pockets and found nothing but an almost empty pack of cigarettes. He remembered suddenly that he had torn up the check sometime during the evening. He remembered the bits fluttering away behind him. Money from Peter. Clothes and passport from the house.

Lena's long seductive body crossed his mind's eye again. It was too late to catch the afternoon boat. He wouldn't be able to get away until tomorrow morning. The police chief wasn't likely to put special transportation at his disposition. If life had to be rebuilt from the beginning, a body was as good a start as any. Forget for a moment the big experiences, the big aspirations and passions and commitments. Were people incapable of bearing happiness? Had life been too good? Had Sarah's impulse to destroy felicity been a normal and inevitable one? Begin all over again with a body. Lena's was a lovely one.

At the next juncture of small stepped streets, he altered his course once more and headed across on the level for Joe Peterson's house.

Charlie was dissatisfied with his afternoon's work. He put down his brushes and took a turn around the studio, stroking his naked chest as he paused in front of the half-dozen unfinished canvases propped up here and there, trying to redefine his intentions in each. Their cool mathematical elegance, which had won him considerable fame, stirred a curious uneasiness in him. Were they as dead as they seemed to him now?

He had been restless ever since he had found Peter's note on the bed before lunch. A sudden crisis had apparently arisen, but he couldn't adjust to this unexpected departure. He was glad Peter was having fun with the girl, but their being off on the yacht together changed it somehow, cut him off more completely than he found easy to accept.

Martha had returned from the port late for lunch bearing strange tales of arrests and additional departures. Jeff and Mike Cochran. Jeff and George's money. Apparently Peter was to play some part in untangling the snarl. Jeff was gone, and Peter had gone after him.

The thought nagged at him all afternoon. Peter was with the girl, he repeatedly reminded himself. Jeff was with Mike. If they saw each other it would be only about the money business. Or perhaps Martha had got it wrong. Perhaps Jeff hadn't gone off with Mike in the way everybody was assuming, but was fleeing justice in his overwrought way and would be sent back by Peter. Since they were all traveling on yachts or under police auspices, anybody could turn up at any time, independently of the regular boats. He would go down and find out what was going on as soon as he was finished for the day.

He returned to his brushes and cleaned them carefully. It was early to quit, but his concentration was broken. He crossed terraces and courtyards and went to his room to shower. Drying himself, he stood in front of the full-length mirror and checked his body critically. Bearing up. *And there was that,* he thought wryly as he dropped his eyes down to the base of his flat abdomen. After a good toweling, it was startlingly conspicuous, exaggerated aesthetically, throwing the lines of his body out of balance. Monumental. It was the reason why parading naked in front of somebody seemed to him very nearly a sexual act. Considering the attention it had always commanded, it was surprising that he had been able to discipline it so easily into assuming the relatively minor role it now played. Ridiculous what power this length of flesh had wielded—over himself and others. Peter was still fascinated by it and would still gladly offer his body to its demands, but his craving for it had been broken, and he wouldn't do him the disservice of subjecting him to its tyranny again. After the years of taking, it was a joy to be able to give himself for Peter's satisfaction. A joy, and so much safer. At times, he was filled with a wild urge, directed at nobody in particular nor toward any particular act, to give full rein to the extraordinary instrument, to let it rage through life as it had once done. The fire was not completely extinguished.

He looked at it in the mirror, long and jutting massively after the toweling, an entity that seemed somehow separate from himself, the adversary identified in his mind with the baseless sense of superiority that had been bred in him in his youth. *Rather a waste to keep it so thoroughly under wraps,* he thought wryly, *but that is the way it is.* He moved a hand to it, startled as usual at what a handful it was, and gave it a few long strokes, watching it lengthen, swell, stiffen with the reinforcement of blood. That was all it was—a flexible vessel filled and stretched to capacity with blood until it was forced to stand upright. Ridiculous.

He dressed in well-cut, closely fitting linen slacks and a pale blue sports shirt that showed off his deeply bronzed body to advantage, taking more trouble with his appearance than he generally did, feeling like showing off a bit in spite of himself. He heard the children clattering about somewhere in the house, and his private smile broadened. He hoped Peter would come back tomorrow. The children missed him almost as much as their senior daddy did.

He went down through the house to Martha's quarters and found her just emerging from the bath in a peignoir, looking sweetly plump and dewy. Her eyes lighted as he entered.

"My. Aren't we looking gorgeous this evening," she greeted.

"Hi, honey. How about going down to the port for a drink? I feel like a stroll and a gossip."

"Oh, darling, do you mind going without me? I promised the children I'd read to them. I'm luxuriating in the house now that that ghastly heat has broken."

"That's all right. Mostly, I wanted to talk to Sid."

"Do. You've been working too hard. Thanks for asking me, sir."

He laughed and approached her from behind where she had seated herself at her dressing table. He leaned over and kissed the top of her blonde head. She held his big hands and dropped her head back briefly against him. He gave her hands a squeeze. "I won't be long. There might be some new developments."

In the old days, at the start of Peter's business trips, he had always been slightly self-conscious with her, sensing in her a suppressed keyed-up anticipation that corresponded to nothing he felt in himself, but it was a phase that had passed. She might still want him to make love to her, but it no longer seemed a great need. Perhaps they would get together tonight. It was probably the break in the heat that was making him feel sexy. He wished Peter were here.

He dropped her hands and turned from her. "See you in an hour or so."

He found the port looking oddly deserted. A few men, young and old, were scattered around the tables in front of the cafés. The only females in sight were at Lambraiki's, where the big table was only half-occupied. *Everybody recovering from the earthquake?* He saw that Sid was there and the Varnums and the nice writer-painter male couple and Sarah without George. He was greeted with an enthusiasm that made him feel like the fellow survivor of shipwreck. He started to sit with Sarah, his best friend on the island, but he didn't know how much she knew about Jeff and decided he'd better be briefed by Sid. By the time he had pulled up a chair beside him, half a dozen conversations had been resumed.

"You're just the man I wanted to see, friend." Sid kept his voice down and muted his usual theatrical extravagance so that, although they were surrounded by people, he achieved the effect of privacy. "Did you know Dimitri has been let out?"

"Martha said she'd heard he was going to be."

"In the clear—for the moment. Now, get this." Sid lowered his voice still further. "It wasn't easy, but I've made him promise to give the money back in the morning. I'll take it to George, no questions asked, until we find out what story Peter has fixed with Jeff."

"At least that's cleared up. I wish Peter knew. It would make it easier for him to spring Costa."

"He'll probably find out from the police up there. George will make sure they're informed."

"Where *is* George?"

"Haven't you heard? He's shacked up with Joe's bunch and won't come out. I'm going to go see him in a little while and give him the word. Good old George. He's broken out at last."

"For Christ's sake. How's Sarah taking all this?"

Sid seemed to vibrate with inner glee. His bold Semitic head bobbed closer. "She's being noble and long-suffering. We haven't told her where the money went. Part of their house fell down last night."

"Oh, great." Charlie was distressed for both of them, but his sympathy was tempered by impatience. He found it difficult to understand why intelligent adults couldn't come to terms with their problems as long as there was love between them. "Does she know about Jeff? I mean, is Cochran definitely for boys? Is that what that's all about?"

"Oh, man. Even *I* saw that. I think Jeff has really fallen for him, but I haven't mentioned sex to Sarah. Jeff asked me not to."

Laughter broke out around them. Charlie stole a glance at Sarah. She was sitting slightly withdrawn, a brave little smile playing across her lovely face, but there was something crushed in the way she sat, and her eyes were liquid with the suggestion of tears. "Well. Maybe I'd better try to break it to her gently. Just as a possibility. Peter's going to have his hands full in Athens."

"He was looking great today. What a guy. And that broad. You guys have all the fun. Things were really humming between them. You know what? I think I ought to broaden my experience. Take Jeff, for instance. I could almost have had a thing about him. His mouth is like a goddamn jewel. I want to take it and wear it like an ornament. Hey, how's that for queer? My big problem is, guys don't seem to go for me."

"Maybe wearing Jeff's mouth will help."

Sid roared with laughter. Charlie smiled and wondered. Humming? It was an apt description of Peter's euphoric high spirits, but he had never thought of him being like that with a girl. It wasn't like him to go off without making contact, touching hands, reaffirming their interdependence. Should he go to Athens too? It was important for Peter to be up to date on developments. He didn't want to look as if he were interfering with Judy, but he was as anxious as Peter to help Costa. Telephoning was out of the question; it took the better part of the day. Peter had said he might come back tomorrow; it would be stupid for them to cross. He didn't want it to break into his work. No, Peter could handle it.

He took the glass and the little pot of ouzo that had been brought to him and carried them around the table to Sarah. She looked up at him with welcome as he pulled a chair up behind her. She turned in her chair to face him, cutting them off from the others.

"It looks as if the earthquake has shaken us all up," he said.

"Dear Charlie. I've been longing to talk to you. You've heard about Jeff? Can you imagine anybody doing such a thing—abducting a boy who's little more than a child?"

"There may be some reasonable explanation. He didn't leave any word?"

"Jeff? Just through Sid that we weren't to worry and that he'd be at Harvard on time. I know George had a talk with him yesterday. Maybe he said something tactless. I'm sure Mike leaped at the chance to take him. I spotted what he was after immediately, but that part of it doesn't really worry me. Jeff has seen it going on all around him and has never shown the slightest interest. The thought of Mike putting a hand on him makes me quite sick, but Jeff wouldn't allow anything to happen. Have you ever seen the faintest sign that he might develop in that way?"

"Well, is the idea so loathsome to you? Frankly, yes. I've always had the feeling he might."

"Why? How could you?" Her eyes were more wounded than reproachful. "He's always been so manly and clean and straight."

Charlie smiled slightly and held her eyes for a beat or two longer than necessary. "What does that make me, the opposite of all those things?"

"Oh, darling, I'm not talking about you. You and Peter are different. You have Martha and the children."

Charlie's smile broadened. "The children? In the beginning, I thought of them as just one more way of making sure Peter wouldn't stray. Lots of queers have wives and children, if that's all you're worried about."

"Yes, but Mike!"

"I don't know him, but stop thinking of him as a seducer of children. Jeff's old enough to know what he wants. Eighteen-year-old boys aren't turned queer by older men making passes at them. Quite the contrary. You may be right. There may be nothing at all going on between them, but if you don't want to lose Jeff entirely, you've got to accept the fact that he might find happiness in ways that could seem odd or even distasteful to you." He paused, and his smoky purple eyes darkened. "I wish somebody had dropped that thought into the heads of some of my female relatives when I was his age."

Sarah put her hand out impulsively and took his. Her eyes swam with sympathy. "Darling Charlie. If that's the way he turns out, I'll try. Just, pray God, not Mike."

"I'd probably go along with you there. The age difference is too great, for one thing. What's all this about George?"

She drew back and folded her hands in her lap, bending her head over them. "It couldn't be worse, but for some reason I feel more hopeful than I have for a long time. It's all out in the open at last. We had the most frightful scene last night. He said things I thought he could never say. Ugly. Cruel. He's apparently off on a binge now. When it's over, perhaps we'll be able to talk to each other again. At least he didn't leave. That's what I was terrified of."

"George? Walk out on you? He couldn't possibly."

She lifted tear-filled eyes to him. "It's so difficult to live with a man with strict ideals. He can't understand that others can't always live up to them. Haven't you ever been tempted? You know what I mean."

He hesitated, arranging the facts to fit the meaning of her words. "No. Not really. I haven't let myself be. Are you talking about Pavlo?"

She dropped her eyes and nodded. "George can't possibly know. I just can't believe I'm so much worse than other people. What about Peter? *Did* the children keep him from straying?"

"With boys?"

The subject obviously flustered her. "No, of course not. But there was a girl who came here—"

"I know about the girls," he interrupted. "They're part of the contract. I know people are naturally promiscuous, men probably more than women. I thought I couldn't stand living with it, but things work out. I can understand what George has been going through since—"

"He's made me suffer enough for that," she interjected.

"When it happened with Peter—with a boy—I thought I could never make him suffer enough. I tore our lives apart and very nearly killed myself into the bargain. That's when Martha and having the children came into it. I thought having a family would hold us together if the rest of it grew stale with time. George maybe loves less selfishly than I do. I don't think he's wanted to make you suffer. If he had, he would've fought back the way I did. He's taken all the suffering into himself. You've got to find a way to take it from him. Making eyes at Pavlo isn't the answer."

Her eyes darted up to his and dropped again. Her mouth moved. "No," she murmured. "That's finished." She took a deep breath that lifted her breasts and faced him squarely. "You've told me something amazing. I'll have to think about it before I see exactly what it

196

means. You're a wonderful person."

Charlie made a little grimace and looked away. "I've looked at myself a lot over the years. There's nothing very wonderful there." He felt the coldness hidden away deep within him. Peter was off "humming" with his beautiful girl, and he didn't really mind. For some reason, his indifference made his throat ache. He swallowed. "No matter what we learn, it doesn't seem to change us much. What it does do is make it possible to act out what we know is right. I try to put on a good act. I don't mean being in love, loving the family—all that isn't an act. I think all the civilized, ordered things we bring into our lives—that's where the act begins. We remain children in lots of ways, bawling our heads off. 'Gimme this. I want that.' Not very dignified." He watched a hot rosy glow suffuse the houses strung out along the eastern promontory. A silence fell over the assembly as fire sprang up in all the windows. For an instant, every element of rock and wall and tree was sheathed in light and defined with three-dimensional precision. The fire was extinguished, and the glow began to fade. The sun had set.

Everybody began to talk at once. Charlie turned back to Sarah. "You really shouldn't worry about Jeff. When Peter gets back, he'll probably be able to tell you all about it. Why don't you have Kate stay on with her friend in Athens? Have the house to yourselves for a bit. Make George stop drinking so much. You're both too intelligent not to work things out."

"I don't quite see what I can do about his drinking if he stays with his alcoholic theologian."

He had always admired her style. There was an astringency in her that cut through the facade of otherworldly nobility she liked to present to the world. He looked into her wide expressive eyes and was briefly reminded of her son. "Something must've brought on this new twist. You say he can't possibly know. There *is* something he might have found out?"

"I can't explain it all. I hope you can understand. Yes. Yesterday afternoon. He was with Mike the whole time. I had to get it out of my system."

Charlie's expression hardened. "I've heard that line before. Christ, Sarah. I don't know what to say. There're certain things we *can't* get out of our systems, but we sure as hell can tie them down, strangle them, even if it means killing something in ourselves. I know you've asked him to forgive you for the other time. You can't go on asking to be forgiven. Make love to him. Make him make love to you. It may sound sort of clinical and calculated, but sometimes it's the only way to get through."

"If you only knew how much I've longed for it. Why do you think yesterday happened?"

They exchanged a look that, in its recognition of carnality, was as basic as desire. Charlie's lips twitched with a smile. "Get in there and pitch, baby. Stop acting the model wife and mother. Tear his pants off. Give him everything in the book. You know how to stir a man up as well as I do."

Their laughter was faintly tremulous with the knowledge they had shared.

"Can you imagine anybody tearing George's pants off?" she asked. "Where is this unlikely scene supposed to take place, since he won't come home?"

"If he isn't home by tomorrow, I'll go try to reason with him. Peter wouldn't have any trouble at all."

"Don't underestimate yourself. He admires you enormously. Thank you, darling. You're a great help. I'll remember everything you've said."

They allowed themselves to be drawn into the group. Charlie stayed on until it was almost time for the children's supper. His restlessness had passed; Sarah had reminded him that he and Peter had got beyond the petty conflicts that plagued most people.

He laughed and chatted with the children while they ate. He received Peter's share of kisses when they were being sent off to bed. Little Pete clung to his neck and demanded clamorously, "Daddy, when is Daddy coming home?" as if the child sensed their shared need of his father. He assured the child that this wasn't to be a long trip, and the children where herded off by the young Greek girl who took care of them.

Because they were alone, Martha had Kyria Tula set up a small table on the colonnaded loggia for their dinner. Charlie had a few more ouzos before they ate. Peter had trained Kyria Tula in more sophisticated cooking than that generally known on the island, and they had an excellent meal while they gossiped about the gossip gleaned by Charlie at the port. They spoke about Jeff in a way he hadn't felt free to do with Sarah, and they agreed that he might be better off with Mike than he would have been if his infatuation with Dimitri had developed.

They left the table and moved for coffee to comfortable chairs at the outer edge of the loggia so that a vast panorama of star-filled sky and still sea was opened out to them. Charlie carried a bottle of wine with him.

"I'm glad you've finally had a serious talk with Sarah," Martha said. "You think it's definitely over with Pavlo?"

"Oh, yes, but that's not much help if George has the slightest suspicion."

"Can't you go find him and tell him he's wrong? She's not likely to've done anything so stupid that he can be sure."

"Oh, I'll go talk to him, but Peter would be more effective. I wonder. Peter'll probably see Jeff this evening sometime. They're all bound to find each other at the Grande Bretagne. Then he's got to stir the police into action. The way things work in Athens, he can't possibly do anything for Costa in less than a day. Plus whatever this Bertin business is. I don't see how he can be back before day after tomorrow."

"If then," Martha said.

"If then?" he repeated. "He said day after tomorrow at the latest."

"Leave him." Martha sat back, and her body seemed to go slack as if she had performed a heavy chore. She smiled across at him. "You know what I'm talking about."

Charlie stared at her. He felt the cold steel in his soul. He prayed that she wouldn't say what she seemed to mean. "I haven't a clue," he said.

"Oh, darling." Her laugh was gay and playful. "You certainly saw it happening last night. I've been expecting it for years. He's fallen in love with her."

Charlie sprang from his chair, took a turn around the furniture, and ended up back at his chair, pouring a glass of wine with hands that trembled slightly. He swallowed half of it in a gulp and felt calm restored. She had said the words, and they were completely meaningless. "If you really think that, I don't quite see what there is to laugh about," he said reasonably.

"They were so sweet together. It makes me laugh just thinking about them." A dangerous subject, but he seemed in a peaceful mood tonight, and she wanted to prepare him for something he would try to avoid seeing for himself. She had never known Peter the way he had been last night. Even in his devotion to Charlie she had never felt in him quite the same electrifying quality. It was doubtless the way he had been way back when he had met Charlie— absurdly young, ardent, aflame. Thinking of him fondly, she said, "Peter really is delicious. And Judy. Her eyes were glued to him the entire evening. She's fallen for him completely."

"I told him so myself." He dismissed Judy with another long swallow of wine and refilled his glass.

"It's mutual. Don't worry. I wouldn't have had to know Peter for ten years to recognize all the signs. He's in love. That's why I say 'leave him.' Give them time to work it out between themselves. Jeff, Costa, Mike Cochran, and those pictures—they're just excuses for them to get away alone. Maybe he'll work out some way to include her in the ménage."

"What ménage? Don't be ridiculous." Danger showed through his flat delivery. "Do you think I could live with him if he were in love with somebody else?"

"Don't say that, darling. We've adapted in the past. We accepted a challenge very few people could have managed. We mustn't lose our flexibility now. Peter finding a girl of his own was to be expected from the beginning."

"Why? Because he's discovered it's fun to go to bed with one occasionally? That has nothing to do with what he really is. Do you suppose I wouldn't know it quicker than you? We had a talk together while she was here, you know. If you told me he'd fallen in love with—Jeff, for God's sake—I might take you a little more seriously."

"Then you admit you noticed something different about him last night," she said, still smiling and relaxed and comfortable.

"I don't admit anything of the sort." Humming? Running off without coming to speak to him? That in itself proved that nothing was different. If he were going through some big experience, he would have felt bound to come to him. He gripped his glass so hard that he became aware he risked breaking it. Things were happening inside him that he had sworn he would never allow to happen again. *He isn't with a boy,* he reminded himself. "I wish you'd tell me where you've got this idiotic idea." He had expected to hear violence in his voice, but his controls were working so well that it sounded only mildly petulant.

"But darling, it was so obvious. I tell you. I could see it. You must've seen it too."

"Stop saying that," he shouted. He seized the wine bottle and hurled it across the outdoor living room. It smashed against the wall, and a dark stain spread out over the immaculate whitewash. He dropped into the chair and gripped its arms.

"Oh, darling." Martha rose and hurried to him. She moved in close to him and tried to put an arm around him. He leaped up, pushing her aside roughly, and almost knocked her down. She recovered her balance and seated herself on the arm of the chair. "This isn't the way to take it, you know. We have the children to think about."

"The children!" He turned and faced her, trembling with anguish and rage. "If you don't know by now that he's the one who's kept it all going, you don't know anything. What would we have without him?"

"We'd have each other." All the years of making the best of the leftovers hadn't prepared her for the empty ring of her words. She had always accepted life passively, but now she was seized by unfamiliar anger at being made to feel that she had been given so little. She burst out, "Peter is a man. He's forty years old. At his age men begin to turn toward youth. Judy's perfect for him. Beautiful, intelligent, not too feminine in a tiresome way. You should be happy for him. Think what you'd be like in a few more years when the shine of youth is finally gone. Absurd—two aging men clinging to each other."

"You must be mad," he said in a strangled voice. "I'm warning you. If you say any more, you'll finish it once and for all."

"I'm not saying anything wrong," she protested defensively, incapable of sustained attack. "I've always loved you. I've been loyal and done without things that most women think are essential. It hasn't been a hardship for me. I've made the children my life. I've always loved your body when you'd let me have it. I remember you saying often enough that sex wasn't the most important part with Peter. If that ends and you find you want boys from time to time—" She lifted her shoulders slightly. "We can manage."

"You *are* mad," he said, staring at her. "Manage? How do you think *we'd* look when the shine of youth is gone? An old queen running after boys while his wife tries to cover for him with the children. Children? Do you think Peter would do anything to hurt little Petey? Haven't you understood anything all this time?"

"Perhaps I understand things you don't." The picture he presented so eliminated all care and affection between them that for a moment she floundered. She wasn't prepared for a fight, but she sensed that if she didn't fight now there would be nothing left to fight for when he discovered she was right. She said the first thing that came into her head. "You've turned yourself into a woman in your efforts to hold him. It's an insult to your manhood."

He sprang at her and slapped her hard across the face. She cried out and covered her face with her hands. "You stupid bitch," he raged. "That really does it. I could forgive you if you didn't sound glad of what you think's happened."

She lowered her hands and looked up at him. She was crying silently, and her voice strained against tears. "I am. I'm glad for Peter because I love him. I'm glad for you, even though you don't seem to think that means much. We'll be all right. I know my love for you."

"Whatever made you think I needed that? I've always been honest with you. I won't stop now. Peter and I have considered you and tried to make things good for you. *Peter* and *I*. That's where it begins and ends. Do you understand that?"

"I don't care what you say. Poor darling. I know it's hard for you to believe that Peter needs a life of his own. It needn't change anything very much. We'll work it all out together."

"Work it out?" Charlie roared. "Peter hasn't found somebody else and never will. Two aging men clinging to each other? What's absurd about that? It's heroic. It's as moving as the survival of anything beautiful. Don't ever laugh again at something that's too big and deep for you to know anything about."

She folded her arms over her breast and bowed her head. As she had expected, she felt none of the elation she would once have felt at the prospect of having him a little bit more for herself. If she was right about Peter, she would do everything possible to make it as little disruptive as possible. She had goaded him only to prepare him. His violence had been spent on her, not on Peter. "I haven't laughed in the way you mean," she said. "I don't know what you think I've said."

He stood over her vanquished form, indifferent to this victory. The victory toward which all his thoughts were now turned lay in proving that she was wrong. She couldn't move him even to pity till he had done so. "I know very well what you've said," he replied curtly. "I'll go to Athens in the morning. I'll bring Peter back with me. You can count on that. Good night." He turned and left her, his legs trembling under him so that he moved jerkily. When he was out of sight, he hurried forward, having difficulty with his breathing. He couldn't face the bed he usually shared with Peter. He locked himself in Peter's study and leaned against the door, taking deep breaths to ease the constriction of his chest and stomach. Why did he do it? Why did he feel impelled to demolish her so cruelly on such slight provocation? Slight? She had sat, all smug and cheerful, predicting the end of everything he had built his life on. Only words, probably well meant. It was madness to let her make him physically sick.

The old story. No one could threaten his dominion over his loved one, no one could trespass on the painful commitments of his heart without inviting annihilation from the destructive fury of his cold self-love. He had known only one other person capable of such ruthlessness—his grandmother, whom he had adored. Gay, witty, stylish, passionately responsive to life, with the core of steel he knew so well and an unerring instinct for the weaknesses of others. Having been the victim of her destructive powers, he should have been able to throw off her guiding hand. To keep him for herself, she had exploited his uncertain response to girls but had failed to calculate on the power of the love that can exist between two men. When she learned of her miscalculation, she had cast him aside as ruthlessly as she had cast aside all her failures.

She had been a Southern lady. The blood of slave owners ran in her veins. In his, too. He had put together all that he knew and had heard of her and had arrived at a portrait of himself. Man-devouring, armored, and mad. With time, he had learned to modify the likeness. He had learned that if one demands blind unquestioning submission from others, with banishment as the only alternative, banishment must inevitably follow. He had escaped from her to that extent. The latitude he permitted, had even forced on Peter was a token of some growth of wisdom.

He was aware of her still guiding him while he planned his next move. He would go to Athens in the morning. He had the excuse of Dimitri and the money so as not to appear to be intruding on Peter's privacy. If he detected the faintest possibility that Martha might be on to something, he would know how to break it off without Peter ever knowing.

Except that Martha couldn't be right. He thought of the few minutes he and Peter had had together after the earthquake. That was when he was supposed to have been already madly in love with Judy. Utter nonsense. He would go to Athens and offer to help with the Costa affair, and they would come back together the next day.

He moved erratically about the room, still feeling drained by the scene with Martha, shaken and ashamed. It was the sort of thing they had made no room for in their lives. They bickered and squabbled, particularly about the children, but there had never been conflicts that touched their three-sided relationship. He thought of going to her and telling her he was sorry, but that might lead her to expect more, and he was incapable of offering more now. He didn't want to add insult to injury. She had probably dismissed his outburst sensibly by now as being of no importance. She knew as well as he did that their lives were too fixed to permit any surprises. He went to a window and looked down at the port. Nothing there to distract him. He would sleep eventually.

"They're bound to go back to the hotel sooner or later," Peter said, smiling across the table at Judy. They were having dinner in a garden restaurant high up on the Lycabettus hill, with a view over the whole noisy little city. The Acropolis reflected moonlight palely below them, a hauntingly romantic touch they didn't need to enhance their delight with each other. Peter added, "I'm sure Jeff will call when he gets my message."

When they had checked in at the Grande Bretagne, they had learned that Jeff and Mike had come in only half an hour before them but were already out. When they had left the hotel for dinner, the playwright and his protégé had still not returned.

"You don't think Mike will get the idea that we're chasing him?"

"Why should he? When we talked to him—when was it? Only last night?" Their hands moved across the table and touched. "My goodness. Another age. *Before.* You still make it awfully hard for me to keep my mind on Mike's pictures. Anyway, he couldn't have been more open about them. Jeff must be the only reason for the sudden departure."

"I suppose. Still, the boss's cable makes me feel as if this might not be a total wild goose chase."

A telegram had been waiting for Judy from Peter's old friend, saying, "Definitely informed several Bertin pictures changed hands Athens." It had given them a fresh interest in the chase.

"We should go back to the hotel soon. If Jeff calls at a reasonable hour, I'll go see him right away. There's not going to be any great problem. If Mike had them and he bought them in good faith, we'll turn them over to the police, and that'll be that. If not—well, what can he do? It'll be a bit sticky for him if he wants to protect the seller, but we still have to call in the cops."

"Assuming he has them, what would he do if we weren't around to trip him up? Aren't there customs regulations going into the States? Wouldn't they be seized?"

"You never know with art. You're supposed to declare it, but lots of people don't. I do, but I'm in the business. If Mike wanted to smuggle them in, he wouldn't be running much of a risk. Customs don't bother VIPs."

"It sounds much easier than it ought to. I've always thought of Interpol as sending out tentacles. Mysterious encounters at night. The Casbah. That sort of thing."

"The great international art racket? It's there, but it's pretty prosaic and well organized. Not nearly as exciting as you are. Ready to go?"

Peter called for the bill, and they finished their coffee and left. He had taken adjoining rooms for them at the hotel. The Mills-Martins were well known here, and he wanted to spare the management embarrassment. The doors were thrown open between them, so they had a great deal of space at their disposal, filled with furniture of an ornate but fading grandeur. He rang for room service and when a waiter appeared within seconds, ordered a bottle of champagne. He rang Mike's suite and was told it still didn't answer. All the while, their eyes were on each other, summoning each other, affirming their possession of each other, inciting each other. The waiter returned with a bottle in an ice bucket and started to open it. Peter waved him away. The Greeks weren't safe with a champagne bottle. He had once been shot by a cork in the back of the head at six paces. It had almost knocked him out. Charlie had been there to administer first aid. Charlie. He opened the bottle, filled two glasses, and gave one to Judy.

"He lifted his glass and smiled at her over it. "It's an anniversary. We've been together a whole day."

"What a day. You're really awfully good at everything you do." She laughed as she lifted her glass to him. "Little secretaries from New York don't often get to loll about in hotel suites in Athens sipping champagne."

They drank, and he moved to her side and put his arm around her. "Little secretaries from New York don't generally look like you. If you put your mind to it, you could bathe in champagne." He kissed the side of her head.

"You give me the most outrageous ideas. I wouldn't dare tell you what I just thought of. Shall we have a summing-up?"

"Of your outrageous ideas? Definitely."

"An anniversary roundup. Things learned during a day of bliss."

"What you said earlier? What you found out last night?" He moved her around so that they were facing each other. She put a hand on his shoulder. They stood chest to breast, hip to hip, thigh to thigh. He opened his mouth, and she gave him hers. Peter planted his feet and pulled her closer, making a growling sound in his throat as their mouths parted. "Every time I kiss you I think of the first time I saw your beautiful mouth, and I can't believe it's mine. That's what *I* found out last night. I just can't believe you."

Her eyes roamed over his face. She lifted her hand and teased the hair on his forehead. "You're such a golden creature. You're feeling beautifully heterosexual again. So am I, even if I can't be so obvious about it." They laughed at the shameless responses of their bodies as they swayed lightly against each other. "We're not creating quite the right atmosphere for a summing-up. I'd better say it while I can still speak. We've been in love with each other all day—" She put her fingers on his lips as he started to speak. "We're in love with each other, after a fashion, and we've been trying to find out why it can't mean the same thing for us that it would for most people. How's that?"

"It's an attention-getter. I'll say that for it." They laughed as they released each other. He refilled their glasses and carried the tray with the ice bucket over to a grouping of furniture just inside the long open French windows that gave onto a balcony. He was grateful for the way she had stated their case, not making light of the excitement they found in each other but acknowledging some slight incompleteness in it. He had realized in the past few hours—he didn't quite know why or when—that he had been playing a game of what-might-have-been. If he had met Judy twenty years ago, would the whole course of his life have been altered? West Point, for which family tradition had prepared him before he met Charlie and chose a life with him, marriage as a young officer, a military career with a wife and children, his huge capacity for loving a man untapped and undiscovered? Judy had made him see it as a possibility; if so, he must be two people. Nearly, but not quite. It was a possibility that he couldn't think of as preferable to the course his life had actually taken.

She had touched something in him no woman ever had, and yet there was still the incompleteness, something withheld, some inadequacy. Simply because she was a female? Whatever it was, she had come very close to expressing it for him, and he held out his hand to her. They sat side by side so that they could touch if need be and looked at each other questioningly.

"Do you mind my saying we're in love?" she asked, cocking her head slightly to one side. "I think we are, in a funny sort of way. I've found out I can love a man's body. Good heavens, that's putting it mildly. If I can love yours, I suppose I could love others, yet I can't imagine this happening with anybody else. How can I be in love with you and not mind the thought of being without you?"

It was a point that had worried him. The serenity in her voice as she posed the question made him want to hug her for letting him off that hook. "I haven't wanted to think about that. The setup at home is so nutty already that I've had moments wondering about fitting you into it, but I couldn't quite see it somehow."

She shook her head and looked away. "No. Even if you were free and unattached, I wouldn't be waiting for you to propose; and if you did, I think I'd refuse. That's something else I've found out. I'm too independent and unadventurous. Even making love with you is too demanding for ordinary life. There's something peaceful about being with a woman. I don't know if there's something missing in me or if it's more positive than that, something extra added, something masculine that makes me have to dominate any situation I'm in. I can't do that with you. Talk about helpless females. We wouldn't last for long." She put a hand on his and caressed it lightly.

"You sound as if you know exactly what you're up to," he said with a hint of regret. Even though everything she said was an assurance that they had safely circumvented all the obvious hazards, he was perversely dissatisfied for it to be so neatly resolved. Integral to his male response to her was an impulse to assert and maintain his possession of her. He knew it was an impulse to be kept under control. All through the day, he had felt the twitching birth pangs of potential ties—in looks they had shared, in things she had said, in the feel of a particular part of her body, in her laughter and her intoxicating desire—ties for which there was no room in his life and that she had now calmly denied. She had revealed to him the stranger, more shadow than real, who cohabited with the self he knew; it was a part of him that would flourish for her alone and in a day or two must be excised, a small amputation as amputations went. It looked, though it had been her feelings that he had been at first concerned about, as if he were the one who might be hurt.

He responded to the pressure of her hand and lifted it to kiss it. She caressed his lips with the back of her fingers. He growled. "That's better than champagne. Have we said everything we ought to say? Is that the summing-up?"

"More or less. There's one more thing. Would you be willing to give me a baby?" The look he shot her was startled, and she laughed in her girlish way. "I'm not sure yet I want it. I think I might, but it would have to be the way I say: you giving *me* a baby. I wouldn't want it as part of any elaborate arrangement like you've created with your family. Just mine, with the assistance of that beautiful cock. After all, you weren't in love with Martha when you gave her a baby, were you?"

"No, it was Charlie's idea, and Martha agreed." Peter managed to chuckle as he refilled their glasses, though he couldn't react casually to her suggestion. "You're really something. A girl I'm in love with, even in a funny sort of way, having my baby. How do you think I'd feel?" She had made it clear, if he still had any doubts, that she was already thinking past him, rounding off the interlude to find what she could keep and use from it. Trust a female. It was enough to turn anyone queer; no man could be so cold-bloodedly realistic. A beautiful female fiend.

"I wouldn't go ahead and let it happen without your knowing," she said sensibly. "We can think about it. By the time you get home, I'll know. I'd understand your not wanting to take a chance on it. I think my family would be pleased even if it is a little bastard. They're inclined to wonder about—"

She was cut off by the ringing of the telephone. They exchanged a look, and then he jumped up and went to it.

Jeff's deep voice came on in response to his hello. "Peter? Are you really here?"

"Of course. What's the idea of going off without saying good-bye? You promised to tell me about last night, remember?"

"It was all sort of complicated. I'm sorry. What're you doing here?"

"Odds and ends. I have to see you, for one thing. Did you think I'd let you go without another glimpse of those beautiful eyes?" Peter winked at Judy. There was a rumble on the instrument that might have been brief laughter.

"Did the parents send you?"

"No, but what if they had? Don't you want to see me?"

"Of course. More than anybody I can think of. I just—"

"Is Mike there?" His and Judy's eyes held, and he shook his head at Jeff's monosyllabic negative. "Well, then, can I come see you?"

"You mean now? Here? Oh, God, yes. Please do. Can you?" The deep voice suddenly sounded tormented.

"Of course. I'll be there in two seconds." He hung up and returned to Judy, leaning over to kiss her mouth lightly. "It's perfect. He's alone. I don't think he'll mind my having a snoop around. I'll try not to be long, sweetheart."

"Don't worry about me. I'll have a wallow in the tub and go to bed. That's where I prefer being when you're around."

He gave her shoulders a little hug with his hands and hurried out. He walked down a long corridor, rose several floors in the elevator, followed another long corridor till he found the number and knocked. Jeff immediately opened the door and took his arms and pulled him in and closed it behind them. Peter gave his lips a chaste little kiss and pulled hastily away as he felt them open for more. He stood back and looked at Jeff and laughed.

"I've never seen you with so many clothes on." He was wearing a tie and a summer jacket and slacks. His angular body made the rather ill-fitting, thrown-together costume look as if it was about to fall off.

"Just some things Mike bought for me," he said with a little note of pride.

Peter observed immediately that he seemed more at ease in his body; he slouched less, and there was a slightly feminine provocation in the way he moved. He held Peter's arm again as they headed for chairs. The room was furnished as a living room with doors at each end giving into bedrooms.

"Well, this is a far cry from our stark island simplicity," he said. "You're entering into the big world in style."

"We have separate bedrooms. Mike doesn't like to sleep with anybody. Is Charlie here too?"

"No. I came up with a girl I met yesterday. She has a yacht. We're all pretty stylish."

"Did you really come to see me?"

"There were several things that all sort of worked together. You're the part that interests me most. I want to hear all about it." He stopped and turned to face Jeff, freeing his arm. Adoration shone in his extraordinary eyes before they clouded and dropped. The boy ran his fingers through his hair. "I saw Sid," Peter pointed out. "What in the world have you been up to?"

"Is Dimitri still in jail?"

"I don't know. Come on, Jeff, honey. Tell me the whole story."

The dark eyes lifted in appeal and dropped again. "It's so difficult. You make me feel like such an idiot."

"Don't be silly. We can tell each other anything. I told you that yesterday. I knew you were upset about something." His power over the boy had been confirmed by look and touch. He moved in close to him and took his arms. He could feel the tremor of response run through the young body. "Come on. You told Sid. I want to hear it all from you."

"I don't want you to hate me. Please. I—" He lifted his eyes once more, filled with adoration, young, helpless, touching. "I had no intention of *stealing* it," he asserted vehemently. "I never dreamed Dad would go to the police and get Costa into it. I was going to put it somewhere in the house where he'd find it. That's all there was to it."

"Okay. I didn't think you were a thief." he gave him a hug and disengaged himself and propelled him to a chair. He sat opposite him. "Did Dimitri put you up to it?"

"No." Jeff sprawled in his habitual fashion, but with a difference. His knees were parted, and his hands were on his thighs making a conscious point of his crotch. "Don't you understand? I was ready to do anything to make him pay attention to me. He was short of cash. I told him he could have the money if he'd let me spend the night with him. I don't think I said it quite like that, but that's what it amounted to. He had his customers all lined up and was going to make a quick profit. Then the police loused everything up."

"They certainly did. I hope you realize how bad this is. You've let an innocent man suffer for something you did."

"Oh, God, Peter. It's been driving me crazy." He lifted his hands and clutched at his hair. "I couldn't tell you yesterday when it was still going on with Dimitri. Then it all got so confused that I would've left with Mike even if I weren't in love with him."

"You should've stayed, you know," Peter said. "You should've done everything you could to clear Costa, even if it meant telling your father the truth."

"Oh, God, I suppose I should have." His eyes filled with tears, and he flung his hands out pleadingly. "Please, Peter. Everything's happened all at once. I've hardly known what I was doing. I told Dimitri last night he had to give the money back. He said he has to lie low till the fuss dies down. That may be true as far as the dope goes, but he could get the money somewhere. He just laughed at me. I told Sid to make him see that it's to his own interest to get Costa out of it. What more could I do? Tell me. I'll do anything you say."

Peter was moved by him. He felt things deeply, often excessively, but his instincts were right. He had broken his sexual bonds and needed time now to test the implications and learn discipline. Peter's manner softened. "I think *you* should tell *me* what you ought to do."

Jeff's chest heaved with a deep breath. "Go to the police? Would I have to go back to the island?"

"I don't see why you should. We'll find out who to see here. When are you planning to go to the States?"

"Tomorrow. After lunch. I'm pretty sure Mike wouldn't wait for me. Will they let me go if I tell the truth?"

"You don't have to incriminate yourself. We'll fix up a story. Make it sound like a practical joke. Ha-ha. Are you willing to do it?"

His eyes widened, and his lips struggled to form the word. "Yes."

Peter leaned forward and patted his knee. "Good boy. That's what

I hoped you'd say. Okay. I'll tell you what *I'll* do. To begin with, we have to produce the money. I'll get it in the morning. I want you to write a statement. You can say—say you found it around the house and kept it to show your father how careless he'd been. You lost your head when the police were brought in. Anything like that. You can go with Mike, and I'll carry on from there."

Jeff pulled himself up in his chair and took Peter's hands in his. "You really are my god."

Peter kept his hands motionless and in a moment withdrew them. "I want you to write another statement telling the exact truth, pot and all. That'll be for me. I'd be happy to give you two thousand dollars if you were in a jam, but not Dimitri. I intend to collect from him. In the morning, we'll have your fake statement notarized with your passport."

A ghost of a smile played across Jeff's lips. "I almost forgot to bring it. I had to sneak back to the house this morning to get it. You should see the place. The earthquake cracked open a whole wall."

"No! What a damn shame. Your father's getting it from every direction. I think you ought to write him and tell him what you're doing."

"About Mike and everything?"

"Why not? Remember what I told you. Don't start out feeling guilty."

Jeff sprawled back in his chair. "All right. I will."

"Are you expecting Mike soon?"

"Not for an hour or two. He didn't come home with me just to prove that I don't matter. He says I'm too young to go to the kind of bars he likes. I guess that's the way it's going to be." He uttered the rumble that was intended as laughter. "I haven't told you about last night. I waited for Dimitri for hours until he closed the bar. When he turned up, he had Mike with him. There we were, all three of us together. My first time. Mike tells me he paid Dimitri two hundred dollars to have me."

Peter passed a hand over his eyes. He found his face set in a grimace of disgust. He shook his head. "Christ, Jeff. Get out of it. Go home."

Jeff dropped his head back and closed his eyes. "No. It's not as bad as I make it sound. When he takes me, it's incredible. There's no doubt about his wanting me then. It's just the rest of the time he has to prove he doesn't need me. He knows even less about love than I do. I'm going to show him."

"Then you'd better forget your sophisticated debut. If you can't make it decent, it's not worth what it'll do to you. You can go just so far with sex, and then it loses everything. Love becomes just one more cock up your ass. You don't want to be another Dimitri. It would kill you." He looked at the boy as he lay sprawled out in the chair, eyes closed, as motionless as if he were already dead.

"I'm sorry," Jeff said at last. "You know what the trouble is. I'm still lost in my dreams. Mike's reality. I know that. I know I have to try to make it good."

Peter nodded to himself and rose and looked around the room. There was a litter of letters and papers and magazines everywhere, but no pictures, except for the hotel prints on the walls. He peered into the bedrooms, trying to see which was Mike's. "Has Mike said anything to you about some pictures he bought here?" he asked casually, turning back to Jeff.

The boy opened his eyes and shook his head. "What kind of pictures?"

"French Impressionists, I think he said. He wanted to talk to me about them. We had a date at noon for him to show them to me. Needless to say, he didn't show up. Do you think it would do any harm to look around while I'm here? We're all apt to be busy in the morning."

Jeff pulled himself out of the chair and approached with the new little sensual glide in his walk. "Is it all right now? Do you still mean what you said yesterday, that we'll always belong to each other a little?"

"Of course, but don't let me down again. And don't let Mike mess you up."

"I *am* a mess. I know that. Mike's a pretty tough proposition for somebody who doesn't know much about life, but every time I talk to you I feel I'm getting out of my depth. May I kiss you right?"

"Right, yes." Jeff's kiss was as chaste as Peter's had been. Peter laughed and mussed his untidy hair. "Good boy. Which is Mike's room?"

Jeff led him to it. There was a great deal of luggage about and expensive-looking haberdashery had been dropped here and there on the furniture. Peter looked around the walls where a package of pictures might be propped. He opened closet doors. He was closing one when he caught sight of a flat package on the top shelf of a wardrobe closet. He reached up and took it down. It felt right to his expert hands, stiff and rough and the right weight. The brown wrapping paper had been folded but not taped or tied in any way. Peter looked at Jeff.

"Do you think it would be prying to see what's in here?"

"If it's pictures, he was planning to show them to you. Go ahead."

Peter pushed some silk handkerchiefs out of the way and laid the package out flat on a table. He unfolded the paper carefully and spread it open. Even though he was prepared for them, he felt a little shock at seeing Raoul's pictures here, looking rather shabby without frame or stretcher. He flipped through them quickly and began to fold the paper around them again.

"Wasn't that a Modigliani?" Jeff asked over his shoulder.

"It looks like one. I doubt if it is." He flattened the paper into its former folds and put the package back on the closet shelf. He turned to Jeff. "I don't think you'd better tell him I took a peek," he said with an excited twinkle in his eye. "Tell him I'm here on business and came to see you. I'll call him in the morning and find out if he still wants to talk to me. Do you know what time he usually gets up?"

"He said we had to be up at ten tomorrow. He wants me to do some errands for him before we go."

"Right. Let's see." He took Jeff's arm and they returned to the living room. "How about meeting me downstairs at noon? Have those statements with you. You can make them brief and to the point, but I want all the facts in the one for me. I think we can have the other one notarized in the hotel. If you want to change the time, call me when you get up. I've got a lot of calls to make in the morning, so I'll be here." When they reached the door, he turned Jeff to him and put a hand on his shoulder. "We'll see each other tomorrow, but we might not have a chance to talk. Promise you won't play hooky from school. That's the important thing."

"I promise. Try to convince Dad that I'm not a mental case."

"Oh, I don't think that'll be difficult. Your father is a very wise and understanding guy. I don't think he'll like its being Mike, but neither do I. If it weren't so nearly time for you to leave anyway, I'd do everything I could to stop you. As it is—six weeks—well, you can get awfully hurt in six weeks. Send me your address. I'll come up and see you as soon as I'm home."

Jeff put his hand over Peter's and pressed it against his shoulder. "I want so much to kiss you," he blurted. "I don't think I can do it right again. Say good-bye to Charlie for me. See you at noon."

Peter nodded and smiled and let himself out. He sped along the corridor and ran down a grand staircase, not waiting for the elevator, and arrived panting in front of Judy's door. He knocked and she let him in, and he took her in his arms triumphantly. "A hit. A palpable hit," he exclaimed. "Right on the nose. Tim should give you a whopping bonus for this. Did you finish the champagne?"

She laughed at his excitement. "We'd made rather a dent in it."

He released her to ring for the waiter. When he turned back to her he saw that she was wearing nothing but the dressing gown that made her look so beautifully naked. Her dark hair fell softly around her scrubbed and radiant face. He was supposed to give this adorable creature a baby and think nothing more of it? Beware of scheming females. He threw off his jacket and began to unfasten his tie as he returned to her. There was a knock on the door, and he veered off to it and ordered another bottle of wine. He threw his tie on a chair and went to her.

"Tell me everything," she demanded as she began to unbutton his shirt for him.

"He has five of them," he said, looking at his fingertips as he touched her face lightly with them. "Braque, Modigliani, and three Pissarros. The Braque is real. I know them all well." He traced the exquisite curve of her upper lip with his forefinger. He started to lean forward to kiss it. There was another knock on the door, and he closed his shirt over his chest to admit the waiter and the wine. When the waiter was gone, he opened the bottle and filled their glasses. He gave Judy hers and took a swallow of his before sitting to remove his shoes.

"What do we do now?" Judy asked.

"I'm going to call him in the morning and see if he still wants to talk to me. If he does, I'll tell it to him straight. If not—well, we have a choice of saying the word and letting them put him through the wringer here, or turning it over to Tim and the U.S.A. I'm sort of in favor of the latter. It lets us out, so we have our time to ourselves, and Tim can make sure the pictures get back to their owner. God knows what might become of them here." He pulled off a sock and waved it absentmindedly while he made sure he had checked all the possibilities. "However it works, I hope Mike is ready with a good story."

"Unless I'm much mistaken, he will be. How's the island mystery?"

Peter shrugged and kicked off the other shoe. "All okay. I'll fix it up tomorrow afternoon." Barefoot, he stood and pulled off his shirt.

"You're a very nice man, aren't you?"

"Who? Me? What do you expect? Costa's my friend." He unfastened his trousers and peeled his shorts off with them. His sex sprang out from its confinement. He disentangled his feet and straightened

214

and laughed. "That's more like it. Take that thing off. I like to look at you too, you know."

She unfastened the tie of her dressing gown, bared her shoulders, and let it fall from her, revealing his ideal woman. He made a slow contented survey of the delights of her body. His loins tingled at the thought of filling it with life, but he knew he couldn't accept her conditions and that therefore it mustn't happen. That this was so told him how nearly she had brought his shadow self to life. Nearly, but not quite. If it remained a simple happy romp in the hay, maybe even he wouldn't be hurt.

Peter was awakened by a knock on the door. In the moment it took him to emerge into consciousness, he became aware that the knock was being repeated in a private familiar rhythm. He twisted his head quickly and saw that Judy was still asleep. He slid away from her without making any abrupt movements and then leaped from the bed and ran to the other room, his erection subsiding as he went. He closed the communicating doors and locked them and hurried to the hall door. He stood behind it as he opened it and peered around it. Charlie was standing at the next door. His first thoughts were guilty ones, as if he had been caught red-handed. He reminded himself hastily that he had nothing to hide and had a moment to register his astonishment at this new arrival. "Hey," he called and ducked back behind the door. "What in the world are you doing here?" he exclaimed as Charlie entered. Had something gone wrong at home?

Charlie glanced from the untouched bed to his naked mate and smiled in a way that was immediately reassuring. "You look so beautiful and tousled and sexy. Have you been up all night?"

"Well, in a manner of speaking."

Charlie's smile broadened. He closed the door, dropped a small bag on the floor, and reached for him.

Peter ducked away. "Just a second, darling. Let me brush my teeth. You've just arrived? Is it that late?"

"After ten-thirty."

"Wicked, wicked me. Ring for some coffee, would you?" He trotted off to the bathroom, calling over his shoulder, "It's lovely to see you."

Charlie did as he was told, and in a few moments Peter was back, his hair combed, a towel hitched around his waist. He went directly to where Charlie had seated himself, dropped to a knee, and kissed his mouth. Charlie drew him closer and made it a real kiss, so that

215

Peter could feel his sex stirring against the towel, but Charlie was the first to pull back. Peter remained where he was, propped against the arm of the chair. "Well, tell all. What are you doing here?"

"I wanted to help." He stroked the side of Peter's golden head and smiled teasingly. "I suspected you might have your hands full. I thought I could take over for Costa." He reported what Sid had told him about Dimitri's promise to return the money. Peter was telling about his talk with Jeff when there was a knock on the door, and he rose and went to it, admitting the waiter with his breakfast tray. He poured a cup of coffee and sat on the edge of the bed with it.

"So it's getting straightened out," Charlie said. "Good. I should've known you'd have it all under control."

"It makes it a lot easier if George had the money back. It's good to know about that. How amazing of you to take all the trouble to let me know."

"Sid and I thought I ought to."

As the coffee cleared Peter's mind of the last vestiges of sleep, he was able to assess the situation created by Charlie's arrival. The secret knock on the door had added confusion to the confusion of waking, and he knew that for the first few moments he had resisted, even resented, Charlie's being here; but, if anything, it removed any furtive element in his enjoyment of his girl—being together in rooms Peter was openly sharing with Judy confirmed their total understanding. Nothing quite like it had ever occurred before. It made him want to be near him, to touch him, to hold his hand and put an arm around his shoulder as a physical expression of their deep solidarity. Yet not in a sexual way, not while Judy was here. He laughed to himself. He wanted the impossible: he wanted Charlie to be with him, and he wanted to be alone. The day promised to be odd and interesting. "I was sorry to run off without seeing you yesterday," he said, looking across the room into Charlie's eyes. "I was in a rush, and I didn't want to break up your morning."

"Of course. I understood. Well, what do you think? Can I help out here, or shall I take the afternoon boat back?"

"Oh, no. Just a second." He drank off his coffee, then rose and went to the telephone. He asked for Mike's suite; after a brief wait, he was told that there was no reply. He hung up and told Charlie about finding the pictures.

"You really do have your hands full," Charlie said.

It was an innocuous remark, but Peter caught unfamiliar vibrations between them. Charlie's habitual manner, aloof, amused, affectionate, was more positive this morning: sharper, more engaged and purposeful. He sensed a coiled-up power in him; it related to another period of their lives, before the children. He was intrigued and stimulated, as if they hadn't been together for a long time. They disposed of the topics of immediate concern to them—Costa, Jeff, Mike, Dimitri—in a quick lively exchange laced with private levity.

It confirmed what Charlie had known last night: he was right, and Martha was wrong. Nothing had changed. Peter seemed a bit nervy and preoccupied; his eyes kept darting to the communicating doors, but that was understandable. "Well, if I'm going to stay," Charlie said with decision, "I'd better get another room." He nodded toward the doors. "She's there?"

"Yes, I took two rooms for appearances' sake."

"So they told me downstairs. Very discreet." He laughed. "For appearances' sake, we'd better take a double farther down the hall. Judy can entertain you in her suite. I don't want her to feel that I'm breathing down her neck."

"Okay. She's going tomorrow. We'll go home together. How's the family?"

"All in order. Little Pete is furious with you. He says Daddy's not supposed to go away in the summer. There's nothing like a day without you to remind us that we're living with the most beautiful guy in the world."

"Of course you are." He laughed into Charlie's eyes, moved over to him, and leaned on his shoulder. "I better wake the lady up."

"Just a second. Have you thought who could tell us how to get in touch with Costa?"

"I'm going to call old Pericles. He knows all the big guns in the Interior Ministry."

"Of course. He'll take care of it. I'll call him. You and Judy can concentrate on Raoul's pictures." He noted the alacrity with which pressure was removed from his shoulder.

Peter circled toward the locked doors. "Wonderful. I better get her moving in case Mike calls. After all, it's her baby."

"If Mike cooperates, you'll have the rest of the day to yourselves. I should have Costa clear during the afternoon. Maybe I'd better call somebody and plan an evening."

Peter returned to his side and laid a hand on the back of his neck. "Don't be silly. We'll all do something together. Judy would love it."

Charlie looked up at him. Peter's eyes didn't meet his with quite the directness they had before. He was obviously anxious to bring

217

this tête-à-tête to an end. Natural. Understandable. The girl was only a few feet away; she must be very much on his mind. "She doesn't want me around. Her last night and everything. Actually, there're some people I'd like to see. Pantelis and that crowd." Everything depended on the degree of conviction with which Peter pursued the point. His insisting on spending the evening together would be as suspicious as his letting it drop. He felt the hand slip from his neck and Peter moved away again.

"Really? Well, let's see how it works out. As for Judy's last night, I'm sure she'd find it much more memorable with you along than just with me."

Pretty good. Should he? Shouldn't he? He rose and turned to Peter, who was hovering near the closed doors again.

To Peter, Charlie seemed suddenly to fill the room. He was dressed for the island, in sandals and shorts and a shirt that was only half-buttoned, exposing the froth of blond hair on his chest. His magnificent lover—for a moment he felt their relationship to the exclusion of all else, but he still wanted to avoid any too-intimate contact. He was afraid of failing in the essential responses so long a. Judy had a claim on him. She would be gone tomorrow, and they would belong to each other again. Meanwhile, he marveled at the impact his presence had on him, undimmed by familiarity. He saw the devilish smile come up in Charlie's smoky eyes and was struck again by the purpose and power in him today.

"Beautiful," Charlie said. "You look like the guardian of the temple gates. Is that towel necessary? You were nicely naked when I came in." He saw what he had been watching for. A shadow crossed Peter's face, so faint that it was impossible to isolate its origins, perhaps a slight twitch of the eyelids, perhaps an almost imperceptible tightening of the lips, but unmistakable in its significance. Charlie's decision was made. Something in him contracted, and his muscles tensed and pulled him up straighter. Peter was his. He could accept no confusion on that score.

"I'm not wearing it for you, silly," Peter said with a successful approximation of his usual jauntiness. The shadow had passed.

"Who, then?"

"You don't expect me to wander around naked all day." They drifted toward each other, drawn to each other as always, laughing with each other with their eyes.

"No, I suppose not. She probably wouldn't give you a moment's peace. Martha's convinced she's madly in love with you."

218

"Madly is hardly the word. In love, maybe, in the sense that I'm the first man she's really liked going to bed with. That's about all it amounts to. That, and liking each other enormously. I really must go wake her up."

They were close enough so that they could reach out and touch each other. Another shadow crossed Peter's face, more pronounced because of their proximity, as he made a tentative move to turn. Charlie had never known him to shy away from him in this way. It hurt dangerously. Martha was wrong, but he still felt a need to prove it conclusively. He pulled his shirt out of his shorts, unbuttoned it all the way down, and threw it aside. "If I'm going to be dealing with officials, I'd better put some pants on. Come on. Let's take a shower. I'll scrub your back."

"You're crazy. Honestly. It's getting late." Peter's laughter was exasperated but affectionate. He couldn't refuse outright. They often took companionable showers together; he liked to have his back scrubbed.

Charlie peeled off the rest of his clothes. "A shower will make you feel better after your wild night. I could do with one, too. That sweaty boat trip. Come on."

"It'll have to be quick." Charlie's masterful mood overrode all resistance. Peter pulled off the towel and let Charlie lead him toward the bathroom. Being naked together created an atmosphere of home and ease and contentment.

The lithe, deeply tanned body at his side, though he didn't let his eyes linger over it, filled him with an impression of beauty that no female body could compete with. He was lifted on a sudden crest of excited high spirits. They slapped at each other playfully and pushed each other into the enormous old-fashioned bathroom, half-wrestling their way to the shower cubicle, which was big enough for a basket-ball team. Peter turned the water on, and their eyes and teeth flashed at each other as they splashed about under the spray.

"This *is* good," Peter shouted. "We've got to hurry. Do my back." He stepped slightly out of the spray and turned away from him, making a firm and successful effort not to let his eyes wander below Charlie's waist. This was fine, all easy and loving and happily playful. He felt Charlie's hands on his shoulders, lathered and sliding firmly over him. Peter's male ascendancy had been long established, but he still relished moments such as this when he could slip back into a sensual lethargy of passivity, being handled and cared for by his lover. Charlie scrubbed his back vigorously, the way he liked, with one of the squares of toweling hanging in the cubicle. After a few moments, Peter started to move away, but a hand strayed caressingly over his buttocks and between his legs to stroke his balls. Peter laughed and again started to draw away, but a restraining hand now gripped his shoulder, and the other moved back up between his buttocks, lathering him. A finger entered him so smoothly that for a second he didn't feel it. Then his body gave a leap, and he cried out.

"Hey. That's not allowed in the YMCA."

"You'd be surprised." The finger moved deeper, gently massaging him, making his sex lengthen and begin to lift.

"Jesus, darling. Do you know what you're doing? Is this for real?"

"I'll say."

For proof, Peter felt Charlie's sex nudging the back of his thighs. He reached back and grasped it. It was slick with lather and swelled into full erection in his hand. "Christ. This. You know what it does to me."

"You want it, baby?"

"Yes. God, yes. What have we been waiting for all these years?" He thought briefly of Judy and of his male triumphs on her body, and then thought was banished by the thrilling prospect of being taken again in this way. His legs felt as if they were buckling under him. He stumbled from the shower without bothering to turn off the water and dropped to his knees on the bath mat, pulling Charlie down behind him. He cried out again as hands gripped his hips, and the immense penetration began.

Charlie's heart pounded against his ribs as he reasserted his mastery over Peter's body. *Forget caution, throw away wiles and stratagems. Let the monumental phallus resume its reign.* He exulted in his power and prowess. He had turned himself into a woman? Peter was deliriously in love with a girl? He repeated all the moves that had always made Peter's body leap and sway in welcome of the massive flesh that was driving into him. He made him laugh and moan and shout. He heard knocking on the connecting doors in the next room and a muffled voice calling, but if Peter heard, he gave no sign. His whole body was writhing in a single-minded surrender. Charlie drove them rapidly to a tumultuous climax, accompanied by shouts and laughter, and was toppled by his last triumphant lunge, more ecstatically fulfilled than he had been for years.

They lay crumpled together on the floor, breathing hard, laughing in little spurts, clinging to each other to relieve the strain of the final convulsions of their bodies.

They pulled themselves together and showered again, handling each other, looking at each other gloatingly in the soft aftermath of union. They left the bathroom with their arms around each other and stopped in the middle of the room to hold each other, looking into each other's eyes. Peter shook his head wonderingly.

"Why you think I want girls when you can do that to me, I'll never know," he said. "God, we're good together. Your cock, darling. I didn't realize how much I've longed for it. I'm going to have a word to say about that when we get home." His body made a little convulsive movement toward his mate.

Charlie pulled him closer with authority. He had countered the immediate threat. The habits of years of caution had been broken, and he felt too wonderful to worry about the consequences. Perhaps eventually, they would fit Martha's description of "two aging men clinging to each other." Then he would rest. For the moment, his body felt revived and overflowing with potency. His hold over Peter was assured till the next crisis. Looking at him, he had the feeling that there would be no rest for a long time. "You're so good every way, it's hard for a guy to make up his mind," he said with a sly smile.

"Maybe I *should* go away more often. Come on. We've really got to get cracking." He took Charlie's hand and led him toward a dressing table where he had left some things the day before. He pushed aside a newspaper and his passport and found his watch. "Yeah. I'm due to meet Jeff downstairs in about twenty minutes. Better get into some clothes. Did I say something about waking Judy?" They were both dressed in a moment. Peter remained barefoot. His shoes were next door.

He was heading for Judy's room when there was a noise at the hall door, more a thump than a knock. He stopped and looked at it. There was another noise, this time a sort of sliding, scratching sound. He and Charlie glanced at each other, and then he went to the door and opened it. Jeff was leaning against the frame. He didn't move. His eyes were fixed on the floor. Despite his tan, he looked pale and sick.

"Well, hello," Peter greeted him. "I was just coming down."

Jeff made no move of recognition. After a moment's puzzled hesitation, Peter drew him into the room and closed the door. The boy was an object in his hands, lifeless, without will. Was he drunk? He had become a body without the definition of personality. Drugs? Something was very wrong.

"What's up, for God's sake? What's happened?" He glanced at Charlie again and saw that his eyes were fixed on Jeff. He gave the boy a little shake. "Come on. What's the matter?"

For answer, Jeff lifted his eyes and gazed at him vacantly, unseeingly. Charlie moved in beside them. Peter could see his presence slowly registering in Jeff's consciousness. The boy turned suddenly, and his mouth dropped open as if he were going to cry out, but no sound came. His body swayed, and Charlie took his arm and began to lead him toward the bed.

"Something must've happened to Mike," Charlie said over his shoulder to Peter. He stretched Jeff out on the bed and sat beside him, putting a hand on his shoulder.

Jeff lay on his back without moving, his eyes closed. "He's gone," he said in a hollow voice.

Peter had followed to the foot of the bed. "Mike?" he asked.

Jeff nodded. He pulled his knees up and clutched his head with both hands and began to thrash about convulsively on the bed.

"Take it easy," Charlie said with a note of command. Jeff immediately straightened his legs, dropped his hands on the pillow, and lay still.

"I thought your plane was later," Peter said.

"It is." Jeff's mouth slowly opened, his neck arched, and the muscles knotted as if he were going to give vent to a shout or a scream, but he went limp again without having uttered a sound. "He took an earlier one to London or Paris. I don't know. He sent me out. When I came back, he was gone."

"He took all his things with him?" Peter asked.

"He made me do things—I can't—nobody would believe," Jeff said as if he hadn't heard the question. "I accepted everything. Why should he—" He scrambled up from the bed, his eyes staring wildly, and made a rush for the door. Peter moved to intercept him. Charlie was on his feet behind him.

"You're with us now, honey," Peter said soothingly. "Just let us take care of everything." Charlie moved in close behind him and put an arm around his shoulder. Jeff immediately swung around, flung his arms around him, and buried his head against his shoulder. He began to tremble violently.

"Get him back to bed," Peter suggested. He nodded toward Judy's room. "I've got to speak to her." He remained where he was, watching Charlie almost carry Jeff across the room. Their lovemaking had left him hypersensitive to every movement of Charlie's body. Was it only by accident that Jeff's hand hung close to his crotch? The boy had made it quite plain whom he had chosen to comfort him. He realized that the sudden unpleasant tightening of his nerves was jealousy.

He hadn't felt anything like it for so long that it came as a new and unexplored emotion. He was stunned at his reluctance to leave them alone, even though he was only going to the next room. He forced himself to turn as Charlie eased Jeff down onto the bed, went to the connecting doors, and unlocked them.

Judy was sitting near the French doors, dressed and reading a magazine. The remains of her breakfast were on a tray beside her. She looked up questioningly as he entered.

"Charlie turned up a little while ago," he explained, collecting his shoes and socks.

"I thought I heard voices."

Something about the way she said it made him wonder if she had heard more. Had there been a knock on the door when they were in the bathroom? He had been too carried away to pay attention. "We have Jeff on our hands, too." He sat near her and pulled a sock on. As he did so, he was aware that the amputation had taken place, quite painlessly. Whatever fragile magic they had created together had vanished; he would never feel anything like it again. She was a beautiful girl whom he liked enormously, but he couldn't take his mind off the pair in the next room.

He tried to make his announcement of Mike's departure sound sufficiently dramatic to maintain some surface continuity in their time together. He couldn't see that it would help either of them to make it clear that there was nothing left for them to share. After Charlie, it was difficult to imagine spending another night with her, but he would have to work his way through that when the time came.

"We should put in a call to Tim immediately," he said, standing up in his shoes. "If it doesn't take too long to get through, we'll catch him at home. It's only about five or six in the morning there. I'll explain to him it wasn't our fault he slipped through our fingers."

"What did Charlie come for? Is anything wrong?" she asked, with only a shadow remaining of the reserve he had felt in her when he had joined her.

"More about George Leighton's money. That's all getting straightened out. The kid's in a bad way. I want to keep an eye on him. Will you place the call?"

"Of course, but won't Mr. Thornton want to know where Cochran's gone?"

"That's no problem. We'll find out from the airport. If we can get Jeff quieted down, maybe we can all have lunch up here. Would that be all right?"

"Fine." They stood together briefly, and he took her hand. Her eyes were on him, and he tried to put the immediacy of yesterday's response into his as he met them. He felt a pang of genuine regret that it required an effort.

"I'll be right back." He turned and left her.

He found Charlie seated on the side of the bed again. His hand was on Jeff's shoulder. The latter had shifted his head so that his cheek rested against it. Charlie rose and went to him.

"He's agreed to go home," he said in an undertone. "I've offered to go with him. I don't think he could make it on his own."

"That's wonderful." Jealousy became an unpleasant sensation in the pit of his stomach as he tried to think of some grounds for opposing the suggestion.

"If we go now, we'll have time to catch the afternoon boat. He can do what ever he has to do with the police there. We won't need those statements."

"Absolutely. It's the best possible solution," Peter forced himself to agree. "I'd have suggested it myself, except that I wanted you to stay. You'll obviously be a big help to him. He worships you."

"I'll get him home and let George take over. I wish you could come too."

"Me too, but it isn't just Judy and the blasted pictures. I've got to find out who's handling Costa's case so there can't be any slip-up. I'll try to bring him back with me. It'll be easier with Jeff on the island."

"You'll come back tomorrow?"

"Don't worry. Judy's calling Tim now. That'll take care of the pictures. I'll get hold of the police this afternoon. Make sure George is doing everything at that end. Tim will probably want Judy to come right back. I'll be on the afternoon boat."

"No later. You promise?"

Peter looked into Charlie's eyes and smiled, gratified by his insistence. "Promise? After this morning, do you think I'm apt to get delayed?"

They touched hands, and Charlie picked up his bag and turned back to the bed. "Okay, kiddo. Let's get going."

Jeff opened his eyes and gazed at Charlie. He rose slowly and went to him, standing close to him as if taking shelter against him. Peter was glad that the boy looked too knocked out to attempt a seduction. He could still feel Charlie enormous within him. After the years of being denied that sublime instrument, he was feeling acutely possessive of it. He hadn't had time to wonder what the sudden reversal signified. As he moved to the door, he wished he was going with them.

"I'm sorry, honey," he said to Jeff, "but when you get over the shock you'll see what a shit he is. Not that that's always a big help. Pay attention to anything Charlie tells you. We know something about these things." He gave his mate a quick kiss and stood in the door, exchanging a wave of the hand with him as they started off down the corridor. Jeff stayed close to Charlie, but a step behind, and Peter noted that they didn't touch.

He closed the door and remained beside it for a moment, preparing to return to Judy. Without Charlie to preoccupy his attention, he felt more confident of making her last day a happy one. If he could get his mind off Jeff. Maybe she would help. He called her name as he started for the other room.

Charlie led the way to Mike's suite. He wondered if the boy was going to hold on to himself long enough for them to get to the boat. For the past fifteen minutes, Jeff had seemed to swing from deep plunges into his private torment, when Charlie could feel him moving closer to the edge of total collapse, back to a sort of vast yearning for Charlie to control and protect him, to assume responsibility for the functions of his being. Sex was an almost palpable element in it. If the boy was going mad with unrequited love for Mike, what was the meaning of it? Did he react sexually to everybody? He thought of Peter's afternoon with him and assured himself that there was no chance of his finding himself naked with the boy. He was far from attractive in this distraught state. Touching, yes. He appealed to all his tender protective instincts, but these could quickly give way to impatience if he didn't pull himself together soon. The hysteria wasn't completely convincing; in the midst of it, he was capable of curiously knowing moments. He had proposed going home. When Peter was out of the room, he had become very still, and his passionate eyes had searched Charlie's.

"Would you take me home?" he had asked in his husky voice. "I'd go if you'd come with me. Wouldn't that be the best way?"

He had promised to be such a burden to all of them that Charlie had felt he was doing Peter a favor by agreeing. He was glad to go, anyway; he had accomplished his purpose, but couldn't be accused of horning in on Judy.

They marched down the corridor toward Mike's rooms. Jeff suddenly flung himself against the wall and buried his head in his folded arms. "I can't," he gasped.

Charlie wondered if tears were coming now. Once they started, he wouldn't be able to do anything with the boy. He stepped close to him and put a hand on his back. Jeff was immediately in his arms.

"Not here, for God's sake," he snapped, disengaging himself.

Jeff stood in front of him, his head back, his eyes closed, his prominent Adam's apple working. "I can't go back in there," he said dully.

"That's all right. Give me the key. Are your things all together?"

"There's just a bag. It's packed. There're two envelopes on the desk in the sitting room that Peter wanted."

Charlie took the key and went to the number indicated. He found the envelopes, picked up the bag from the middle of the floor, and returned to Jeff. The boy took the bag, and they fell into step again. The danger of collapse would recede, Charlie hoped, once they were out among people.

They made their way out of the hotel, and he hailed a taxi and hustled Jeff into it. He got in beside him and ran his arm along the top of the seat to give Jeff's back a pat. He felt all of Jeff's body flow to him. Whatever he felt for Mike, he would doubtless soon find someone to console him. He dropped his head back onto Charlie's arm and closed his eyes, only to be seized with another fit of trembling.

"Take it easy, kiddo," Charlie said. "We'll get a cabin on the boat. You'll be able to rest."

He let his eyes roam over the strong profile. The way his long dark hair fell over his forehead was an invitation to toy with it. The straight brows, the straight strong nose, the long hard line of the jaw, and the swelling curve of the neck were all elements that he would like to capture on paper. It was the mouth that his eyes kept returning to. The curve of the lips was exquisitely chiseled, and there was a slight irregular fullness in the middle of the upper one that he found fascinating. It was a masculine face, but its vestiges of androgynous adolescence exerted the pull he had felt before. He suddenly saw Sarah clearly in it. He was holding Sarah's son and being tempted by him.

He felt a welcome little twinge of distaste. Surely he could offer the boy comfort without allowing it to go further. He could understand how his yielding, not quite innocent defenselessness could have incited a Mike Cochran to sadistic excesses, but it aroused only compassion in him. Thoughts of Peter long ago when he had thoughtlessly hurt him passed through his mind. The terrible sorrow

226

of youth. He wanted to heal Jeff with blameless caresses. He hugged the boy closer. Jeff's lips parted, and he turned his face toward him without opening his eyes, closing his mouth on his arm in a simulacrum of a kiss. His trembling stopped.

Charlie's eyes dropped to Jeff's hands where they lay on his thighs. They weren't wide, but had long strong-knuckled fingers and nicely shaped nails—good, sensual, stimulating hands. He gathered this knowledge, along with every other detail about the boy, with an intense interest that people rarely stirred in him. He sat back, cradling him on his arm, glad that lustful thoughts remained in abeyance. His continued scrutiny of the face and body beside him satisfied the sensuous curiosity of his eyes.

When the taxi pulled up amid the bustle surrounding the departing boat in Piraeus, contact between them was broken as they unloaded bags, paid the driver, bought tickets, and mounted the gangplank. Jeff became an automaton at his side. Charlie was greeted expansively by the personnel on board, and he was obliged to exhibit his public personality for a few minutes while a cabin was assigned to them.

When he turned to look for Jeff, he saw him standing at the head of the companionway, clutching the rail, his head averted, his shoulders heaving. Charlie hurried to him, seized his arm, and rushed him down the stairs. He found their cabin, thrust Jeff into it, and locked them in as the flood he had been expecting burst over him. Jeff stood helplessly while his body was wracked with sobs and tears streamed down his face.

Charlie unbuttoned and removed his jacket and supported him to one of the two bunks, safely narrow and uninviting, and got him stretched out on it. Jeff flung himself about on it as the sobs were torn from him. Charlie sat beside him, untied his tie, and unfastened the button of his collar. Handling the boy so intimately, feeling the smooth skin of his neck, uncovering the deep hollow at the juncture of his collarbones, witnessing this explosion of raw emotion, unsettled Charlie's control. He couldn't leave him in this state, but he knew that if he stayed he would be putting himself to a perilous test.

Jeff communicated a child's wild longing to be held. Charlie hesitated another moment and then stretched out beside him and gathered him into his arms. Jeff was so slight that there was plenty of room for both of them. Charlie choked with the sweetness of holding and comforting him, but in this position, body to body, there was no way of concealing any response that might be stirred in him. He doubted if Jeff would be aware of it, as all his hurt and grief and shame poured from him. He murmured comforting words to him, kissing his wet cheeks and stroking his hair. Perhaps he could get them both beyond sex.

Holding him, their bodies clothed and his own motionless, permitting his hands no greater intimacies than those of a man with a child, he found himself approaching something more inexplicably thrilling than the act of love; at moments, he felt himself being carried toward a strange sexless orgasm.

Slowly, Jeff grew quieter and at last was still. In the silence, Charlie heard the anchor being raised. After the passage of more minutes, while the silence was filled with the low throb of engines, Jeff finally opened his tear-cleansed eyes. Their heads were very close together on the pillow, facing each other. Charlie felt as if he were looking into his soul, and his heart began to pound at the passionate surrender he saw there.

"It's going to happen, isn't it?" Jeff said.

He spoke with such a matter-of-fact assumption of an understanding between them that Charlie couldn't immediately believe Jeff knew what he was suggesting. Charlie had been so caught up in the strange delight of holding and comforting the boy that at first he had been scarcely aware of the growing rigidity of his sex. At troubling moments, he had been able to believe that Jeff was past caring about it. Jeff's question made it impossible to ignore it; it suddenly stood up hard against them both.

"Do you think it's a good idea?"

"I know gods sometimes play with mortals. It's nice for the mortals, but it can't really mean anything. I know that."

"I wish I did. You're such a funny one. I've watched you grow up and all of a sudden you're somebody I've never seen."

A pale smile hovered on Jeff's lips. "I know. You've always seemed so aloof and unapproachable, but now you're all alive and beautiful. You seem even younger than Peter."

"Did you make love with him?" Charlie asked, to clear away any possibility of doubt. Peter never lied, but he almost wished he had so that he would be relieved of all scruples.

Charlie stroked his hair and felt for a moment that that was sufficient joy. "I feel very shy with you," he said gently. "You're all knocked out. I don't want to do anything that'll make it tougher for you."

"The only thing that would make it tougher is if you don't take me. I've dreamed of both of you taking me. Now you're holding me and you have an erection. I want so to hold it, but I won't do anything unless you tell me I can. I can feel it growing and growing. It's making it right for Mike to have left me."

"Are you sure of that?"

"Oh, Charlie. If you'd just let us be naked together, like Peter, it would be almost enough. Does it make any sense to be dressed when we both have erections?"

Charlie raised himself on an elbow and looked at the beautiful mouth, and his lips parted. Was it possible *not* to kiss it? If he kissed it, he would never be able to stop there. He could still feel Peter's ecstatically leaping body in every fiber of him. This morning, he had broken through the fixed cold guidelines he had set for himself and awakened in both of them a fresh passion. Peter would probably think it an unforgivable denial of life to reject this young plea for comfort now. He had held Jeff and learned all of him with his eyes, an act of possession very nearly as complete as the meeting of bodies. Anything he did with Jeff had nothing to do with Peter.

He lowered his head slowly and kissed him. To his surprise, Jeff didn't stir. He simply parted his lips and let Charlie do what he liked with his mouth. Charlie had never encountered such an utterly passive body; he found it deeply provocative. Jeff was challenging him to release him from sorrow. He unbuttoned Jeff's shirt while he kissed him and drew back to look at the chest he had laid bare, the chest he had seen a thousand times, transformed now by being uncovered by him. He loved the uncompleted look of his body. It was like a work of art at the point of being brought to fruition, rich with potentialities. He stroked the fine dark down on the chest and ran his hand over the abdomen to the concavity that began above the top of his trousers.

"Go on. Undress me," Jeff whispered without moving.

He opened the fly and pushed the trousers aside, uncovering undershorts with buttons. He unfastened them and eased them down so that the body was naked to the first outcropping of pubic hair. Still, Jeff lay inert. It was like unwrapping a package. He could see where his sex was confined, a significantly straight hard line.

He lifted him enough to work an arm out of a sleeve and then removed the shirt. He stood and went to the floor of the bunk and removed his shoes and socks. He took a grip on the trousers and shorts and drew them down, stripping him. Jeff's sex lay out rigidly on his belly, looking astonishingly adult for the boyish body. He straightened and surveyed all of him, his heart racing, wondering if he could find the source of his potent appeal.

His eyes moved from big feet up long coltish legs to slim hips. They lingered on the concave belly and the bony pelvic formation and moved up over the still-underdeveloped chest to the wide shoulders, and looked into Jeff's eyes. They yearned up into his so unabashedly that his stillness became a miracle of submission, and Charlie's heart accelerated breathlessly. So far, he probably had done little more than his mate had. Simple lack of desire would have made it easy for Peter to check himself.

"Now you. Please," Jeff murmured.

"I'm not going to be as restrained as Peter."

"I have some—" Jeff began in his deep voice.

"So have I." he turned quickly and went back to the door where he had dropped his bag. There was a washbasin and towels and a chair. He took his clothes off, his body exulting in its release. He opened the bag, found the tube, and prepared himself. The hard bulk of the flesh he was handling fanned the fire of his old phallic pride. He took a towel and turned back to the bunk. Jeff's eyes immediately went to his sex and remained there as he approached. His eyes were wide, his lips parted. His body gave a great heave, and then he rolled over onto his stomach, his legs spread, his arms flung out over his head, a performance of total yearning submission.

Charlie sprang forward, straddled him, and lowered himself. He held his sex to guide it. At its first contact, Jeff cried out ecstatically once and then lay docile beneath him while Charlie took possession of him. The ease with which he received him constituted a heroic welcome of him. There was a quality of worship in it, as if he were offering himself up not so much to an individual as to some power that he acknowledged as his master.

Charlie worked himself into him slowly and gently, his soul melting with tenderness and an unfamiliar, selflessly poignant concern for his well-being and happiness. He had never been more aware of the power of possession conferred on him by his prodigious sex. Jeff made him feel that he existed only to be possessed by it. He felt a warmth in the cold core of himself. The fire sprang up and spread all through him, warming his spirit. His throat tightened, and tears welled up in his eyes. He lay still on the boy's body and felt the contact between them all the length of him. He swallowed with difficulty and flung away his defenses. "God, you're incredible," he whispered against Jeff's ear.

Jeff made no response, his quiescence not a rebuff but a vast surrender. Charlie lay on him and felt his sex swelling deep within him.

230

His breath caught with incredulity at what was happening in him, and he uttered a moan that grew in volume as tension gathered and was shatteringly dissolved in orgasm. Jeff grabbed for the towel and pushed it under him as his body leaped with Charlie's. They both lay still once more.

"How extraordinary," Jeff murmured with a deep tremor of wonder in his voice. "We came without moving. We made each other come without even trying. You took me and didn't humiliate me. It doesn't have to be degrading."

"Did you think it did?"

"Mike made me think so. Do you know why I wanted to just lie here and do nothing and let you have me any way you wanted?"

"Maybe. I don't know. Tell me."

"I worship you. I want to know if I could worship you without making it evil. I didn't want to take anything for myself. I'm yours. It's too much for me to grasp. I know gods don't want mortals for long, but I'm yours for now. You're inside me, Charlie. Isn't it amazing? If this had happened a day or two ago, everything would be different."

"You know it couldn't have, but you'd better explain a few things." Without withdrawing from him, Charlie started to shift his weight from his back, but Jeff's hands were immediately on his thighs, holding him.

"Don't move. I want you there. I want to feel all your weight on me. That's obvious. I don't know if I can explain anything else."

"You can't be in love with someone new every day. What *do* you feel about Mike?"

"I'm in love with him. Still. I didn't worship him. I tried to tell Peter. I can't think of you as ordinary mortals. It's on a different level. Peter's a playful Dionysian god. You're a majestic god. You're Apollo. You're probably fatal."

He made a rumble of laughter in his chest.

"I don't feel much like a god. I just want to look after you, take care of you, love you."

"You're being unfaithful to Peter. Can you explain that?"

"I've already tried to justify it in my mind. I can almost convince myself that he would approve. He sort of turned you over to me. Of course, nothing would've happened if you hadn't made me want to give my life to you in some way."

"I make you feel all that?" Jeff asked with a little lilt of incredulity in his voice. "How beautiful. You're still hard, aren't you."

"Again," Charlie said accurately.

"Really? You're so enormous I can't tell the difference. Peter told me about you, but I couldn't imagine it. I want to look at it for hours. I've never seen anything so colossally beautiful. I could go on talking about it all day."

"Talking about it makes me want to do something with it." He withdrew slowly and slowly drove into him again.

Jeff suddenly brought his body into play. He worked his hips and uttered a series of brief cries as Charlie filled him again. "Oh, God! Charlie! Let me pretend you're a mortal this time. Let me do it all with you. Make love—I want you to fuck me hard so it hurts. I want to feel where you've been tomorrow and the next day and the day after that."

"This isn't going to be the last time, you know."

"Isn't it?"

"I want you to stay with me tonight. After that, who knows? It's too much to think about yet." The words tumbled from him, fired by unknown emotions that boiled beneath desire. It was unimaginable that this child could threaten the attachments of a lifetime, but while he held the slim hungry body and moved himself within it, he felt that he could never let it go. "I love you, dammit," he gasped. "Don't you understand?"

Light clear laughter broke from Jeff. "I know it isn't possible, but I love you to say it. Show me. Yes, like that. You *are* Apollo. Nobody else could be so colossal."

They abandoned themselves to their bodies. Charlie was staggered by the frenzy of passion in him. There was nothing artful in what he was doing. He was swept up into a delirium of passion while he strove to satisfy the ravenous hunger that was in the boy. Jeff broke into wild sobs through which he kept crying Charlie's name. When orgasm finally overcame it, the body in Charlie's arms felt as if it would fly apart; he found himself grappling with it like a wrestler, exerting all his strength to hold it while he drove his own orgasm into it.

The silence that followed seemed to echo with their exertions. Charlie lay stunned, spent, appalled but triumphant. Love was in him, love compounded of fury and tenderness, a longing to expose himself fearlessly. He felt Jeff's enormous vulnerability to hurt, and he felt a coward for having surrounded himself with so many guards. Let them go. Loving Jeff was a battle. In the aftermath of this preliminary encounter, it seemed a battle he must win. It might not survive the night, but as long as the fire burned in him he would let it rage.

He felt his sex shrinking, and he roused himself with an effort, withdrew carefully, and sprang up from the bunk. He went to the washbasin. When he was finished, he returned to the bunk, leaned over, and touched the back of Jeff's neck. The boy's body was shaken by a long shudder.

"Hadn't you better wash up?" Charlie asked.

Jeff gathered himself together and sat up on the edge of the bunk, holding the towel against himself. "Don't look," he said, his face averted.

"I won't do anything you don't want me to do, kiddo. Ever, I hope." He turned away as Jeff rose and hurried from him. Charlie tried to keep his mind a blank. There were too many questions crowding in on it. He gave his attention to a stain on the bulkhead in front of him. His eyes found curious forms in it.

"All right," Jeff said after a few minutes.

Charlie turned. Jeff stood halfway between him and the washbasin, one of the small towels hitched around his loins. Slim hips. He was struck anew by the beauty of dark head. Love burned up in him as he looked at the young body he had possessed. He longed to watch it ripen and mature, help him to come to terms with it and himself.

Jeff kept his eyes on Charlie's. "You don't despise me now?"

"Why should I?"

"Because I enjoyed it so much. Because I let myself go like that."

Charlie laughed. "Making love isn't supposed to be a court ballet."

Jeff's eyes cleared. It had the effect of filling his face with youthful carelessness, in such contrast to his habitual melancholy that he might have been wreathed in smiles. "Mike made fun of me. I know there's something wrong with me—I mean, being in love with Mike and loving it so with you. Peter warned me about turning into a whore, but maybe this couldn't happen right now with anybody but you. And Peter, if he wanted me."

Charlie was sharply conscious of the danger signals, but he didn't retreat before them. He couldn't blame Jeff for wanting Peter. Fortunately, there was no chance of his getting him. He went to Jeff and unhitched the towel and threw it aside. "You don't have to cover yourself when you're with me." he studied Jeff's face. "Your mouth is so beautiful. I haven't had time to kiss it properly." He did so.

This time, Jeff responded avidly, letting his body go against Charlie's. As they drew apart, Charlie saw that he had aroused the boy into full erection again. A phenomenon of youth, but it was thrilling to have this power over him. Jeff took Charlie's sex in his hand and dropped his eyes to it.

"At last. If you only knew how often I've dreamed of seeing it and touching it. It's colossal even without an erection. It's obsessive. I want to see it like this, and I want to see it towering up in front of you the way it did a little while ago. Could you get another erection with me now?"

"Given a little time. We've had quite a workout. We don't have to try to set a record. Come on. We better put some clothes on. We have things to talk about before we get there. We won't be very coherent if we're naked together."

"Just one more minute." He dropped down, took Charlie's sex in both hands, and put the head in his mouth. He rolled his tongue around it and released it, then put his hands on Charlie's thighs and gazed at it. "Oh, yes, I can give you an erection," he murmured. "Just hanging, so long and heavy and beginning to get hard, it's absolutely spellbinding. And to know what it will become—huge and demanding and taking anything it wants. If I make it get like that, it will want me."

Charlie put his hand under Jeff's almost beardless chin and caressed it as he lifted him. Jeff's eyes met his. "I love you, you know," Charlie repeated with a further painful opening of his heart. Their eyes held for a moment, Jeff's deep and yearning and strangely impersonal.

They parted and gathered up their clothes and put them on. Charlie pulled the envelopes out of his hip pocket and led Jeff to the other bunk. He sat, pulled Jeff down beside him, and put his arms around him. For the moment, there was peace between them. The way the boy let his body go to him confirmed his total possession of it and heightened his sense of responsibility for him. Jeff was his now. "Well, now. Peter told me all about everything. The only difference is that we don't have to put up the money, after all. Sid is getting it from Dimitri. Peter said something about statements. Is that what these are?"

"Yes. I did the official one in Greek and English."

"We won't really need them, either, now that you're here. Take them to your father. I don't know if he's gone home yet. When last heard of, he was staying at the Gripari house with Joe Peterson."

Jeff turned to him with a rapid little movement of his head. "You mean it? He's left home? He doesn't know about the house?"

"I don't know. Anyway, look for him at Joe's first. I'd like you to talk to him before you see your mother. You'll tell him everything, won't you?"

"Not about us?"

Charlie started to speak and stopped, staggered that there was an "us" to tell about. Us—Peter and I—and Jeff? After the initial shock, it filled him with inexplicable contentment. For this little while, he could continue to act without counting the consequences. He had until Peter's return tomorrow for this freedom to work its transformations. Perhaps by then he might know what "us" meant. "No," he said with some reluctance. "I don't see what we have to do with everything that's been happening the past couple of days. Stick to that. If your father hasn't been to the police yet, tell him that Peter wants him to go right away."

Jeff opened the envelopes and peered into them. He handed one back to Charlie. "You're supposed to keep this for Peter."

"I don't think that matters now. Your father's going to want to know about Mike and why you let Dimitri have the money. Are you ready to talk about that?"

"Tell him I'm a raging faggot? I don't see how I can, but I'll try to answer truthfully if he asks me anything. Hold me, Charlie."

The piteous note in his voice cut straight through to all Charlie's tenderness and love. He gripped him closer, lifted a hand to his face, turned to him, and kissed his mouth again. He had to shift his legs to accommodate the burgeoning of his sex. Jeff's hands found it. Charlie relinquished his mouth. "We don't have to set a record. You want to spend the night with me, don't you?"

"Of course, but that's hours away. We haven't even got to Poros yet." Very deliberately, he unbuttoned Charlie's shirt and ran his hands exploringly over his torso, his eyes intent on it. He slipped from the bunk to his knees, pushed Charlie's legs apart, and moved in between them. "There's plenty of time," he said, his hands working unhurriedly to attain their goal. When they had done so, their touch brought Charlie's sex surging up between them. Jeff sat back, and his eyes roamed over it. "Ye gods, how it soars. Right up to your chest. I could sit here and stare at it for hours." Jeff tugged at the shorts, and Charlie lifted his hips and allowed his thighs to be stripped. Jeff held the sex and stroked his cheeks and forehead with it, held it against his eyes, leaned the side of his head against it. "I hurt so everywhere. Wherever I touch myself with this, I feel healed."

It was explicit, almost ritualized worship, filled with awe and a terrible passion, not for Charlie but for the towering flesh and the male principle it embodied. The reign of the monumental phallus had returned with a vengeance. It seemed to Charlie that he would scarcely have had the right to deny access to an object that inspired such fervor in its disciple. His self-imposed reticence about it seemed perverse before the extravagance of this adulation. He knew that the worship hadn't opened out to include all of him. Jeff was capable of love—he could feel it trembling in him, like an unshed tear, on the rim of his sexuality—but Charlie hadn't made it spill over. There were moments during the strange rite—rapt, remote, ecstatic—in which Jeff's eyes and hands and mouth were mesmerically engaged, when Charlie had to fight back an impulse to seize him and force himself on his attention. Instead, Jeff led him into the ritual, placing Charlie's hands on himself, indicating how he wanted him to hold and caress himself, while his own hands and mouth conducted additional ceremonies.

At last, he pulled off the unbuttoned shirt and placed Charlie's hands on the mattress so that he was leaning back, propped on his arms, his legs sprawling, all of his body slack and disengaged so that the sex seemed to stand free with an immense thrusting power of its own. Jeff once more took possession of it with both hands, stroking it slowly with tantalizing adoration, holding it all over, working every possible variation until he found the combination that brought it immediately to the edge of orgasm. Charlie cried out as he felt it coming. Jeff had dropped down so that he was staring up wide-eyed at the point of emission. He let the first jet leap into the air and then scrambled up to draw the rest into his mouth. When it was over, he wiped his face with the back of his hands and gazed up at Charlie from eyes soft with wonder and gratitude. "Charlie," he murmured.

It brought Charlie forward with his arms out to hold him, touched by his young indifference to the fragility of the love he could offer him. He held his head against his bare chest and kissed his hair. "It was a bit lonely," he said, "but I'm glad for anything I can give you."

Jeff pulled back from him and looked him searchingly in the eyes. "Anything? Everything! Don't you understand what that meant to me? I've been waiting for it all my life. It's the fulfillment of my destiny. So many things have come clear."

Charlie looked into the face that seemed to grow more beautiful with familiarity and smiled at the grandiloquent phrases. "I'd like you to tell me later. We'd better pull ourselves together. We're almost there."

Charlie dressed again while Jeff put on his jacket and stuffed his tie into a pocket. At the door, Charlie kissed his lips and looked into his eyes. "I wish I could tell you to come right up as soon as you can, but I'll need a little time. I left things in mild disorder at the house.

There'll be the kids and Martha and so forth to cope with. Come at ten. I'll be waiting for you in Peter's room. You know."

Jeff ran his hand over his crotch. "I'll find you," he said.

In the confusion of arrival and debarkation, he clung to Charlie's side. They were jostled by the crowd and could allow themselves furtive little contacts of their hands. When they were off and headed in toward town, Charlie kept a hand on his shoulder. He passed the steps he usually took up to the house and continued into a tangle of narrow streets. They offered a sense of semiprivacy. Charlie stopped and faced him. "I've got to leave you somewhere," he said. "I guess this is as good a place as any. I'd like to kiss you before I let you go."

"Why don't you?"

"Here?"

"The Greeks don't care. They kiss each other all the time. Nobody else matters."

"I suppose you're right." He laughed, and their mouths met. He allowed himself only an instant to savor the eagerly parted lips and then drew hastily back, but doing it in the open, here on home territory, made him realize more vividly what the day had done for him. Life had become an adventure once more. All the stale old patterns had been smashed. Anything could happen. "I'll be waiting," he said. He turned abruptly and strode off.

Jeff stood where he was and watched him go, spellbound by the carriage of the masterful body, his mind filled with images of the great phallus. The magnificent figure turned a corner and was gone. Even if he never saw Charlie again, he would always hold him in his mind. He had no need of fantasies anymore.

He set off through the familiar streets, scarcely seeing them. He felt as if he had been gone for a long time and had no real sense of returning. He had gone forever, had, in a sense, departed life. There was a new confidence in his body—he was aware of an impulse to flaunt it; it had been so stupendously used and loved—but there was only darkness in his soul.

If anybody could have dispelled it, it was Charlie, but he hadn't and couldn't. Mike had shown him the level of his needs. There had been a fierce bestiality in their moments of intimacy that had exposed the extent of what he labeled dispassionately as his depravity. He still longed to sacrifice himself to the limitless cruelty of Mike's ego. The air he breathed with Charlie was too rarefied. He didn't want the beauty he offered him except for the beauty of his colossal cock taking him. He had come into possession of himself overnight, and what he had found filled him with despair. He was in love; he had been broken by his love and couldn't be mended.

He listened to Charlie's words as his mind replayed them. Love? The way Charlie said it evoked security and solicitude and devotion. He had gone beyond all such concepts. He was in headlong collision with his destiny. He no longer feared even a meeting with his father.

He found Joe's courtyard door open. Like all the residents, he didn't regard this as an invitation to enter. Doors often wouldn't close. He knocked and waited. When there was no reply, he entered hesitantly and set his bag down inside the door. He heard voices. He was shy of seeing his father with others. He advanced into the seedy courtyard and called "Hello."

A girl he didn't know appeared in a window above him. She smiled down at him. "A beautiful boy," she said in accented English. "Come in, beautiful boy."

"Is my father here?" he asked. "I mean, is George Leighton here?"

The girl looked down at him and laughed maddeningly. He was spared further communication with her by the appearance of his father at the door. He had to stoop to pass through it. For a moment, his face held an expression of blank astonishment, then it brightened with welcome. He approached Jeff, seeming to tower over him as he always had, though there was no great difference in height between them now.

"You're back. What a wonderful surprise. Somebody gave me the impression that you'd left for good."

"I had." Jeff saw instantly that his father was drunk, not stumbling drunk, but cheerful drunk. His clothes looked as if he had been sleeping in them for days, but he was more or less freshly shaved and looked clear-eyed and quite capable of dealing with business. "I have something important to talk to you about."

George put a hand on Jeff's shoulder and gave him a friendly little shake. "You don't look any the worse for wear. Did your mother send you?"

"No. Why? When did you go home last?"

"Well, now. Let's see. You left yesterday? Yes, I was going to Athens this morning, but it turned out there was no need to. Sid pulled my money out of a hat. He won't tell me where he got it."

"That's what I have to talk to you about. Can't we go somewhere private?"

"Come over here. They won't bother us." George took the boy's arm and led him to a corner of the courtyard where there was a

238

derelict table with the paint peeling from it, a kitchen chair, and an upended box. George sat on the box and waved to the chair. Jeff noted it as typical of his unfailing courtesy. It always put him at a disadvantage.

"There," Jeff said, sitting and putting the envelope containing his statement on the table.

George looked at it. "There what?"

"Read it. No. Don't bother. It doesn't tell the whole story. I took your money. I gave it to Dimitri." He filled out the details less emotionally than he had to Peter, not attempting to exculpate himself any more than he felt the facts justified.

When he had finished, George propped his elbow on the table, rested his forehead in his hand, and gave the envelope a little spin with his forefinger. "You're in love with Dimitri?" he asked.

"I thought I might be."

George toyed with the envelope for a silent moment. "So now we're going to have the truth. That's good. I want to understand. We're apt to lose our heads when we're in love. Oh, I don't mean thinking you could borrow the money for a day. I can see how you were thinking. But not to come to me when you knew an innocent man was in trouble—that's rotten, Jeff."

"I know. All I can say is that it got out of control. Dimitri and the police. Mike and the chance to go away with him. I told Sid so he would go on working on Dimitri after I left. At least he succeeded. I'm not pleased with myself." He pushed the envelope closer to his father. "Peter told me to write it that way. He didn't see any point involving Dimitri, since it was all my idea. So long as Costa is let out, he didn't think it mattered if I arranged it a bit. He thought I was going away."

George lifted his head, drew the sheet of paper from the envelope, glanced at it, and dropped it. "You have good friends. Forget it. I've already told the police I found it in the house. They have let Costa go. I've managed to do that much. Why *are* you back? Aren't you going away with Mike?"

"I thought I was. He left without me this morning."

"I see. I mean, I don't see at all. What did the son of a bitch do? Did he lead you on and ditch you? Did he offer you the trip so he could get you into bed with him? I don't know. I'm just talking. I hope you can tell me."

"It wasn't like that." Jeff averted his face. George could see his Adam's apple working. "I—he was—he was—in his way, he fell in love with me. I was—I'm in love with him."

George hunched his shoulders to absorb the blow. He shook his head to clear it. "You're not making sense. In love with Dimitri? In love with Mike? Don't you mean you wanted to go to bed with them? You can look me in the eye when you say it."

"That's not why—" Jeff flung himself forward and banged the table with clenched fists. "Don't you understand? It's tearing me apart. I've heard you call guys screaming queens. Well, that's what I am. It would've been all right with Mike. There was something between us that was good for both of us. It's gone. All right. Now I just want to go to bed with men."

George reached out and gripped his arm. "Easy. I'm sorry. I was being stupid." He wished he hadn't had anything to drink. Although Jeff's grief was evident, he couldn't identify with it. He hadn't experienced anything like it in his youth. There had been the casual affairs and then there had been Sarah and as much happiness as a man could reasonably expect—until recently. Because the very idea of Mike encouraging the boy in any way repelled and outraged him, there was a stoppage of his sympathies. He waited while his son got himself under control.

"*I'm* being stupid," Jeff said at last. "I know. It's over. He obviously couldn't accept what he felt for me. He prides himself on not caring about anybody. I wish that when things are over you could stop feeling them."

"Yes, that would be convenient. But then I suppose we'd never learn anything." Something about his attitude about Sarah shifted profoundly as he spoke. For two days, he had been trying to convince himself that it was over with her. He had even had Lena as an enthusiastic bed partner on several occasions in the past twenty-four hours. Nothing had changed; it was time for him to face it. "You know, you won't go down in history as the only boy who ever wanted to go to bed with a man. That's all I meant about looking me in the eye. I was being dim. I thought you were embarrassed. There's no need to be, of course. I don't condemn homosexuality. I just don't understand it. I wish we could find a new word for it. It's too loaded with opprobrium. There certainly aren't many people I admire more than Peter and Charlie. If that's going to be your life, do it as well as they have. The hell with Martha and her children. Those two are complete in each other. I should think it would be awfully difficult, but apparently it can happen."

Jeff's cheeks were burning as the colossal phallus rose in his mind's eye, the network of living veins, the deep backward sweep of the dark flanged head, the thick base from which the great column sprang of equal monolithic thickness all its length, lifting with such force that it seemed to be in motion, propelling itself toward conquest. Complete in each other. They were, of course. Yet he had held the secret sacred flesh. It had entered deep within him and made him its slave. He had drunk its mysterious leaping fluid. To that extent, for an hour or two, he had partaken of their completeness. Charlie's arms around him. Peter's. Peter's mouth sweet and instructive, Charlie's passionately healing. He had glimpsed their secret, and there was nowhere in him for it to take hold and nourish him.

"I doubt if it can happen to me," he said with a touch of self-mockery. "I'd have to go back to Plato and renounce the lusts of the flesh. It's always struck me that Socrates must've had an awful lot of boys before he came around to that point of view."

George was shocked by the jocular note, though he knew he should have been prepared for it. The boy was a mass of contradictions. Somehow, he preferred torment to flippancy. More stupidity on his part. "Well, since we seem to be having some straight talk, maybe you won't mind telling me more. Have you been leading an active sex life for long?"

A ghost of a smile played across Jeff's lips. "Since night before last. Yesterday. Morning, actually."

"You mean, never before? Not with Dimitri?"

"Never before."

"And you're convinced on the basis of twenty-four hours' experience that that's the way you're going to be? You've never been faintly attracted to a girl?"

"Never. I've always known. Don't ask me why. Even Charlie and Peter can't tell me that."

"You've talked to them? I'm glad."

Their eyes met, and neither flinched. George found himself looking into Sarah's eyes, and love overcame his regret and bewilderment. The child in Jeff was dead; they could talk to each other as equals. "I'm sorry you've had such a rough start, but love is where most of the suffering comes from, as well as the joy. I couldn't want you to be spared it. Just remember that this is only the beginning."

"That's a pretty horrible thought. No, you're being very—well, I appreciate it. Don't worry about me."

"I do, naturally. But I will a lot less if you'll talk to me. You'll have to take the initiative. It's not for me to put ideas into your head. I respect you for coming clean about the money, even if you should've done it sooner."

"Peter made me."

"Nobody could make you if you hadn't known you should. You're not perfect, but you don't have to make yourself out worse than you are. It might be a good idea for you to tell the police you hid the money. It makes my story more convincing. Anything to get Costa completely off the hook."

"That's what Peter wants. He's working on it in Athens."

"He's in Athens? Yes, I guess Sid told me. Christ, I'm not a very inspiring example. Everybody doing something while I sit here getting drunk." He ran his fingers through his hair and felt the muscles of his face stiffening as he phrased his next question. "Listen Jeff, yesterday there would've been lots of things I couldn't talk to you about. That's changed. You've had a look at the adult world. It isn't always pretty. There's something I've got to know. You *were* telling the truth the other day, weren't you? About seeing your mother?"

Jeff drew back and dropped his eyes. "I don't know what made me say it, but I'm not a liar. Dimitri's house is up near there." He paused and lifted his eyes again. They were full of fierce ardent reproach. "Does it matter? If you love someone, you love them, no matter what they do."

George sighed and propped his head on his hand again, thinking of the impossible confrontation with Sarah that lay ahead. Nothing could come of it, but his will would remain paralyzed until he had forced himself through it. "Yes, well, I wonder how long you'll be able to hang on to that thought. It takes an awful lot of generosity to live by it. I'm glad you said it, though. It sounds simple, but there may be something in it."

"What's fidelity and jealousy and all the rest of it? It's just being selfish with somebody else's body. I'd never expect anybody to be faithful to me."

George marshaled his thoughts; if he couldn't make Jeff understand, what could he say to Sarah? "That may be an insight into your particular tastes," he said, "but you'll have to take my word for it that it doesn't work that way for ordinary couples. Because of the way we're built, maybe a man feels more possessive toward a woman than he would toward another man. He doesn't want used goods. Could it be as dismal as that? It doesn't have to be a question of morals. Any valid morality is primarily based on self-interest anyway, so let's say it's self-interest. It's to the interest of the man *and* the woman, if they love each other, to keep themselves whole for each other in order to create a relationship that's always alive and growing and always moving toward completion. You can't do this if you're giving something so essential as physical passion to others. Being forgiving and unselfish doesn't replace the loss. This is pretty old stuff, but it's not something that changes from year to year."

"Why do you talk old stuff?" Jeff burst out. He made a quick swipe at the hair on his forehead, and his eyes grew brooding and faltered, and he bowed his head over the table. "Maybe it's all wrong. Maybe it's impossible to make the kind of relationship you're talking about. What about the people who give something to everybody who comes along? Like Dimitri, even. I don't know. You're a great man. You can tell people what life is all about. You should hear the way Mike talks about you. You're worth a thousand of him—all he knows about is destruction and hate—why do you do things that make him look right? Why are you here unless you know that we can find something better than anywhere else? Mike says it's because you can't face reality. Reality to him is hitting somebody when he's down. You, Charlie, and Peter—you see beauty and meaning in life. Are you kidding yourselves? Can't you spell it out so the rest of us can understand? I want to see beauty, but all I see is the beauty of a male body. Is that enough?" His breath caught on a shudder that shook him. "Life is impossible," he ended with deep pained melancholy.

"It's a bit soon for you to be coming to that conclusion." George reached out and ran a hand down his arm, gripping his elbow. "You've asked some important questions and made me feel fairly ashamed of myself, but that's nothing new. Life *is* impossible without a lot of strength and patience and discipline. I've let it become impossible recently, but that must be my fault, though I haven't quite figured out what it is. I'm still trying. Does your mother know you're back?"

"No. Just Charlie. He came with me. I'd never have made it without him."

"They're being very good to you. You've given us a lot to talk about, but there's nothing I can say yet except that if I can't answer your questions by tomorrow I might as well throw in the sponge. Let's clear the decks. For whatever it's worth, I'll take your statement to the police. I'd appreciate it if you'd go home and tell your mother I'll be along in a little while."

"Am I supposed to tell her about—well, about me and Mike and so forth?"

"I'd soft-pedal the sex angle until I've had a talk with her. There's no point her getting worked up for nothing. She's inclined to take the natural woman's view that it's a great loss not to have a wife and children and all that goes with them. I think so too, of course, but I can see there might be compensations. If it's not too much to ask, it might be a good idea for you to go out for a couple hours. Have something to eat at the port. Needless to say, your mother and I aren't on the best of terms at the moment. If I'm going to try to hammer out some hope for the future, I'll want privacy."

"Of course. I want to see Dimitri anyway. Don't be surprised if I stay out all night."

"With Dimitri? Sorry. Don't answer if you don't want to."

"That's all right. Not Dimitri. I'd rather not say more. I'm not feeling very cheerful. If I'm going to make sense, I'll need all the help I can get. I won't hang around the bar, if that's what you're afraid of."

George had almost forgotten having forbidden the bar. It seemed like weeks ago and no longer had any relevance to the young man he was talking to now. "Don't bother about that. I doubt if anybody will be fooling around with dope for a while. That's all I was worried about. You're turning into a very handsome guy, Jeff. Lots of people will be after you. Discriminate, for God's sake. At your age, sex just for the hell of it never did anybody any harm. If you find beauty in a male body, make the most of it. That is, respect your emotions as well as your desires. You feel things deeply, but it's not condescending to say that you're bound to be immature still in some ways. Don't pour yourself out for anybody who isn't worthy of you. That's all. I don't expect you to pay attention to anything I say. It's the sort of thing a father feels he has to say to his son. Shall we go?"

"Don't you have to say good-bye?"

"They won't even notice I'm gone. I'll thank Joe for his hospitality when I see him." He pocketed the envelope and rose. Jeff followed suit, and they walked together to the gate, where Jeff stopped to pick up his bag. "I suppose the police might want you to come in and tell your story in person, but I'll try to stall them off. The sooner we forget this the better."

"I'll go if they want me. I want to do whatever's necessary."

"Good. You're going to be all right." They left the courtyard. George gave him a little slap on the back and a push in the direction of home.

Jeff took a step and turned back. "I believe in you." His Adam's apple worked, and his great eyes brooded at George. "This may sound sort of fresh for a son to say to his father, but I know *you're*

244

going to be all right. That matters a lot more than my silly little problems. I have sense enough to know that." He swung away and set off with a new grace in his step.

George stood speechless, staring after him. He became aware of a lump in his throat and swallowed. Was this the turning of the tide? Was he recovering his touch? Had he handled himself that well with Jeff? He was beginning to feel quite sober as he turned down toward town.

What was a man supposed to do when his son announced he was queer? Beat him up? Shoot himself? Mike stuck in the craw, but Mike was gone, thank God, before the atavistic repugnance Mike touched off in him threw him completely off the track. He could think of his son in the arms of some other male lover without horror and even with approval if the guy were decent. He devoutly hoped that Jeff would soon find somebody to love him. His unbalanced intensity was frightening at moments. He needed somebody desperately who could hold him steady. He would offer him all the support he could, but no parent was ever enough.

At least, affection and understanding had had an inning, with promising results. He had little left for Sarah. Jeff had been telling him things that still lingered unresolved in his mind. A vote of confidence. They had much to give each other. Was that enough to have salvaged from the ruin? He had leaned on Sarah long enough, demanding loyalty, unable to offer what she needed. A living, growing relationship? Mutilated. Murdered. Discard it in a clean and manly way. He must go to her with the strength to cope with life alone.

As he neared the police station, he bridled at the atmosphere of blind complacent authority he would encounter there. The captain had glared at his money this morning as if willing it to disappear. It interfered with his routine and was therefore offensive. Coached by George, Joe had followed him to say that his money had been returned by a foreigner who had borrowed it without mentioning it. What foreigner? He had left on the morning boat. The case against Costa had evaporated. Did the captain's threats still hold good? The fact that Peter was pulling strings in Athens was reassuring. Perhaps he would blunt the captain's wrath. He didn't care, no matter how it turned out. Alone, without the support of place or person.

He wasn't sorry to find the captain absent. He displayed Jeff's statement and countersigned the signature and turned it in. He left word for the captain that he and Jeff were at his disposal to answer any questions and made his getaway.

Once home, he was so intent on finding Sarah that he was halfway across the courtyard before he noticed the rent in the wall. He stopped dead in his tracks and stared. He blinked and stared again. Why hadn't anybody said anything about this? What in the world had happened? If he weren't feeling quite sober now, he would suspect his eyes of inventing it.

It started up near the roof and continued down below the bedroom floor, above and alongside and under one of the bedroom windows, so that the window frame was standing almost free and furniture was visible within. After stupefaction, his first reaction was outrage. Who was responsible? How could it have happened? He remembered vaguely some talk about a structural weakness when they had bought the house. Something about earthquakes and the builder airily pointing out that there hadn't been an earthquake of consequence in—he couldn't remember how many years.

The earthquake. It had been like this since the night before last, and nobody had told him. Briefly and unreasonably, he felt it as an additional grievance against Sarah. All of his pride in the house gathered in a knot of protest. The house was his single creation about which there could be no question. It was, in a way that had nothing to do with architecture or aesthetics, perfect. It had even shut Mike Cochran up. Their ruined lives? The symbolism was so neat as to make it absurd. If the house was ruined, their lives must be flourishing. Total ruin was visited on a man only to illustrate divine retribution. Was he Job?

He noticed that some effort had been made to gather the rubble of the wall into neat piles, but one whole bank of their finest saffron geraniums had been destroyed. He laughed softly, a strange sound that caught in his throat with dismay. What could he do but laugh? *And rebuild it,* he thought with instant decision. He wasn't as impervious to the police chief's threats as he had thought. He wouldn't go until the house was repaired. He would pull strings, go to the press, fight back. This was where he lived. He was going to stay. He was pleased to find that there was so much left in him.

He caught movement out of the corner of his eye and realized that Sarah had appeared in the door. He turned slowly and looked at her. He felt so at odds with her, so deeply estranged that for a moment he wondered why he had thought he had something important to say to her.

"Is Jeff here?" he asked without a word or gesture of greeting.

"He came a little while ago. I was so relieved to see him that I was

246

careful not to fuss over him. He just put down his bag and left."

As he had asked him to do, but George was sorry he wasn't here. He wanted to talk to him about the wall. Wanting him to be here was like thinking of a beloved friend. Curiously, his liking men brought him closer, quickened George's protective feelings toward him, broadened his responses to him. Without having given it much thought, he found that his acceptance of it had already grown more positive; he would like to help him prove to the world that it wasn't a misfortune.

Sarah emerged from the house and approached him cautiously. "You hadn't heard about that?" she asked, facing the wall. "It's one of the major casualties of the earthquake."

He admired her for making no reference to his absence. "Is there any other damage?"

"Just what you see. It's hard to say how far it goes. We'll have to get Pano here and see about fixing it. Sid told me you have the money back. I don't care of it takes all of it. It has to be fixed."

George looked at her with a spark of interest. "I'm glad we agree about that." This much agreement reestablished some semblance of normal contact between them. He supposed they could go on from here and pretend that the last three days hadn't existed. They could, but he was determined not to do so.

Sarah turned and took a few aimless steps toward the grouping of outdoor furniture. "How odd of Jeff to have wanted to lend it to Dimitri. I mean, Dimitri is—do you think there's anything—well, anything unhealthy about their friendship?"

It was just what he had been waiting for. He had plenty to say to her. "I think they've been to bed together, if that's what you mean," he said bluntly. "That sounds healthy enough to me. Some of our best friends prefer their own sex. It's not surprising if Jeff does too. I want you to get that through your head right from the start."

Sarah turned back to him with an anguished look. "But darling, you can't just accept it and condemn him for life. He's extricated himself from Mike, but I knew he would if there was anything of that sort involved in it. He needs help. There must be something we can do. Couldn't you arrange for him to have a girl? Men sometimes do that for their sons."

"Sure. I could deliver him to Joe Peterson's doorstep. He could have three girls, with a boy or two thrown in. Good God Almighty, do you think he's not old enough to know what he wants? He's extricated himself from Mike because Mike dumped him. He's madly in love with him, poor kid."

"How can you say that? How can you talk about it as if it didn't matter? I don't understand it from you, of all people. You've said yourself you don't like what's happening here—so many of them beginning to turn up."

"I was talking about a particular type. There's no need for Jeff to be like that. If he's inherited his tastes from you, I certainly intend to help him." It was an oblique attack, but he had had to steel his nerves to say it. It prepared the way for words he couldn't imagine saying to her sober. He saw only a mild reproof come into her expressive eyes before it melted into her distress.

"If you can't feel any normal concern for him, I wish at least you wouldn't be flippant," she said.

"That wasn't meant to be flippant, and you know it. Okay. I have another word or two to say on the subject, and then we can get on to more disagreeable matters. I intend to encourage Jeff to be perfectly open about his emotional life, his sex life, whatever you want to call it. If he wants to bring a friend home to go to bed with, he's welcome. He's not going to feel any guilt with me. I don't ever want to hear you say a disapproving word or make him feel that there's anything wrong. If you do, I'll leave you and take him with me. That's how flippant I feel about it. Right? As for the rest of what I have to say, we'd better go inside. It doesn't lend itself to alfresco discussion." He saw her straighten to assert herself, but at the same time he felt her acceptance of his authority. All the years of attempting to achieve an equal partnership had probably been a waste of time.

"You're certainly giving yourself airs this evening," she said, not without humor. "You disappear for two days. You make it sufficiently clear that you've been with three girls, and then you move back in as if you were the lord of the manor."

"That's what I am, though I've allowed you to lose sight of the fact more often than I should have. Only one girl, incidentally. Shall we go in?" Again, he had to make an effort to speak so plainly. All the years when they hadn't had such things to talk about made it difficult to break the habit of gentle loving intercourse that had grown up between them. He had managed it the other night in front of Mike, when he had been drunk, but even then he hadn't been able to bring himself to name names and cite facts. In spite of his violence, he remembered skirting an outright accusation. It mustn't be like that again.

She stood for a moment musingly, studying the nails of one hand, making a small point of making up her own mind, and then started for the house. As she passed him, she gave him a look that was as nearly flirtatious as any she had ever given him, having never been inclined to obvious feminine wiles. Why should she flirt with him now, when she had found herself a new love, when he had insulted her in public and as good as left her? Did she think she could obliterate all that had gone wrong between them with a suggestive glance? He felt his fists clenching for the blow she so richly deserved. He accompanied her into the house without looking at her. "Go up to my study," he ordered her. "We'll be private there."

"Do you want to take a drink?" ،

"This isn't going to be a social event. No, no drinks. If I can't do it sober, it's not worth doing at all."

Some sense of the gravity of the occasion seemed to get through to her. She kept her distance as they crossed rooms and mounted stairs and came out at the top of the last difficult ones. He glanced at the smashed window. The broken lamp lay where he had left it.

"Oh," she said when she caught sight of it. It was a small stricken sound.

"Yes. 'Oh.' I had a little temper tantrum when I found out what you'd been doing while I was with Mike the other afternoon." Dread made his heart beat heavily. When it had all been said, when it had been clothed in words so that it lay ugly and explicit between them, what would be left to carry them over into the future? Perhaps nothing. That was the risk he was taking.

"I wish you'd get to the point," she said as she seated herself beside a table piled with books. "What is this all about?" She watched him closely as he went to the bed that doubled as a couch and let himself down on it. *He can't know,* she repeated to herself. It had been her main source of support for the past two days. She mustn't betray her guilt by the slightest quiver of hesitancy. She had to carry it off—for his sake more than her own. If he were anybody else, she could imagine breaking down and confessing and hoping to patch things up. That was the ordinary human way, but he wasn't one for patching.

"I told you I was leaving the other night," he said conversationally. "What did you make of that?"

"I was terribly frightened, of course," she said, welcoming what seemed to be a reprieve. "Actually I was sitting here wondering what I could do to stop you when the earthquake happened. When I saw the wall was gone, the first thing I thought was that you'd have to stay to take care of the repairs."

"How very touching. I haven't been all that much fun recently. Why were you so anxious for me to stay?"

"Oh, George. Because I love you, darling, and always have. What a question."

"Love me in your fashion? Love having me around while you have other men to satisfy you?"

She knew his calm was deceptive. She could hear the shout barely contained in his voice. She blanked Pavlo from her mind so that she could look at him with eyes shining with sincerity. "I've begged and begged you to forgive me my one bad mistake. There's something I never wanted to tell you—it's a subject I've tried not to think about—but I suppose I should now. I had the feeling that he was torn between me and Jeff. It was one reason he was able to get under my defenses. I felt he needed an experience with a woman so desperately. I don't say that as an excuse but so you'll understand that I didn't just lose my head."

"Oh, God. This ridiculous idea that homosexuality is some sort of disease that can be cured." He ran his fingers through his hair. Her composure made an accusation indecent. She looked fresh and cool and lovely in her simple summer dress. He would never believe in her again. "You know perfectly well I'm not talking about silly fucking Ronnie. I said 'men.' "

"I heard you. You're sometimes capable of poetic license."

"Splendid. You're really good, Sarah. All right. Before I can expect you to tell the truth, I suppose I ought to tell the truth myself." He paused to conquer his shame. He had guarded the fairly obvious secret for a year, drowned it in alcohol, drowned them both in alcohol rather than reveal the pitiable fact. Now that he was prepared to speak, he was suddenly filled with hope. Perhaps a confession would solve everything. He had been withholding something that was essential to their understanding of each other. If he could open himself to her totally, as he had always believed in doing, love might flow from him once more. "You talk about my forgiving you," he began. "I had. My mind found all the necessary excuses. I was a more eloquent advocate for you than you could ever be for yourself. There was one thing, though, that I should think you might've guessed. You made me impotent. I've always thought of our bodies as belonging so exclusively to each other that I stopped wanting yours when I knew somebody else had had it. I'm not impotent in a general way, just with you, but that doesn't mean I've been running

250

after the other girls, as you very well know. I've made the best of celibacy, waiting to get back to you. I've punished myself with drink in order to keep myself concentrated on you. It was self-defeating, of course, but I think something had begun to happen. There've been moments recently when I've felt the dam breaking. I'd hoped you might accept celibacy too." He watched her face as he spoke. It had filled with a sort of grieving sympathy when he said the key word, but he had penetrated deeper now. He watched as her grieving seemed to turn in on herself. He had struck genuine regret. It was a clear admission of guilt, but it left him at his most vulnerable, filled with the old desire to protect her from hurt. He was drawn by her.

He started to his feet, but as he thought of taking her in his arms, the specter of her latest infidelity intervened. He would be imitating Pavlo on her body. He couldn't bear it. He had failed to overcome the refusal in him. He would have to go on until everything had been said between them, no matter what the consequences. He slumped on the bed and dropped his eyes and ran his fingers through his hair.

"Oh, darling, why didn't you tell me?" Her dark voice trembled with a plea. "What do you expect me to do when you cut yourself off from me?"

"I guess a man's pride in his sexual powers is pretty basic," he said, offering it as an apology. "The guy who can't get it up is a joke."

"You couldn't be a joke to me. If you'd told me, we could've done something. We'd have found a way around it."

He sat up and stared at her incredulously. "If you think it's as simple as that, why didn't you? Do I have to make an announcement? Do you think I want to turn it into a project, you working over me, trying to recapture something that's always been marvelous and spontaneous between us?" As he said it, his mind countered with another question: *Why not?* The surrender of pride was a small price to pay for restored happiness. Yet wasn't pride intrinsic to their happiness? They were neither of them grovelers. "I've tried to find a way around too many things. It's time to meet them head-on, fight through them or be beaten in the attempt. That's what I intend to do now." He sprang up and took a turn around the room and stopped behind her. He didn't want to watch her while she lied. She did it too well. He would like to retain some scrap of faith in her. "I'm afraid we can't get around the afternoon Mike was here. Was it only day before yesterday? It seems longer. What did you do after we left you?"

"Don't loom behind me like that, darling. It's not nice."

"I'm not trying to be nice. I'm trying to get you to tell me the truth.

It might be easier for you if you don't have to face me. I want you to answer my question."

"What question?" *He couldn't know,* she reminded herself as she realized that she wasn't going to escape an interrogation. She took a deep breath to steady herself. "You mean about the other afternoon? You know perfectly well what I did."

"Yes, I do, but I think it's important for you to tell me."

"I took a nap. I—this is absurd. What do you expect me to tell you?"

"The truth."

Had somebody seen her? She mustn't say anything he could catch her up on. "I—oh, of course. I remember now. I went for a walk."

"On the hottest day of the century? That sounds pretty eccentric."

"That's why. I woke up in a pool of sweat. The house was an oven, so I went out."

"Where did you go?"

"Really, darling. What *are* you trying to get at? Just around. Up toward the school. Nowhere."

"You know perfectly well what I'm getting at. Why do you want to prolong the agony?"

So he did know something. She was glad he wasn't looking at her. She could control her voice despite the erratic beating of her heart, but she didn't know what was happening to her face. She was aware that she was gripping the arms of the chair with her hands. She shifted in her seat. Had she gone too far to backtrack? She had no choice. "Oh, I see," she said with a little laugh, as if she had been caught in a naughty prank. "Somebody saw me going into Pavlo's house, or coming out, whichever, and couldn't wait to tell you. People really are extraordinary."

He came slowly around from behind the chair and stood looking down at her. She forced herself to lift her head with a little smile. His expression made the smile inappropriate, and it was quickly effaced. She was more frightened than she had ever been in her life with him. He look of cold pained disgust told her that she risked losing him forever. Disaster confronted her, and she talked fast, hoping that something would come out that would deflect the force of what she felt was going to be a punishing end to everything. "If you'd asked me if I'd been to Pavlo's house, I would have told you. Why all this beating around the bush? It never occurred to me you'd be interested. Besides, we've had no chance to talk. You haven't been here. I'd made friends with him on the rocks. I was hot. I just dropped in to see if I could cool off. Stop staring at me like that, darling. I drop in

252

on people all the time. I don't always remember to report all my comings and goings to you."

He looked at her, watching all her composure crumble. He felt a small sad vindictive satisfaction in knowing that he had her on the run at last. It wasn't the sort of satisfaction he wanted to live with. "You've made a *friend* of a creature like that? My respect for you has worn pretty thin, but there's enough left for me not to want to believe that. I prefer the truth. Sex is sex. Before we go on, I'll offer you an alternative. I've decided not to leave. Do you want to? Leave here, leave me, take Kate, and go? Jeff doesn't belong to either of us anymore."

"Don't be ridiculous, George," she said, astonished at being given this opportunity to fight back. "Where would I go? You can't afford for us to leave, even if I wanted to. I don't, of course. You're my life. You know that. We've made our life here. Neither of us is going anywhere."

"I wouldn't be too sure about that. Maybe we'll be thrown out. I haven't told you about that possibility."

"What are you talking about now?"

"I won't go into it at the moment, but it might be best. Perhaps Mike is right. Maybe I should be back in the States, taking part in whatever is going on over there. After seeing Mike, I don't believe it, but it's worth thinking about. Keep in mind. If you stay with me, you may not be living here long."

"I'm going to stay with you, George, no matter where we live."

The heartfelt simplicity with which she said it made tears spring to his eyes, and he turned away from her. She knew how to play on his vulnerability. The temptation to let her off was greater than ever, but he had to resist it. Nothing had been accomplished, nothing had changed. He cleared his throat and turned back to her. "In that case, we'll have to go back to Pavlo before I can decide whether I want you to stay. Tell me what happened."

"What do you think happened?" The respite had given her an opportunity to rally her confidence. Now that she had admitted going to the house, there was no reason why she couldn't maintain to the end the innocence of the visit. "We talked for a few minutes. As a matter of fact, it *was* cooler there. It was quite a relief after my walk."

"Sarah, you know perfectly well I know why you were there. If you can't tell me, I definitely don't want you to stay. If you can—well, truth hasn't been the most common commodity between us recently. Maybe a little more of it would clear the air. I really don't know. It's the risk you have to take."

"Why do you talk such nonsense? What risk? This is getting very boring, you know. I don't like the suggestion that I can't go visit a man without misbehaving." A cloak of indifference descended over her, as if she had suddenly passed beyond his reach and achieved total independence. It was undoubtedly play-acting, but it chilled him because it corresponded to something he was beginning to be aware of in himself. Some part of him was free of her. It *was* boring to go on trying to make her state the obvious. He could almost believe that he wanted to be completely free of her.

"Christ," he explained. His voice rose to a shout. "You went there to get fucked. Do you think I'm an idiot? You're still attractive enough, goddamn you. It's obvious what he's thinking about every waking minute. It's on display for everybody to see. How was it? Is it as big as it looks? Did he really get it in there and make you feel it?"

"Please, George. Don't be disgusting." She sat inviolate in the dignity of her indifference and distaste. "What's come over you? We don't talk like that. I've never seen you like this."

"It's high time you did. You grab a young twerp who's after your son. Aren't we supposed to mention that? You go panting after a beach boy with a big cock. What a dreadful word. Christ. You're no more or less sluttish than any other woman. If you're not getting it at home, you go out and find it. Can't we say it?" Rage was boiling in him. He was freeing himself with every word he said. He had only to revive the earthy crudeness that had once been in her to reduce them both to the half-tamed animals they both essentially were. He had been born and bred a sham, sham gentleness, sham consideration of others, sham cultivation of his mind and senses. If her betrayal helped him to break through the layers of sham, at least he would be more nearly a man.

"I won't listen to this," she said in infuriatingly superior tones. "You must be mad. What about all the decency and happiness we've created together? You're throwing it all away."

"You're damn right I am. Decency is incompatible with the human condition. People can't endure happiness. You haven't had sex for a year, but what about before? Weren't you happy when you met Ronnie? Who cares? You had to be sure you weren't missing something. Shit on decency." He sprang forward and swung his open hand hard across her face. She cried out and rocked in her chair. "Go on. I want you to say it. I want you to hear yourself say it. *Pavlo fucked me.* Get it out loud and clear. Then maybe we can talk about decency and happiness."

Tears were rolling silently down her cheeks. "You don't hit people," she protested incredulously.

"Don't I, though." He swung his other hand and hit her harder. He could scarcely believe that it was he who was doing and saying these things, but he was filled with a wild exhilaration. Let the animal take over; civilized man had had his day. "You're going to say it, do you understand?" he shouted. "I'm going to hit you till you do."

She had lifted her hands in front of her in fragile self-defense. She shook her head as sobs began to shake her. "You can't make me," she asserted in a choked voice.

"That's what you think." He swung both hands, one after the other, and hit her twice again.

She cried out with pain and bowed her head, holding it in her hands. Her body swayed and twisted as if she were wrestling with some inner demon. "All right, damn you." Her voice rose suddenly, hard and coarse and almost exultant. "Pavlo fucked me. He fucked me. I wanted him to fuck—"

He was on her, his arms flailing, beating her on the head and back and shoulders. He seized her hair and shook her until he heard her teeth clattering. He released her and struck her again so that she almost toppled from the chair. She managed to twist out of it and dart up from under his arm. He turned and seized her and sent her hurtling against the bed. She fell back on it, her skirt up around her thighs. She tried to struggle upright, her hair falling in a tangle across her face. He had stripped her of all pretense to dignity at last. She pushed her hair back, and their eyes met, hers brimming with tears and an unmistakable message. This wretched, sobbing, battered creature wanted him. He lifted a hand to his forehead. His mouth stretched wide to emit an animal howl of outrage. No sound came. He covered his mouth with his hand to contain his revulsion. His mind once again posed the question: *Why not?* If this was the way back to her, take it. So much for tenderness and solicitude and understanding. They could wallow in the gutter together. He was on the bed in a bound. He grabbed her arm and dragged her up to him. He seized the top of her dress and gave a great yank. It ripped down the middle.

"You disgusting—" she panted. "Don't touch me. I won't ever—" Her eyes contradicted her words. They were full of astonished, wounded desire. "What about yesterday? Did you go let him fuck you again?"

"No. I did it so I would stop wanting him. It worked."

255

"You bitch. How many more men are you going to have so you'll stop wanting them?" He tore the remnants of the dress from her. She was wearing nothing under it but brief underpants. Her body had no need of being trussed. He yanked at cloth again. Elastic held, but enough came away in his hands. Shreds of the garment circled her waist, but the center of her was exposed. The effect satisfied the brutality he had found in himself. She looked like the victim of rape. Her arms were lifted instinctively to shield her breasts. He tore them away and held them out while he looked at her and flung her back into the bed.

"You're vile. Filthy," she cried. "If you go on I'll never speak to you again."

He stood over her and tore off his shirt. The feel of her skin against his hands, her obscene nakedness exposed to him after all the months of averting his eyes from it, were sending commanding orders tingling through his body. He wasn't impotent now. He stripped and straightened and thrust his hips toward her. He caught a strong whiff of body smell. Ordinarily, he would have been fastidiously offended by himself, but now it contributed to his intoxication. He was glad to stink of humanity. "I'm not a body boy, but I'm the only man you'll have as long as I'm around," he raged. He lunged for her hair and pulled her face up close to his lifted sex. "There. All I needed was to see you for what you are. An available body. If it's going for free, I'll have some too. Go on. Take it. I'll bet you were panting to suck Pavlo's. It must've been quite a mouthful. I'm easy for you."

"Why do you want to make it hideous?" she sobbed. "I loathe you. I never want you to touch me again. It's all over."

"You're damned right it is. It was all over day before yesterday. What's hideous about sucking my cock? You sucked his, didn't you? I'm sure he didn't have to insist. Tell me. I want you to say it."

"Yes, I sucked his cock." Her voice was once more hard and coarse.

His sex strained upward. He yanked her head closer. "Then do it, goddamn you. Open your mouth and do it."

She did as she was told, and in an instant all inhibitions vanished from her obedience. He felt no pleasure in it. There was a great wrenching within him, and his spirit seemed flooded with tears. All that was left to him was the harsh sordid satisfaction of making her grovel before him at last. He steeled himself to accept this shameful obeisance and swarmed up onto the bed over her, gripping her frail shoulders roughly to keep his sex in her mouth.

256

When he had exploited his command of her to the limit of his endurance, he pulled away from her. "That's enough of that," he said harshly. "We know you like it. Now I'm going to fuck you. I'm sorry you like that too. I'm not going to do it to give you pleasure."

His hands were rough on her, handling her beauty with cold authority, while he placed her as he wanted her and dropped down onto her, driving cruelly into her. She cried out, but he could feel her body offer itself to him. He closed his heart to its appeal. He was determined to reestablish his possession of her without yielding his newfound freedom. He forced himself to take her selfishly, forced his nature to retreat before the liberation of his basest urges, resisted the love that flowed out of the very act of their lying together again after their long privation.

Orgasm became a hope of final freedom. He drove hard to achieve it, knowing that it must come quickly if he was to save himself from being ensnared by her again. He had recovered the power to accomplish a mechanical act on her body, nothing more. It was dehumanized, depersonalized, independent of the desire he felt charging her body with electrifying responses.

He burst into her with a shout before she could impinge on the cold solitary enactment of his triumph over her. He lay on her with his eyes closed, blessedly drained of thought or feeling. When he opened them again, the room was afire with the copper rays of the setting sun. The glory of it transfigured what had just taken place between them. He withdrew from her hastily and sat up on the edge of the bed, fighting back tears.

"That's fucking for you. It has all the emotional impact of brushing your teeth." After the violence he had unleashed in himself, words sounded peculiarly sterile and superfluous. Using them was a habit he had yet to overcome. "Is that all you wanted from your body boy and your pretty fairy?"

There was a silence, and then she spoke in a constricted voice. "You've punished me more horribly than I thought possible. You had the right. I didn't know you had such cruelty in you."

"I didn't either. We still have things to discover in each other." His voice caught, and he bowed his head, resting it in his hands. "Oh, Christ, Sal, why did we have to do this to each other? Were we so wrong for so long? It's never going to be the same again, you know."

"No. Never."

"Maybe we'll discover that's a good thing. I wonder."

"How can ugliness be good?"

"Ugliness can be true. I've tried never to shut my eyes to ugliness or truth. The truth you had to tell me was ugly enough. Don't you forget it. I'm glad I made you tell me. It was stupid to pretend there was less ugliness in us than there is in most people. Things were going our way for so long that I guess we forgot. Loving each other so much right from the start maybe wasn't an unmixed blessing. We've always been sort of above the battle. My goddamn success. Living here has been part of it too, I suppose. Our island idyll. We're not above the battle any more."

"We are and always will be. You're still you. Nobody sees the beauty in life the way you do." She said it with conviction while she thought what a relief it would be not to be so in awe of him anymore. He wasn't perfect. He had been unfaithful to her now. He had dismissed it as if it had no importance, but it would surely count in the way they dealt with each other in the future.

"We're right back where we started, with all of it to be done all over again," he said, reminding her of the harsh facts as he saw them. "Do you think we can make it?"

"I didn't mean any of the things I said. You were terrifying, but—" She dropped her voice almost to a whisper. "It was horrible but exciting."

He suppressed a pang of revulsion. She was right to say it. A fuck was a fuck, and the hell with their otherworldly sensibilities. "Don't expect me to be that exciting often," he said. "It's there, but I have to dig for it. A lot of it was pretty forced." He lifted his head. The light had lost its piercing clarity. He looked out the window at the swirls of gold and green and rose and purple that were spilling out across the western sky. This prodigal display to mark the ending of a day spoke to him of time. They had time. That was one reason he had to be here. Time was running out everywhere else in the world. Where else could he have disappeared for two days to allow himself to fall apart so thoroughly that he had had no choice but to pull himself together? At home, there would have been engagements and commitments, all the things Mike had offered him as salvation, so that he should have been too busy to be aware of a need for salvation. A scene such as they had just had would have been inconceivable to his old self. He could see that all the years here had been a preparation for it, had in a sense been leading up to it. Their total freedom, coupled with the obligation of creating their own rules out of their real needs, had made it possible finally for him to reveal himself to her.

He had found an answer to one of Jeff's questions. Not much, if he was supposed to tell people what life was all about. He might have something to say to a few backward souls. Mike, for one. If Mike had constituted a threat, a test, a challenge to his beliefs, he had been soundly routed. Jeff had told him that. Mike hadn't the courage of his own vicious convictions.

He sighed with an almost peaceful exhaustion. After all the shouting and obscenity and violence, what had he achieved? He had staked out some new little area of freedom in himself; he would never again hide anything of himself from her. There was a new inconsequential element of fatigue in his feeling for her; he couldn't imagine expending quite so much passionate attention on her in the future. Otherwise, love was intact. Everything was pretty much the same. That was the miracle. They would go on, as he had known they must despite his brief rebellion, adapting—yes, growing. Knowledge was growth.

He turned and looked at Sarah. There was a puffiness in her cheeks and along her jaw. One eye was bloodshot. The skin along her shoulders was beginning to show marks of discoloration. His bruised love. He reached out to her, pulled her up, and drew her in beside him on the edge of the bed. She folded herself against him in the way he had longed for her to do, had been terrified that she might do, for so many months.

He held her close with one arm and smoothed her hair. "Poor darling. Did I hurt you badly?"

"Yes, you did," she said with spirit.

"No more than you hurt me. I'll never get over Ronnie, but I do understand finally. I guess we were in a rut. A rut of contentment. That's what people can't endure. They long for the heights and don't worry about the depths they'll fall into if they fail to reach them. It keeps things moving. Gain and loss."

"I thought it was going to be all loss from now on. Thank God you've taken charge again."

He turned her face to him and gently kissed her swollen lips. He dropped a hand to her sweet breasts and bent down to kiss each nipple. He straightened and looked into her eyes. "Such a pretty girl. I really don't want anybody else to have you."

"Nobody ever has—nobody ever could the way you do."

He parted his legs and allowed his freshly erect sex to lift from its confinement. He laughed and put her hand on it. "That's in charge again. Poor Jeff, he'll never know how awful and fascinating women are. And yet, my God. How magnificent it might be. I hope it will be

259

for him. Two hard bodies and two hard minds butting up against each other, wringing love from an impossible clash. There's a sort of mad valor about it. None of us can have everything. Gain and loss. It's a rule of life."

"Can I have you now the way it's always been?"

He looked at her and smiled ruefully. "We agreed it would never be the same again. Well. Life is a slow wearing away. We'll see." They fell back on the couch together, and he moved her with tender care and removed the ugly shreds of cloth from around her waist, making her comfortable before he lifted himself over her and prepared to celebrate his slightly worn, slightly damaged love.

Charlie sat at Peter's desk and tried to draw Jeff's head from memory. It kept coming out rather hawklike. He must have missed some quirk in the features that was the clue to a likeness. He wished the model would hurry up and get here so that he could rectify the omission. He couldn't bear the thought of his sitting alone somewhere, tormented, feeling abandoned. He hoped his parents hadn't given him a bad time. He could count on George, if sober, to deal reasonably with him. He was less sure of Sarah. The boy was already strained to the breaking point; he tensed at the thought of what a careless word could do to him.

Everything had gone more easily with Martha than he had expected, and the household had received him comfortably. There was evidently to be no further reference to the night before. He had been able to announce Peter's return for the next day as if it had never been questioned. As he had done so, he had been nervously aware of tempting fate by allowing himself to think of Jeff while Peter was still away.

But he *had* thought of Jeff, without stopping. He had worked his way through the whole situation in his mind, presenting it to himself in the most extreme terms.

He was half in love with a boy half his age. At any moment, he might say the word or make the move that would release the flood of love he had sensed so precariously balanced in the boy. They would be two people in love. They would have to be together. He would move to Boston. Farewell to the family. He would watch over Jeff, guide him, help launch him on whatever career he might choose. There would be no fear of Jeff being tempted by others so long as he remained spellbound by the monumental phallus. Charlie had known a good many male bodies in his time and had encountered only one or two that might have qualified as competition. As for himself, something in his spirit had been captured by Jeff's great undirected, undisciplined yearning. His body ached to fill Jeff's young unformed body with joy. His eyes longed to learn the moods that filled Jeff's eyes with mysterious beauty, that touched the beautiful curve of Jeff's lips with adorable tenderness. It would mean building a new life. A life with Jeff. Us.

Each step in his thoughts caused a wrench, but when he got that far he was overwhelmed with desolation. He had to be with Peter. He would wither and die without the familiar touch of Peter's glorious body, without the known safe brilliance of his presence. He could think of having them both, but wasn't there any sane solution? Adopt Jeff as a son, integrate him into the family, have him secretly until the ache slowly eased? Perhaps tonight would still his craving to display himself to Jeff's worshiping eyes. Wasn't that what his being "in love" amounted to? Whatever words he used to describe it didn't diminish the fire that burned in him.

His hand flew over the paper as he created another hawklike image. It was the extraordinary depth and sensitivity of the eyes that foiled him. He could see them as clearly as if he were looking into them and he longed to sink his own into the depths of their surrender. Jeff would be here any minute.

The thought made his mind race in preparation. What had he said? What would he say? He had spoken of love, and Jeff had acted as if he hadn't heard him. Avoid commitments and declarations. Let their bodies speak for them until tomorrow, when something would have to be said. There need be no secret of Jeff having slept here. He had told Martha he was coming, telling her of the circumstances in which they had found him. She had made a point of accepting it as quite natural that he should take care of him.

He heard the thud of the front door below. All the surface of his body seemed instantly sensitized as if a thousand centers of erotic pleasure had flowered on his skin. He stood, naked except for the sarong hitched around his waist, and felt his sex stretch with the weight of desire. He crossed the room and opened the door. Jeff's pace quickened to reach him across the dark adjoining room. Charlie closed the door after him, turned the key, and opened his arms to the slim body that flung itself against him.

Jeff's hands were busy, disposing of the sarong, rushing to grasp rigid flesh. He wrenched his mouth away from Charlie's and looked down at it. "It happens so quickly," he said with wonder. "You'd suppose it would take time to get so enormous." He removed his hands slowly and took a step back, continuing to gaze at it as he began to unbutton his shirt.

"How did everything go?" Charlie asked, moving toward him, wanting to engage his mind as well as his senses.

Jeff retreated, his eyes still fixed on his sex. "It doesn't matter much when I can look at that." He turned and headed toward the bed-side table where he knew the lubricant was kept, discarding clothes along the way. "Dad was fine. He really is a wonderful man. If you ever get a chance, tell him I said so." He faced Charlie naked, a hand behind his back applying the lubricant, his eyes lowered and worshiping.The sight of the willowy angular body being unabashedly prepared to receive him engaged all of Charlie's responsibility once more. So young. So damn defenseless. He wanted to protect him from further hurt. He stepped quickly to him, and Jeff reached for his sex. He gripped it and gasped and closed his eyes.

"God, yes. Once more," he muttered as if to himself. He turned his back, lifted Charlie's hands, put them on his chest, and swayed into the circle of Charlie's arms. His hair brushed softly against the side of Charlie's face. "Once more and forever," he whispered mysteriously. He pulled them forward and fell onto the bed, bringing Charlie down on top of him. "Oh, God, Charlie, make me yours," Jeff begged in a deep strangled voice. "Save me." He burst into sobs again as their bodies began to struggle, locked in the combat that Jeff seemed to demand. There was a note of terror in his voice as he kept calling Charlie's name. Charlie gripped him hard, digging his fingernails into spare flesh, tangling his fingers in his hair and beating his face down into the pillow as he fought to allay the terrible longing that remained in the body beneath him. Their orgasms were a wrenching interruption rather than a release. They left Charlie with a feeling of failure. The more passionately he gave himself, the more Jeff seemed to retreat into his wild secret sorrow.

After he had rested briefly, he pulled away and sprang up, reaching over for Jeff and hurrying him into the bathroom. Perhaps connection would be made in small everyday acts. He pushed him under the shower and stood close to him while they washed. He thought of Peter this morning and of the sunny gaiety he generated between them. He thought of their being together tomorrow evening and the joy they would share in resuming pleasures he had long denied them. His body tingled at the thought. What was he doing here with this boy? Did he seriously contemplate having two lovers, the lover of the

262

dark, the lover of the light? Perhaps in another age or place it wouldn't be so absurd, but here and now he had only a night and a day to find the dimensions of reality.

Jeff's great eyes were on his face now, fixed and still and contemplative. Charlie couldn't bring himself to meet them. Jeff spoke. "If you knew what it does to me, being able to look at you at last, being with you like this so naturally. It devours me. I couldn't survive it a week." The words came from somewhere deep and remote in him, muffled and strangely passionless.

Charlie put out a hand to him impulsively, gripped his neck, and bowed his head so that their foreheads touched. He turned off the water and drew Jeff out of the shower. His sleek slim body seemed to have no will of its own in Charlie's hands. His sex was erect once more.

"I'm insatiable," Jeff said when Charlie released him and handed him a towel. There was no flirtatiousness in the statement; it was said as a melancholy fact. "You're so *young*. I feel a hundred compared to you. I suppose it's because you're immortal."

"You talk such nonsense. I have some very mortal things to say to you."

"I love your gray hair. Every year when you first arrive you look so beautiful and distinguished. After you've been here a while, the sun makes it all streaked with gold, and the gray doesn't show anymore." He lifted his hand and brushed his fingers through the hair on Charlie's temples.

Charlie trembled within himself at the touch. This was as close as Jeff had come to recognizing him as a person. Perhaps it would happen now. Perhaps love would begin to flow out to him. He remained silent and motionless so as not to divert its course.

"If only you could make me part of you, everything would be different," Jeff went on musingly. "I mean literally, so that your great cock could be in me always. Today has made my life complete. I could never want anything more."

Their eyes met. Charlie felt as if he were falling into appalling depths of unappeasable longing. Every nerve and muscle and fiber in him wanted to clasp the boy to him and bring him peace. He broke the unbearable contact and finished drying himself hurriedly, then took Jeff's arm and led him back to the bed. They were both damp as they clamped themselves to each other, and Charlie took the boy's mouth gently and lingeringly. He was met with a passion that seemed to have no connection with anything Jeff said. Charlie drew away and rested his forehead on Jeff's shoulder, where he could see the marks of teeth.

"I ought to go," Jeff said.

Charlie jerked his head up. "Don't be silly. You're staying the night."

Jeff lay with his eyes closed. "Peter would find out," he said.

"Jesus Christ," Charlie exclaimed. "Don't you understand? Peter's got find out something."

"You didn't mean those things you said on the boat, did you?"

"I usually mean what I say. We haven't had a chance to talk. I want to now." Despite his resolution to avoid declarations, he knew he had to speak to clear the confusion in his own mind.

"Don't. Please don't. You must understand. This is all we can have. You know that."

"Why do I know that?" he protested, while part of him accepted the words with relief. It would be easier if Jeff clung to his curious detachment when they weren't making love. As long as they were lying together, it seemed to matter less what happened tomorrow. Still, there were things he felt he should say, things that eluded him. The talk about gods created an aura of fantasy that he hadn't penetrated, and he felt it essential for Jeff's sake that he should. The depths of despair he felt in him frightened him. He tightened his grip around him. "Jeff. Look at me." He slowly opened his eyes. Again Charlie felt as if he were falling into them. For a moment, he couldn't speak. The words finally came, strained and difficult. "I told you I love you. I've come awfully close to saying I'm *in* love with you, but I can't because—well, because I'm in love with Peter, and it's supposed to be impossible to be in love with two people at once."

A faint smile played across Jeff's lips. "That's foolish. I could be in love with dozens of people at once. It'd be nice to hear it even if it doesn't mean anything. It won't make any difference. Believe me."

"All right. I'm—in love with you. I—" He had said the words to only one other person in his life. To say them now was a monstrous betrayal, but the fire soared up in him. He had never felt so exposed or carefree. He couldn't think what else he had been going to say.

Jeff's smile became more pronounced. "I'll never forget your saying it. That makes it really complete. I've had a very full life. I've been in love with a big theatrical celebrity. A famous painter says he's in love with me. He's made me his. Don't ever tell Peter anything."

So much for the monstrous words. They didn't mean anything.

Jeff was making it easier for him than he wanted. "Don't you realize I want him to know? Not about our making love. That's something I've still got to think about. I mean, how to handle it, how to control it. But—"

"I wondered if you were going to get around to that." Laughter rumbled in Jeff's chest. "There's nothing to think about. You'll see. Your colossal cock. It's taken me, once and for all. You don't have to do it again."

"But you want it," he exclaimed, still trying to fit Jeff's behavior with his words.

"Oh, God, yes. But I want so many things. Most of all, I want Peter to love me always. Not that I deserve it. He probably knew what was going to happen with us. He knew it was the only thing that might've kept me sane. He's so damn sweet; I want to think he'd understand. I love him. I love you both as an indivisible pair. That must never change, or nothing will ever make sense. Promise you'll never let him know anything."

"How can I promise that? I'd have to promise not to see you again when he's back."

"I'm not worried about that. Just remember, whatever happens, you've made my life complete. You've given me everything. Don't ever think you could have given me more. This might not seem to make much sense to you now, but you'll understand."

"I wish you wouldn't always talk in riddles." His eyes followed the curve of the boy's mouth. He could feel Jeff's hard sex against him. He knew from the weight of his own that he would soon be ready to make love to him again, but he wanted to postpone another combat of their bodies until they had said things to each other that might take them a step toward a future he was trying to imagine and shape. He longed to bring a light to Jeff's eyes and see them shine with youth and happiness. That was what this was really all about—leading him out of the shadow of despair—his mind committed to it as well as his body. "We've got to talk about simple things, like tomorrow and the next day," he said. "One day, you're going to fall in love with somebody your own age. That's simple enough. Until you do, we're here, Peter and I, loving you. You know Peter doesn't want you, thank God, but I do. We've got all night to find out what we want from each other. Almost anything's possible, except as you say, to let anything come between me and Peter. I know what I want most of all. I want to help you to be happy."

A smile still hovered around Jeff's lips. "I don't think I want to be happy, not the way people usually seem to mean. I can't imagine settling down the way you're supposed to, the way you and Peter have. I'm not good enough. I was with Dimitri this evening. I made him fuck me. It was the first time he'd ever done it with anybody."

Charlie stared at the nearly expressionless face, trying to absorb the words. This mind tried to reject them, and then he was frantically disentangling himself from Jeff as if he were lying in a bed of glowing coals. He struggled up and flung himself headlong across the room to put space between them. Without knowing what he was doing, he retrieved his sarong and fastened it around him. There was a roaring in his ears. He bent over the desk and pounded on it with his fist. "You little shit," he shouted. "Haven't you understood anything? You've torn the guts out of me. I was ready to do anything for you. You talk about worship and you—you—" He choked on tears of rage.

"I had to know," Jeff said with limpid clarity. "If he hadn't been able to do anything for me, I would've known I was all right. His cock is smaller than mine, but it was thrilling all the same. Nothing like you, of course, but he was a man exercising his masculinity in me. Because I worship you, I want to give myself to every beautiful man I find and discover the little bit of you that's in him. I'd fill the world with a rage of male love. I know it's impossible. I know I'd make a mess of myself, but that wouldn't stop me. People go to church and worship their gods with hope and prayer, but when they leave they go on with their little mortal lives. You and Peter are my temple. You could never be my daily lot in life. Please remember, always. You've given me everything I could ever want or hope for."

"Get out. Go," Charlie said dully, while the pain of saying it ate into him until his legs would no longer hold him. He dropped into the chair at the desk and sat very straight with his fists clenched in front of him. The hurt in him was a sickness that unhinged his mind and paralyzed his senses. Why had he thought he could allow the caution of a lifetime to go unheeded? He wanted to tear the house apart. He wanted to beat Jeff. He had to keep himself very still to stave off violence.

The flame Jeff had brought leaping up in him had seemed a precious gift of life; he had somehow convinced himself that it would cripple him to stamp it out. He would cultivate detachment once again; if he was to preserve himself for the long haul of the future, he must maintain an even keel, keep all fires banked.

He had never considered jeopardizing his life with Peter. His thoughts had flown around the possibility of accommodations without having had time to come to grips with the practical problems involved. Peter would be back tomorrow. He could count on Peter. He thought of Martha last night and what had taken place in the hotel room this morning. Peter was his. He would be back. He had promised.

Charlie's ears had been deaf to Jeff's movements in the room, and he was startled by the proximity of his voice when he spoke.

"I knew you wouldn't want me again when I told you," he said. "That's the way it should be."

Charlie lifted his head, his expression neutral. Jeff was dressed and stood beside the desk. His long dark hair fell softly across his brow. His head had never been more beautiful. "You're right, of course," Charlie agreed with cool reserve.

"All the same, I hope you don't hate me. I've lived in my mind for too long. When I finally began doing things, nothing seemed to fit with what I expected. I've got to go a long way away where I won't be at odds with life anymore."

Something in his voice sharpened Charlie's attention. "What are you saying now?"

"Oh." He shrugged, and his voice became matter-of-fact. "Harvard's pretty far away, I guess."

Charlie was suddenly on his feet. He stepped out from behind the desk but stopped short of touching the boy. "Stay, for God's sake," he begged, feeling acutely that it was vital to keep him here. "Stay for tonight anyway. Let me try to satisfy you at least once. I know I haven't yet. It might be important for both of us."

"I told you I was insatiable. Especially with you. Do you want me still? Do you want me as much as I want you?"

"You know I do, goddamn it."

Jeff stepped quickly to him and took him in his arms possessively, kissing his mouth with a fierceness that threatened to shatter Charlie's barely reintegrated control. His hands dropped to the sarong and pulled it away again, moving over the flesh that obsessed him. He drew his head back. His eyes blazed briefly into Charlie's. "There. For once. The way it should be. Man to man and nobody else counting." He released Charlie and backed away from him, his eyes on his body. "It happens so quickly. I'll remember you forever like that. I mustn't topple that tower." He uttered laughter that threatened to end in a sob. When he lifted his eyes, they were flooded with his unbearable longing. "Good-bye, Apollo. Good-bye, my lover," he said softly. He turned and moved quickly to the door and unlocked it and was gone without looking back.

He heard Charlie call his name as he hurried across a room and downstairs and out the front door. Tears slid silently down his cheeks. He dashed them from his eyes so that he could see in the dark and set off at a rapid pace for his next rendezvous. He had known since noon that it awaited him. Without the day with Charlie, he would have gone to it in blind despair. Now he was buoyed by a sense of victory. He had said everything necessary so that Charlie would feel no guilt. When he heard, he would surely know that he had come as close to saving him as anybody could. When Mike heard, he would know the truth. Perhaps it would touch him at last. Perhaps he would understand what he had meant when he said that he loved him more than life. He dashed tears from his eyes again and reminded himself that he would soon be free.

He crossed the quiet port. People waved from a table, and he waved back without seeing who they were. He took one of the main stepped streets that led up through the town. He was panting when he reached the upper rim of the amphitheater. The road dipped over a crest and led off on a level between walls toward open country. He passed through a sort of suburb, well back from the sea and high above it. He was breathing easily again as he entered the only bit of pastoral landscape the island offered. Land sloped gently away on both sides of him. There were a few farms here, some fields where grain had been harvested, almond and olive groves. It was one of Jeff's favorite places, time-haunted, biblical in its rustic simplicity, Pan land. He had always felt close to the gods here. The night was vast and luminous around him. He felt totally alone on earth, unfettered by ties to any human creature. Thoughts of Mike could no longer hurt him. There was only a riot of pagan dedication in him.

He turned off the rough road into an even rougher lane, under trees, that dipped down toward a house, rose again, and petered out among great boulders. Jeff picked his way over them, jumping from pinnacle to pinnacle, climbing the back of a high cliff face that dropped sheer to the sea. He knew his way.

He came out on a fairly even plateau of rock hanging over the huge panorama of westering sea. The moon was sinking into it. He stood and caught his breath after his exertions and then ventured closer to the edge. When he was a few feet from it, a prickling in his legs and all down his spine stopped him. It must have been like this that the ancients imagined the edge of the universe—an abrupt clean drop into space. He backed away until he felt safe and took all his clothes off, arranging them in a neat pile. It was important that it should look as if he had planned everything carefully and rationally.

He stood with his feet apart and lifted his arms straight out from his body so that he could feel the soft night air on every pore. Standing naked under the sky stirred him. He ran his hands over his body and brought them to rest on his buttocks. He arched his spine backward and stretched all of himself while he recaptured the sensations of being taken by Charlie. His fingers strayed caressingly, and his hips swayed as his sex lifted into erection. His hand moved forward and stroked it slowly. This was a familiar ritual. He had consecrated the place with his sperm long ago.

Mental images of the colossal phallus that was part of his experience were more potent than anything he had ever imagined. He could feel it inside him. He threw his head back and stretched his mouth wide to receive it. It multiplied until it seemed to press on every part of his body, a mighty web of hard flesh that held his mind spellbound. He had been loved by Apollo. He had aroused the jealousy of the gods. The discus had been arrested and reversed in its course. He could sense it hurtling toward him.

The movement of his hand accelerated. His body writhed and leaped and drifted in an orgiastic dance of self-hypnosis. He wasn't mindful of his footing, he knew he hadn't far to go. His loins were congested with the ultimate experience that his being yearned for. His sex swelled in his hand until it felt as if it should burst.

At the first huge jet of his orgasm, he sprang forward, his knees buckled, and his body was convulsed as he hurtled out into space, his legs flailing, his mind reeling with astonishment and ecstasy, until gravity reached out for him and he plunged.

Charlie awoke early from a restless night feeling as if he had been involved in some catastrophe. He wasn't quite sure he had survived it. Guilt, apprehension, and exhaustion formed a knot in him and blurred his thoughts. He had slept again in Peter's room because guilt kept him from the bed they shared.

And on the off chance that Jeff might come back? Yes, he had been able to sleep only after he had talked himself out of hoping that he might. Jeff had understood better than he that they had had all that time permitted them, but he was totally unpredictable. Given the opportunity, he might offer himself again in the days to come. Charlie would have to take care to avoid seeing him alone.

His head cleared as he went through his morning routine. Underlying the guilt and apprehension, sharpened perhaps by exhaustion, he became aware of an odd sense of anticipation in himself. Of what? Of life itself? He was prepared for the unexpected in a way he hadn't been for years. He collected a spartan breakfast tray from Kyria Tula and took it up to his studio. A glance around him told him that his mood alienated him from his work. The highly disciplined, intellectual cold-bloodedness of it made him want to let loose and fling paint about, get his hands in it and throw away the rules. He finished his coffee hastily, got out a virgin canvas, and went to work, the final result he wanted to achieve for once eluding him. When he stepped back to survey his progress, he laughed out loud at what he was doing. Let his public make what they would of it. He felt reckless and inspired. Perhaps he was entering a new Period. This was the area in which to consolidate his new sense of liberation, not with treacherous young lovers. He couldn't wait to show Peter.

Thoughts of Peter and Jeff hovered on the edges of his concentration. Peter tonight. Feeling it as a constraint, he pulled off his sarong and tossed it aside. This was the way to work, naked, his whole body engaged. He might throw in a few touches with his cock. He laughed out loud again while he worked. Jeff. Of course he wouldn't avoid him. He loved him, was in love with him in a way he could explain to Peter. He was too young to have deserved last night's fury. Let him fall into bed with every man in sight. He'd be back, his great eyes yearning. Perhaps then he could give him peace.

He was absentminded during the midday break with the family. His work was exciting him, as well as other things. When he returned to his studio, he was tempted to masturbate for the first time in more than twenty years; Jeff had accustomed the Monumental Phallus to constant attention. It felt very much in the way, but he made himself wait. Peter was already en route by now.

He went down to meet the boat earlier than necessary, having told Martha that he wanted to go alone, and was pleased to run into George Leighton as he strolled toward the landing area. They settled down at a café near where the boat tied up and ordered coffee. Charlie noticed that there wasn't a trace of the alcoholic fumbling that had been characteristic of him lately. He looked cheerful and relaxed. What had taken place with Jeff added warmth to his affection for George. There was the bond of shared love.

"Peter's due back, is he?" George asked when the coffee had been served.

"Yes," Charlie said firmly, to still any doubt he might have.

270

"I came along to see if Costa's aboard."

"You know Peter. He wouldn't come back until he succeeded." He was drawing on the reserve of confidence he had stored up in himself. Something might turn up involving Costa that would delay him. If he had sent a wire, it wouldn't arrive till tomorrow.

"Have you seen Jeff today?" George asked.

"No. I haven't seen anybody. I haven't been out of the house until this minute."

"I just wondered. He didn't come home last night. It doesn't matter. He said he might stay out. Nobody seems to've seen him."

A little tremor of anxiety fluttered around Charlie's heart. "I saw him last night," he said.

"Oh, good. Look. I know he has no secrets from you. He's talked quite openly with me. I'm not in a state about—well, about the way he's turning out. You know me well enough to know that. I mention it just so you won't feel you're compromising him if you can give me an idea of what he's up to."

"I haven't the slightest. He came by the house after dinner. You know I came out with him yesterday? I told him he could spend the night—you know, kids sometimes feel more at ease with a friend than with their parents—but he seemed to have something on his mind and took off." *God knows, I tried to keep him,* Charlie thought.

"I gather you and Peter have been very good to him. Your being fond of him makes me very proud of him."

"He's a fascinating kid. Mike knocked the stuffings out of him. I've tried to help him as best I could."

"I hope I have, too. You'd know the right things to say better than I would, but yesterday I felt as if we could talk to each other like friends at last. When your two are older you'll find that's one of the most satisfying things that can happen to a parent."

"He said you're a wonderful man. He told me to tell you."

"Really? My God. I think I'm blushing." A smile of great sweetness passed across his face. "I hope he's found somebody to cheer him up."

Charlie's hands tightened on the arms of his chair. It still wasn't pleasant to think of Jeff giving himself to others. "I wouldn't be surprised," he said with an ease that he felt deserved congratulations. "You know how promiscuous we all are at that age, especially if we've been kicked in the teeth by someone we love. It's the first cure we think of." He found himself searching for some other explanation for his disappearance. Had his making a point of saying good-bye meant anything? "Do you suppose he could have gone back to Athens? If he did, Peter will know. He'd be bound to go see Peter." To offer himself again and complete his conquest of his twin gods? Peter simply wouldn't be interested.

"I don't believe he'd clear out again without telling me. I have a feeling he's going to be all right now. After all, I retired from life myself for a couple of days. Whatever he's doing, I hope he's having fun. He's always been inclined to take things too seriously."

"I know. I kept thinking yesterday how much I'd like to make him laugh."

George put down his cup and looked at him intently across the table. "You care about him that much?"

Charlie looked into keen, understanding eyes and nodded. "Let's say that if I were younger, I could really fall for him. That's just between us."

"Of course. Thanks for telling me. I hope you don't mind my asking a personal question. There's a lot I'd like to understand. Is he attractive? I mean to men. If you were playing the field, would you pick him out?"

Charlie resolutely held his eyes on George's. "He's a beautiful boy, George. You can see that for yourself. If you accept the fact that men can be attracted to each other, it doesn't require any special understanding. It's just people."

"Then you think Mike took him away because he really wanted him, not just—I don't know. I guess what I'm really asking is whether you think Mike had anything to do with his deciding he's homosexual."

"Good God, no. He told Peter all about it—when? Day before yesterday. He was still a virgin then."

"So he told me. Well, it was time he cleared that hurdle. You think it's reasonable to hope that he'll find a guy and make something good like you two have?"

"He doesn't think he can. That's the only thing that bothers me. I'd like to convince him he's wrong."

"Good. I'll probably get over wanting to kill Mike. I'm glad it's all out in the open. I want to help him find everything that's good in it. I know you and Peter will, too."

"I want to. I hope we'll see a lot of him before he goes. And in the States too, of course. It's nice to know we'll be so close. It's funny. I've been thinking of him as a child until the last day or two."

They gossiped of other island matters. George was in good form.

272

Charlie gathered from several chance words that he and Sarah were on good terms again, which pleased him. Reconciliation was in the air; he felt it as a support for his own eagerness to close ranks with Peter. For moments at a time, his ears stopped straining for the ship's whistle. When it sounded, he was immediately on his feet and had taken up his position at the barrier, barely aware that George had followed him and was at his side. The boat had not yet appeared around the eastern promontory.

When it did, he straightened and watched tensely as it slid in bow-on toward the *quai*. Engines were reversed with a swirling of water, and it swung around broadside as lines were thrown. His heart stopped as his eyes swept the decks. He had only an instant of agonized suspense. He saw him immediately, standing at the rail beside where the gangplank would be hoisted aboard so that he would be one of the first off. Their eyes met. Across the narrowing gap of water, he learned all that he needed to know: Peter was his. It was a great deal. It was everything. The fire was still in him; it warmed his love for Peter. They signaled to each other how glad they were to be together again and that all was well at home.

"He looks as if all his news is good," George said at Charlie's side.

As soon as the gangplank was in place, Peter sprang lightly down it and was with him in a blaze of golden radiance. Their arms went around each other's shoulders in a quick embrace, Peter shook George's hand, and they all started to talk at once. Amid the shouts and the excited babble of returning travelers, Charlie made no effort to follow what was being said. Jeff's name caught Peter's attention.

"What do you mean, nobody's seen him?" He turned to Charlie with an air of reproach. "Why didn't you keep him with you last night?"

"I told him he could stay. He didn't want to. I thought he might've gone back to Athens."

"I don't think so," George said. "He'd have let me know. You didn't bring Costa with you?"

Peter gave Charlie a puzzled glance before turning back to George. "He's out. Everything's all right."

They had moved away from the crowd and conversation had become possible.

"Good for you," George said gratefully. "Where is he? I've got to make up for my stupidity."

"I gave him money. He's having a little rest cure. He had to sign a paper saying that the police had treated him with exquisite courtesy. He promised not to come back until there're no signs to the contrary."

"Christ. Was he badly beaten?"

"Oh, he didn't look as if they'd really put their hearts into it. He'll be all right in a week or so."

"If you know where he is, I'll go up in the next couple of days and have a talk with him."

"I think he'd like that. He's a good guy. He was really sorry about having to get Jeff into it."

Peter was setting a brisk pace. They had time for only a few more exchanges before they had reached the turnoff where the climb up to the Mills-Martin house began. They all stopped.

"I can't thank you guys enough for everything." George said.

"All for the common cause," Peter said. "You're looking good, George."

"Persevere, lads. That's my message for the day. Most of all, thanks for helping me to get to know Jeff. If we can cover our losses with a few gains, I guess we can't complain."

They exchanged fond smiles and lifted their hands in parting, and Peter started up the steps as if he were in a hurry to get home. As soon as they were out of sight of George, he slowed to a more normal pace.

"Tell me about Jeff, for God's sake," he demanded. "Is he all right?"

"I suppose so." Charlie had had a few moments of worry about Jeff—he had assumed responsibility for him, and the note of farewell at the end had been a bit odd—but he was so happy to see Peter that he didn't see any need to worry more about him now. "He's probably filling the world with a rage of male love. I think that's the way he put it."

Peter uttered brief rueful laughter. "Oh, dear. Is that the next phase? It sounds like him."

Charlie knew he had no right to feel this deep singing contentment; having Peter once more at his side was a prize he had won by cheating. Running after him, taking him, not with real need but with calculation, seizing the opportunity to balance accounts with him for his display of nakedness—yes, that must have been in the back of his mind at first with Jeff, before it became so much more appalling. Scoring off Jeff to put Peter off the scent was the last straw—cheap and unworthy of Peter's faith in him. He was assailed again by guilt for all the unforgivable things he had done since Peter's departure. "Listen. I think we'd better have a talk before we go home." He felt rather than saw Peter's quick glance before they both returned their attention to the uneven steps. They were beginning to pant slightly with the climb.

"I wonder." Peter interrupted himself for a breath. He had read the signs, heard the warnings in Charlie's voice. Above all, they must avoid confessions. He didn't want to have it all made explicit, for Charlie's sake more than for his own. "We both probably have things to talk about. I hope we stick to the things that matter. We can sit up there on the wall and watch the sun set."

The stepped street opened out just ahead of them and became a sloping path where the houses dwindled off and were scattered about in their own rocky grounds. Farther ahead of them, they could see the rambling walls of their own impressive establishment. They continued to climb the rock-strewn path in silence until they reached the low wall above the steep drop of rock where Peter had first kissed Judy. A significant landmark now, a reminder. He turned off the path toward it, and Charlie automatically followed without missing a pace. They moved in complete unison. Although they stayed close together, there was no friction in the touch of their bodies, no moment of getting in each other's way. Every move they made was synchronized by time and a long awareness of each other. It made Charlie more wretchedly conscious of the outrages he had committed and deepened his guilt.

Peter dropped his bag and sat on the wall facing the sinking sun, his feet propped on the narrow rock formation that dropped away to the circle of the port. Charlie sat beside him, facing the opposite direction. They turned to each other and their eyes met, clear blue in cloudy purple, not seeing details but registering an ensemble that represented for both of them the sum of delight in human intercourse. Peter leaned forward, and their mouths met. Their tongues strayed briefly along each other's lips, and they drew apart. It was a casual kiss of a sort they exchanged a dozen times a day, exciting nevertheless for all it implied of the physical nature of their relationship. It made even a moment's infatuation with Jeff wrong. Peter laid a hand in Charlie's lap and chuckled at what he felt there.

"Everything seems to be in order," he said.

"Christ, don't do that," Charlie burst out in an accumulation of self-loathing. "You're so damn sweet, and I'm a total shit. I'm really appalled by myself."

Peter withdrew his hand and looked at his mate with instant concern. "Now, listen. I meant what I said about sticking to what matters. If this has anything to do with Jeff, all I want to know is whether you think he's getting over it."

"Why do you go on harping on Jeff?" Charlie demanded, choos-

ing indignation to mask guilt until he knew how much he was prepared to tell. Jeff was only part of it, and he could talk about the rest
more easily. "I'm talking about myself. Rushing after you yesterday,
taking you on the bathroom floor to prove that I could do something
for you that your girl couldn't. I thought I'd got over that sort of
thing. It was disgusting."

"Oh, darling. No." His voice was reproachful but rippled with
laughter. "It was absolute bliss, and you know it. All right. I'll come
clean. It's what *I* want to talk about. I got in pretty deep with Judy. I
couldn't get it up for her afterward. And I was *glad,* you silly shit. It
was heaven feeling that I belonged so completely to you again."

"Jesus." Charlie almost groaned with despair. How could he hope
to recover an even keel, retreat to the safety of their carefully disciplined life, if he didn't curb once more the exhibitionistic schoolboy
craving of his cock for attention? Peter seemed bent on encouraging
it. He felt Jeff's skinny young body under him, arms and legs flailing, his big cock deep within it feeling almost as big as Jeff himself,
claiming the boy as his own. He took a deep breath in an effort to
loosen the grip of guilt. "I'm the one who talks about keeping ourselves open to new experience, I've carried on about not getting so
turned in on ourselves that we can't breathe, and then when something comes along that might be important for you I do everything I
can to kill it. It *is* disgusting."

"But that's what I'm trying to tell you," Peter broke in with exasperated laughter, reading his mind. After twenty years, they could
still play games with each other. What had Jeff said? Something
about coming forth into light, in his usual literary way. They had
come forth and lived in the harsh glare of their own reality and suffered the consequences of exposure. A necessary and beneficial
experience, teaching them about essentials. They could allow themselves now to play in the tempting shadows. Still, he preferred the
light. "I don't want experience. I want your cock. I know you don't
like me to talk about it, but I've got to. I know it's not the biggest in
the world, because I've seen a couple that were maybe bigger; but
they weren't attached to the right guy. Yours will have to do. It's a
fact of life. Our life. Let me be mad for it if I want. It's ridiculous to
pretend it isn't there. I should think a moment would come when
you'd want to wave it at the whole world. That's why I say Jeff
doesn't matter. I was feeling very ready yesterday to hold him and
comfort him. When that starts, especially with a kid like Jeff, there's
no telling where it might end."

"What if it ends with my falling in love with him?"

"Did it?"

There was a silence of shock, shared by both of them. Peter straightened. He began to talk rapidly as if to keep up his courage. "Well, well, well. Yes, I can see you'd almost have to. Well, if taking me the way you did yesterday arouses the old hunter's instincts, that's a risk I'm ready to take. I've always suspected that's what it was all about. When you see how wild you drive me, you must be tempted to spread it around. Your theory about my being fucked by you making me want to be fucked by every guy in town never did make much sense. If I set out to find another cock that could do what yours does to me, it would probably take the rest of—" He broke off abruptly. "I'd better shut up a minute and let you tell me." He lifted his fists to his forehead and held them there a moment, then dropped them. "If I can stand it."

There was a knot in Charlie's throat that made it impossible to speak. He swallowed several times, then flung his arm across Peter's chest, found his shoulder, and pulled him close. "No," he managed in a constricted voice. He had to clear his throat before he could say more. "There's nothing to tell. Let's say that I got in pretty deep with him for a few hours. That's hardly being in love. It just seemed like a good idea to mention the possibility." He felt his mate's body go slack against him.

Peter exhaled a long breath. "Wow. That's the scariest moment I've had in a long time. I'm glad you said it. We may yet find we can say anything to each other. I've wanted to talk about your cock for a long time but—oh, lord, darling, when two people want each other as much as we do, it doesn't matter how we do it. I love taking you, but when that giant charges into me and makes me really part of you, I know the things you worry about can't possibly happen. I'm glad you got in deep with Jeff. It proves my point. Of course, if you hadn't worried all these years, God knows what might have become of us. We haven't shut ourselves off from the world the way we might have, and sacrificed all for our guilty love. We have the family, thanks to you. Judy made me realize how special Martha is. It's all worked better than we had any right to expect. After twenty years, I think we can safely say we've made it."

Charlie doubted if they could say anything of the sort until they had both dropped into their graves. All the same, since he had blurted out the near-truth about Jeff, something extraordinary was happening to him, growing and taking hold in him. He moved his hand

277

along Peter's shoulder, feeling the beloved bone and sinew under his fingers, until it reached the strong neck. He folded his hand around it and held it firmly. It aroused the fierce possessiveness that had always frightened him. He wasn't frightened now. *Mine.* But yesterday he had applied the same word to another. "I guess we *can* say it, baby, but I don't think we'd better. It's tempting fate."

Peter smiled into his eyes. "I'm even ready to do that. You're my fate, and I want to tempt you. You were pretty clever about the girls— they've had a lot to do with making me more mature. I don't think there'll be any more. Judy's the only one that really mattered, and it came too damn close to being rough on her. There're not many girls who can be faced with a limp cock, and know why, and not want to spit in my face. Fortunately, she likes girls and understood, so we were able to end happily. I'm glad of that. I learned something. I'm forty, for God's sake. I think we might almost agree that I'm grown-up."

Charlie saw the love in his eyes flowing to him deep and strong and direct. It blinded him. He looked past him across his shoulders to the limitless expanse of dazzling sea and waited for guilt to bite into him again and poison all his responses. He had paralyzed Peter sexually for the sake of his goddamn phallic pride. But was it only that? He had dared assert his will to keep what was his and had risked defeat. Guilt receded.

Sitting here alone with him, detached from the world, created a sense of indestructible solidarity between them that made his habit of caution seem alien; more appropriate was the reckless courage to gamble all of himself for the man he called his mate. Jeff was part of the gamble. He had a feeling that Jeff wouldn't need him again, but if he did, they would be here, as Charlie had promised. Us. *They* would deal with it. They had perhaps achieved at last an odd perilous balance in which each dominated and submitted to the other. There was the danger of conflict in it and the promise of challenges he had disciplined himself to avoid during what seemed to him now a long stagnation. If he trusted their love fearlessly, in Peter's way, perhaps he would be rewarded with some measure of Peter's buoyant optimism.

He burst into laughter that startled them both. "Yeah, yeah," he exclaimed, almost incoherently. "I can't wait to show you. You're going to have a new commodity to peddle. How about that? My Cock Period. If you—" His voice broke, and tears started up in his eyes. The tensions of the last two days gathered and crashed in him, then were dispersed. All he needed to know was that here beside him was the source of all the peace he had ever known, all the joy and simple fun, the delight and agony. He couldn't look at Peter; he felt shy with what seemed absurdly like the dawn of love. He gave his neck a little squeeze and stood up.

Peter picked up his bag and fell into step beside him. The sun was setting spectacularly, but neither of them noticed it. Peter was aware that Charlie was moved in some way that involved them both profoundly. Explanations might be found, but he wasn't interested in searching for them. It was enough to know that they were as close as they had ever been, as close as two people could ever be.

Neither of them spoke until they had pushed open the heavy front door, crossed the threshold, and stood at the foot of the marble stairs that led up to the first courtyard. There, Charlie drew Peter to him, and they held each other and kissed with an intensified loving excitement.

"Thank God for you," Charlie said as they drew apart.

"That's *my* line," Peter said. "Still, I sort of like the way you say it. My God, there's still so much to tell you. I haven't even told you about Mike being arrested, have I? Wait till you hear about that. He's in for some trouble. He'll pull strings and worm his way out of it, but all the same—Jeff has the last laugh."

A small blond figure came prancing into view at the top of the stairs. "Daddy," he shouted to the household in general. "It's my daddies." Little Pete came hurtling down the stairs, a brief golden streak in space (*God, how beautiful,* Peter thought; and then with quick alarm: *Take it easy, darling*), hurtling down the stairs (*Oh, lord,* Charlie thought, his chest stretching with uncontainable love for this splinter of Peter's magic, reproduced in gold), hurtling down the stairs to greet them.

Jeff was found the next morning at dawn by some fishermen, his bloody and broken body impaled on a rock above the sea, his upturned eyes staring at the sky, a terrible smile on his face.

A cursory examination of his body revealed that shortly before his death he had engaged in carnal pleasure of a sort that many spoke of as unspeakable. Animals were mentioned in whispers. Had he been pushed? Had he slipped? Had he chosen to leap? He entered into island legend, an example to sinners, as a lovelorn boy who had been driven to destroy himself by the enormity of his unnatural crimes.

Books 1 and 2 of Gordon Merrick's beloved Peter and Charlie trilogy

ALSO AVAILABLE FROM ALYSON PUBLICATIONS

In **THE LORD WON'T MIND,** Merrick explored the coming-out of a young homosexual and the stormy, painful, and abiding love he finds with another man. When the book was first published, Merrick's startling frankness and open affirmation caused shouts of praise and howls of protest, but *The Lord Won't Mind* rode out the storm securely lashed to *The New York Times* best-seller list.

In **ONE FOR THE GODS,** Charlie and Peter have everything: beauty, wealth, and the good fortune to spend their lives in exotic places. Enter Martha, a passionate temptress intent on seducing both men. Witness their triangle of romance and desire as it unfolds against the sun-drenched backdrop of St. Tropez and Athens.

CALL 1-800-5-ALYSON TO ORDER

Other books of interest from
ALYSON PUBLICATIONS

❏ **B-BOY BLUES,** by James Earl Hardy. A seriously sexy, fiercely funny black-on-black love story. A walk on the wild side turns into more than Mitchell Crawford ever expected. An Alyson best-seller you shouldn't miss.

❏ **BECOMING VISIBLE,** edited by Kevin Jennings. The *Lambda Book Report* states that *"Becoming Visible* is a groundbreaking text and a fascinating read. This book will challenge teens and teachers who think contemporary sex and gender roles are 'natural' and help break down the walls of isolation surrounding lesbian, gay, and bisexual youth."

❏ **CODY,** by Keith Hale. Trottingham Taylor, "Trotsky" to his friends, is new to Little Rock. Washington Damon Cody has lived there all his life. Yet when they meet, there's a familiarity, a sense that they've known each other before. Their friendship grows and develops a rare intensity, although one is gay and the other is straight.

❏ **THE GAY FIRESIDE COMPANION,** by Leigh W. Rutledge. "Rutledge, 'The Gay Trivia Queen,' has compiled a myriad gay facts in an easy-to-read volume. This book offers up the offbeat, trivial, and fascinating from the history and life of gays in America." —Buzz Bryan in *Lambda Book Report*

❏ **MY BIGGEST O,** edited by Jack Hart. What was the best sex you ever had? Jack Hart asked that question of hundreds of gay men, and got some fascinating answers. Here are summaries of the most intriguing of them. Together, they provide an engaging picture of the sexual tastes of gay men.

❏ **MY FIRST TIME,** edited by Jack Hart. Hart has compiled a fascinating collection of true stories by men across the country, describing their first same-sex encounters. *My First Time* is an intriguing look at just how gay men begin the process of exploring their sexuality.

❏ **THE PRESIDENT'S SON,** by Krandall Kraus. "President Marshall's son is gay. The president, who is beginning a tough battle for reelection, knows it but can't handle it. *The President's Son* is a delicious, oh-so-thinly-veiled tale of a political empire gone insane. A great read." —Marvin Shaw in *The Advocate*

These books and other Alyson titles are available at your local bookstore. If you can't find a book listed above or would like more information, please call us directly at 1-800-5-ALYSON.

a